THE
FIRE LORD'S LOVER

KATHRYNE
KENNEDY

Published by Sourcebooks Casablanca, an imprint of Sourcebooks,
Inc.
P.O. Box 4410, Naperville, Illinois 60567-4410
(630) 961-3900
FAX: (630) 961-2168
www.sourcebooks.com

Printed and bound in Canada
WC   10   9   8   7   6   5   4   3   2   1

About the Author

Kathryne Kennedy is the award-winning author of the Relics of Merlin series and is acclaimed for her world building. She's lived in Guam, Okinawa, and several states in the United States, and currently lives in Arizona with her wonderful family—which includes two very tiny Chihuahuas. She welcomes readers to visit her website, where she has ongoing contests, at: www.KathryneKennedy.com.

Acknowledgments

I would like to thank Christine Witthohn, Deb Werksman, and Dominique Raccah. This world would never have been created if not for them.

The link between the world of man and Elfhame had sundered long ago, the elven people and their magic fading to legend. Tall beings of extraordinary beauty, the fae preferred a world of peace. But seven elves—considered mad by their own people—longed for power and war. They stole sacred magical scepters, created their dragon-steeds, and opened the gate to the realm of man again and flew through.

Each elf carved a sovereign land within England, replacing the baronies that had so recently been formed by William the Conqueror. They acquired willing and unwilling slaves to serve in their palaces and till their lands. And fight their wars. Like mythical gods they set armies of humans against each other, battling for the right to win the king, who'd become nothing more than a trophy. They bred with their human slaves, producing children to become champions of their war games.

The elven lords maintained a unified pact, using the scepters in a united will to place a barrier around England, with only a few guarded borders open to commerce. Elven magic provided unique goods and the world turned a blind eye to the plight of the people, persuaded by greed to leave England to its own, as long as the elven did not seek to expand their rule into neighboring lands.

But many of the English people formed a secret rebellion to fight their oppressors. Some of the elven's children considered themselves human despite their foreign blood and joined the cause. And over the centuries these half-breeds became their only hope.

One

London, England, 1724

THE PEOPLE LINING THE STREETS OF LONDON CHEERED while General Dominic Raikes rode to his doom. Not that they had any idea what awaited him at Firehame Palace, and if they did, he doubted they would care. He resembled the elven lord too much for that. Yet he had won the final battle and they hailed him as their champion despite his elven white hair and pointed ears.

Young women threw flowers from upper-story windows, the petals flickering through the air like snow and coating the dusty streets with color. Gray skies covered the sun and in some places the buildings nearly met above the streets, further shadowing the riders' passage with gloom. The glass-fronted shops had been locked up as their owners joined the throng in the streets: painted harlots, street urchins, costermongers, servants, and the occasional prosperous Cit, distinguishable by his white wig. The fishy smell of the Thames overlaid the stench of the streets as his troops approached Westminster Bridge.

Over the murky waters the flaming turrets of Firehame Palace beckoned Dominic onward.

He shook back his war braids and straightened his spine and glanced back at his men. They had cleaned their red woolen coats as best they could, and lacking wigs, had powdered their hair to resemble the elven silver-white. They had polished their boots and buttons, brushed their cocked hats. Despite their stern faces, Dominic could see the glitter of pride in their eyes and nodded his approval at them. They returned his gesture with wary respect.

Dominic turned and sighed. They were brave, good men, every one. Some he owed his victory and life to. He would like to oversee their promotions himself but it would be too dangerous. He didn't know the personal life of a single man, nor did they know of his. Dominic had grown used to his solitary existence, yet sometimes he regretted the necessity of it.

The hooves of his horse met the road at the end of the bridge with a crunch of pebbles. The noise of the crowd faded as they neared the open gates of Firehame Palace. Red flame jutted from the top of the stone pillars flanking the entrance, danced along the outlying curtain walls. Dominic halted his mount for the span of a breath, studying his home with the unfamiliar gaze of one after a long absence. Elven magic had tinted the stone walls a glossy, brilliant red. Warm yellow flame slithered up the stone, whorled over the buttresses, making the entire structure shimmer in his sight. The towers soared above the three-storied palace and Dominic's black eyes quickly sought out the tallest, looking for a flicker of wing, a jet of red fire. But he could see no sign of the dragon and so flicked his reins, urging his horse into the courtyard.

Dominic wanted nothing more than a bath and then the quiet of his garden or the sanctuary of the dragon's tower. He knew he wouldn't manage any of his comforts until he'd been tested in fire.

He thrust away the memory of pain and dismounted, feeling his face turn to stone, his body conform to rigid military posture as he crossed the paved courtyard and ascended the steps into the opulence of Firehame Palace. Several of his officers followed, although many decided to forgo the privilege of coming to the attention of the Imperial Lord of the sovereignty of Firehame.

The back hallways they marched through displayed the magic and wealth of the elven lord. Delicate tapestries that rewove their pictures every few minutes covered the walls, and thick rugs of rippling ponds and bottomless chasms carpeted the floors. Dominic breathed in the scent of candle wax, perfume, and elfweed, ignoring the portraits framed in gold with their moving eyes that followed his passage. At the end of summer the air in the corridor still felt chill against his cheeks. His ears rang from the silence.

Then Dominic opened the door leading to the great room and the thunder of applause broke that brief moment of quiet. He paused, waiting for his men to compose themselves, then started down the middle of the enormous room through the crowd of gentry that awaited them.

Fluted columns lined the sides of the hall, capped with ornately carved capitals that supported archways even more ornately carved with golems, gremlins, and gargoyles. Courtiers milled between the stone supports, a riot of colorful silk skirts and gold-trimmed coats. Full court wigs of powdered white sparkled with the addition of the ground stone the nobles used to imitate the silver luster of elven hair. Buckled shoes flashed with diamonds; ceremonial swords sparkled with ruby and jet.

The smell of perfume became overwhelming, and Dominic suppressed the urge to sneeze. He kept his gaze fixed on his goal, the dais of gold where the elven lord Mor'ded waited, but he caught the faces of the courtiers from the corners of his eyes. The lustful gazes of women—and more than a few men— followed his every movement. Despite their fear of the elven, humans could not resist their beauty, and Dominic had inherited more elven allure than his half blood warranted.

When he reached the Imperial Lord's throne, Dominic stared at Mor'ded for longer than he intended. Silvery white hair cascaded past broad shoulders in a river broken only by the tips of the elven lord's pointed ears. Black, fathomless eyes stared coldly into Dominic's own, the expression robbing them of their almost crystalline brilliance. Smooth, pale skin glistened like the finest porcelain over high cheekbones and strong chin. A full mouth, straight nose, high brow.

When Dominic looked at the Imperial Lord, he might as well have been gazing into a mirror of his future, for although his father must be over seven hundred years old, he did not look a day over five and thirty. And despite the thickness of his elven blood, Dominic aged at a normal human pace. In ten years, Dominic would look like the man before him.

Dominic dropped to one knee and bowed his head, war braids dangling beside his cheeks and eyes fixed on the marble floor. A wave of silence rolled across the room until he could hear nothing but the breathing of his men and the rustle of the ladies' silk skirts. "I have won the king, my lord."

At his words, the room erupted in applause again and Dominic stood, gazing at his father, hoping to see a glimmer of pride in those cold black eyes. He had fought for years to achieve such acknowledgment.

Imperial Lord Mor'ded smiled, revealing even white teeth, and cut his hand through the air, signaling the court to silence. He stood with a grace no human could possess and stepped down from the dais, one hand wrapped around the black scepter that enhanced his magic. Dominic's eyes flicked to the rod, the runes carved on it swirling momentarily in his sight before he quickly looked away.

As a child he'd been constantly hungry. He'd been stealing food off the sideboard in the grand dining room when his father and court had entered. He'd hidden under the table and his father had sat, the triangular-shaped head of the scepter jutting beneath the crisp white linen. Dominic didn't know what made him reach out and stroke the forbidden talisman, for everyone knew only one of true elven blood could hold it without being flamed to ash. But he hadn't tried to wield it, had only touched it, and since then he couldn't look at it without feeling strange. As if the thing possessed a conscious awareness of him. It bothered him that he had such a fanciful thought.

Mor'ded reached his side and placed his other hand on Dominic's shoulder. The chill of his long fingers penetrated the heavy wool of Dominic's coat. "After a hundred years the king will finally be returned to his rightful place. Thanks to my son, the champion of all Firehame."

Applause thundered again. The elven lord's words echoed in Dominic's ears. His father had publicly acknowledged him as his son. Fierce pleasure rose in Dominic's chest and he had to force himself to concentrate on Mor'ded's next words.

"General Raikes has defeated Imperial Lord Breden's forces, and we have won the ultimate trophy—King George and his royal court. London will again be the center of taste and fashion. The sovereignty of Firehame will house the man who decides what color breeches you wear."

A ripple of excited pleasure ran through the courtiers, and Dominic stared coldly at the assemblage. Did they not hear the disdain in his father's voice? Did they not understand the mockery toward the king who should be their rightful ruler?

Mor'ded's fingers tightened on Dominic's shoulder, and the elven lord's magic shivered through his spine. Dominic forced himself to relax under the painful grip. It did not matter if the ton understood or not. They could do nothing about it, anyway.

"Tonight we will feast in my son's honor."

His fingers gave Dominic one last painful squeeze before he released his grip and climbed back up on his dais. With a flourish of his scepter, Mor'ded filled the long great room with sparkling white fire, the flames harmlessly bouncing off the wigs of the men and the silk skirts of the ladies. The courtiers laughed and wove their bodies through the magic, and Dominic watched them with hooded eyes until his father grew tired of amusing his playthings.

When Mor'ded swept the skirts of his red silk coat through the door behind the throne, Dominic followed, resisting the sudden urge to draw his sword and run it through his father's back.

He'd tried it once. It had cost him the life of his best friend.

His father lit their way through the gloomy passage with white fire that slithered on the ceiling above them. Dominic knew most of the passageways behind the walls of the palace. He'd spent hours as a youth exploring them. This particular one led from the throne to Mor'ded's private chambers and branched off only once by means of a tunnel that his father told him twisted far beneath the palace, finally opening onto an entrance to the fabled land of Elfhame. Of course, only a chosen one could pass into that land, and Dominic had still failed to prove worthy. They both ignored the heavily warded door blocking the tunnel as they continued on to the end of the passage.

Mor'ded opened the door to his chamber, and Dominic followed him into the room and suppressed a shudder. Very few people were allowed into the Imperial Lord's private chamber, and he didn't count himself lucky to be one of them. The walls glowed with iridescent color, a copy, Mor'ded had once told him, of the truly living walls of his old rooms in his homeland of fabled Elfhame. Plants grew in the corners of the room, pale pink pods that occasionally liked to dine on warm meat through some corrosive process Dominic didn't want to understand. A striated crystal sat next to the double doors that led out onto a balcony broad enough for a dragon to land. The stone picked up the color of the gray skies and threw it into the room. Large enough for a table, and yet shaped like a cone, the crystal held a hole in the top of it that Mor'ded often slipped his scepter into.

Chairs that resembled flower petals, a bed that could be some sort of deformed swan, and a desk that snapped closed like the jaws of some great beast completed the room.

Dominic always felt displaced here, as if a part of his mind rejected the surroundings. But then again, he'd become quite skilled at projecting his mind out of his body. It was the only way he'd survived the trials with his sanity intact.

Mor'ded slid into one of his petal-chairs, the scepter carelessly laid across his lap. He liked to play with Dominic a bit before he began, taunting him to display any human weakness.

"You used magic to gain your victory."

Dominic clasped his hands behind his back and widened his stance. No use in denying it. He'd seen the shadow of the dragon hovering over the battlefield, his father atop the great beast, enjoying the sight of the games. "I used it to save the lives of my men."

That handsome mouth crooked, so like Dominic's own. "It looked to be quite a firestorm."

Dominic shrugged.

Mor'ded shifted, the swish of his silk coats loud in the silent room. "Breden is furious, of course. He says we should not allow any of our bastards to play in the games. Indeed, that we should cull any of those possessing the slightest degree of power."

Dominic kept his face impassive. He did not doubt that the elven lords would destroy all their offspring on a whim, for he knew of their madness better than anyone. "One of Breden's bastards tried to quench my fire with a wave of water from the Bristol Channel."

"Which I pointed out to Breden," replied Mor'ded. He waved a graceful hand. "It matters not what he says. His pride has been injured by the loss of the king. He had become complacent, and we elven must never succumb to that human weakness, eh, Dominic?"

"Never, my lord."

"Aah, but it makes me wonder. Have I allowed *myself* to become complacent?" Mor'ded leaned forward, his glittering eyes intent on his son's face, baiting him with the agony of anticipation.

Dominic clenched his teeth.

Mor'ded collapsed back in his chair, the petal swaying with his laughter, a ringing song emanating from the depths of the flower. "You were one of my greatest mistakes, and yet a most amusing one. We elven procreate with you animals so rarely, and yet a brief rut with a common kitchen maid produced a bastard with enough of my blood to bear a marked resemblance to me. And sometimes I swear your heart is all elven." He shook his head, pale locks winking with silver. "Still, who knew that when I saw you fighting with the other kitchen boys and threw you into the game, you would rise to claim the king one day? Not I."

"You've taught me well, Father."

"Indeed. And now we must again test your worthiness. You know what has to come, do you not?"

Dominic lifted his chin.

His father stood, the scepter held before him with both hands, calling on the additional power the talisman gave him. "There is no other way to be sure of your power. Defend yourself, boy." And he unleashed the black flame.

It engulfed Dominic with a hiss and a scream, licking at his feet, shivering down his arms. His clothes appeared unaffected by the flame, and yet he felt them melting into his flesh, fusing into him. His skin still looked whole, and yet he felt it searing into ash. The black flame only burned in the mind, but ah, even the worse for that. He gritted his teeth and vowed that this time he would not fall. His own little game he always played against his father.

Dominic held up his hands, his own magic instinctively responding to the assault. White, blue, gray—he could call the entire spectrum of fire magic except for the black, but only the red fire did any damage, and his father easily squelched the blaze before it could sizzle the tiny fibrous hairs off his monstrous plants.

"Come on, lad. You can do better than that," said Mor'ded. And increased the magic twofold.

Dominic gasped for breath. The blackness slid down

his throat and into his lungs, charring them until he could not breathe. The pain he could withstand, but the suffocation always defeated him. He dropped to one knee. His magic flared again, and he imagined he felt the power of the black fire within him, the flame that burned only in the mind. Dominic tried to call it forth, but as always, nothing happened.

He always forgot how bad the pain could be. How could he forget?

Dominic had been wounded in battle many times. His men whispered that his elven blood made him impervious to pain. They did not know his mind had been tempered in fire, that the cut of a sword or sting of a bullet seemed a minor ache compared to the agony of his father's magic.

And Dominic knew he couldn't possess the power of black fire, as much as he wished for it. The gift would have been revealed when he reached puberty, when any elven powers first appeared, and he would have been sent to Elfhame with the rest of the chosen children. Only those with small magics stayed in the human world.

Yet his father continued to test him again and again, as if he suspected his son held stronger power as well. Or perhaps Mor'ded just enjoyed torturing him.

Dominic's lungs began to falter, his breath reduced to no more than a strangled wheeze of agony. His other knee collapsed and he fell to all fours, cursing his weakness. Cursing his father.

And suddenly the burning fire ceased.

Blessedly cool air caressed his cheeks and he sucked in a deep breath. Dominic resisted the urge to run his hands over his face, his hair—to reassure himself that he stood unharmed as he'd done the first time he'd endured one of his father's trials. Mor'ded had laughed at him, and Dominic had vowed never to give the man the satisfaction of that pleasure again.

Dominic rose with elven grace.

Mor'ded studied him with narrowed eyes. "No elf could withstand such pain and not instinctively call forth his own magic in defense. Again you've proven how truly weak you are... and yet..."

Dominic let out a tired sigh. He did not bother using the blue healing fire. His body might be whole, but it always took some time for his mind to heal from the memory of the pain. And he rarely used so much of his power; he felt tired unto death. "Either destroy me completely or allow me to leave. I'm half-human, you know."

"Indeed, indeed." Mor'ded chuckled, lifted his scepter, and the door of his chamber flew open with a breath of fire. "You look so elven I forget you're half animal. Go lick your wounds, then. I want you rested for the feast tonight, and of course, your marriage tomorrow."

Dominic halted in midstep. He had forgotten the date. Easy to do, since he'd almost forgotten what his intended looked like. He'd met Lady Cassandra a few times and could only recall a plain wisp of a girl with brownish hair and eyes. "Is it tomorrow, then? I suppose it's best to get it over with."

Mor'ded rolled the scepter between his palms, his black eyes glittering. "It will make the humans happy, seeing my son wed to one of their finest aristocrats.

And who knows? Perhaps you will breed true and produce another champion."

Dominic sighed. Fatigue shrouded him and it took all his will to pick up his feet and put one before the other again. He had realized years ago that it would be pointless to fight the destiny his father had forced upon him. If Mor'ded wanted him to take a wife and breed champions, so be it.

It mattered only that Dominic never allowed them to be used against him.

When he left Mor'ded's room his feet took him to the tower stairs and not his own chambers. Halfway up the curving staircase a wave of nausea overtook him, and he allowed himself a brief moment of weakness. In the dark, where none could see. He felt again the searing of his flesh and the constriction of his lungs. Sweat broke out on his forehead while his body trembled in wave upon wave of remembered pain. But he gritted his teeth against the sobs that threatened to rise from his chest, and for a brief moment pictured his father's slim neck between his battle-hardened hands.

He thrust the futile image away and began to climb again. The elven lord could level London if he so chose. Dominic's strength would never be a match against Mor'ded's, and he'd been forced to accept that.

But he had won a victory today. He'd made his father proud enough to call him son before the entire court. Dominic would grasp that slender victory, as he'd grasped even smaller accomplishments over the years.

He shoved open the wooden door and stepped out

onto the flat roof of the tower. Humid air caressed his skin; a light breeze swept his silver hair against his cheeks. The metallic smell of the dragon teased his nose, and he glanced across the rooftop at the huge beast.

Ador raised his black-scaled head and blinked at Dominic, his red eyes glowing even in the overcast day. Strange eyes with elongated pupils with black lines radiating from them, separating the red color like pieces of a pie. The dragon's leatherlike wings lay tucked against his sides, appearing deceptively small against his long, sinuous body.

Dominic removed his woolen coat and spread it out in his usual place at the base of a merlon and sat, his back against the stone. He leaned his head against the hard surface and closed his eyes with a sigh of utter weariness.

The dragon shifted. Dominic heard it in the slide of scale on stone, felt it in the tremble of the floor beneath his feet. It had once frightened him, the sheer size of the beast. But no more. He'd gotten used to the beast and Ador… well, the dragon had finally managed to tolerate him.

"Do you remember the first time I came up here, Ador?" Dominic didn't wait for the dragon to answer. He rarely received a response to his musings. But for Dominic it was enough that someone listened. "Father had tested my magic by burning Mongrel to ashes. He was a good dog and a loyal friend. I didn't think I'd ever forgive myself for not having enough magic to protect him."

The pungent smell of the Thames swept across the tower, even at this height, and for a moment,

Dominic thought he could hear the muffled sounds of the city below them.

"It was the first time I realized I could no longer allow myself to care for anyone. Man nor beast. For Father would always use them to test my magic." Dominic blocked the images of those who had suffered because of him. He'd found it much easier to bear the pain himself. "But my human weakness for companionship made me think of you. All alone, atop your tower. And then I realized Father would never harm his dragon-steed. That I could care for you, at least. Even if you couldn't return the sentiment." Dominic cracked a hopeful eye. But Ador appeared to have fallen back to sleep, his lungs like a great bellows pumping beneath those black, shiny scales.

Dominic sighed and allowed the solitude of their high perch to settle over him. The world seemed very far away up here. The wars, the court, his father—all dwindled to minute specks of matter. One final small tremor shook him, dispelling the last memory of pain. And when he spoke again his voice held the coldly rigid control it always did.

"I have done well, in most respects, to be like my father. Remote and untouchable, concerned only with my own pleasure. But you know the truth of me, don't you, Ador? Whether you willed it or not, you've been forced to hear my true thoughts over the years." Dominic scrubbed a weary hand across his brow. "This elven face of mine is deceiving, for I've been cursed with an all-too-human heart."

Ador snorted and his wing twitched, his only reaction to Dominic's damning statement. Ah well.

Dominic should consider that a remarkable response. Usually the dragon resembled nothing more than a still lump of shiny black coal.

Dominic rose and arched his back, wincing at a stab of pain. Just an ordinary pain, though, from an old bullet wound in battle. He smiled with relief that it held none of the taint of black fire magic. "Are you aware I'm to be married on the morrow? A dangerous proposition for one such as I. I almost feel sorry for the girl… but the aristocracy are used to being breeding stock, are they not?"

He picked up his coat and slung it over his back. His mind felt settled again, the memory of the burning fading to a manageable degree. Dominic couldn't be sure if the dragon's quiet presence soothed him or if the release of his thoughts brought him peace. He knew only that he always healed faster atop the tower.

He'd taken a few steps toward the door when the dragon's rumbling words stopped him.

"I smell a change in the wind."

Dominic turned and stared into those red eyes. "What do you mean?"

Ador, of course, did not answer. He closed his eyes again and huffed a small stream of smoke through his nostrils.

Dominic considered the implications of the dragon's words. Ador had once told him his father was mad. An obvious statement, it seemed, and yet those words had allowed Dominic to deal with his father time and again. So he did not think the dragon referred to something as simple as the coming of the king. Yet no matter how he twisted the statement around in his head, he could not fathom it.

Ah well. How could Dominic know the turnings of a dragon's mind? It would become clear in time... or until Ador chose to make it clear.

Two

Lady Cassandra Bridges knelt on the wooden step of the pew in front of her and pressed her palms together. The small chapel lay shrouded in shadow, the gray clouds failing to light the stained-glass windows above the altar. Several students surrounded her, and so Cassandra kept her voice to lower than a whisper. "Almighty God, please let my new husband be happy with me tomorrow—"

She started at the light touch on her shoulder, turning to face Sister Mary, who only nodded her veiled head toward the open chapel door. Cassandra mutely followed the sister down the aisle, noting with satisfaction that none of her classmates noticed her departure. She'd worked hard to make herself almost invisible to them, fostering no friendships or acquaintances.

They stepped out into the long hall with its arched roof and mosaic-tiled floor, their footsteps echoing softly over scenes of glorious battles and cherubic angels. Sister Mary slowed to walk beside Cassandra.

"You must be sure to pay extra attention during your private lesson today," said the blue-eyed nun.

Cassandra mutely nodded, waiting for the other woman to explain herself. She'd learned that if she kept her mouth closed, people talked more freely than if she asked them a hundred questions.

Sister Mary clasped her hands before her bosom. "General Raikes—your intended—has won the king today. So you must be even more diligent in your studies, for when you go to court, you will not only have to impress the Imperial Lord, but King George as well."

Cassandra's heart fluttered with excitement. Not because her future husband had accomplished what no other man had done for over a hundred years. Not because she would live under the same roof as the king. But because the king's most trusted advisor, Sir Robert Walpole, would be coming to Firehame. Having the counsel of the leader of the Rebellion might make her task easier.

"So you must listen well to Father Thomas," continued Sister Mary, a slight hitch to her breath at the mention of the handsome priest. "Practice your curtsies and table manners and forms of address, so you will do our school proud."

Cassandra glanced at the nun. She required a response. "Yes, sister."

The nun nodded with satisfaction. Sister Mary had elven blood somewhere in her family line, for Cassandra caught the brief flash of a halo around the other woman's head, the brilliant white plumage of angel's wings behind her shoulders. The illusion faded, though, at Sister Mary's next words. "Although I can't imagine anyone not paying close attention to Father Thomas." A small sigh escaped her pretty mouth.

Cassandra stifled a smile. She didn't blame the nun, despite the other woman's vows of chastity. The handsome priest would cause any woman's heart to yearn for just a touch of his hand. Indeed, Cass had even once thought herself in love with him, when he'd first come to tutor her.

Sister Mary stopped just outside a heavy wooden door, a relief of elven figures being warmed by rays of light from heaven carved into the oak surface. "Do you wish me to accompany you inside?"

Cassandra heard the note of longing in that request but had to shake her head. The staff had strict instructions from the headmaster to never enter this room. And despite Sister Mary's longing to catch a glimpse of Father Thomas, it would be safer for her not to become too familiar with the priest.

The nun sighed and left, the long sweep of her robes floating back down the hall, her wings reappearing and flowing in her wake like some feathered train. Cassandra took a breath and slowly turned the doorknob, allowing not a hint of a squeak, a ghost of a sound, to announce her presence. Although her fellow students chose to wear the silk gowns befitting their aristocratic status, Cass had years ago traded them for soft, brushed wool and modest-sized hoops. Her skirts did not rustle, nor did her hoops catch on the door frame.

She closed the door as silently as she'd opened it.

Father Thomas stood with his back to the room, his hands on the windowsill, contemplating London's dreary skies. Tables littered the room where he'd taught her all the card games with which the court amused itself. Near the columned fireplace sat two velvet chairs and a tea tray, arrayed with meticulous precision. A pianoforte waited on the left wall, music sheets carefully arranged for her instruction.

But the middle of the room lay bare, nary a rug or carpet to break the smooth expanse of flagstone. Her true lessons took place within that empty space.

Cassandra waited with bated breath. Father Thomas appeared deep in thought, unaware of his surroundings. One of his ancestors had ties to Dreamhame, for the man possessed some of that sovereignty's elven power of illusion and glamour. He often startled Cass by appearing silently at her side. Had her tutor really made such a mistake, or had he orchestrated a clever trap?

She slowly removed the cloth-of-gold belt from around her waist. A tune formed in her head. She felt the slight shiver of elven magic run through her blood as her feet began to move to the tempo of the music in her mind. Her body trembled in anticipation of the dance; the kettledrum pounding a growing beat, the flute twittering its notes, the bassoon growling beneath the increasing tempo.

Cassandra wrapped the ends of her belt firmly in both hands and allowed the music to possess her. It fired her blood, strengthened her muscles, gave her a speed that surpassed all but an elven lord's. She danced across the room within the blink of an eye. Looped the belt around Father Thomas's neck and twisted.

His hands scrabbled at the cloth around his throat.

She could feel his magic rising within him in defense of the attack. But speed and surprise aided her. His body's need for air overwhelmed his instinct for the magic. He fell, his heavier weight bringing Cass to the floor with him, knocking over a small mahogany table and shattering the pale blue vase that sat atop it.

Lady Cassandra squeezed until Father Thomas stopped struggling. Had she really caught him by surprise, then? Had he broken the rule he'd pounded into her over the years? "You were distracted," she accused him.

He didn't respond. Fear fluttered in her stomach, and she loosened her hold. "Thomas?"

He grunted and she slid her belt off his neck, then tossed it aside as she crawled over his body to look into his face. Despite the slight blue tinge to his full lips and the scowl tightening his brow, he still managed to look incredibly handsome. The annoyance in his gray eyes softened to something else as Cass continued to study him with genuine alarm.

"Have I hurt you?"

He smiled. "My pride more than anything else."

Lady Cassandra humphed. "Because you were bested by a woman?"

"No. Because I was bested by my student."

She suddenly realized their faces lay only inches apart. That she sat close enough to him to smell the scent of his cologne. Cass scrambled backward, smashing her hoops against the wall. "Well I should think," she continued, "that you'd be pleased with yourself, Viscount Althorp. Isn't the best teacher the one whose student surpasses him?"

He sat up, rubbing at the red mark around his throat, his priestly garb twisted around his lean body. Cass never understood how he'd managed to fool so many with that clothing. He had the eyes of a wicked man.

They looked at her with a glitter of wickedness even now. "Perhaps. And I suppose the timing is fortuitous, since you're to be married on the morrow."

Cassandra abruptly rose and he copied her movement, his eyes never leaving hers. He reached out to touch her hand and she turned away, facing out the same window he'd been standing at but a moment ago. "You've heard that he has won the king?"

"Of course."

Cassandra didn't need to name her intended. They both knew of whom she spoke. And suddenly her doubts overwhelmed her. If only she had inherited some of that elven beauty, perhaps she wouldn't be so unsure of winning him over. Her brown hair had a hint of red, her brown eyes a touch of gold, but her appearance held nothing unusual enough to tempt him. Fie, the nuns likened her to a little brown wren. She lowered her voice to a near whisper. "The very thought of him frightens me sometimes. I think he is more elven than human. I worry I shan't be able to please him."

"Cass." Thomas's own voice lowered to a husky timbre. "Look at me."

She never should have spoken of her fears. Not to him. Truly, not to anyone. But her marriage had always seemed a distant thing, something she needn't worry about for a long time. The day had come faster than she had been prepared for.

When she didn't turn around, Thomas clasped her shoulders and spun her, forcing her to look at him. "You don't have to go through with this."

She looked into those gray eyes and saw to her utter astonishment that he meant what he said. "Do not allow me to give in to a moment of cowardice, Thomas."

"I'm serious." His hand brushed her cheek.

When he'd first come to tutor her, she would have given her life for that touch. But Thomas had kept himself aloof, recognizing her infatuation for what it was. Or so she had thought.

"Come away with me," he said. "You don't have to go through with this. The Rebellion will find someone else to marry the bastard."

Just the thought that she would stray from the path laid out for her dizzied Cassandra for a moment. Nearly every day of her life had been in preparation for her marriage to the Imperial Lord's champion. The thought that she wouldn't fulfill her destiny set her adrift. "It would be impossible."

He misunderstood her. "No, it wouldn't. I've given this a lot of thought over the past few days. I'm the most skilled spy in the Rebellion, Cass. I can get you out of Firehame and into one of the neighboring sovereignties before anyone suspects you're even missing. I can keep you safe."

She shook her head and his temper flared. "You are going to your death, Lady Cassandra."

Her own temper retaliated in response. "You've known this for years. Need I remind you that you are the one who taught me the death dances? You are the one who swayed me to the Rebellion's cause. How dare you take advantage of my cowardice to offer me this false hope."

"It's not false." He picked up her hands and went down on one knee. "Marry me."

"I cannot."

"Why?"

"Because I don't love you."

His breath hitched. She hadn't meant to put it so baldly. "You don't love the bastard either. And you can't marry *him*."

She pulled her hands out of his. "I can. I will. That's different and you know it. It's a path I decided to take long ago. I've made my peace with God and am willing to risk my immortal soul."

"Don't spout that holy drivel at me, Cassandra. This priestly garb is nothing but a disguise, you know."

She couldn't help the half smile that formed on her mouth. "And well do I know it, Viscount Thomas Althorp."

He stood, raking his gold hair away from his eyes, scowling at her stubbornness. "You used to love me, once."

"I admit I was infatuated with you. How could I not be? Besides my father, you're the only man with whom I've spent any company." She didn't mention her betrothed. She'd been allowed out of the confines of the school to meet with him on several occasions. But they had all been formal functions, and Dominic Raikes had barely seemed to notice her.

Thomas made a strangled sound, stepped forward, and roughly took her into his arms. And then he kissed her.

Cassandra had never been kissed before. He caught her completely unawares, and at first she could do nothing but study the peculiar sensation of having a man's mouth on her own. Warm, wet... and decidedly odd. She couldn't quite decide whether she liked the experience.

Thomas pulled back his head and stared down into her face. "You don't feel a thing, do you?"

She frowned. "What exactly am I supposed to be feeling?"

He let out a sigh of exasperation and kissed her again.

Cass wondered if it would feel the same when her intended finally kissed her. Although she couldn't be sure if he would, not knowing if it was necessary for the act of... procreation. He'd made it very clear he would do only his duty and nothing more. That he viewed her as his breeding stock.

The thought made her try to respond to Thomas. This might be her only chance to experience a true kiss. She cautiously curled her hands around his shoulders, which made him moan and lean even closer to her, nearly bending her backward with the force of his mouth.

Cassandra could think of nothing other than the pain in her back and the need to breathe.

Thomas pulled away and raised his golden brows. "Despite your lack of enthusiasm, I know you aren't frigid," he muttered.

"What do you mean? I'm not the slightest bit cold. Indeed, your hold is nearly suffocating me with warmth."

He straightened and set her away from him. "You could come to love me, you know."

"I'm not destined for love. I knew that the moment I decided to join the Rebellion."

He spun and sought out the chair by the fireplace, sat with his elbows propped on his knees and stared into the embers. "You've always been stubborn. Once you set your sight on something, there's no changing your mind. I had to try though." He glanced up at her, gold hair tumbling over his brow. "Do you know how many assassins we've set on the elven lords? And they've all failed, Lady Cassandra. Every last one of them."

The look in his eyes frightened her. She prayed to God for courage and took a moment to compose herself. She smoothed her sleeves, fluffed her skirts. Their lesson today had not gone as she had thought it would. Fie, she had never imagined having such a conversation with Lord Althorp. Had never imagined that the man who'd always reassured her would now require that same sentiment back.

She folded her hands in front of her and gave him a cheeky grin. "How many of them managed to nearly strangle you to death, Thomas?"

He couldn't seem to resist smiling back at her. "Confound it, girl. I can't help but admire you. There's nothing I can say to change your mind, is there?"

"No." She felt her smile falter as she thought of the enormity of her task. "I cannot think of myself, Thomas. Nor you, nor my father... nor the elven bastard, for that matter. The freedom of the people of England is at stake. And just the chance"—she clasped her hands tight—"the mere chance of ending these ridiculous war games and setting the king in power once more is worth my soul."

"Not to me." She opened her mouth again and he held up a pale hand to quiet her. "Enough. Do you know your eyes glaze over like a nun at prayer when you say such things?"

"Had I not been chosen for this task, I would have liked to have taken the vows."

Thomas laughed at her, slapping his knees. "Oh no, my girl. Becoming a nun is not for the likes of you."

Cass raised her chin, miffed at his opinion of her. "I would make a very good nun."

He laughed harder, wiped the tears from those wicked gray eyes. "Sometimes I think I know you better than you know yourself. There's a fire within you, Lady Cassandra. I felt it in your kiss. And one day it will be set free, and heaven help the man who stokes it." He motioned her to the chair across from him and Cassandra took it, although her back stayed as stiff as a rod. He eyed her for a time in silence, only the crackle of the fire and the muted sounds of a carriage rumbling past the window disturbing the quiet.

All trace of humor vanished from his expression, and he leaned forward, his brow creased in earnestness. "I do not think your father did you a favor by having you raised among all this religious dogma. You've taken it to heart and I'm not sure if it will help or hinder you."

Cass frowned. She'd always considered Thomas's lack of faith a peculiarity, another oddity to his character compared to those she'd always been surrounded by. She pitied him for it.

Thomas sighed. "Well then, there's no help for it. Despite my teaching, the nuns have managed to keep you pure, anyway. What a paradox you are, my dear. The court won't know what to make of you."

"Unless they get in my way, they hardly matter."

"I daresay. Now, this will probably be the last time we will be able to meet privately."

Cassandra felt her stomach twist. In many ways, Thomas had been her only friend. How would she manage without his company?

He patted her hand, then snatched his away, as if he had to force himself not to hold onto her. Their conversation today, that kiss of his, had changed their relationship, it seemed. Perhaps it would be better if they did not meet again.

"Don't worry," he assured her. "You shall still see me. But not as Father Thomas. Viscount Althorp, however, will reappear at court, to the surprise and delight of all, I am sure." He gave her that crooked grin that had once made her younger self swoon. "But it wouldn't be safe for us to talk often or privately, so listen closely."

She nodded, relieved they had resumed their familiar roles as tutor and student.

"I don't know," he said, "if having the king's court in Firehame will make your task easier. See if you can aid Sir Robert Walpole, but do not risk your task for his sake. We've never had an assassin this close to an Imperial Lord before. Your mission is far more important than the leader of the Rebellion, do you understand?"

Cassandra nodded.

"Your magic for the dance will not be enough. You never would have returned home after your trials if you had enough magic to truly threaten the elven lord. Only surprise and skill will overcome him."

Although Cass vaguely remembered her trials, she knew her father had been disappointed when she hadn't possessed enough magic to be sent to the elvens' home world, the fabled Elfhame. His friend, Lord Welton, had bragged for years that his son had been a chosen one, and the duke had been decidedly put out when he could not say the same of his only child.

It had soothed her father somewhat when she'd become affianced to General Raikes. And now that her intended had won the king...

"It may take you years to get close to the Imperial Lord," continued the viscount. "It will help you immensely if you can manage to make your new husband trust you. But even then do not rush forward blindly. Remember your most important lesson."

The words fell from her mouth without thought. "Patience."

"Just so. Practice it with Dominic Raikes. I'm sure he will tax it."

Cassandra smiled. Thomas did not return it this time. Instead he leaned forward, his gray eyes hard as steel. "Make sure of your opportunity before you seize it. If nothing else, remember that, my girl."

"I will. I promise."

The bell rang, signaling the end of prayer, and made both of them jump. Thomas smiled at her rather sheepishly, and Cassandra feared the smile she gave him in turn held too much sadness in it.

He walked her to the door, bowed low over her

hand. "If you ever need me, leave a message for Father Thomas. I will come... if it's safe."

She understood. From this moment forward, she should depend only upon herself. She turned to leave, but he would not let go of her hand.

"Are you sure?" he murmured.

"Yes." Oh, how confident she sounded! Was it false or true? She supposed the next few days would tell.

His grip loosened and she felt her entire body grow cold. Would she ever be truly warm again?

"Farewell, then, Lady Cassandra. You have been a most excellent student."

She might never see him again, at least in this guise. She wondered what he would be like in the full role of Viscount Althorp. "Good-bye, Father Thomas."

Cass slipped out the door almost as quietly as she'd entered. Some of her training had become pure habit. The hall flowed with the colorful skirts of the ladies of quality, and she insinuated herself within the crowd of students with barely a notice. She knew she should go to her rooms, that her father had sent his servants along with her wedding gown so she would be prepared for tomorrow.

But the entire encounter with Thomas had shaken her belief in the path she had chosen to take. Her widowed father had no idea of her involvement with the Rebellion; he would have disowned her, since he stood to gain status and funds with her union to the champion.

She'd missed her mother over the years, but never as much as she did at this moment.

So when Cass passed by the chapel, she slipped

inside and closed the door behind her. She'd always had God to talk to. For a moment she enjoyed the silence, the chatter of the girls muffled behind the walls. Prayer time had ended, and so she had the entire place to herself.

She passed the pews and went straight to the altar, then sank to her knees on the bare stone, as close to the cross as propriety would allow. She bowed her head, pressed her palms together, and continued her interrupted prayer, her words barely above a whisper.

"Almighty God, please let my new husband be happy with me tomorrow so I can murder his father."

⁂

Cassandra sat within the carriage, trying not to rumple the silk of her wedding dress. The sunshine streamed through the windows and struck the silver edging decorating the cream fabric and shot tiny sparks of light around her. Father had insisted on the silk, had chosen the pleated gown himself. He wanted his daughter to shine.

Cass wanted only to disappear.

She glanced across the coach at her father. The press of traffic to Westminster Abbey impeded their progress, and the Duke of Chandos grumbled again.

"Devilishly foolish of the lot. They're all here to see the wedding, and they can't have one without the bride. We shall be late because of all the gawkers."

He checked his gold watch for the hundredth time. Age had not diminished her father's handsome looks. His silver-white wig made his hazel eyes appear lighter, and they made a striking contrast against his tan face. He loved to hunt, spent a great deal of time outdoors, which had kept up his youthful physique. He had not mourned Cassandra's mother for long, although she supposed she couldn't blame him, when women kept throwing themselves at his feet.

He'd inherited only a pretty face from his elven blood.

"Please, Father, don't be concerned. They will wait for us."

"Eh?" He glanced up, as if he'd forgotten her presence. "Yes, quite right." The Duke of Chandos leaned over and patted her hand. "As you are my only child, your son will inherit the title. Of course they'll wait."

Cassandra gave him a weak smile and turned to stare out the window. Her new stays itched. And Father had insisted she wear the most outlandishly wide hoops; as a consequence they kept popping up in her seated position. She gave a sigh of relief when she saw the Gothic arches of the Abbey. The carriage stopped in front of the ornately carved entry. The area had been roped off to hold back the crowd, and a line of uniformed officers standing in rigid military attention created an aisle for her to walk through.

Their uniformed escort leaped down from the back of the coach and opened the door, stepping aside to create another barrier against the watching crowd. Cass felt as if she were on display and confined all at the same time.

A sudden flare of cool white fire highlighted the officers and the entrance to the church, dancing upward past the tops of the spires in curling waves of crystal scintillation. Cass could feel the strength of the

Imperial Lord's magic like a shiver in the very air. Her hands began to sweat inside her silk gloves.

Father stared out the window and swallowed. "Don't worry, my dear. We'll do just fine."

She couldn't be sure if his words were to reassure her or himself.

Father exited the carriage first, adjusted the lace at the sleeves of his satin coat, and held out his hand to her. Her fingers trembled as she clasped it. The sweep of her gown preceded her from the carriage, and when she raised her head a sudden beam of fire touched her satin pinner, radiating outward to join the already swirling beams. Her knees felt like pudding and for the first time in her life, she thought she might swoon.

Cass muttered a prayer, took a deep breath, and walked forward to her doom.

But the moment she entered the grand abbey, the carved images of saints and apostles calmed her. Statues of angels stared lovingly down at her, the feathers in their wings, the very folds of their robes, appearing softly real from the skill of the artisan that had sculpted them. Father led her down the nave, and she ignored the hundreds of staring eyes of the nobles who sat in the pews, keeping her gaze focused on the great cross over the high altar. The music of the choir soared above and beyond the Imperial Lord's magical fire that had led them inside, and she let the melody carry her slippered feet down the very, very long aisle.

She didn't trip on her gown. Father didn't stumble in his new high-heeled shoes. Cassandra thought she might manage this public display without too much fuss after all, until they neared the altar. And she saw her intended. And his father.

General Dominic Raikes's handsome features had always flustered her. But today she realized the elven-kind had brought the beauty of angels to earth for them... and Dominic looked so strikingly similar to his elven-lord father. Her intended stood with military precision; indeed, he'd worn his uniform, although she doubted he wore this version in battle. The red wool had been replaced by red velvet, with gold trim about the sleeves and flared skirt of the coat. Dozens of gold buttons trimmed the wide cuffs of the coat and down the opening, although only one clasped it closed at the waist. His cravat and sleeves dripped with black lace, and that color matched his shiny boots and the velvet cloak slung over his shoulders.

Not the normal dress for a marriage, but it suited him well.

He wore no wig, of course, since after all, the reason the gentry wore them was to copy the elvens' silver blond hair, and the general had inherited the original. As she drew closer to him, she noticed he wore battle braids in his hair, but they'd been drawn back and fastened behind his head, revealing his pointed ears and the high cheekbones in his face.

Cass had her attention riveted on him, but he didn't return the favor. Indeed, his gaze roamed the vaulted ceiling and he looked... bored.

She glanced over at Imperial Lord Mor'ded. He'd dressed in the same manner as his son, although Cassandra imagined he'd never fought on a real battlefield in his life. His face looked slightly paler than his son's, his shoulders narrower, his legs less muscular. And his black eyes…

Cass's face swiveled between the two of them. Large elven eyes, as shiny and black as coal—they almost looked like they had facets in them. Both their eyes would be beautiful—glittering like exotic jewels—if they hadn't looked so very cold. So very cruel.

Instead of the angels to whom she'd compared them, she should have been thinking devils.

Cass turned her attention toward the archbishop and kept it there as her father brought her to stand next to General Raikes. He didn't so much as blink to acknowledge her presence. Her head just topped his shoulders, and she fancied she could feel the heat of his body.

She refused to allow her intended to intimidate her by his mere presence.

The entire wedding party waited in a frozen tableau while the choir finished its song. Yet beneath Cass's dress her toes continued to tap in time to the music. She felt the dance swell inside of her, seeking direction. A brief thought came to her and made her stomach flip. Could she kill Mor'ded now and put an end to this farce? She'd resigned herself to the knowledge that she wouldn't survive the assassination. Surely the Imperial Lord's son would kill her if she moved now. What better way to send the sovereignty into chaos and advance the tide of the Rebellion?

Her heels lifted. Her knees swayed.

General Dominic Raikes leaned down and whispered in her ear. "Do you have an itch?"

The archbishop frowned at them. Imperial Lord Mor'ded fastened those cold eyes on her.

Cass froze. Had she detected a note of mockery in the general's deep voice? She stole a glance at him. His emotionless eyes stayed fixed on the archbishop as well, but the corner of his mouth twitched. She vowed she'd seen it twitch.

She felt a flush creep from belly to nose and knew her face had turned a deep red. And knew her opportunity to act had passed. The choir ended with a crescendo of glorious song, and without further ado the archbishop began the ceremony.

Perhaps it was just as well. Thomas had cautioned her for patience and she'd almost rushed forward. And as she stood through the painfully long ceremony and went through the motions required of her, she chided herself.

Imperial Lord Mor'ded's body nearly vibrated with tension, his eyes watching the assembled guests without appearing to. His white fire magic still swirled among the guests, and she suddenly wondered if it had all been for show. Could he search for hidden dangers with it? Could he sense an attack, whether magical or physical, with his power?

Cass couldn't be sure. The information that the Rebellion had on the elven lords was sketchy. Thomas had done the best he could, but she suddenly realized she'd been ill prepared for her task. She could feel the power of Mor'ded's magic, and the tiny bit she possessed seemed negligible by comparison. Perhaps the wiser course would be to discover all she could about the elven lords and their magic before she acted at all.

Cass now stood facing her... new husband. She supposed she'd have to get used to that idea. Although she didn't think she could ever get used to the coldness of his beautiful eyes. She'd hoped she could use the general to gather information about the elven, but right now he did not look like a man who could be used. Indeed, when his eyes met hers for a moment, a shiver of dread went through her.

The few times she'd visited him, he had treated her with a disinterest bordering on contempt. She'd foolishly thought that when she became his wife that might change, but it appeared the ceremony affected him not at all. Faith, how would she manage to share his bed tonight? Best not to think of that.

She blanched as her new husband slid a ring on her finger. A band of gold with a rose carved atop it. But the rose looked so real, the edges of the petals as delicate as the true flower. Cass couldn't resist the impulse to bring it closer to her face, then nearly jumped when the petals curled closed, changing the carving to a tight bud.

He'd given her a ring crafted with elven magic.

Her eyes flew up to his in alarm.

General Raikes lowered his head. "It won't harm you," he muttered, a note of exasperation in his velvety voice. And then he lowered his head and kissed her, signaling an end to the ceremony.

Cass's heart flipped over. She stood quite frozen, unsure of what had come over her. The general had done nothing more than press his lips to hers. And her entire body had shivered. From that one dispassionate touch.

As the onlookers broke into polite applause, Mor'ded leaned close to his son and said, "Surely the champion can do better than that."

She watched her husband glance at his father. Saw his face harden with challenge. Then the general wrapped his arms around her and roughly pulled her against his chest, and Cass could only pray.

Her new husband kissed her again. But this time he kissed her like Thomas had, bending her backward in his arms, moving his mouth over hers as if he sought to eat her alive. But the experience was totally unlike the one she'd shared with Thomas.

The world seemed to fall away. Cass became aware of nothing and no one but the man holding her in his arms. The heat of his mouth, the fire that ran through her body, the sheer exhilaration of the taste of him. Her senses heightened. She felt her breasts tighten and strain toward him. Felt a wetness between her legs that frightened and excited her all at the same time. His tongue pressed against her lips, and lacking any experience of what to do, she opened her mouth and he invaded it, stroking and tasting until she just forgot to breathe.

Her new husband abruptly let her go and set her away from him. Cass swayed. The applause in the room had risen in volume, and she blushed again to realize she'd behaved in such a manner in front of an archbishop, half the country, and in the house of the Lord, no less. She couldn't account for what had come over her.

General Raikes gave his father a heated look. "Will that do?"

Mor'ded chuckled.

When Dominic took her hand and led her back down the nave, Cass could do nothing but weakly follow. But she noticed the rose in her ring had come unfurled, spreading out into a glorious open blossom.

Three

CASS SAT AT HER WEDDING BREAKFAST WITHIN THE great hall of Firehame Palace, still slightly dazed. Her new husband hadn't spoken a word to her in the short carriage ride back to the palace. Indeed, he had appeared to be furious with her... but surely she must have been mistaken, for the general would have to possess feelings for her to arouse them so.

When they'd arrived at the palace, he'd turned back into the man with whom she'd become familiar. Cold, disinterested, and aloof. He sat across from her at table, next to a beautiful woman with hair pale enough to require only the lightest touches of powder. He completely ignored his new wife in favor of the blue-eyed creature.

Mor'ded sat at the head of the table and leaned to his right to speak to Cassandra. "That's my son's mistress, Lady Agnes."

Cass dropped her spoon and it clanged atop the china. The rose on her wedding ring twisted into a tight bud. General Raikes finally turned to look at her. How dare he bring his mistress to their wedding breakfast? Is this how the court behaved? Well, she didn't give a fig what the others considered acceptable. She glared at her husband and his beautiful companion.

Again, a twitch of the lip. So she continued to amuse him, did she?

The elven lord laughed. "Don't worry, my dear. You will have your husband's full attention until he gets you with child. He knows what's expected of him... as should you."

She heard the threat and squashed down her anger. She reminded herself that her marriage to the champion was nothing but a falsehood, a way to get close to the elven lord. She must appear to be as cold and unconcerned as he. Cassandra kept her voice steady. "I look forward to giving you a grandson, my lord."

Mor'ded scowled, the expression not diminishing his beauty one whit, and leaned back in his chair. "The devil to that. I want a new champion."

If Cass had any doubts as to her new role, the elven lord had just made it clear. If she didn't already have the task of killing her new father-in-law, she'd surely wish to do so now.

Mor'ded tapped the triangular-shaped head of his magical scepter against his cheek, watching her with narrowed eyes. She didn't know what expression might be on her face and quickly bowed her head. She watched the room through her lashes, practicing the skill she'd nearly perfected over the years. Despite her position at the head table, she almost succeeded in making herself unnoticeable.

But she felt the Imperial Lord's gaze fall on her time and again throughout the meal.

"Lord Blevin," said Mor'ded, "I grow bored. I daresay I can count on you to liven up the meal."

The lord in question sported a wig with such a long fall of silver-white hair that he'd curled it in his lap. In an attempt to imitate the flawless pale complexion of the elven, he'd covered his face with too much powder, and it cracked as he beamed at being singled out. "Indeed, Imperial Lord, I have just perfected a new spell."

Titters flowed up and down the crystal-laden table.

Lord Blevin puffed up his chest beneath his bright yellow waistcoat. "Although some may laugh at my lack of fire magic, I assure you my smoke can be just as powerful."

Mor'ded nodded, but Cass detected a slight stiffening in his posture. Surely the elven lord couldn't be concerned about the magical powers of his courtiers? Not when he held trials thrice a year to test the children born with the elven gifts.

Lord Blevin had scrunched up his face and now held out his hands before him. Smoke did indeed form between his palms, and his hands shook while he shaped it into the figure of a tiny person. He then added wings, and Cass thought he meant to create a smoke angel, but she should have known better. The wings took the shape of a bat and white smoke formed pointy, long teeth hanging from the mouth. The small bat-person hissed and flew at Lady Agnes, who shrieked a laugh and begged the general to protect her. The man looked quite unmoved by her plight.

Lord Blevin created another much more quickly than he had formed the first, and the ones that followed with even more speed. Soon the entire table lay covered in the beings of smoke, their wings flapping in the faces of ladies and their teeth snapping at the gentlemen who tried to defend them.

One of the nasty beasts lunged at Cassandra, and she waved her hand through it. The smoke parted and then resumed its previous shape. She sighed and then ducked her head, determined to ignore the nuisance but the creature hugged her face, making her cough. She waved her hand again, her eyes burning and causing tears to run down her face.

Several ladies had started to scream right along with Lady Agnes, and the sound of chairs being pushed back hurriedly from the table added to the cacophony.

Imperial Lord Mor'ded laughed. "Well done, Blevin."

"Ho, ho, it's just smoke," declared another gentleman. "Watch what I can do." And he pointed at one of the smoke creatures; a loud pop of displaced air sounded, and the thing exploded into tiny bits of gray wisps.

"Devil a bit," said a portly courtier. "I can top that, man!" And with a flourish of his arms, the wine in every glass and decanter poured *up*, burgundy waves of color, dousing several smoke creatures and more than one lady. The screams escalated.

Lady Cassandra glanced at her father, who had sat on her other side as still as a stone throughout the entire meal. His hazel eyes had widened in stunned disbelief at the chaos around him.

"This is my wedding breakfast," she said to him.

He turned and gave her a look of apology, glanced at the elven lord, and patted her hand. "Best get used to the whims of the court, girl."

Sudden rage drove Cass to her feet. Mor'ded had collapsed into whoops of laughter. General Raikes watched the antics of the nobles with disdainful interest, like a man studying a group of monkeys at play. She slapped her hands on the table, rattling the china, finally gaining the notice of her husband. "This is my wedding breakfast," she repeated, but this time with such force that the courtiers froze, turning to stare at her as if she'd just sprouted horns.

Mor'ded stilled. The guests breathed in a collective breath.

"You've got spunk," said the Imperial Lord into the silence. "I'll give you that. But I find spunk amusing only in small doses, girl."

She felt his power throb like the beat of a heart. It made her knees weak, and she collapsed back into her chair. Slowly the other nobles regained their seats, wiped faces streaming with port, and dabbed handkerchiefs at spotted silk.

Dominic Raikes continued to stare coldly at her, as if she'd turned into one of the monkeys. Cass gave him a look of entreaty.

Mor'ded snorted. "Don't expect support from that direction. If anything, my son's heart is colder than my own."

He said it with pride. Her husband's chin lifted with pride. Cass prayed for guidance.

Mor'ded turned his attention to Cassandra's father. "You there, Chandos. Elven blood runs in your veins.

Since your daughter has deprived me of entertainment, perhaps you can show us your own power."

Father tried not to squirm. Tried not to look around at the other nobles. "You forget I have no power other than the gift of my charm, Your Most High."

Humphs of disgust from the gentlemen. Titters of scorn from the ladies.

"Yet I'm sure I remember that your daughter has the gift of dance." Those glittering black eyes narrowed. "She'd best have enough of the blood to breed true." His gaze pierced Cass yet again. "So girl, it looks like it's up to you to entertain me." He rose, a flutter of velvet and lace and deadly magic. He clasped her shoulder and nearly dragged her from her chair, through the hall into the great ballroom. Cass shied away from his scepter, afraid it would accidentally brush against her skin. Rumor had it that no one could touch it but a true elven lord, and she wouldn't relish finding out the truth of it.

Lady Cassandra could hear the excited whispers of the court as they followed.

Startled slaves quickly dropped their tasks and vanished behind stately columns and cleverly hidden doors. The long tables at the end of the ballroom appeared half-full. Weak light filtered in from double doors and the candles hadn't been lit yet, so the room lay shrouded in gloom. Mor'ded uttered a word and the ceiling lit with a blazing light, causing several of the musicians to break their strings while in the middle of their rehearsal.

Mor'ded hauled her into the middle of the floor. "Play," he commanded them.

They quickly organized themselves and struck up a tune while the lords and ladies spread around the room, vying for the best view.

Cass swallowed. She'd made a complete muck of things and now he sought to punish her. Instead of impressing the elven lord with her innocence and demure nature, she'd incited his anger... something she guessed few rarely did. But perhaps. Perhaps she could turn this to her advantage. She could get close enough to the lord for a killing blow once her strength was enhanced by the music.

"Will you partner me then, dearest father-in-law?"

He looked down his nose at her with disdain. "Dominic," he called. And he thrust Cass into the arms of her new husband, then strode across the polished floor to settle himself on his golden throne.

The music rose in volume and she felt it creep into her bones. Without further ado, General Raikes swept her into a dance, one that swirled her silk skirts across the floor, made the silver in her dress sparkle like the sun's reflection on water.

Despite her annoyance at herself for inciting the elven lord's wrath, she couldn't regret that her husband finally held her in his arms. He had strong, warm arms.

"I shall endeavor to behave better in the future," she said to him.

He didn't blink. Didn't shrug. Just danced her around the room like an angel of grace. His elven blood made his movements smooth and lithe, but she could tell he did not embrace the music. Did not become one with the magic of it, as she could.

She feared he had no feelings—but if he did, he surely regretted the choice of bride that had been thrust upon him. She had asked God to allow her to make him happy, but since he seemed to lack that emotion, she must seek to impress her husband, at the least. She must bridge this gap between them in some way.

So Cass let the music swell through her. Her feet caught the rhythm and moved of their own accord. Her body swayed with the beat of the drums; her arms fluttered with the soulful sound of the strings. She felt Dominic's intake of breath, and the dance between them subtly shifted. He still led—she doubted if it could have been otherwise—but his body molded to hers, and soon they did more than the practiced steps of the minuet. Motions that came from the music itself shaped their dance until what they performed no longer resembled any of the movements defined by man.

Cass had danced only with Thomas and her father. Neither of them possessed the elven grace the way her new husband did. She felt almost as if he became one with her, and she danced as she'd never done before, twirling around him to be caught again in his grasp, sliding across the floor by turns of their heels. He seemed to sense her next move and stayed with her, so she didn't fear that when she leaned back in an arch, he would not be there to catch her. That when she trailed her arm down his own and twirled at the tips of his fingers, he would not be ready to pull her back into his arms. She knew not what to call this dance they devised, but she felt sure it would shock the court.

She noticed her rose ring had blossomed again. Elven magic, indeed. Did it predict so accurately her mood, then?

When the music finally ended and they swayed to a stop, not a sound could be heard within the vast room. Her husband looked at her then. Truly looked at her as if for the first time. But she could tell nothing of his thoughts from the cold glitter of his black eyes.

"That's a very old elven dance," said Mor'ded. Cass turned and saw the flicker of a smile on the Imperial Lord's face. "I never thought to see it performed as if I watched my own people at a fete in Elfhame. You do indeed *dance*, Lady Cassandra."

She suspected that would be the highest praise she would receive and bowed, turned to see if she'd also managed to please her new husband, and realized she stood alone.

Indeed, she stayed alone throughout the entire day, except for the company of her father, who kept a silent vigil by her side. Once, he managed to whisper to her, "Perhaps I have made a mistake in giving you over to this man." But Cassandra quickly shushed him, assuring him all would be well. That her husband's heart would eventually warm to her, and he would seek her company.

Lady Agnes pranced by at that moment in Dominic's arms, her laughter denouncing Cass a liar. Lady

Cassandra didn't need to look at her ring to know it had tightened into a small bud again.

She plucked a glass off a footman's tray and downed the contents. It burned; she coughed but immediately felt better. She knew her marriage was nothing but a charade, that her new husband didn't have a heart. But she'd had enough humiliation for one day. And if she continued to attend a ball where her husband flaunted his mistress in her face, she would hate him. And that would not serve the Rebellion's cause one whit.

So she kissed her father and quietly left the ball, hesitating outside the grand room. She had no idea which direction to take. Up, most likely, and then perhaps she could ask a chambermaid for the directions to the general's rooms.

From the corner of her eye she caught a furtive movement, quite like her own stealthy habit of slipping around door frames. Without thinking she reached out, snagging the shoulder of the boy's shirt. He struggled for a moment, gave a sigh of defeat, and looked up at her with the largest hazel eyes Cass had ever seen. Faceted, elven eyes.

"Don't be frightened," said Cass. "I just need some directions."

The lad looked at her face, then down to a meat pie he held—which he'd obviously stolen from the banquet table—and quickly stuffed it into a ragged tear in his shirt. Cass ignored the pilfered item. A child needed to eat.

"What's your name?"

"Do ye need to know that?"

Cass smiled. Cheeky little thing. "I suppose not, but I would like the pleasure of knowing whom I am addressing."

The formality of her request appeared to make an impression. Cass released her hold and the boy squared his shoulders, smoothed back the silver-white hair tangled about his face, and curtsied. "My name is Gwendolyn, but everybody calls me Gwen."

Cass started. Well, at that age, and with the amount of dirt covering the child, she shouldn't be surprised she'd mistaken the gender.

"Did I do it wrong? I never curtsied before, but I've watched lots of times when the ladies do it."

"Ah no. You curtsied quite well. How clever of you to teach yourself."

The child beamed. Cass tried to suppress her discomfort. They employed servants in her home and at her school. The gentry considered it a show of their status that they could afford paid servants, and if they kept slaves, they were assigned the most menial tasks… and were hidden from view. So she didn't have much experience with slaves. The child looked ragged enough to have come from the workhouses of the East End of London. And even there they didn't put little girls in boy's breeches.

"Well, Gwen, my name is Lady Cassandra, but you may call me Lady Cass. And I'm looking for General Raikes's bedchamber. Can you direct me?"

"Yer his new wife, ain't ye? Why ye leaving yer party so early? Did ye see all the food they laid out fer ye?"

"I'm quite full, you see."

The child nodded in relief, as if glad Cass hadn't neglected the feast. "Ye don't want to go to his old place, do ye? They gave him a new set of rooms, ye see."

"Indeed. You can direct me to the new rooms."

"Ye might get lost. I could take ye there, but I'm not really supposed to be up in them. I might get in trouble."

Cass reached in the slit of her skirt and pulled out a coin from her bag. "If anyone should stop us, I shall say you are my guide. And this will be for your trouble."

The coin disappeared as quickly as the meat pie had, and in the same place. "That's all right, then." The child skipped off. Cass lifted her skirts and rushed to follow. "I'm supposed to stay in the kitchens, see. But I know me ways around. There's secret passages behind the walls, did ye know?"

Cassandra shook her head and tried to look suitably impressed.

"The general showed me. He used to work in the kitchens too, when he was little."

So Cass had heard, but she'd hardly credited it. "Did he?"

The child stopped at a winding staircase, the mahogany handrails polished to a brilliant shine, the treads carpeted in plush red. "I don't use these. The servants' stairs are back there." And she pointed to a closed door. "But I suppose it's all right since I'm with ye."

Cass nodded, lifted her silk skirts a bit more, and started up the stairs, the child right on her heels. "So you know the general, Gwen?"

"Oh aye. We likes to call him champion, ye know. But only when he ain't around, 'cause he don't like it."

Cass waited, hoping the girl wouldn't need any further prodding.

"He don't pay us no mind either. But he likes to snatch food from Cook, says it's a habit he can't break." They had reached the landing, and Gwen pointed down a long hall. "This here floor is for guests. Yer one more up."

Cass nodded and started up again.

"He don't like us none. He don't like anyone."

"I hope he'll like me, Gwen."

"Maybe. But he don't seem to like the women he sleeps with neither. At least, that's what Cook says."

Cassandra thought she might take a little trip to the kitchens on the morrow and meet this Cook. She couldn't imagine that the churlish general went to the kitchens for nostalgia. What might be his true purpose?

"Don't worry about not knowing him, Lady Cass. Nobody does, that's what Cook says. Now me, I think the dragon knows him. He spends a lot of time up there in the tower."

"With Mor'ded's dragon-steed?" What would he want with such a dread beast?

"Aye, his name's Ador, and I'm scared of him. But I don't think the general's scared of nothing."

"Indeed."

"But I only have finding magic. If I had the champion's fire magic, maybe I wouldn't be scared neither."

"Finding magic?"

"Oh aye. I can find lost stuff. If ye ever need anything found, lady, just let me know."

They had reached the second landing, and the child skipped in front of Cassandra, taking the lead down the vast hall. Urns filled with blue fire lit the passage and gave it an eerie glow. Treasures littered the cabinets and niches in the walls, and Cass vowed to explore them in the light of day. But for now her guide hurried her along.

Gwen stopped at two large double doors covered in gilt. "This is where yer new rooms are. I haven't been inside yet; they just finished with them."

Cass nodded and reached for the gold handle.

Gwen tugged at Cassandra's skirt. "Down there," she whispered, pointing a grubby finger at the end of the corridor, "is the Imperial Lord's rooms. Nobody's ever been in there, 'cept maybe the general. Don't go there, Lady Cass. There's things in there that'll eat ye if Mor'ded don't flame ye first."

Cassandra frowned, wondering if Mor'ded had started the rumor to ensure his privacy. If it was indeed a rumor.

"But don't ye worry about the champion hurting ye. He don't flame women or children."

For some reason Cass didn't feel reassured by that statement. "Would you like to come inside with me, Gwen?"

Those hazel eyes widened even farther. "Oh aye, my lady." Then she hastily added, "Cook says my curiosity will get me flogged one day."

"They flog you?"

"Oh aye. Ye can do anything ye want with a slave. Ain't got no rights, ye see. Ye don't seem to know much, lady. Where ye come from?"

Cass smiled. "A private school."

"Not a very good 'un, then." She sucked in a sharp breath and added, "No offense, my lady. Cook says I talk too much. Probably get flogged for that someday too."

"Not if I have any say about it," muttered Cass as she pushed open the door. She walked into what might have been a parlor if it had held more than two chairs by the fireplace and a footstool. She went into the adjacent room, which looked to be a private dining room by the bare table sitting in the middle of it. Another door led into a small sitting room, which held another door that led into an empty bedchamber with two bare bedsteads. Beyond the sitting room lay the master bedchamber, boasting a large box bed with black drapery, a wardrobe, and her own trunks. A small door led to a washroom, with a wooden seat above the chamber pot and a washstand. She hadn't been sure what to expect after the glorious richness within the rest of the palace, but the austerity of the apartments rivaled that of her boarding rooms. At least there, furnishings from home had surrounded her.

The only light came from the fireplaces, so Cass lit a candle and viewed her rooms again. They did not improve with illumination.

"The general don't like frippery," piped Gwen. "He says it makes ye soft."

"I see. Does he not like servants as well?"

"He makes do for himself, 'cause he says—"

"It makes him soft; yes, Gwen, I begin to understand." Cass walked over to the bed and sat on the edge of it with a bounce. Hard, of course. "Well, at least he allows servants to make the bed and lay the fire. I daresay I'm glad you came with me. I shall have someone to undo my buttons."

Gwen frowned. "I don't have much practice with those, my lady, but I'm a fast learner."

Cassandra eyed Gwen, a sudden brilliant idea forming in her head. "I believe you are. I find I'm in need of servants, Gwen. How would you like to work for me?"

The child rocked back on her heels. "Oh, my lady. Ye can't go hiring slaves. The servants won't stand for it."

Cass swept her head about the room. "I don't see any here to complain."

"But, but... the Imperial Lord won't like it."

And Cassandra certainly couldn't afford to anger him any further. "Well then. I shan't officially pay you. But if you are to attend me, I shall have to buy you new clothes and fatten you up a bit, for a lady cannot have you waiting on her looking as you do now."

Gwen screwed up her face. "I suppose not."

"That's settled, then. In fact, I believe I shall visit the kitchens tomorrow, for surely I will need more than one helper."

"If... if yer sure, my lady."

"Quite. Now, for your first instruction." Cass squatted, held down her hoops, and showed her back. "Take one side of the cloth and push the button through while gently tugging on the other side."

"I know how," Gwen said in disgust. "Just don't have much practice." The girl's little fingers started fumbling, and Cass suppressed a giggle because it tickled. "Lor', there must be a hundred of them, lady."

Gwen loosed her giggle. "I'm sure you're up to the task."

"Oh yes. This is much easier than turning a pig roast."

Cassandra continued to laugh while Gwen helped her undress. The lacing of her stays proved too difficult for the child to undo, so Cass just left it on over her chemise. She'd purchased a lovely nightgown to please her new husband, but despite Mor'ded's assurances, she felt sure the general would be spending the night with his mistress so it wouldn't signify anyway.

Cass crawled up on the hard bed and yawned.

"Is there anything else I can do for ye, lady?"

"No, dear, I think it's time you were off to bed yourself. Tomorrow we will see about making up the servants' bedchamber for you, but tonight I'm afraid you'll have to go back to the kitchens."

"Oh, I can sleep anywheres. Sometimes I go to the kennels with the dogs when it's cold."

Cassandra widened her eyes in horror. "Then we shall have to give you a good scrubbing before you return."

Gwen returned her look of horror. "But the water will make me sick."

"I promise it shan't. The nuns at my school taught me better."

Gwen humphed, already having given her opinion of Cass's education, but dragged her feet to the door. "I suppose," she sighed. "It will be hard to work for ye."

"I suppose." Cass yawned again. The stress of the day seemed to have caught up with her. Despite the hardness of the bed, she found herself falling back onto it.

"Yep, likely to be more of a chore 'n scraping carrots." The patter of her bare feet sounded all the way to the double doors leading out to the hall. Cass realized she should see about shoes for the girl as well.

Gwen's voice drifted through the quiet length of rooms. "Ye won't forget to come fetch me, will ye?"

"Of course not, Gwendolyn," called Cass. "Who shall unbutton me tomorrow night?"

And with that assurance, the door closed with a rattle, and alone in a strange room, Cass chided herself. What did she think she was doing? Setting up a household as if she had a right to. Why did she have to keep reminding herself that her marriage was nothing more than a falsehood? That this would never be her home, nor would she ever wish it to be. She had a larger task than improving the lives of a few slaves; indeed, she had the means to free them all. If she succeeded.

But it could be months before she found the right opportunity. Her mind balked at the thought that it could be years, for she couldn't imagine living years with these heathen people in this dreadful place. Besides, she had resigned herself to a short life. And the herbs she used to prevent a child might not be as reliable as she hoped. No, she could not be in this situation for long.

"But still," she whispered to the empty walls, "I will have to have my buttons undone in the meantime."

And with those words she must have dozed off, for a sudden loud noise made her jump up in bed, blink sleepily at the clock over the hearth. Late night or early morning, she could take her pick, but hadn't the time to decide before a large shadow entered the room. Her husband had decided to forgo his mistress tonight after all. Cass's heart started pounding, and all vestiges of sleep fled as General Dominic Raikes's cold gaze surveyed the room and then finally settled on her.

"Take off your clothes."

Good Heavenly Lord. Cass could only stare at him in sheer terror.

"Are you deaf, wife? I said undress." He stood with his hands on his hips, in nothing but his breeches and hose. Had he shed his clothes on the way to their bedchamber, or were they strewn about his mistress's rooms?

The thought managed to pump a bit of anger through Cass. Another humiliation to add to the ones he'd already subjected her to today. "I cannot undo the laces of my stays. And there were no servants to help me."

She thought he scowled, but it might have been her imagination, for the candle she'd lit had burned down, and she had only the light from the dying fire to see him.

"You should learn to do for yourself. Depending on others only makes you weak."

She swallowed a retort that he didn't have back-lacing stays or hundreds of buttons where one couldn't reach, because he started for her and fear locked her throat. When he stood close enough to touch, she began to tremble. She'd heard the other girls in school whisper about the act. Nothing she'd heard had prepared her for this moment. Her husband was a horrible monster and would show her no mercy.

She didn't know whether to scream or kill him.

Four

CASS COULD DO NEITHER. NOR COULD SHE AFFORD TO hate him, as much as she would like to. It would not serve the Rebellion's cause.

"Turn around," he ordered. She obeyed and braced herself, expecting him to rip the laces from the fabric. But his fingers barely touched her skin, his hands gentle as he unlaced the ties and eased the stays off her. Then he made a noise in his throat, and Cass looked over her shoulder.

Fie, how she wished he weren't so beautiful. The firelight gleamed in his silver hair, danced along the muscled planes of his naked chest. His eyes appeared enormous in the half-light, dark and mysterious and capable of stealing her soul. Her fear of him didn't stop her from wanting to run her hands down that smooth, pale skin just to feel the texture of it.

His lip quirked at her inspection and her eyes flew to his mouth, remembering his kiss, wondering if he would kiss her again. Hoping and dreading it all at the same time.

"Turn around," he ordered again, then reached

out, seized the cloth at the shoulders of her chemise, and ripped it off over her head.

Lady Cassandra gasped and tried to cover herself with her hands.

"Don't," he said, then spread his arms, and Cass felt the force of his magic. The fire flared to new life, lighting up the room, making her blink. She hadn't realized the strength of his magic and it made her fear him all the more.

She kept her arms by her sides by sheer force of will, feeling a flush crawl up her body to her face. He studied her the same way she had him; but she had only a touch of the elven blood, couldn't compare herself to his beauty, and feared he found her lacking.

Her goal had been to please her new husband, to gain his trust if not his affection. Cass lifted her chin. She needed to stop acting like some innocent school-girl and try to please him but didn't have the faintest idea how to go about doing that. Why hadn't Thomas taught her how to manage this?

"Lie down," he said as he moved to the other side of the bed, released the tie from around the canopy curtain. The black cloth fell, casting her into shadow, making it easier to lie flat on her back, her body exposed to his gaze. He untied the curtain at the foot of the bed but held it for a moment, his black gaze fastened on her rigid body. "Spread your legs."

Lord of mercy. Please help me. He would have a view of... She couldn't do it. The thought of her most private area exposed to his emotionless gaze set her trembling even harder. Did he purposely seek to embarrass her? Or did his mistress treat him to the sight this evening and he expected only the same from her?

"I… I can't."

His mouth twisted. "Don't you want to please your husband?"

"No. I mean, yes. I mean—"

He laughed, allowed the curtain to fall, cutting him off from view. "You are the innocent I was promised," he said from behind the barrier of the drapery, his voice low and muffled. "Well done, Father."

When he appeared again next to her, she suppressed a yelp and chided herself. Her fear would only make this worse. She closed her eyes and froze. She would just hold still and endure. That's what the other girls in school had advised each other. There would be some pain, but if one held still and silent, the man would finish all the more quickly.

And right now, all Cassandra could hope for was a quick end to her husband's attentions.

The fire subsided to a normal glow and he sat next to her, dropped the one remaining curtain, shutting them inside the box bed, effectively cutting them off from the rest of the room, the rest of the world. Plunging them into complete darkness.

Nothing could save Cassandra now.

She widened her eyes, unable to see a thing, hoping he couldn't either regardless of his superior elven sight. It made her relax a bit, feel a little less exposed. She heard him move, felt the warmth of his fingers touch her arm.

Cass jumped then froze again.

She waited for him to give her another order. Waited for him to violate her with that cold harshness he always used with her.

But his hand trailed up to her neck, gently stroking, smoothing back her tousled hair. His touch sent little shivers racing through her body and she gritted her teeth against the shock of it. He stilled, and she could hear only her little pants, the smooth rhythm of his breathing. She sensed a change in him, felt him relax, as if he released some barrier and it eased him.

Then he curled one arm beneath her shoulders and his other beneath her bottom and gathered her up against the smooth warmth of his chest. He held her there for the longest time, until her trembling eased and her muscles went lax. Until she slowly became aware of the hardening length of him beneath her backside.

He smelled like some exotic spice and she breathed in the delicious scent. She could feel the beat of his heart, and it comforted her that although he looked like an angel, he felt very much like an ordinary man.

Her husband kissed her hair and it made her tremble, but not with fear this time. With something else, a wanting she couldn't quite define. His lips trailed kisses down to her brow and the heat of them, the tender soft feel of his mouth, made her bold. Cass leaned back her head and met his lips with her own.

It happened again. Just like when he had kissed her in the abbey. She became aware of nothing but the feel of his mouth on hers, the texture of his tongue as he slipped inside her own welcoming warmth. The fire that spread from her breasts to her most private place. Time stopped and she didn't know how long he held her, tasting her, showing her the pleasure he could bring her.

He shifted and she barely noticed, too intent on the feelings his kiss evoked. She moaned, the sound loud in the silence of their cocoon, and lifted her arms, curling them around his broad shoulders. She could feel the strength of his muscles beneath the silk of his skin, could tell he held that strength in check. For her.

The realization emboldened her. Since the first time she had seen him, she'd longed to touch that silver-white hair. Her hands crept up to his neck and she buried her fingers in the silky softness of it. Fine as the strand of a spider's web, but so thick it created a heavy fall that reached the lower part of his back. Cass stroked it, resisting the urge to purr with utter delight.

She didn't know when his hand had covered her breast. When the warmth of his palm finally penetrated her senses, she didn't start or tremble with fear. She moaned and pressed against his touch. His mouth slipped away from hers, traveled down her throat. He shifted her and pressed kisses along her collarbone, and then lower until she felt his mouth replace his hand, circling her nipple in some slow dance.

Her fingers clenched in his hair when he drew her nipple into his mouth. She had never imagined such a thing. Couldn't have anticipated the jolt that went through her. As he drew on her bud again and again, her body responded with an answering ache of need. Cass squirmed with the want of it, not understanding what was happening to her but hoping he knew how to soothe it.

He continued to hold her with one arm, arching her back, turning his attention to her other breast. It happened all over again and Cass moaned.

Then he touched her thigh, spread his fingers wide, and smoothed his large hand down over her knee, then to her calf. Her attention strayed from his mouth for a moment. No one had ever touched her so intimately before and yet it seemed as natural as if he had always owned the right to her body.

And then he stroked her other leg with the same rhythmic movements, came back to her thigh, and hesitated a moment. Cass unclenched her fingers from his hair, felt the tie that had held his battle braids away from his face come loose and fall forward. When he lifted his head the braids fell across her sensitized breasts, the strands of fine hair at the ends of them tickling her skin.

His mouth again found hers. She eagerly opened for him, welcoming the raspy feel of his tongue, the salty-sweet taste of him. This time Cass pressed herself against him, tightening her hold around his neck, wanting him closer and yet feeling he still wasn't close enough.

She felt his hand cover the triangle of hair between her legs. She would have flushed with embarrassment if she hadn't been so involved in learning how to kiss him properly. He stroked her mouth with his tongue in the same gentle movements that he stroked her downy hair with his fingers. He did it long enough that when his finger dipped lower Cass had become so used to his touch that she barely flushed at the intrusion. He slid his finger deep inside of her and the sensations that caused made her break the kiss with a gasp.

She wanted to push his hand away, wanted him to stroke her more deeply.

Cass froze in confusion.

But the general had no doubts about what she wanted. His fingers continued to stroke and fondle while he buried his face in her neck, licking and sucking at the sensitive skin there. Making her entire body come alive with some need that soon had Cass bucking against his hand, clutching desperately at his muscular shoulders.

She had never imagined the act of making children would be like this. Cass couldn't quite grasp what had happened to her. He made her body feel things it had never felt before, and heaven help her, she loved it.

His fingers grew so slick with her wetness that when he sought the nub hidden within her downy hair, it brought wonderful new sensations coursing through her. A sudden tightening replaced the deeper longing that had risen in her womb. What new magic did he perform on her now?

Tiny tremors shook her as she squirmed beneath his touch. Something lay just within her reach, something that built within her, and Cass couldn't imagine what it might be. But shouldn't she be doing the same to him? Shouldn't she be discovering his body as well? She couldn't learn to please him too if she didn't try.

Her hands drifted down his shoulders, across his chest. Smooth, hot skin. Rigid muscles beneath. Her fingertips grazed his nipples, and she wondered if he would experience the same pleasure that she had. She gently pushed at his chest until he lifted his head and she could bring her own mouth to his neck. In the darkness she missed and found her lips on the curve of skin that defined the middle of his chest. He tasted salty and clean. Like spring water and ocean spray all at the same time.

Cass found the peak of his nipple and sucked at it the same way he'd done hers.

Dominic groaned. A deep sound that she felt rumble in his chest, on her lips.

And then he pulled away from her.

For a moment her heart stopped. Had she displeased him then? She feared to ask. Just listened to the harshness of his breathing as he seemed to struggle for control. Then he laughed, a low chuckle that made the hair on her body rise. "You learn quickly, don't you?" he whispered.

She opened her mouth to respond, but in one graceful movement his entire body covered the length of hers, and she sucked in a breath at the heat of him. The sheer strength and size of his body atop hers. But he didn't crush her. He kept his full weight suspended just above her, while touching every inch of her body with the heat of his skin.

Cassandra sighed.

"Spread your legs," he whispered in her ear. But this time it wasn't a command. It sounded almost like… a plea. A prayer.

Her heart gave a funny little twist and she moved her legs, felt him settle between them. Felt something round and hard and soft and exhilarating prod at the wetness he'd created between her thighs. Felt the resistance within her as he pushed forward. Felt it break as she forgot to be frightened and bucked up to meet him, a small exhalation of pain escaping through her lips.

And then the pain faded and the general taught her a new dance. A dance she never could have conceived of, that held beauty and grace and a desperate longing to somehow make two people become one. A dance so intimate that she thought she felt his very soul.

Cass threw back her head and gloried in the sensations he made her feel. No, she could never have imagined anything like this. The feel, the smell, the strength of him...

She wrapped her arms around his shoulders and buried her fingers in his hair again. One moment she thought him a devil and then the next, an angel, and she truly couldn't decide what sort of man she had married.

He took long smooth strokes inside of her, making that deep ache in her womb grow again, this time even more fiercely. Cass clenched her teeth against the need to cry out, to demand that he dance faster, harder. She needed... needed...

He abruptly halted the dance and pulled his upper body away from hers, tearing her arms away from him, and she knew him to be a devil.

His hand sought the nub just above where their bodies joined, stroking it with a gentle finger while he took up the rhythm of the dance again, and she knew him to be an angel.

Because now the fierce longing in her womb joined with another feeling, one that made her shiver, made her squirm beneath him, and she could no longer hold back her cries. And then. And then the world split asunder and a wave of glorious pleasure ripped through her, like a swelling tide that continued to rise and fall, rocking her on a tempest of radiant delight.

"Oh," she cried, startled and amazed.

The demon laughed. He pulled his hand away and lowered his chest atop hers again, kissing her forehead, her cheek, her lips. Then he lunged inside of her so swiftly, so deeply, that she thought it would hurt. But somehow he knew, knew it was exactly what she needed, knew she could encompass the full length of him.

Indeed, Cassandra fought for more.

She clutched at his shoulders, lifted her hips up to meet his. Her fingers roughly tangled in his hair, and she wrapped her legs around him, digging her heels into his bottom, forcing him ever deeper inside of her. She didn't beg, she demanded.

And her husband complied with a growl of feral pleasure.

The world split asunder for Cass again, but this time it was a deeper pleasure. As she rode it, she felt Dominic's body stiffen, heard his intake of breath, and then he shook as well, his harsh pants mingling with her own sighs. His release made her buck against him again, take him deeper, as if she sought to take his seed completely into her womb.

Cassandra came to herself with a start. Despite what her body urged, she couldn't afford to become pregnant. How could she have forgotten so easily the reason she'd married this man?

She lay beneath him for a time, fighting for calm, until she finally nudged him to roll off her and he allowed it, landing heavily on the hard bed. Cass fought at the bed curtain until she found the opening, then slipped outside and into the cooler air of the room. She took a few deep breaths, fighting for her sense of self again. How had he managed to make her lose it?

She looked down at her naked body in the firelight and grimaced. Thomas should have warned her about this. Should have prepared some defense against it. But how could he have known this cold elven bastard could light such a fire within her? She had never suspected her new husband would be such a gentle lover. Thomas surely wouldn't have.

Cassandra waited, listening to the even breathing behind the curtained bed. Thank heavens, it sounded as if the general had drifted off to sleep. She wasn't sure she could withstand his attentions again. Her heart thrummed at the thought and she chided her body to behave itself. Went to her chest and put on her nightgown, then removed her bag of herbs and favorite teapot. She inspected the room as she hung the pot over the fire. She should have brought more of her belongings with her, by the looks of things. After she acquired some servants she would go shopping.

She stoked the fire and her wedding ring glinted, the rose open to a full blossom. While she waited for her tea to steep she stared at the black curtain, wondering what type of man she had truly married. In public he treated her coldly, yet the moment he'd closed the curtains behind them he had touched her so gently. Had prepared her so skillfully for his love-making. She'd barely felt any pain and her shyness had fled with his ministrations.

There appeared to be more to General Dominic Raikes than he allowed others to see. Could she possibly gain enough of his trust to allow her to use him?

Cassandra's head spun in useless conjecture while she sipped her tea, then tucked the herbs back into her trunk and finally returned to the bed. She slowly parted the curtains, the glow of the fire revealing the nude body of her sleeping husband. Her breath caught.

She'd felt every inch of him and yet hadn't seen him at all. That thick silvery hair of his—which had felt like spun silk in her hands—parted slightly over the tips of his ears and spread out around him like a sparkling halo. He lay on his back, one arm thrown above his head, his face softer in sleep, the angles less harsh. His pale skin appeared to glow in the darkness, highlighting the muscles of his chest, the ridges in his abdomen. The long sinews in his thighs. She averted her gaze from the part of him that had brought her so much pleasure, and blushed. She hadn't the boldness for that. Not after one night.

Suddenly his lids flew open, that black gaze of his seeming to swallow her whole, seeming to know her every thought. The fire reflected in the crystalline brilliance of his eyes and Cassandra shuddered. He was so very beautiful.

"You're cold," he said, his voice deep and low.

She nodded and crawled into the shelter, lay down next to him as rigidly as her favorite parasol. Then she heard the bedcovers move and felt the heat of him against her back. He pulled her against him, his mouth nuzzling her hair, his arms enfolding her in a gentle cage of firm muscle. He sighed and slowly resumed the deep, even breathing of sleep.

Cassandra lay awake for a long time, listening to that oddly comforting sound.

❦

She awoke the next morning alone. Parted the curtains around the bed and squinted at the brilliant sunlight. It looked as if she'd slept half the day away, an unusual occurrence for her. She slipped from the bed, donned a robe, and padded through the rooms. No sign of her new husband, not even the slightest trace of a dropped glove or a dirty teacup. Faith, he did manage to take care of himself without need of a servant.

She returned to the bedchamber and stared at the black velvet curtains. Had she dreamed it then? That night of lovemaking with a passionate yet gentle lover? If only he had been here this morning, she wouldn't be so confused. He would touch her with familiar intimacy and then she would know it had been real. Perhaps they could even… perhaps she could go find him and then…

Did she so long for him to make love to her again? Had she no shame?

Her breasts tingled and she crossed her arms over her chest. Apparently not. But she reassured herself it had nothing to do with the general or his extraordinary beauty. He had just introduced her to a new delight and her body craved more. Quite simple, really.

A knock sounded at the door and she nearly ran to open it. But only Gwen stood outside in the hallway and Cass struggled to suppress her frown of disappointment.

Gwen performed her awkward curtsy. "Morning, my lady. I got to thinking ye might need help with yer buttons. 'Cause how can ye come fetch me if ye can't get dressed proper?"

"You were right to come," replied Cassandra, stepping aside to let the waif in. The child followed her to her trunks and watched with wide eyes as Cass pulled forth one gown after another, finally choosing an ivory sacque dress of heavily embroidered linen. Burgundy, pink, and lavender roses climbed up the loose skirt and pleated back, creating a garden of summer color. Cassandra loved it. Her father had exquisite taste in clothing, but she'd chosen it for its lack of buttons and ease of movement.

Gwen found it difficult enough to lace Cass's stays, which remained looser than she usually wore them, and she could see the tip of the girl's tongue as she concentrated on lacing her stomacher to it. But in a surprisingly short time Cass was clothed and searching the trunks for shoes.

"My dear papa," she said, tossing another set of high-heeled shoes over her shoulder, "provided a most fashionable wardrobe. But I refuse to wear"—and she tossed out another pair stitched with fleur-de-lis—"heels that I can barely walk in." Cassandra sat back, brushing her hair off her forehead with the back of her hand. "Somewhere among these trunks are my sensible shoes."

Gwen's crystal eyes sparkled with an ethereal light, a hint of gold within the hazel, and then she pointed to the third trunk on the left. "They's in there, my lady."

Cassandra's eyebrows rose but she opened the trunk the child indicated, and down near the bottom sat her collection of low heels and slippers. "Your finding magic is most impressive, Gwendolyn."

The girl beamed.

"Now, then." Cass slid into her shoes. "I must find a vanity for my cosmetics, as I suppose I'll have to get used to using them now that I'm at court." She shoved her hair up off her forehead again. "And a hairdresser."

Gwen practically leaped to her toes. "My friend May does weaving near as fine as ye can get."

"I'm not sure—"

"Oh, she does all the horses' tails for the grand processions. And," Gwen lowered her voice to a mere whisper, "I've seen her weave the sunlight, my lady. Truly I have."

Cassandra smiled. "Magic appears to run strongly in the kitchens."

"La, it does. The looks too." And Gwen preened her silvery hair.

"Well then, let's go find your May and see if her talented fingers can be trained to a lady's coiffure." Cass ran a quick brush through her hair, twisted it into a simple bun, and then followed an eager Gwen from her rooms.

Thank heavens she had the girl for a guide, for she couldn't yet make sense of the sprawling layout of Firehame Palace. It seemed to be designed purposely to confuse, and magical artifacts and items lay around every corner. Stationary walls appeared to breathe and shift, mirrors reflected imaginary scenes with her face floating inside them, carpets flowed like water, and ceilings trembled, threatening to come down upon her head. Gwen cautioned her not to touch this or that, and Cass could only wonder if the griffin statue would have come alive and pecked off her fingers if she had stroked that mighty beak. Or would it be capable of doing something much worse? The elven lord protected his palace in subtle ways and had an odd sense of humor, so Cass obeyed the young slave girl's advice.

Her unusual companion drew only a few startled looks from the nobles they passed, but Cass still breathed a sigh of relief when they reached the basement kitchens. She must get Gwen suitably attired before any gossip spread.

Cook stood nearly as tall as the general, a robust woman with red cheeks and matching hair. She wielded her spoon like a sword, but it seemed most of her helpers had acquired a certain skill at dodging it. Roasts stewed and pastries baked, and the delicious aromas made Cass think that Cook had a bit of elven magic herself.

"So," she said, eyeing Cass with a frown, "yer the champion's new bride."

Cassandra froze, feeling as if the other woman sought to strip her bare and expose her soul.

"Ye just might do."

"Indeed?" snapped Cass, refusing to let a servant weigh her worth.

"No offense, my lady. It's just glad I am that the champion has someone to take care of him now."

Cass's annoyance evaporated in the hopes of finding out more about her new husband. "I've never met a man *less* in need of being taken care of, Cook. Why would you say such a thing?"

Cook leaned forward and lowered her voice to a whisper, strands of red hair flopping over her forehead. "Have ye not heard that appearances can be deceiving? Haven't ye wondered what made the man so cold?"

"It's the elven blood."

"Aye, so do many think. But consider his father, lady, and why he might need to act the way he does. Ask the general about Jack... Nay, he wouldn't speak of his best friend. Ask him about Mongrel, my lady. He might talk of him."

Cass's head spun. General Raikes had a friend? The elven did not make friends, possessed with such cold hearts. And Thomas had told her that her husband had no friends. Jack must be a part of the general's childhood, yet what had happened to alter him so in his adulthood that he now spurned all friendships? And who might this Mongrel be?

"A dog," said Lady Cassandra. "General Raikes has a pet?"

"Oh aye, he once had—" Cook spun and whacked a small lad with her spoon. "'Ere, now, none of that. I told ye to keep yer fingers outta the pudding." She cast her gaze about the kitchen suspiciously. "The champion once had many things, my lady. And perhaps ye will be the one to give them back to him. But, please, don't breathe a word of what I said to none other than himself."

The big woman straightened and raised her voice. "I'm sorry, m'lady, but what with the champion's marriage guests, I don't have the time to sit and chat. Been cookin' near round the clock, I have."

Cook had looked at the brick walls as if they had ears. Cass took the hint. "We've come only to find May."

Cook's red brows climbed up her broad forehead. "Has she done somethin' wrong? That girl's forever neglecting her duties and—"

The kitchen door flew open and an older girl with Gwen's coloring flew into the room. "Cook, look what I made fer ye!" And she held out a shawl that glittered in the morning sunshine flooding through the open door. Cass had never seen anything like the pale gray material before. May draped it over Cook's shoulders. "See there, it will not fall off while yer stirring the dough."

Cook eyed the thing suspiciously. "What's it made of this time?"

May's hazel eyes sparkled. "Spider's webs. Ah, they're tricky to weave, mind, but I managed to figure out how. Ye see—"

"Ugh," said Cook, removing the scarf from her shoulders with the handle of her spoon. "Ye were supposed to be fetchin' parsley fer the stew."

May's lovely face fell. "Oh dear, I forgot. I'll go back to the garden right now."

"Never ye mind," huffed Cook. "Ye'll probably come back with a fine green hat fer me to wear. Besides, this here lady wishes to speak with ye." She turned back to her oven while May's eyes widened as she looked at Cassandra.

But before Cass could speak, Gwen darted over to May's side and yanked on the older girl's ragged dress. "I told the lady that ye could fix her hair right fine and she wants to bring us upstairs to wait on her."

May's eyes widened even farther. "But the servants—"

"The lady says she don't see no servants in her rooms to bother with."

"Gwen," admonished Cassandra, "allow me to get a word in. I find myself in need of assistance, Miss May, and if Cook doesn't mind, I would like you both to come and live in my new apartments."

May gasped, wavered on her feet for a moment, then settled a wistful gaze on Cass's hair. "Oh my, ye have a lot, don't ye?" And her fingers began to twitch.

Cook glanced up at the three of them and harrumphed. "Both of those girls are nothin' but a bother to me. If ye want them, I have no objection."

Gwen ran to Cook and gave her a quick hug, then darted back to May's side, yanking at her hand. "Let's get our things afore either one of them changes their mind."

Cass followed them to the back of the kitchen, into a small storage room that held two cots made of woven grass. She waited while they gathered their meager belongings, trying not to breathe too deeply of the musty smell of rotting potatoes. "Are you sisters?" she wondered aloud.

Gwen shrugged. "No, m'lady."

"You look so similar."

"'Tis the elven blood. We both got too much of it in our looks." She sighed. "But not enough in our magic to be sent to Elfhame, eh, May? I wonder what it's like there, with trees that weep honeyed fruit and skies that rain wine and—"

"Are ye sure we should be doing this, Gwen? What of the champion?"

"Ah, May, ye know he doesn't give a fig 'bout anyone."

"But he notices everything. And the steward knows he goes to the kitchens, so he makes sure we're tidy and have proper beds and Cook has clean kitchens…"

Cassandra kept her mouth closed and let the girls continue to talk, although her mind spun with questions. Dominic had grown up in the kitchens, neglected by all accounts. Did he visit to make sure the other slaves weren't treated as badly as he had been? Or did he just come here from habit? Rumor had it he cared for nothing but the games, and yet his lovemaking had been so gentle. Was she trying to credit him with some human feeling because of that? What manner of man had she truly married?

"Ye worry too much, May."

"But when he finds us in his rooms… Ye know he doesn't like servants about."

"But I do," interjected Cass. "And I've quite made

up my mind. Now, if you've got your things, we shall call a coach."

Gwen clapped her hands. "I've never ridden in a carriage before. Where are we going, my lady?"

Both of their hazel eyes widened when Cass replied. "Shopping."

᪣

When Cassandra joined the court at dinner later that evening, she felt exhausted but entirely pleased with herself. Gwen and May looked lovely in their new gowns—although Gwen had stubbornly fought the need of stays. But they both vowed they would happily get used to their uncomfortable new shoes, and admired the shiny buckles at every opportunity. New feather mattresses and linens for their beds had sent both girls into complete rapture, and Cass had made all the rooms much more comfortable with the addition of mahogany tables and plush velvet chairs and soft tapestries to adorn the walls.

With a sigh of satisfaction, Lady Cassandra entered the dining hall, smoothing the folds of her satin dress and knowing she looked her best. May did indeed have magical fingers, arranging Cass's hair into curls and weaves without benefit of an iron or a single hairpin. Her lace cap had long lappets that trailed down past her shoulders and matched the trim on her skirts and sleeves. She missed the comfort of her wool gowns but decided the look on her husband's face when he saw her would be worth the trouble.

She'd been entirely wrong.

When the general looked up at her standing in the doorway, he looked right through her. Cass's own heart did a leap at the sight of him in a white satin coat trimmed with silver, his pale hair brushed in a smooth fall about his broad shoulders. His handsome face looked hard and implacable, but she remembered the gentle softness of his lips on hers and started toward him as if pulled on a string.

She wanted to be near him. She yearned for just the touch of his hand upon her skin.

He stood. She sucked in a breath as he headed in her direction. And then let it loose with a gasp as he strode by her and picked up the hand of the Lady Agnes, leading the woman over to his chair to sit beside him.

Cass heard the titters of the other nobles at the blatant rebuff. It took all of her courage to settle into the same chair she had the previous day. Across from her husband and mistress. Next to the smiling Lord Mor'ded.

Had she truly given some human attributes to her husband's character? If he'd shown some gentleness in his lovemaking it had been only a ruse… or her own imagination. He had awakened her body to pleasure and she'd overreacted, thinking some feeling must lie behind the act. She felt like a fool for thinking he'd allow her to rush into his arms this evening. That he'd been as enchanted with her as she had been with him. She'd even thought he had some generous motive to his visits to the kitchens.

His blood ran as cold as his father's. She'd best get over her attraction to his angelic beauty and remember that he was the devil in disguise.

"You've barely touched your plate," said Lord

Mor'ded, leaning close to her. "You'll need your strength, dear girl."

Cass fought the urge to move away from him. Two devils sat at the table, and she'd best not forget it. With a nod, she lifted a spoonful of pudding to her mouth, trying not to choke as the greasy mass slid down her throat.

"That's better." He sat back, those black glittering eyes studying the guests, his mouth twisted into a mocking smile. "Lords and ladies," he began, barely raising his voice. Yet they all turned to him as one, even those at the end of the long table. "On the morrow your champion will fetch the king and his ministers. A toast to General Raikes!"

They rose, a clatter of screeching chair legs and clinking glasses. Apparently Cass didn't stand fast enough, for the gentleman at her side scowled and hissed at her, "Get up, you fool."

Lady Cassandra bristled at his tone. How dare he speak to her that way? And yet, what better treatment could she expect when her husband set the example for the court? She rose and pretended to sip her wine until the full implication of the elven lord's words hit her; then she drained the glass.

Not that she cared a whit about the king's coming to Firehame. But his prime minister, Sir Robert Walpole, would be with him. Even to speak to the leader of the Rebellion would bring her a great amount of comfort, which she most assuredly needed right now. And it might be possible to have a private moment alone with him on the road, something she might not manage within the walls of the palace.

Cassandra suppressed a smile. She could turn her obvious fascination with her new husband to her advantage. She looked over at Dominic, who had studiously avoided her gaze, and allowed the newly awakened lust of her body to show in her brown eyes. "But surely you won't leave my bed so soon?"

A startled silence followed, and then Mor'ded chuckled and the entire assemblage broke into mocking laughter.

"Egads, you broke her into her traces good, eh, Raikes?" said the man who'd made the wicked smoke creatures, leering at Lady Agnes. "Now you've got two of them panting after you."

"Three," the woman to his left said, laughing and coyly smacking Lord Blevin with her closed fan.

Dominic sat stone-faced, not a blink of his thick lashes to acknowledge their words. Cassandra spoke again before the conversation could degenerate any further, transferring her gaze to Lord Mor'ded. "May I be allowed to go with him? Surely the more we… well, the quicker you will have your new champion."

The elven lord appeared to be proud of his son's prowess, whether on the battlefield or in the bedroom, because his eyes showed no suspicion as he shrugged. "Go with him if you wish. I care not."

"But that's preposterous," said the Lady Agnes, her voice at odds with her beauty, a nasally squeak to her words. "There's danger on the road. Bandits, wild magic. And I vow I will not sleep upon the hard ground."

Cass smiled at her sweetly. "Then you need not come."

Dominic turned to his father. "She will be a nuisance."

Cassandra knew he referred to her and not Lady Agnes.

Mor'ded rolled his black scepter between his palms. "So will the king. Surely you can protect them both?" His eyes searched his son's face, as if looking for something.

"Of course. But I value the king more than I do her. Do not blame me if your breeding mare is harmed."

Mor'ded smiled with satisfaction, as if some unspoken question had been answered, and threw back his head with a laugh. Cass couldn't figure out what had passed between the two, but she felt the silent battle of wills as if it were a solid wall. How would she ever discover the secrets between them?

But she had gotten her way and counted that a small victory.

Five

DOMINIC ENTERED HIS APARTMENTS LATER THAT
evening, after having consumed a bit too much wine
and fighting off the advances of Agnes. Demanding
wench. She annoyed him most of the time—which
was precisely the reason he kept her as his mistress.
He never felt in danger of becoming attached to her.

But at this moment he felt that his new wife annoyed
him more. What business had she to invite herself
along on this journey? It would be dangerous and most
arduous for a lady, especially one as tiny and frail as
Cassandra. Had she no sense of self-preservation?

His shin met the edge of a table and he let out
a startled curse. He didn't remember a table in the
middle of the room. With a call to the magic in his
blood, he lit up the apartments with cold white fire
and narrowed his eyes.

What had she done?

Instead of the sparsely furnished rooms he had
demanded, a confusing array of color greeted him.
Red velvet chairs littered the floor, along with tables
of assorted shapes and sizes. Colorful tapestries hung

from the previously clean walls, with country scenes and fanciful creatures and flowers.

"Flowers," he muttered, weaving his way through the room.

He paused in the sitting room, his senses alert, the same ones that had saved his life amid many a war. He quietly opened the door to the servants' room, which he'd intended to stay empty. Owners often became fond of their servants and he couldn't afford for that to happen. Nor could he allow possible spies around him, reporting to his father and endangering anyone for whom he showed a weakness. So when he heard soft breathing coming from both beds his annoyance rose. He closed the door as softly as he'd opened it and quickly strode to his bedchamber.

The curtains of the bed had been pulled back and Lady Cassandra lay in the middle of the mattress, arrayed in some gossamer gown that left little to the imagination. And made his groin stir in anticipation. He ignored it, strode over to the bed, and put his hands on his hips.

"I forbid you to go with me tomorrow."

She opened her eyes with a start, looking tousled and frightened and entirely delicious, damn her. "I beg your pardon?"

"You heard me—and pray tell me the meaning of all this?" He spread his arms, his magic flaring to new life, lighting up the room to a white-hot glow.

She sat up, rubbing at her eyes. "I'm not sure I understand."

Dominic held back a growl of impatience. "You've ruined our apartments and hired two servants."

She frowned at him and he forced his eyes to stay on her face. Her pert nipples thrust at the fabric of her gown and did their best to gain his attention. But the charms of a woman had never distracted him from his purpose, and so it didn't worry him overly much.

"I didn't hire any servants," she said. "And I couldn't bear the coldness of these apartments. Isn't it enough that I must bear the coldness of the court?"

Her soft brown eyes looked at him accusingly and he knew he was to be blamed for the way the court treated her. He shrugged. "It can't be helped."

Her lovely full mouth curled into a frown. "I don't understand."

Dominic spun, refusing to be sympathetic to her, knowing he couldn't afford to involve himself with any feelings his new wife might display. He shrugged out of his coat and then his waistcoat, amused that instead of looking away, his wife eyed him with eager curiosity. "It's not your place to understand, Lady Cassandra. You are to do as you are told and breed another champion; that is all." He sat in one of her velvet chairs and kicked off his shoes, unbuttoned his hose from his breeches and rolled them down his legs. "You will disengage the servants tomorrow."

She crawled to the edge of the bed, her gown shifting up over her knees. "I told you, they're not servants."

"Then what, pray tell, are they? Creatures created by the elven lords?"

He could hear the soft sound of her breath as it escaped through her lips. "Like the smoke beings at our wedding breakfast?"

"Not hardly. Those were created by a courtier with but a hint of true power. Now answer my question."

The daft woman completely changed the subject. "Did you enjoy our dance?"

Dominic's mouth twitched. "Which one?"

He enjoyed her blush. "The one at the ball."

"I enjoyed the one in our bed much more."

"As did I." She clapped a hand over her mouth, as if the words had escaped unthinkingly. Dominic tried very hard not to think it charming. Instead he concentrated on finding the buttons of his shirt through all the ruffled trim and began to unbutton them.

She slid off the bed and stood, the light shining through her transparent gown. "And yet you ignore me in front of the court and prefer your mistress by your side."

Dominic allowed his white fire magic to fade to shadow. "Of course. You would do well not to mistake duty with pleasure."

She bristled at that. He admired her courage.

"Duty? You consider it just an obligation to lie with me?"

He removed his shirt, not bothering to stifle a yawn. Let that be her answer. He'd drunk too much tonight, and felt tired unto death of his father's games and the jostling of his minions for his attention. He had no patience for any further pretense, especially with this confusing woman. He'd thought he would marry a boring, biddable girl. At least, that had been his impression before he'd bedded her last night. The realization he'd been gravely mistaken worried him.

"About those servants—"

"That's my magic, you know."

Dominic rubbed his bare chest. She had the oddest way of confounding him. "What?"

"I dance, General Raikes. That's my magical gift."

"Oh." He yawned again, reaching for the buttons of his breeches. He preferred to sleep in the nude when not on the battlefield. It might take several days to fetch the king from the sovereignty of Dewhame. It wouldn't surprise him if Imperial Lord Breden made the task as difficult as possible. He'd sleep in comfort while he could.

"I know many kinds of dances," she continued, her voice suddenly a bit unsure. "Shall I dance for you?"

Dominic leaned back in the chair with a groan, reminding himself to dismiss the servants on the morrow. "There's no music."

"I need none."

And she began to dance.

For the first time in his life, a woman distracted Dominic. More than distracted. Entranced.

The first sway of her body held him frozen in his seat. The slight flutter of her arm became the most erotic movement he'd ever seen. She had a grace that far surpassed those of pure elven blood. The sound of his heart pounded in his ears, the rhythm a perfect accompaniment to her dance.

Dominic could not take his eyes off her. She used her long brown hair as a cape, spinning and revealing parts of her body teasingly, then allowing the silky tendrils to cover her once again. Her brown eyes glazed to a dark luminosity, a fascinating mixture of sultry innocence. Her nightgown hid nothing and yet when she lifted the hem above a thigh, the sight of her smooth skin inflamed him even more.

He had thought her pleasing to look at, exquisitely shaped. But as she danced, she became ethereally beautiful.

Her complete innocence in his bed and genuine faith convinced him she'd been raised religiously, and yet somewhere she'd learned an elven love dance. What manner of woman had he married?

Lady Cassandra ended her dance on her knees in front of him, her head thrown back, breasts thrust forward. Thighs parted and welcoming.

Dominic didn't hesitate. He picked her up, carried her to the bed, and covered her body with his. He'd never felt such lust before, such an overwhelming need to possess a woman. He couldn't even prepare her for entry… but he needn't have worried. She was wet and hot and oh so welcoming. As if performing the dance for him had excited her as well.

When his senses managed to return he found himself flat on his back, staring at the engraving on the ceiling of the box bed, wondering how he would manage to avoid becoming infatuated with the little minx by his side. He quickly closed the curtains around the bed, reached out, and pulled Cassandra near.

She wiggled against him and then gave a satisfied sigh. "Just duty, sir?"

He smiled at her smug tone and refused to answer, his eyes drifting closed.

"May I keep the slaves?"

That brought him alert more quickly than the sound of gunfire. "What slaves?"

"Why, the ones I hired to help me."

So that's what she'd meant by saying they weren't servants.

He had worked in the kitchens as a slave for long dreary years. If she had purposely sought a way into his frighteningly human heart, she could not have done better than by caring for a slave.

"They will steal you blind," he finally said.

"They shan't."

His eyes drifted closed again. "Let it be your worry, then. Just keep them from my sight." And he realized he'd just given her his agreement. Against all likelihood, Lady Cassandra had bewitched him. His only recourse was to stay away from her and her new household. God forbid his father should learn he'd become fond of his wife or took pity on slaves. Not a one of them would be safe from fire.

∾

Dominic awoke before the sun rose and realized with dismay that his wife had already left the apartments. The stubborn hoyden seemed bound and determined to accompany him to fetch the king. Or to stay by his side. He supposed that becoming pregnant with his child and securing her place as mother of a champion was more important to her than her own safety. But producing a champion would be no easy task; most children were born with either too much power and sent to Elfhame, or too little, like the nobles of his father's court. But he supposed he had a better chance than most of producing a child with acceptable magic.

He parted the curtains and got out of bed, surprised to find his uniform laid out neatly atop his trunk and a kettle of tea warming on the hob. A small basket with fresh biscuits inside sat next to the pot, and he ate them quickly before getting dressed. He rarely broke his fast in the morning but he supposed it would be easy to get used to.

Damn her.

It would not be the last time he cursed her today, for when he entered the courtyard it appeared that half the court had also taken it into their heads to accompany him. The fools had brought carriages and trunks and servants. They had dressed as if they attended a festival, a riot of silks and garish color. Dominic fought back the urge to tell them all to return to their soft beds. Only a few of them had packed lightly and sat atop a horse, so he would lose most on the road anyway.

Unfortunately, one of those who sat a horse happened to be his wife. His eyes narrowed at her sensible riding habit and jaunty hat, the way the rising sun caught the auburn in her brown hair and changed her eyes to golden amber. Had he once truly thought her ordinary? She held the reins with such delicate hands, her slight form straight and graceful in the saddle. His groin stirred as he remembered her love dance, and he realized with a start of alarm that if he'd had a choice, he would rather have spent the day in bed with her than riding out to fetch his prize.

She caught his gaze and held it for a long moment. He felt sure his face revealed nothing—he'd trained it too well over the years—but he couldn't be sure whether his eyes showed a bit of his yearning. For Lady Cassandra smiled with pleasure while a blush of bright red crept into her cheeks. Then her mount snorted and reared, and her attention centered on the huge beast she'd been given to ride.

Dominic frowned, wondering what half-wit had given her the black stallion, who was known for his volatile temperament. Even the best of riders had difficulty controlling the horse. He checked himself as he opened his mouth to demand another mount for his wife, feeling a pair of eyes upon him like a heavy shroud.

Dominic turned. Mor'ded stood on the steps, his black gaze going from his son to Cassandra.

Women always gazed at the elven lords with lustful admiration and he looked enough like his father to be given the same attention. But Dominic couldn't be sure what his own eyes revealed and if he should show the slightest concern for Cassandra's safety...

The general turned his back on his wife, indeed upon all the court, and mounted his own horse, signaling his troops forward. Despite the shrill outcry of alarm from a few of the nobles, Dominic and his men pounded through the gates. By necessity they had to slow through the streets of London and many of the court managed to catch up to them. But when they reached the countryside Dominic set a brisk pace for his men, and as he had predicted, most of the fools fell behind.

A sudden flash of black seething muscle galloped past him, Lady Cassandra clinging to the back of the stallion like a burr. Dominic leaned forward, fully intending to ride after the runaway horse, afraid his new wife would be thrown from the beast and likely break her neck.

A shadow fell over him and he glanced skyward. Ador rode the winds, his father mounted on the dragon's back. So Mor'ded had come to watch the return of the king as well.

He cursed beneath his breath and sat back in the saddle. Mor'ded would wonder if Dominic rode after the girl, wife or no. An elven lord should be concerned only with himself, and humans were but dumb creatures to be used at a whim.

He would kill the half-wit who had given her that horse.

The general continued the brisk pace he had set, perhaps increasing it a bit as he searched far down the road. When he saw the black speck, with a rider still astride, he grunted with relief. Lady Cassandra waited for them to catch up, patting the neck of the lathered, shivering beast. Somehow she had tamed the black stallion. As his troop passed her, she gently flicked the reins and the beast rode smartly along with the rest of the horses, his ears occasionally flicking back at Cassandra as if eager to comply with her slightest wish. He couldn't help but feel a trickle of admiration for his new wife.

Dominic straightened his spine and slowed the pace. He didn't see a need to tire his horses any more than necessary. It would take them several days to reach Devizes in the Wilts, the town that lay on the border between the sovereignties of Dewhame and Firehame, where the exchange of the king was to be made. For now the general fully intended to take advantage of the peaceful countryside to calm the anger his wife had managed to provoke by almost getting herself killed.

He loved the land. The rolling hills and green meadows and quiet ponds. Although he knew that when the elven lords had chosen and conquered each of their sovereignties they had altered the land with their magic, he could still see the original beauty of England beneath the huge elven flame trees with fire red blooms that dotted the green swards of Firehame. Dewhame, where the elven lord Breden ruled with the magic of sky and water, boasted hidden grottos, natural fountains, and enchanted lakes. The eastern sovereignty, where Mi'cal ruled with his green scepter, sported tracks of barely impenetrable forests with a wealth of plants that defied description.

Dominic hadn't visited the remaining four sovereignties but supposed he would fight battles within them some day. His curiosity about them could wait. He hoped he would still be able to recognize the original countryside of England within them, though.

For now he avoided the pockets of flame that shimmered among hill and vale, taking the road less traveled, bringing their party through silent forests and sleepy meadows. The preautumn leaves almost rivaled that of the elven lord's flame trees with their tints of red and orange color. Dominic allowed the beauty and peace to settle over him, storing it up as usual for when he would need to call on it within the palace walls of Firehame.

By the time he found a good place to stop for the night he felt saddle weary but calm. He chose to camp near a small stream within a circle of flame trees, their fire red blooms lighting up the area within and around the clearing. The glow from the blossoms should discourage any surprise attacks.

He signaled for his men to help the ladies—and more than a few gentlemen—to dismount. Each time they had rested the courtiers had scrambled from the saddle with increasing stiffness. If his men hadn't aided them now, they would be sprawled about the ground in all their silks and satin.

His men pitched their tents, including his, the largest of the lot, and built the fires to prepare the meal. Dominic washed up with the other male courtiers at the far end of camp, allowing the ladies some privacy for their own ablutions. His camp cook must have planned for guests for the stew tasted better than usual. Mor'ded did not join them. Ador could fly far faster than the swiftest horse could gallop, and the elven lord would sleep in his own bed tonight back at Firehame Palace.

Dominic hadn't looked at Lady Cassandra the entire day, yet he knew exactly where she rode in their column, knew right now her position around the campfire. He supposed she hadn't thought to bring a tent and he would have to invite her into his. His heart soared at the thought and then he stilled. Granted, he enjoyed bedding her. But he'd never felt such anticipation for a woman before and feared where it might lead.

"Why, General Raikes, I do believe you lost half the court on purpose."

Dominic didn't know whether to feel relief or dismay at the sound of Lady Agnes's whiny voice. "My intention had been to lose them all."

As usual, Aggie laughed, ignoring his cold demeanor and tone of voice.

Few dared approach him. Two of his lieutenants sat next to him but the rest of their party gave him a wide berth.

Lady Cassandra seemed content surrounded by the rest of his men, avoiding the company of the courtiers, who either had the tendency to ignore her or treat her with indifferent disdain. Dominic knew he was to blame, for the dunderheads took their cues from him. He tried to ignore a sudden wash of guilt.

Agnes sat in his lap. "Oh la, it appears that I forgot to bring a tent." She leaned forward and whispered into his ear. "Would you perhaps have room in yours, my champion?"

Dominic winced. He hated when she called him that. In one smooth movement he picked her up and rose, then set her on her feet. "I'm sorry, my dear, but I have a duty to perform."

Agnes glanced over at Cassandra and frowned. "It's a sad situation, sir, to so deny your pleasure for duty, but I suppose it can't be helped. I'm sure I will find another tent with a bit of room." She smiled coyly at that, her eyes roaming the officers, and then sighed. "Not a one of them could compare to you. If you should need some... comfort during the night, you have but to ask."

Dominic bowed. "I will endeavor to keep that in mind." And then he headed straight for his wife.

Discussion stilled when he approached and by the time he reached her side, complete silence reigned among the previously boisterous group. He said nothing, only held out his hand. She looked up at him, those soft brown eyes wide with surprise, and placed her hand in his.

"We have a duty, madam," he said. "Surely that is why you have so inconvenienced me this day." The courtiers overheard. Several of the women gasped and more than a few men snickered. His soldiers just looked at him with dismay.

Cassandra's brilliant eyes dulled but she allowed him to lead her to his tent.

"Even though you may feel I am only your duty," she whispered, "must you say it in front of everyone?"

The sadness in her voice managed to bother him and his words came out harsher than he intended. "I have no feelings, Lady Cassandra. I thought I had made that obvious. You must cease in this ridiculous tendency to be hurt by that fact."

She ducked inside the tent, and he tied the flap closed, shutting out the glow of the fire. He could just make out the outline of her delicate nose, the gleam of her large eyes.

"But you do take pleasure with me," she said, keeping her voice low, knowing those outside could hear everything within their shelter. "What have I done for you to treat me so coldly?"

"I told you not to come. *You* chose to ignore my wishes. You must accept the consequences of your actions."

"Oh." Her voice shivered, sounding very small.

Devil a bit, he felt no sympathy for her. That horse could have killed her. "Come here."

Her skirts rustled as she moved closer to him. At least she had dressed more sensibly than Aggie, wearing petticoats instead of hoops. Dominic grabbed her shoulders and roughly kissed her. Damn, he had wanted to do that all day.

She melted against him and despite everything, his kiss turned gentle. He brought his mouth to her ear, speaking in nothing but a breath of sound. "It's just fortunate for you that I happen to honor my obligations."

"What…?"

"Your dance, my lady. It brought me satisfaction and yet you had none of your own."

Her breath caught. He laid her down and pulled up her skirts before she had a chance to reply. Her legs shone whitely against the dark rug blanketing the floor of the tent. Dominic ran his hands up and down that smooth skin, pulling down her stockings in the process, until she quit trembling. When had he ever been so concerned about the satisfaction of his bed partner? And yet he could not shake the longing to see her face glowing with pleasure.

Dominic lowered his head and kissed a knee.

She jumped. He kissed the other knee, then began to trail kisses up her thighs, first one, and then the other, until he reached the dark triangle of hair between them.

"You… this… it's shocking."

He smiled and continued his explorations, finding the little nub nestled in her hair, flicking it with his tongue until she started to pant. Dominic raised himself up and picked up her hand, looking at her wedding ring. The petals of the rose had bloomed wide open, and he raised a silver brow at her. "Have I shocked you enough?"

"I don't… I don't think so."

"Excellent." He kissed the tip of her nose and slid down her body and resumed his ministrations. When he suckled her she cried out, and he distantly became aware that the conversation outside had ceased. Well, he was known for his prowess as a lover so he saw no harm in continuing.

She squirmed and cried out again. When her body loosened into spasms, the sounds of pleasure his wife made stirred his rod into painful hardness. But he had resolved not to take her. To deny himself, thereby proving he had nothing to fear from her.

When Lady Cassandra finally stilled, Dominic pulled down her skirts and gathered her into his arms. She lay quietly for a few moments and then said, "What about your duty, sir?"

He smiled for the second time that night and quickly wiped the expression from his face. He would have to be more careful, lest he betray himself that way when others were looking. "I don't feel the need."

"But…" Her hand brushed the hardness within his breeches.

"Hush, go to sleep. Haven't you caused me enough trouble for one day?"

Thank the devil, she listened to him. He felt sure the long ride contributed to her quick obedience to his words, for he soon felt the even rhythm of her sleep.

But sleep eluded him for a long time, and when he awoke the next morning he felt as if he hadn't slept at all. He saw to the disbandment of camp, his words surlier than usual. His men avoided his eyes but the courtiers watched him with eager speculation.

That day the journey seemed twice as long as the day before. He forced himself to ignore Cassandra, for if he looked at her, his groin quickly stirred to life. It made him even more determined to deny the ridiculous attraction he had for her and he took refuge within the elven side of his nature.

But damn his human passion, he could not stop thinking about her and chose a camp for the night before the sun had even passed below the horizon.

Dominic ignored the curious glances of his men, the whispered comments of the court while they made camp, and he used his magic to light the fires. He washed quickly, wolfed down his food, and went to her before she'd eaten half of hers. But she didn't protest as he dragged her into the tent.

They sat on the rug facing each other, an undeniable chemistry crackling between them.

Daylight flooded their small chamber and he looked his fill of her, from her soft brown eyes to her mahogany hair, until she blushed and looked down at her skirts, which puddled about her hips as she sat on the floor across from him.

She looked stunning, a mix of innocence and fortitude that made his desire for her uncontrollable. He'd never lost his control over a mere woman before. Had never felt the urge to possess her mind as well as her body. Had she thought of him today as he'd thought of her? Had *she* come to him out of duty?

Dominic unbuttoned his breeches and reached for her. Shoved her skirts up her thighs. Pulled her toward his kneeling legs.

"I've been thinking about what you showed me last night—" she started.

He kissed her, trying to devour her.

"—all day—" she managed.

Dominic plunged his tongue inside the sweet softness of her mouth, trying to still her tongue with his own.

Again, she managed to pull away and speak. "I should like to try—"

Dominic covered her lips again, holding her with one arm while his hand quested with the other. He quickly found her hot opening and groaned with relief. Wet. Ready for him. Physically, at least, she wanted him, and he should not have felt so grateful. With his elven beauty he'd yet to find a woman who could resist him. And yet that didn't seem quite enough. Dominic wanted more from her, wanted her spirit as much as he needed her body... and cursed himself for the mere thought. He could not have such a void inside of him that needed filling. He *would* not.

He grabbed her bare bottom with both hands and pulled her onto his lap. A bit higher and the tip of his shaft met her soft flesh. He groaned.

Cassandra spoke no more. She clutched his shoulders and pulled herself closer to him, fully encasing him within her. His fingers tightened on her buttocks, and he rocked her back and forth on his lap, the pressure of her weight on him pulling him deeper inside her than he'd ever dared. She threw her head back, the velvet skin of her throat bared to him. Dominic buried his mouth in that softness as he set a rhythm that had her panting his name.

He sucked at the skin of her neck, trying to smother his own groan of release as his body exploded. He was just as unsuccessful as Cassandra as her own climax quickly broke.

His foolish attempt at denying himself the day before had only made his want of her even stronger. Dominic didn't even try to suppress his groans when he took her the second time that night. And late into the morning, the third. And when he stepped out of the tent, he knew he'd made a mistake.

Aggie studied him with shrewd eyes. He had never made such sounds of pleasure with her. His officers quickly hid their grins but the nobles felt no such compunction, jabbing each other with their elbows and snickering behind their hands. He could imagine their gossip—a woman had finally snared the elven bastard. Could he be more human than elven after all?

For the entire day a trickle of worry kept him even farther away from Lady Cassandra than usual. But he noticed a few of the male nobles rode alongside her, trying to engage her in conversation and curry her favor. Fortunately the women stayed huddled around Lady Agnes, continuing their cold treatment of Cassandra but now occasionally throwing her looks of disgust.

Perhaps he hadn't blundered too badly, then.

Still, Dominic breathed a sigh of relief when they reached the town of Devizes. Despite the lateness of the day the market bustled with activity. It distracted the courtiers and fortunately his wife as well. They passed stalls and tables of every cloth imaginable, draped to show the sheen, arranged to reflect the softness of the weave. He did not stop and did not concern himself with the nobles who chose to linger in the marketplace. Lady Cassandra stayed with his troops.

Dominic knew something had gone wrong the moment he reached the Fire and Water Inn. It should have been filled with the king's advisors and court. Only an old man and a drunk sat at the wooden tables.

General Raikes called for the innkeeper, who emerged from the back room, wiping his hands nervously on a cloth, a tremor in the jowls of his cheeks.

"Where is he?"

The innkeeper bowed his head. "I know not, my lord. His rooms have been prepared, I assure you."

Dominic waved a hand dismissively. "There must be rumors. There are always rumors. What have you heard?"

The portly man glanced up, his eyes flitting nervously from Dominic's face to the sword at his side. The pistol in his belt.

"They say..." His voice broke. "Arumph. They say that the king refuses to leave Bath. His court is quite comfortable there and he has no desire to take up residence in London."

Dominic's lip twitched. Surely the king realized he had little choice in the matter. But Imperial

Lord Breden obviously supported him, making their victory as difficult as possible or just extending the game. Only the lord of Dewhame knew what that game might be. The elven lords had a unique sense of what relieved their boredom.

Dominic spun. "Mount up," he barked to his troops, heading for the door.

"But my lord," called the innkeeper, "night is falling, and your horses—"

If the man hadn't sounded so genuinely concerned for the beasts, Dominic would have ignored him. The roads to Bath were notorious for their ruts and deep pits, and a horse could easily break a leg traveling on a dark night.

Dominic raised a hand and lit the ceiling of the inn with cold white fire. The drunkard fell off his chair and the old man covered his bald pate with his thin arms. The innkeeper squinted at the brilliance that would light any road the general chose to ride.

"Don't forget whom you are speaking to again."

"No, no, my lord, most assuredly I won't."

But the innkeeper had done him a favor, for the light revealed a small figure huddled in the corner, her brown eyes wide and her lovely hair curling about her cheeks. Dominic couldn't tear his own eyes away from hers.

"Innkeeper," he barked as he neared her. "See that my new bride is well cared for."

"Oh… oh yes, my lord. Of course, my lord."

Lady Cassandra rose, as if fully intending to follow him despite his words. He gave her a cold look that should have frozen her in place. "You will stay here."

She looked confused, as if she couldn't fathom why he would deny her company. "But Sir Ro—the king. Perhaps I can help convince him to come."

"I will do the convincing," snapped Dominic, completely out of patience. "Something is afoot and I will not allow you to be caught up in an elven game. And you *will* obey me this time." He couldn't afford a drain on his power if he faced a battle in Dewhame but he had to be sure of her safety and held up his palms, surrounding her in a ring of dull gray fire.

Her mouth dropped open quite becomingly; he could just make out her features through the gray flames. She held out her arms and touched the walls of her prison, and then shoved at them. Gray fire wouldn't hurt her but it would remain impenetrable until he snuffed it, which he would not do for several hours. By then his men would be well on the road to Bath and she could not follow.

Dominic gave a grunt of satisfaction and strode out of the inn, mounting his horse in one smooth leap. When darkness fell he lit their way with white fire and they made good time on the road. Halfway to Bath he called a halt, sudden winds buffeting his horse and men.

Ador landed just beyond his magical light, a black gleaming shape in a dark meadow. Mor'ded slid down from his perch and waited for his son to come to him.

Dominic remembered to release the spell of gray fire from around Cassandra, wishing he could have been there to see her face, then quickly dismissed her from his mind as he reached his father. He glanced at Ador and the dragon blinked one red eye at him in acknowledgment.

"Where are you going?" demanded Mor'ded.

The general stiffened. "The king is not in Devizes. It is said that he refuses to leave the comfort of Bath."

"Interesting. So Breden wants to extend the game."

"So it seems."

Mor'ded almost smiled. "I wonder what is on his clever mind. Too bad it can't be anything on a grand scale. He knows better than to interfere directly in the game."

"He can only support the king's folly, nothing more. I will take care of this, Father. Your presence here might be misconstrued." The Imperial Lords rarely consulted with their commanders once a game had begun. It broke their rules of giving the orders and watching the humans try to follow them. For them, that was the most amusing part of the game. But Breden had technically started a new one, so Mor'ded had a right to discover the nature of it and perhaps issue a few new orders.

But it would look better among the elven lords if he allowed his champion to decide what action to take. Mor'ded nodded and returned to his dragon-steed, mounting in one fluid motion.

The horses and his men looked better for the halt and they made good time for the rest of the journey, arriving in Bath with the dawn.

His men narrowed their eyes against the glare of the sun's rays as they rode through the cobbled streets. It always appeared brighter in Bath, indeed, in the entire sovereignty of Dewhame, due to the reflection of the light bouncing off so much water. Small fountains of flowing urns and spouting creatures decorated every doorstep. Larger fountains stood within every square, their spray a loud hiss in the quiet morning, a cold spatter against Dominic's face. The buildings lining the streets had been painted in muted tones of blues and greens, and they all lacked a single straight line, the walls and roofs rounded like the swell of a wave.

But they could not compare to Dewhame Palace, the home of Imperial Lord Breden. As Dominic and his men approached the looming structure, he marveled again that something so seemingly *soft* could be so impregnable. The walls surrounding the palace had been crafted to resemble ocean waves, one rolling atop the other to create one large barrier. Elven magic made the waves appear to actually flow, but the palace walls themselves really did move with water. It erupted from the top turrets of the palace to cascade down the ridged walls, a translucent shimmer of color in the morning sunlight.

A flood of water drenched Dominic as they passed through the open gate and he didn't get any drier when he reached the waterfall-surrounded court-yard. Water rained down from the palace walls and splattered from the waterfalls and swirled about his horse's hooves. The general's wool coat stuck to his shoulders and back and made him itch. He scowled. Wet wool stank.

And the king didn't want to leave this place?

Dominic's scowl faded a bit though, as a welcoming party splashed forward to meet him. Two liveried footmen held an enormous umbrella shaped like the wings of a seagull over the wigged head of a heavyset gentleman. His bearing struck Dominic as someone of importance, and as he neared, the piercing intelligence in the man's darkish-colored eyes confirmed it.

"Lord Raikes?" the man inquired, his voice raised to a shout to be heard above the waterfalls.

"*General* Raikes," Dominic replied. He had no aspirations to be a lord. Although he supposed that because of Cassandra his children would have that distinction—He cut off the thought.

"Yes, of course. Well met, General Raikes. Allow me to introduce myself. Sir Robert Walpole, at your service. My most humble apologies, sir, to both you and your men, for having to come an additional distance to fetch your king. But we would be most honored to have your escort to Devizes, and then, of course, on to Firehame Palace."

"Indeed? The king has reconsidered his attachment to Bath?"

Something flickered in those intelligent eyes, but too quickly for Dominic to guess the emotion behind it.

"Not quite, General Raikes. However, I have packed up the court and we await you at the side gate."

"And the king?"

"You will find him in the Royal Bath. Down this street a ways. A large statue of Zeus fronts the building."

The general raised a brow.

"His royal carriage will be waiting for him by the time you… escort him forth."

"I see. It's a pleasure to meet such a sensible man, Sir Robert."

"The pleasure is all mine, I assure you. I've heard much about the champion's exploits on the battlefield."

Dominic nodded his head brusquely, tired of the polite speech, the hidden implications. He turned his mount and sloshed back through the courtyard into the relatively dry streets, easily finding the large statue of Zeus. His men circled the front of the building, his lieutenant ordering half of them to surround the back exits without having to be told.

Dominic expected Breden's army, or what was left of it, anyway, to appear within moments. His men readied themselves, drawing forth their pistols and frowning, wondering if the shot was still dry. Most of them drew their swords.

Dominic waved off the men who tried to accompany him, entering the building by himself. A mosaic of Zeus decorated the floor, sea monsters and mermaids frolicking about him. Not a single guard stood attention at the door to the baths and with no opposition Dominic strode into a marble-tiled room.

A very small old man sat up to his neck in the waters, two women his only companions, one thin and the other heavyset. Dominic didn't waste time with words—he already knew what the situation required. He reached down and pulled the king out of the water, grateful that propriety required a bathing costume. He did not relish having a man's naked buttocks so close to his face.

He set the king on his feet, gave him a respectful bow, and before the old man could protest, slung him over his shoulder.

The king cursed at him in heavily accented English, then switched to his native German. The two women scrambled from the bath and followed, screaming for help throughout the now long walk across the mosaic hall.

Dominic hesitated before he stepped outside, fully expecting to hear the sounds of battle. But only his troops waited for him and as promised, the king's gilded coach. Dominic handed his burden off to Sir Robert, who waited inside. The two ladies quickly followed their monarch and the general slammed the door behind them and nodded at the driver to move.

His troops surrounded the ornately decorated coach as it made its way through the empty streets. The men who had covered the back of the building joined them.

"Nothing?" asked the general.

"No, sir. I don't like it, sir."

Dominic felt the same way, waiting for an ambush as they journeyed back to Devizes. But when that failed to happen it set him to wondering. Why had Breden allowed the king this ridiculous little rebellion if the elven lord didn't wish to engage in a last desperate battle? Perhaps he hadn't expected Dominic himself to fetch his prize, and the Imperial Lord couldn't afford to lose any more men in another battle with the champion. It would take Dewhame another generation of breeding before it built its army back up enough for a decent invasion.

Still, Dominic refused to take any chances, escorting the king's carriage directly back to the inn, not waiting

for his court to catch up. His Majesty could wait for
the rest of them in Devizes.

It took them twice as long to make the journey
back, arriving far after midnight. The innkeeper met
him in the doorway, twisting his pudgy hands around
a mop cloth, ignoring the arrival of the king and
approaching Dominic first.

"She's been taken, my lord," he said without
preamble, "along with several of the other ladies."

He didn't need to ask to whom the man referred.
He should have kept her imprisoned in gray fire. A
deathly calm settled over Dominic. Now he knew
Breden's game. Firehame would gain the king, but
Breden would deprive them of their champion's
new bride.

"Lieutenant," barked the general.

"Aye, sir."

"Get us fresh mounts." Dominic turned to the best
tracker in his company. "Captain Wilkes."

"Sir."

"Go with the innkeeper; find their trail."

"Yes, sir!"

Dominic clenched his fists. Cassandra belonged
to him. Damn what Mor'ded might say about the
matter; he would get her back.

Damn if he would allow Breden this petty victory.

Fire bled from between his fingers and he took a
deep breath, dispelling that telltale flame and slowly
uncurling his hands. His rage didn't come from caring
about the girl. That had nothing at all to do with it.

Six

CASS WOKE TO THE SOUND OF WEEPING AND THE SMELL of stale urine. She blinked at the single ray of sunlight that shone through a tiny window far above her head, slanting across the room to fall on the barred door. She rose and tried the handle.

"It's locked," said Lady Agnes, a bit unnecessarily.

"Where are we?"

The lady shrugged, her arms around another woman who wept rather piteously. "There's several old castles in the area. I imagine we're in the dungeons of one of them. It could be worse. At least we're a bit aboveground."

Cassandra nodded and studied the ladies in the room. Like her, they all wore their nightgowns. She couldn't remember their names; indeed, she doubted they'd ever been introduced to her. They had purposely kept her out of their circle. Since it appeared that only Lady Agnes had kept her presence of mind, she directed her words to her husband's mistress.

"Who has taken us? What do they want?"

Lady Agnes glared at Cass. "How should I know? I just woke up myself. To a dreadful headache, mind. They must have drugged us with something."

Cassandra swallowed. Indeed, her mouth felt full of cotton, her limbs weak and shaky. She began to pace the cell, trying to flush the rest of the drug from her system. Had it been put in their wine or last night's meal? She couldn't be sure. After Dominic had released that wall of dull gray fire about her, most of the nobles had already retired and she'd been given dinner in her room by a lackey.

After that, she vaguely remembered a bumpy wagon and being smothered in hay.

She plucked a piece of straw from her hair. She supposed when they got out of here, her husband would be able to ferret out who had drugged them. If they got out of here.

Cass stopped pacing and addressed her words to the entire room. "What magical skills do you have?"

They all looked at her with shock and disdain, refusing to answer, but at least they managed to stop weeping. Lady Agnes smiled triumphantly. Rather foolish, given their current situation. "Do you propose that we try to save *ourselves*?" she asked. "With our paltry magical gifts? My dear, we shall do what any proper lady would. We wait for rescue."

"Surely we shall be ransomed," agreed the woman sitting next to her.

"They wouldn't dare harm a lady of the court," said another.

Cassandra hoped they were right. But if not... she couldn't perform a death dance in front of them if it came down to a fight. It would expose her to too much speculation. "I apologize. I'm sure Lord Mor'ded will never allow the ladies of his court to be harmed. It's well-known how much the elven lords care for their people."

The ladies suddenly looked worried.

"That is, if he's not too busy with the king," continued Cassandra. "But if something *were* to happen to us, we shall be comforted in the thought that another war will be fought in retribution. They might even name their new game after us."

A tall woman stood, the feathers adorning her nightdress trembling with the movement. "I can sing. But I doubt that would be much help." She waved a hand at each woman. "Lady Somers can make fiery sparkles in the air. Lady Ursula can shape clay into any form and animate it for a few minutes. Viscountess Rothermere can play the harpsichord so beautifully you can barely see her fingers move. Lady Agnes…"

The blonde tossed her head. "I don't need any magic. I have the elven beauty."

And she was right. Even bedraggled with bits of hay stuck in her hair, she looked stunningly beautiful.

Cass sighed, trying to keep the disappointment from her face. Their elven gifts might manage to distract their captors but she didn't think it would help them escape.

The tall woman stepped closer. "I am Lady Verney, the Marchioness of Verney. Perhaps we can put our heads together and think of some way to use our skills to best advantage?"

Cassandra looked up at the taller woman with a

smile, thinking it might be difficult to bridge the distance between them to put their heads on a level. Lady Verney appeared to read her mind, for her eyes sparkled with understanding.

"Indeed, we can try," started Cass. "If we made some sort of commotion—" A door slammed and they all jumped, staring at the small barred opening of their own cell. Laughter, the sound of booted feet making their way toward them. Two men, possibly three.

Lady Verney backed up against the wall and two of the women started weeping again. Cass shushed them and ran to the door.

"Heh, ye got it right, Martin. If we has to kill 'em anyways, we might as well have us some fun first."

The ladies gasped in unison. Cass turned. Lady Agnes clutched her throat and Lady Verney's feathers shook.

The men's laughter rang against the stone walls.

"I'll go with them," whispered Cassandra, wishing she had a belt... a string holding her nightgown closed... anything. But alas, she had worn to bed a filmy gown with only a petticoat beneath for warmth. Asking for one of the ladies to share a part of their wardrobe would have raised questions that would jeopardize her secret. "It should give you more time to think of a way to save yourselves."

Lady Verney's eyes widened. "We can't let you sacrifice—"

"Oh, yes, we can," interjected Lady Agnes.

The other ladies nodded, and they had no further time for discussion as two dirty faces peered into their cell. Silence reigned as the men studied them.

"I like the blonde," pronounced the man with a scar running from eye to jaw.

"And I likes the little brown-haired one. Lookee her eyes. She'll put up a good fight. I likes them lively."

Cassandra wrinkled her nose. Their body odor drifted through the bars into the room, and the one who liked her smelled the worst.

"Let's flip for it then," said Scar Face. "Toss a shilling—we gots plenty to spare after this job, eh?"

Their faces disappeared for a moment. The lock on the door jiggled, and it slowly opened. The stinky one entered the room and Cass gave a sigh of relief.

"Come along, little 'un," he said, waving a pistol at her face.

Lady Verney made a strangled sound, but the rest of the ladies stayed mute as she followed the man out of the cell. When she stood in the dank corridor outside the room, he gave her a quite unnecessary shove and Cass pretended to fall, landing in a heap of material. She quickly tore a strip from the hem of her petticoat.

"I'll be back fer ye," shouted Scar Face into the cell door, and Lady Agnes yelped. Both men laughed.

"Get up," said Scar Face, giving her a kick when she didn't move quickly enough. Cass rose and glared at him, balling up the strip of cloth in her hand. She then stuck her nose in the air and headed down the corridor.

"Tol' ye." Stinky Man chuckled. "No snivelin' from this 'un."

Lady Cassandra preceded them down the corridor, up winding stairs and into another long hall, this one with stones missing in several places, giving her tantalizing glimpses of freedom. She felt the gun on her back as an itch that grew worse with each passing footstep. She took a deep breath. She'd been trained to dance to kill an elven lord; two ordinary men shouldn't present her with much of a challenge.

But she'd killed a man only once. Thomas had told her it was necessary to make sure she could follow through with her task when the time came. He'd chosen a man slated for the gallows for killing his wife and five children. Thomas told her she'd done the man a favor.

Cass had still felt sick afterward. It had taken her weeks of prayer and meditation before she'd managed to eat a full meal again.

She told herself to stop thinking, to concentrate on the thrum of blood in her ears, on the sound of their boots on the floor. They had a rhythm, and she immersed herself in the beat, allowing the song of a dance to take over her body and awaken the magic in her blood. Hoping the torn cloth balled up in her hand would be long enough for the deed.

"Stop here," said Stinky Man. "Open the door."

The door opened with a wobbly swing onto a filthy room with a pile of straw in the corner. Her captor motioned her over to the makeshift bed with a jerk of his pistol. Cass's feet refused to cooperate, her body swaying with invisible music.

He pushed her hard this time, clear across the room and into the crackly grass. Cassandra truly fell, her head meeting the ground with a sickly thud. Her vision sparkled with starlight, and if it hadn't been for her graceful roll she would have been knocked senseless.

"I'm first," panted Stinky Man, shoving his gun in his belt while he walked over to her.

Cass suppressed a grin at his action, fisting her hand around the torn strip of cloth, adding the sound of his soft footsteps to the dance already flowing through her. He stood above her, unbuttoning the flap of his breeches. Then he glanced at his mate. "Turn around."

Scar Face rolled his eyes but turned his back, as if this wasn't the first time he'd complied with such a request.

This time Cass couldn't suppress her grin. If they continued to make it easy for her, she might not have to kill them. The dunderheaded stinker smiled back at her. "Decided ye'd like it, eh?" He shoved up her skirts and then lowered himself on top of her. She held her breath against the stench and slapped his face. But not too hard, just enough to distract him while she shook out the cloth in her hand.

Scar Face chuckled to the wall. "Ye said ye wanted a fighter, Martin. Sounds like ye got one."

Martin's eyes lit up with evil glee as he rubbed his red face. Before she could blink, he hauled his fist back and punched her. The room spun for a sickening moment. Cass started to sob—loudly, covering the sounds the stinker made as his excitement rose.

"See, Martin. Thass why I don't like fighters— they's too noisy."

Cassandra's gown had gotten tangled up, and Martin ignored his friend, swearing and grunting in his efforts to find her legs while supporting himself above her.

The dance shivered in her blood and lent strength to her arms. Cass wrapped the strip of cloth around his neck and pulled. It took him a few moments to even realize what had happened. When he finally managed it, he didn't have the breath to cry out. She sobbed louder to cover his harsh gasps for air.

And then her makeshift garrote ripped.

And several things happened at once.

She returned his favor, punching him in the throat, making him choke, allowing her to use leverage to roll him off her. Scar Face either sensed something wrong or felt impatient of his view, for he turned around. His muddy-colored eyes widened and he drew his pistol.

Cass pulled Martin's pistol out of his belt and pointed it at the other man. They fired at the same time, both of their shots going wild. But she'd expected that, for guns were notorious for their misdirection even at close range.

Scar Face grinned and drew his sword while Cass took Martin's sword... and knife.

"Don't make me kill you," she said.

He laughed and lunged at her. Martin must have recovered his senses because he grabbed her leg at the same time. Lady Cassandra could no longer consider her options. She let the dance consume her, allowed the magic full rein. Time slowed as her senses heightened, her muscles strengthened. As her body performed the steps with no conscious thought of her own.

Martin's knife hit Scar Face square between the eyes. Martin's sword relieved his own head from his body.

Cass could not stop dancing for several minutes.

When the magic finally released her, she looked with regret at the two dead men. She covered Martin's face with straw, used Scar Face's soiled neck cloth to cover his. Then took a deep breath, knelt between the two of them, and began to pray for their souls. "Please, God, forgive them for their sins. And forgive me for what I was forced to do—although I took this path knowingly, so perhaps that's asking for too much."

Lady Cassandra sighed with fatigue from using so much of her magic, but bent over Martin and recited the Our Father, then went to Scar Face's still body and prayed the same for him.

That's where Dominic found her when he burst into the room.

He didn't say anything at first, thankfully allowing her to finish. When she looked up at him she blanched, for his eyes looked so deadly cold, and fire flickered up and down the length of his bloody sword.

"The others are in the dungeon. D-down that corridor."

The general nodded and turned to his men, motioning them onward, then turned back to her. "Are you harmed?"

Cass touched her face, the area already starting to swell from Martin's blow. "Not much."

Suddenly his cold eyes flickered with anger. An anger directed not at her, but at the man who had harmed her. For just a moment she saw fear mixed with that emotion, as if he had come to her rescue because he had truly cared for her safety. Then the look faded, and he cleaned his sword on Scar Face's shirt before sheathing it with deadly calm. "What happened to them?"

Lady Cassandra glanced from one dead man to the other. What could she possibly say? That she knew more death dances than she did any other? That the Rebellion had taught her from secret information they had gleaned with their spies? He would have to kill her where she stood.

Over the past few days she'd pushed her true task to the back of her mind, forgetting their relationship was naught but a falsehood. She had lost herself in his loving, in his beauty and kisses and the sheer pleasure he brought to her body. She had no other goal than to win him over.

He waited for her answer patiently, with that inhuman elven calm. Her beloved enemy.

"They… they fought over me… to see who would be first. They wanted to…" Cass covered her face and sobbed, surprised to find that this time her tears were real. She felt so very tired. She hadn't wanted to kill them, truly. She might have been able to render them unconscious, tie them up, and then escape. But she'd been trained in the dance too well; they hadn't given her time to consider her options…

And she still recoiled from the thought of Martin's foul hands on her body.

So she jumped when she felt Dominic's arms around her. He loosened them for a moment, as if to draw away, and Cass flung herself at him. Dominic gave a great sigh and lifted her off her feet so she could bury her face against his neck. He held her for a time, caressing her hair and face and whatever else he could touch, as if assuring himself that she was unharmed. Then he carried her out of that room, into the open air, where the wind blew and the sun hid behind the clouds.

Cassandra no longer cried for the men she had killed, for the fright they had given her. As soon as she'd seen Dominic at the door, his sword dripping with blood from the men he'd killed while coming to her rescue, she'd wanted this mockery of a marriage to be real. So she cried because she wanted to love this man, wanted him to love her. And it could never be.

When she calmed he set her back on her feet, removed his cloak, and settled it about her shoulders with a gentle touch. "Close your eyes."

"Why?"

"So the light doesn't hurt them."

Cass closed them. Even then she could see the blue fire from behind her lids. The powerful throb of pain in her face faded and she regained some of her spent strength. Even the sadness she felt inside eased a bit.

"How do you feel?"

She opened her eyes and stared at his impassive face. The wind threw his silver hair against his strong cheeks, across his stern mouth. His voice had held such concern, she'd thought for a moment… "Much better, thank you."

"Good." And then he leaned down and kissed her breath away. It felt different from the other kisses he'd given her. More tenderness than passion within it. But then she threw her arms around him and kissed him back with fervor and it changed again, that passion that always lay between them sparking to life. Her knees grew weak and she thought of the small tent that they'd shared and the pleasure he'd given her, and she wished they had someplace they could go away from the demands of their world, to just be together. For despite his denials she knew she gave him pleasure. That second night in the tent he had wanted her so badly she'd felt it shimmer in the air between them, and the moment he had her alone he'd claimed her…

She pulled away from him and stared in wonder. Her husband had managed to make her forget the horrors of the past few hours.

He set her from him again, picked up her hand, and studied the unfurled petals of the rose ring. "You are fully recovered now."

Cass nodded, even though she still felt a bit weak. But rest and a good meal would fix that.

"Then next time I tell you something, woman, you will listen."

"I… I beg your pardon?"

The wind shushed through the tall grass and whispered in the trees. "This never would have happened if you'd obeyed my wishes and stayed back at Firehame Palace."

He sounded as if he blamed *her* for being abducted. "Surely, sir, you could have used your gray fire to keep me there, as you did back at the inn."

"I can't afford to always be wasting my magic on a disobedient wife."

Lady Cassandra realized that despite his stoic demeanor, he was still very angry with her. Could she hope that he had truly feared for her? That what she'd glimpsed in his eyes had been real? Or did this anger really come from injured pride because someone had dared to take something of his? "Then I'm sorry to say, dear husband, that you'd best get used to it, for I cannot promise to obey your every command."

His lip twitched. And not from amusement, she felt sure.

"You could have been killed." He said it as if he commented on the weather, but his voice had dropped dangerously low.

"I can take care of myself."

"Indeed?" And those crystal eyes of his glittered, a deep black full of dangerous intelligence, and he stared at her a long time. Cassandra feared she had aroused his suspicions and mentally scolded herself for a fool. She could at least pretend to agree to obey him.

She opened her mouth, but he spun on his heel, stalking back into the ruined castle without a backward glance. Cass wavered in indecision for a moment and then trudged after him, skirting several dead bodies near the entrance of the keep.

"General Raikes," called Lady Agnes as soon as they entered the long hall. She swayed toward them, an officer on each arm. "I knew you would come and rescue us. I told her you would." And she glared briefly at Cassandra before batting her blue eyes at him again. The rest of the ladies followed behind, avoiding Cass's eyes, except for Lady Verney, who gave her a nod and a hesitant smile.

The wind blew harder from outside, reaching into the hall, plastering the ladies' gowns against their bodies. They pulled borrowed cloaks closer about their shoulders.

Her husband raised a brow. "My wife doubted me?"

Lady Agnes tittered. "She said we should use our magic to protect ourselves, can you imagine? As if sparkles in the air and nimble fingers could save us."

Lady Verney stepped forward, her height commanding attention. "Lady Cassandra offered herself in order to give us time to gather our resources, sir. It was the most selfless act I have ever witnessed." She stepped over to Cass and took her hand. "Please tell me you suffered no harm. I shan't be able to live with myself if you have."

Cassandra didn't know how to react to this sudden support. She glanced over at Dominic, but if anything, his black eyes glittered more dangerously than they had but moments ago. Was she the only one who noticed the fury beneath that calm expression? "I assure you I'm fine, Lady Verney."

"Sophia. Please, call me Sophia."

"As you wish—"

"I do believe I shall faint," announced Lady Agnes. The men holding her tightened their grips and she turned and scowled at them. They let go. She staggered over to Dominic. The bastard caught her in his arms. "You have no idea what horrors we suffered through, General."

"No doubt, madam." He glanced through the hall to the outside. "Let's see if we can make it to the Fire and Water Inn before the storm breaks." He picked up Lady Agnes, who squealed in delight, and carried her out to his horse. The wagon that must have brought them here sat next to the mounts but the officers ignored it, each taking a lady and riding double.

After giving his general a swift glance, a young man with fiery hair and a wide mouth assisted Cass up into his saddle. Apparently Dominic intended to ignore his wife and ride with his mistress. If he thought to punish Cassandra this way for his ridiculous notion of her rebellious behavior, it wouldn't work. She could not afford to subjugate herself to his will.

But the general acted as if he hadn't given his wife another thought once he had her back in his possession. When they had all mounted up he motioned for them to ride, except for his own horse, Lady Agnes still perched in the saddle. He walked back to the ruins alone. Cass watched over her shoulder as he raised his muscular arms, red fire blazing from his palms. It first touched the dead men surrounding the entrance, then surged within the keep, flaring out the windows and jagged openings and roofless chambers. The fire rumbled and hissed, shaking the stones from the walls and making the entire structure waver in her sight.

Her husband had used magical red fire, and as far as she knew, the most potent of his arsenal. Within a few hours, nothing but black rubble would remain of their prison.

Lady Cassandra shivered.

Her escort gave her a squeeze of reassurance. She sat in front of him, one leg thrown over the pommel to help her sit sidesaddle, even though the saddle wasn't meant for it. He had one arm wrapped around her waist, the other holding the reins. He leaned down and whispered into her ear, "Our enemies will think twice before trying to abduct you again, my lady."

His voice reeked with pride.

Cassandra fought to stop her shivering. She had never seen such a potent display of power, had never witnessed the destructive strength of her husband's magic. And she thought she could assassinate his father, whose power far surpassed his? Perhaps Thomas had been right. Perhaps she should have run from this task God had given her.

She prayed for courage.

The sound of hoofbeats approaching made her glance up into the smiling face of Lady Agnes and the expressionless face of her husband as they rode up to her. But her escort must have read something in those elven features, for he quickly removed his arm from about her waist. The general nodded at his officer and then urged his horse to the front of their column.

Lady Cassandra struggled to maintain her seat the rest of the way to Devizes, for her escort refused to touch her after that.

And yet Dominic had no qualms about touching the woman sharing his saddle. Fie, he barely kept his hands off her. Unfortunately, Cass had an unob-structed view of them in front of her. How the general managed to direct his horse while his mistress rubbed her hands all over him and held his face while she kissed him was beyond Cassandra's understanding.

She decided she could keep her face as stoic as her husband usually kept his.

And then Lady Agnes wrapped her hands in Dominic's hair.

Cass narrowed her eyes, tightened her grip on the edges of the saddle. She loved the feel of his hair, those satiny strands beneath her palms, the silvery mass of it twined about her fingers. Damn the woman, that was *her* territory, *her* favorite way of touching him.

The beat of the horse's hooves, the wild swish of the wind in the trees, the sway of the bushes beside their path all combined to form a single harmony. A song that crept in with her jealousy and started to form a dance of magic.

"Lady Cassandra," said a female voice.

Cass turned and blinked. Lady Verney and her escort had ridden up beside her. The tall lady reached over and patted her shoulder, glancing at Dominic and his mistress with contempt. "The elven lack human feeling," she said. "You cannot judge them by our standards."

"He's half human," muttered Cassandra, grateful for Sophia's timely appearance. When had she ever allowed the dance to come upon her without willing it to? Not since she'd had her trials.

Lady Verney hadn't heard her, but the man sitting behind her said, "Not enough to notice, lady."

Cass ignored him.

"I daresay," said Sophia, "that Lady Agnes has a way about her."

Cassandra grimaced. Sophia laughed.

"What I mean," continued the lady, "is that she actually made us feel as if *you* were the interloper. That a new wife would steal her lover from her." Her thin lips curled down. "Faith, I wonder how she managed to hoodwink us into believing such nonsense?"

"She charms women as easily as she does men."

"Indeed." Lady Verney's watery eyes narrowed. "It's hard to withstand that elven allure when they choose to apply it." Her gaze strayed to Dominic's firm back and muscular shoulders. "None of us blame you, you know. For being unable to resist him."

Cass shrugged. "Why should I? I do not know the art of being coy, Lady Verney, having never been taught it."

"Sophia, dear, and yes, I'd heard of your... insular schooling. Your innocence is quite refreshing, and yet..."

She let the thought trail off while the sky overhead rumbled.

"I do believe we shan't beat the downpour." Lady Verney turned her head and nodded at the ladies behind them. "They will come around as well, my dear. You shan't be so alone anymore."

Cassandra's eyes burned, but fortunately rain started to fall, so Sophia did not see the start of her tears. She'd had to be kept apart to keep her secret, to pursue God's purpose for her. But that didn't mean she had ever liked it. Indeed, it might be half the reason for her infatuation with her new husband. Besides Thomas, she'd never been as close to anyone as she had become with Dominic.

The rain washed away her thoughts, and Cass pulled Dominic's cloak up over her head against the sudden downpour. It smelled of him. A clean, spicy scent that made her head spin and her body ache with desire. She felt only relief when her escort bent his body over hers and they broke into a gallop, racing for the comfort of the inn. By the time they reached Devizes, the rain had soaked the material and banished any scent of her husband.

The general and his mistress had entered the Fire and Water Inn well before them, so Cassandra had the advantage of walking in unseen. Dominic must have changed the king's mind about coming to Firehame, because His Majesty looked quite pleased with the company at the moment. On his left sat Mor'ded, his elven beauty like a shining light next to the small older king, and on his right must be...

Cass almost fell to her knees. She'd heard so much about Sir Robert Walpole, the leader of the Rebellion. Despite his gentle smile and affable expression, Cassandra could see the intelligence in his dark piercing eyes. For a moment she could see nothing but him.

"Ah, Your Majesty," drawled Imperial Lord Mor'ded, "this is my champion, General Dominic Raikes. Without his services we would never have had the esteemed pleasure of your company."

The king turned his bug-eyed gaze upon Dominic and regally nodded. "He looks very much like you."

"Indeed," replied the Imperial Lord. "Except he always dresses like a soldier. Perhaps you can educate him on the benefits of court attire, now that the ruler of fashion will reside in Firehame Palace."

Dominic bowed stiffly.

Cassandra heard the mocking tone in Mor'ded's voice when he addressed the king. Sir Robert did as well, for he watched the king like a hawk, as if waiting for any sign of eruption. But if the king noticed Mor'ded's tone he did not give any indication of it. And indeed, what could he have done about it anyway? He signed the papers the elven lords gave him for new laws, new titles, the transfer of land. They hardly needed the king's stamp yet used him as if it gained them credibility among the people. Cass sighed. Which it surely had to the general populace anyway.

"You have returned the ladies as well, I see," said Mor'ded to his son.

"Of course," answered Dominic as if there had been no doubt of it.

The king opened his mouth to say something and Mor'ded shushed him, his cold black eyes focused on his son's face. "And they are all unharmed?"

"As you see." Dominic put his arm around Lady Agnes, who gave him a beatific smile.

"But what of your wife? For surely she is the reason you charged out to rescue them, leaving the king behind and defenseless."

Cassandra frowned. Something lay beneath this conversation. Some threat or insinuation, for the king had hardly been left defenseless. The general had taken only a few of his troops with him, leaving the bulk of his force to guard the king. She glanced over at Sir Robert—who had distracted the king from his miff of being shushed with a tray of sweetmeats, but whose sharp eyes stayed riveted on the elven lord and his son.

He sensed something as well. Cass hoped she would have an opportunity to ask him about it. Perhaps he could figure it out.

Dominic did not respond to the accusation that he had left the king defenseless. "Breden sought to trick us. To take what is ours because we took what is his." He raised one elegant brow. "I disabused him of the notion he could best you in a game."

"And your wife? Where is she?"

Dominic shrugged. "With one of my men. She is back in our possession—what else matters?"

And then Mor'ded threw back his long thick hair and laughed, truly an evil sound. Cass wished he would refrain from it, even though it broke the tension in the room. Sir Robert blinked and collapsed into his chair with a frown. The Imperial Lord turned back to the king. "My court was so eager to meet you that several of them journeyed to Devizes for the privilege. Shall I introduce you to them? Lord Somers, in particular, wishes to know what color hose you deem fit for the winter season."

The king lifted his chin and gave a regal nod, holding out his beringed fingers to Lord Somers.

Lady Cassandra felt a sympathetic hand fall on her shoulder and looked up into the thin face of Lady Verney. The other woman's eyes shone with indignant shame for her and Cass suddenly felt very small. A very insignificant personage, by her husband's own words.

Cassandra gave her new friend a false smile and then faded backward into the shadows of the inn, finding the staircase and her room with little trouble. A servant waited in her room and she directed the young girl to fetch her dinner, for she refused to go back downstairs and subject herself to further humili-ation in front of Sir Robert.

She fumed while she ate, attacking her dinner with the cutlery, cursing her husband by the only means at her disposal. By using the words she'd heard him use. She decided that she had finished with trying to please her husband. Indeed, she would now demand he show her at least a little respect.

By the time the frivolity in the main room had quieted, Cassandra had changed her mind. Dominic had not come to her room. Surely he would not choose that viper over her? She then decided she wouldn't scold him. She would perform a love dance for him instead, proving that Lady Agnes's charms were no match for her own.

By the time she fell asleep, quite alone in the large bed, she'd gone back to cursing him, the gold rose on her finger clenched into a tight bud.

Seven

With Mor'ded accompanying them back to Firehame Palace, Dominic had no difficulty ignoring Cassandra. His father had tested his feelings for the girl back at the inn, and fortunately he'd disabused the man of the notion that he'd so fallen in love with his new wife he'd rushed to her rescue.

Although he couldn't be sure of that himself. And it worried Dominic that it might have had nothing to do with who had won Breden's game; that he had indeed rushed off to the rescue because he might have become fond of the girl. And when he saw her standing in that filthy room, rage had near overwhelmed him. The thought that another man had even touched her...

And yet something else nagged at him. Cassandra's story of how the two men had fought each other didn't quite add up to the condition of the dead bodies. She'd been lying and it made him suspicious, gave him another reason to keep her at arm's length. There was more to his wife than it appeared.

Dominic noted the redness of Cassandra's eyes as

they journeyed, the way Aggie gloated over her. But he refused to pity her and kept his mistress at his side like a shield—although he couldn't seem to stomach her in his bed. She pouted about it but continued to share his tent.

Cassandra slept with the other ladies. At least his wife now had the friendship of Lady Verney to comfort her. His estimation of the tall woman's sensibilities rose considerably.

And Mor'ded no longer watched Cassandra and Dominic with calculating eyes.

Of course, with the king's retinue in tow, it took twice as long to return to the palace, and Dominic spent a weary day getting the new court settled into their home. And a long evening getting drunk enough at the fete that night to drown his anger at Cassandra's near brush with death. Fortunately she did not attend the celebration, and Mor'ded taunted the king so mercilessly that Dominic did manage to stay distracted.

Sometime during the night he must have made his way up the stairs of the dragon's tower and passed out on the hard flagstone, for he woke the next morning with an aching back and a pounding head. He sat up and then immediately folded over, covering his face with his hands.

"Egads, the sun is too bright this morn."

A huff of breath that might have been mistaken for laughter if it hadn't come from a dragon.

Dominic slowly dropped his hands and cracked his eyes open. Ador seemed to swallow the sunlight with his black scales, his even darker wings. A fine stream of smoke seeped from his left nostril to catch the breeze and drift over the side of the tower wall.

"I have brought home my prize. The king now resides in Firehame."

Ador didn't even blink. The dragon probably knew everything that went on in Firehame and didn't need Dominic to tell him. But he had only the dragon to confide in for many years and spoke from habit, nothing more. Ador had never betrayed any of Dominic's secrets but the dragon also rarely spoke. The general certainly hadn't expected a response.

"It won't work, you know," said Ador.

His voice sounded like rock scraping over stone. Dominic winced. "Of course it will," he replied. "I have earned my father's respect at last. We will no longer be so at odds with one another."

"I don't speak of mad elven lords, human. I speak of your wife."

Dominic lifted his head in surprise and met those red-striated eyes. For a moment his fear for her made him unable to speak. For if his father's thoughts were alien to him, Ador's were indecipherable. That either of them took too much notice of Cassandra gave him pause. Ador had spoken of a change in the wind, and indeed, it appeared the dragon, at least, had shown a great deal by breaking his near silence after so many years.

But Dominic could not help but take advantage of it. He'd won many a battle by gaining as much knowledge as he could from the most unlikely sources. "And what do you know of her?"

Ador rose, his claws scraping new gouges into

the flagstone, his wings unfolding to stretch to awe-inspiring proportions. He blocked the sun, casting Dominic in the shade of his shadow. The general had long ago become accustomed to the sheer size of the beast, but betimes it still took his breath away.

"I know hiding your affection for her won't work for very long."

Those veined wings stroked the air, plastering Dominic's bedraggled shirt to his chest, throwing his coat open and slapping his hair against his face. He narrowed his eyes again against the force of the dragon's tempest. Although he would deny it to Mor'ded with his last breath, he did not attempt to dispute Ador's words. "How do I stop from caring for her?"

"You cannot." The dragon leaped atop the wall, each leg straddling a merlon, claws gripping the red stone.

Dominic rose when Ador launched into flight, bracing his feet against the buffet of wind. The dragon had a simple way of ending a conversation. The general watched the beast circle the tower a few times, admiring the beauty of the dragon's scales glimmering in the sun, the majesty of his wings as they moved smoothly among the currents. Ah, how he longed to ride the beast but Ador had never offered, and Dominic would never ask.

"I will stop from caring for her," he muttered as the dragon dwindled from his sight. "I must," he sighed, turning and making his way back down the tower stairs. "It's the only way I can protect her."

So he avoided returning to his apartments to say farewell to his new wife before leaving the palace

to check on the borders of Firehame. Dominic
knew the other Imperial Lords would eventually
test their defenses. With the king in residence, every
sovereignty in England would now conspire to attack
them. Their only reprieve was the harvest. Most of
the soldiers had returned to their homes to bring in
the crops. The elven lords wouldn't risk starvation of
their people for the game, for they needed strength of
numbers to win.

The fighting wouldn't begin in earnest until the
new snow.

·✦·

After several weeks Dominic returned to Firehame
Palace, satisfied that for the moment, at least, they
could withstand any small skirmishes a bored Imperial
Lord would send against them. And confident he now
had firm control over the growing affection he'd felt
toward his new wife. He wanted to bed her, indeed,
but he no longer felt the burning desire to possess
her that had overwhelmed him on their journey to
Devizes. His anger that she might have come to harm
when she'd been captured had completely faded.
Ador's words be damned. He had enough elven blood
to prove the dragon wrong.

The general wearily dismounted in the main
courtyard, accustomed himself to the warmth of the
flame-covered walls, and entered the hall. He passed
the blue withdrawing room, surprised to see that his
father held court within, apparently in benign humor
today, for the blue room had been designed with
healing magic. Watered blue silk covered the walls,

blue puddles of carpets littered the floors, and magical ornaments of blue glass and silver created a calming effect. Dominic stood for a moment, idly slapping his hat against his thigh, studying the scene before him.

Mor'ded sat in a velvet chair with a high enough back to look like a throne, the king to his left in a seat with legs short enough to require that he look up at the Imperial Lord. The king's advisor, Sir Robert, sat at a table next to an open window, yellow flame occasionally flickering around the sill. The king's two mistresses sat at his side, the skinny one laughing at something Lady Agnes had said. The blonde beauty had wasted no time in ingratiating herself with the royal court.

Mor'ded looked up, his cold black eyes fastening on him immediately. "So the champion has returned. What's your report on our borders?"

Dominic stepped into the room amid a round of admiring sighs. He'd been on the road for days, dust covered his hair and cloak, and he needed a bath. And still he could feel their lust like a palpable thing. He ignored it as he strode to his father's throne, tucked his hat under his arm, and bowed.

"I'm satisfied to report that our borders are secure, my lord. His Majesty will be safe within your realm."

"Naturally," Mor'ded said with a nod, although Dominic saw a flicker of boredom in those dark eyes. And boredom made an Imperial Lord doubly dangerous.

"There are reports of unrest in the city, however," added Dominic.

Mor'ded leaned forward. "Such as?"

"Rumors that children are being hidden from the upcoming trials."

The court gasped in unison, causing several blue vases to erupt in a shower of blue powder. Those sitting closest to the ornaments breathed in deeply, their faces relaxing into dreamy smiles.

"Ignorant peasants," snapped the plumper of the king's mistresses, popping a chocolate into her mouth. "Who would not want their child to go to fabled Elfhame?"

"Who, indeed?" said Mor'ded, a twist to his lips. "If we had not been given the task of finding worthy humans to populate our homeland, we would return in a trice. A land of sweet rivers and lush forests. Trees laden with fruit so delectable to the palate that no human could imagine the ecstasy of a single bite. Peasants become kings in Elfhame, wear robes woven of soft *narish* and spun gold. Who would dare deny his child the right to be a chosen one?"

"Yes, indeed," interjected Sir Robert. "Why would anyone be so foolish, General Raikes?" The man's negligent pose seemed at odds with the intensity of his gaze as he waited for Dominic to answer.

The general shrugged. "I do not pretend to understand. It seems some people care for their children and do not want to be parted from them, however much it may benefit the child." He turned back to his father, his face impassive. "Shall I dispatch some spies to find these families?"

"No." Mor'ded gracefully settled back into his chair, rolled his black scepter excitedly. "I think I shall handle this myself. You are dismissed."

Dominic bowed, turned to the king and nodded, and attempted to leave the room.

Aggie waylaid him first, her perfume rolling over him like a cloud, her delicate feet sinking into a puddle of blue carpet that appeared to ripple about her skirts. "You will come to the ball tonight, will you not? It is in honor of the king's return and the costumes promise to be grand."

He lifted a brow.

"Oh, I know you don't care a fig about that, but I assure you *my* costume will delight you. Will you come?"

Dominic didn't know how he could get out of it without insulting the king, so he nodded and strode toward the door.

Viscount Rothermere hesitantly touched his arm, then quickly snatched it back as if he'd been burned when Dominic turned to him. "Pardon me, General. But your wife—"

"Yes? Speak up, man! What about her?"

"Err, um, yes. No offense, sir, but she has been upsetting the servants."

Dominic gave his lordship a cold glance and took a step to pass the man, and another insolent fool stepped up to him.

"I daresay, sir, since you don't employ servants yourself, you can't imagine how… difficult they can make one's life."

"Then perhaps you should accustom yourself to doing without them."

Dominic took another step.

"Devil a bit," said Lord Blevin. "Just look at my wig, man! Tangled! And my new velvet coat. Spots!"

A small mob of disheveled-looking men now surrounded him. Dominic crossed his arms over his chest. He had known Cassandra would cause a stir by hiring those slaves, but he didn't give a damn about the nobles' vanity… or the servants who felt their orderly universe had been threatened by the invasion of slaves into their territory.

"My biscuits have been burned every morning," said another courtier. "Now, General, you must take your wife to task. It's a man's duty, after all."

Orange flame sprouted on Dominic's hands and he idly played with it as he waited until the fools ran out of bluster, until the room quieted, including the king and his courtiers. Orange fire was cooler than red but could burn just as easily. All eyes had riveted on the fire in his palms, watching with fascination as he tossed it about like a juggler, his hands showing no sign of being burned by the flame. When he could hear the sound of his own soft breath, he squelched the blaze and said, very slowly, "What my wife does is no concern of mine. You mistake me, gentlemen, for someone who gives a damn."

He took a step and the astonished courtiers hastily cleared a path out of his way. He heard his father's laughter behind him, the soft clap of his hands as he applauded his son's deportment. The sky-painted ceiling above them suddenly shivered, and a rain of blue vapor fell, the calming magic swirling around the assemblage. Dominic waved a wisp of it off his nose and strode out of the room without a backward glance.

Perhaps it had been fortuitous that Mor'ded had held court in the blue room today.

He trod up the carpeted stairs to his new apartments, feeling the start of a smile on his lips and then banishing it. The woman was a nuisance. He should chastise her for causing him difficulty with the court and annoying him. He did not particularly care to see her again. He returned to his apartments only because he needed a bath and a change of clothing.

Dominic's footsteps became swifter and lighter as he neared the door to his rooms. He threw open the double doors with a bit too much force.

His apartments had grown even more cluttered in his absence.

He made his way through the parlor and the sitting room, noting the lace-edged pillows and thick carpets and elaborate wall hangings. By the time he reached the bedroom, he could no longer continue the catalog of frippery; it simply boggled the mind. His apartments now looked as ostentatious as the king's.

She sat in front of a mirrored table in a carved chair painted with climbing roses, a young girl dressing her brown hair and an even younger one holding a patch-box up to her face.

"But, my lady," said the younger one, "ye shall put us to shame if ye don't wear at least one."

His wife smiled. "Now, Gwen, I've already agreed to the rouge, so you must be content with that. I'll not have those spots on my face—they look like bugs."

The girl giggled. "So they do. But what if I cuts them into shapes? Per'aps a star right near yer cheek? Won't that look grand?"

His wife's soft brown eyes met his in the reflection of her mirror. "I'm not sure. What do you think, sir?"

Dominic could do naught but stare. She looked lovely in her dressing gown of pale satin, her hair woven into an intricate design that layered in strands of champagne pearls and gold ribbons. Her loosely belted gown revealed the swell of her breasts and the brocade fabric of her stays.

She continued to gaze at him, a smile playing about the corners of her lovely mouth. Dominic had had enough experience with women to know she should have greeted him with pique, if not downright hostility. He had dismissed her person as unimportant to the king, had not slept with her since she'd been captured in Devizes, and had left for weeks with nary a farewell.

Any other woman would have thrown something at him, hoping for some kind of emotional response. Women had always tried to goad him into some acknowledgment of their *feelings*. Dominic had become quite adept at dodging glassware.

Cassandra worried him. And he'd vowed not to let her affect him in any way.

"I don't care. I need a bath."

Her delicate face collapsed into a frown. "Of course, how thoughtless of me. I'd heard you've been riding the borders for days, making sure our people are protected." She turned to her two helpers. "May, dear, I believe my hair holds enough pearls; you may stop now."

The slave pulled her fingers out of his wife's silken hair, the girl's hazel eyes still fixed upon Dominic.

The younger girl stared at him in terrified fascination as well. A swarm of flies could make their way into such open mouths.

Except for their hazel eyes, they could have been his sisters, with their silver hair and flawless complexions. He couldn't tell which elven lord they might be descended from because of the mix of color in their eyes, nor could he recall which battle had brought them here as slaves. But obviously no one had paid their ransom to return them home.

"You have dressed them as fine as any noble's servants," said Dominic. "No wonder the court is in a huff."

"Does your father care?"

"No more than I."

"Then it doesn't signify. Gwen, fetch the kettles off the fire and pour them in the bath. My husband eschews fashion and likes to soak, do you not?"

He nodded, wondering how long she'd stared at his wooden tub before she had figured out what he did with it. The two girls disappeared behind an oriental silk screen painted with red-plumed birds. *That* hadn't been there before either. He hadn't needed a privacy screen.

Dominic began to undress. By the time the slaves reappeared, he'd stripped down to his breeches.

"Does he need our help bathing, my ladyship?" asked the younger one with a terrified warble in her voice.

"Gwen," replied Cass before Dominic could reply, "remember what we discussed?"

They both blinked at her then rounded their eyes to him and with a quick curtsy, they disappeared.

Dominic shed his breeches. "I take it you told them you completely disregarded my wishes by hiring servants who will only be a nuisance to me?"

Her gaze ran up and down his body with appreciation. "Don't be odious, Dominic," she replied a bit breathlessly. "Why frighten them any more than they already are?"

He liked the sound of his name on her lips. He liked the cheeky way she spoke to him, as if, unlike the rest of the court, she didn't fear him a whit. Indeed, he found that instead of being annoyed by having his routine interrupted by a new wife and servants, he rather… enjoyed the attention.

When he stepped behind the screen and saw the steaming tub, the cake soap laid out neatly atop thick drying cloths, and rose petals floating atop the water, he decided he could get used to this. "You'll make me soft," he mumbled.

"Pardon, sir?"

Dominic lowered himself into the tub and closed his eyes in rapture. "I said," he replied, raising his voice, "that I need my back washed."

A moment of silence and then her dainty face peeked around the screen. "But I thought you liked to do for yourself."

"I've changed my mind."

Her eyes closed for a moment, and her lips moved as though she whispered a prayer. Then she gingerly walked over to the tub, grasped the soap with a trembling hand and dunked it in the water.

Dominic smiled and leaned forward. The first touch of the soap sliding across his skin made his member swell. "I've been weeks without a woman."

He heard her swallow. "Indeed, I am most surprised, sir."

"How so?"

"I assumed you had more than one mistress scattered about the sovereignty."

"If that were so, it wouldn't matter now. It seems I must save myself to get you with child."

"How… disagreeable for you." She dunked the soap and slapped it across his back, rubbing vigorously.

"Mm. I assume you want a child as quickly as possible, madam?"

"Naturally."

"Then take off your clothes."

The soap plopped into the water. "I… I cannot muss my hair. It took May hours to weave it."

"Faith, woman, I shan't touch a hair on your head."

For a moment he could hear nothing but the crackle of the fire.

And then she rounded the tub to face him, hands on hips, brown eyes flashing. "I have tried to make myself agreeable to you, sir. I have done my best to please you. And yet you still treat me with little respect, ordering me about as if I were some lackey. I care naught for your feeling but I demand at least a little consideration."

Ah, so Lady Cassandra did not scream and throw things, she silently simmered to a boil. Interesting.

Dominic studied the controlled rage on her face, and his admiration for her grew. But what could he say? That he could not afford to show her any consideration because it might lead to an affection that could be her doom? That he did it to protect her?

But even if he trusted her enough to confide in her, he would not risk getting any closer to her by exchanging secrets, for therein lay disaster. No, he would hold himself as aloof from his wife as he did with everyone, no matter what Ador had said. For Lady Cassandra was a danger to him. As soon as he got her with child, he would avoid her like the plague.

So Dominic ignored his wife's words and slowly stood, revealing the firmness of his arousal. The water sluiced down his skin, dripping over the muscles in his chest and the ripples in his abdomen. Elven blood made him physically perfect and he knew that with a crook of his finger, no woman could refuse him.

Lady Cassandra's brown eyes widened, and she turned her face away and then just as quickly spun back around to stare at him, her eyes glazing as they traveled over every softly ridged curve, every glowing inch of his skin. Her feet stayed rooted to the floor, but her upper body swayed toward him at an almost perilous angle.

Dominic held out his hand.

Cassandra's fingers twitched. And then she spun again, disappearing behind the screen. He heard the bedroom door slam.

Dominic stared at the empty space where she had stood, utterly bewildered. A woman had never rejected him before, much less run away from the sight of him. He stood there for a long moment, not quite knowing how to react, while the water dried on his skin.

And then a wicked smile spread across his face, an expression his father would heartily approve of. So the wench had tossed him a challenge, had she? The thought so inflamed him he felt hard-pressed not to shout a battle cry.

She would see who could hold out the longest. Her resistance would fall long before he allowed his to.

❧

Dominic's resolve lasted until he glimpsed her at the ball.

He had dressed more carefully than he ever had before in his life. He chose all black to suit his mood, in the style of his uniform. But this outfit had been crafted of velvet, from his coat to his waistcoat to his breeches. He wore new cuffed boots, polished to a high sheen, and a dress sword lay at his hip, the sheath and pommel encrusted with diamonds. He left his hair loose to flow down his back and shoulders, the silvery white a stark contrast to his black attire.

When he strode purposefully into the ballroom, his fur-trimmed velvet cape fluttered behind him like the wings of some predatory bird.

His father had outdone himself this time with his display of power, whether to impress the king or the nobles visiting from other sovereignties, Dominic couldn't be sure. White fire formed columns of glittering swirls of harmless flame. The mellow warmth of yellow fire danced atop the ceiling, creating starbursts that splintered every few seconds, scattering harmless embers onto the heads of the crowd, falling on shoulders and wigs to sparkle like diamonds.

A glowing carpet of red lava made a path through the throng and Dominic stepped upon it, hoping the soles of his boots wouldn't melt. But his father had tempered the heat in the same way Dominic could temper the fire magic he summoned. Yet it seemed that the rest of the nobles didn't care to test the path, for he trod it alone.

As he made his way to the dais where Mor'ded and the king sat, conversation stopped around him. He felt desire emanate from the crowd as hot as any flame. Women sighed and men murmured in admiration, and that wicked smile formed on his lips again. Several young girls swooned.

But the general did not look for *her* in the crowd. Not yet.

He bowed to his father when he reached the dais. The Imperial Lord sat ensconced in his golden throne, the king in a smaller one a step below him. Yellow fire dulled to gold shimmered in a curtain behind the dais like a waterfall of unimaginable wealth.

Mor'ded wore red satin, the skirt of his coat stiffened with whalebone to flare out dramatically over his seat. His black eyes studied Dominic with cold calculation. "You have dressed with care this evening. Do you honor the king, or is there some other reason for such a dashing display?"

Dominic erased the smile from his face, turned, and bowed to the king. But carefully, making sure his head did not dip lower than the obeisance he had bestowed on his father. "My salutations, Your Majesty."

The king gave him a regal nod, his brow beaded with perspiration. The room felt cool despite Father's magic, and Dominic thought the king would soon become accustomed to the suggestion of heat. Surely it would be a relief from the foul dampness of Breden's sovereignty.

Several of the king's highest ranked courtiers stood to his left, although Dominic noticed that Sir Robert appeared to be missing this evening. The original court of Firehame stood on Mor'ded's right, a division that might soon create problems if the elven lord wasn't careful.

Although knowing his father, Mor'ded had probably instigated the division. If it started to annoy instead of entertain him, he would call in Dominic to take care of it.

The general sighed.

"Good," pronounced King George, drawing Dominic's attention back to him. The king's protruding eyes surveyed Dominic's costume with enthusiasm. "Good for man who won the king to boast of it with a soldier costume. Fur is a nice touch, but you should wear shoes. High-heeled, yes?"

The general nodded politely, his face rigid enough to hide his contempt for the subject of heels.

"And your wife?" continued the king. "I still have not met this woman. She has not yet recovered from her ordeal?"

Dominic couldn't fathom why the man wanted to exchange pleasantries with him. It would take him some time to accidentally run into his wife and he itched to get started. He stole a glance at his father, noting the interest that still shone in those cold eyes. Did the man guess Dominic had dressed to entice Cassandra?

Father's courtiers leaned forward to hear his reply.

"My pardon, Your Majesty, but I don't really concern myself over my wife's health."

The old man's face twisted in confusion and his courtiers gasped in outrage. But his father's court nodded their heads, as if they'd expected no less from the elven bastard, and threw superior looks at His Majesty's court.

"Come now," said Mor'ded, his black eyes almost twinkling. "You want the chit to bear you a healthy child, don't you?"

"That is your desire, sir. Not mine."

The Imperial Lord laughed, relaxing back into his throne.

"I do not understand," mumbled the king.

"Ah well," replied Mor'ded. "No doubt you're used to Breden's bastards, Your Majesty, who are weak with human blood. My champion has an elven heart."

He said it with pride and despite himself, Dominic felt a thrill of pleasure course through him. And a sense of relief that Mor'ded did not suspect his... possessiveness of his wife.

With impeccable timing, Lady Agnes chose that moment to materialize at his side. Dominic bowed. "If you will excuse me?"

The king gave him a regal nod, his face betraying a hint of his fear of Dominic. Mor'ded dismissed him with a negligent wave of his hand, *his* face already stiff with boredom, his gaze roving the crowd, looking for another distraction.

Dominic led Agnes among the dancers, as far from the dais as possible. He would have to be even more careful this evening. He'd had every intention of pretending to ignore his wife while dancing with every other woman in the room, reminding her that he could have his choice of bed partners. That she should be honored that he shared his bed with her. Then he would have centered his attention upon her, and she would have melted in his arms...

But now he could not afford to be seen showing the slightest interest in Lady Cassandra. He would have to wait out the entire evening until she returned to their room in order to charm her. And once he got her behind the privacy of the bed curtains...

As they clasped hands, Aggie looked up at him, her beautiful lips twisted in a pout. "You haven't commented on my costume, sir."

Dominic blinked, lowering his head. He'd forgotten about her.

"Indeed," he muttered, raking her with his gaze. She looked like a flame, the color of her dress shifting from yellow to red, triangles of cloth floating about her neck and shoulders, lapping at her skin like true fire. "Very nice."

"Nice? I'll have you know that this cloth came all the way from Dreamhame. It's been woven with an illusion of your magic and cost me—well! You can at least offer me a better compliment than that, sir."

"It suits you."

"Hmph. The Duke of Claridge offered me a much bolder compliment. He said—"

They slid sideways in the pattern of the dance. "I care naught what other men say to you. And don't expect such flattery from me."

Agnes rolled her eyes. "I'm quite aware you haven't a romantic notion in your head. But you could at least *try*, Dominic."

His lip twitched. Perhaps she was right. He bowed and she curtsied. "You must know you're the most desirable woman in the room. I chose to dance with you, didn't I?"

She flung back her head and laughed, drawing several envious gazes their way. "La! Be grateful for the amount of elven blood that runs through my veins, General. For otherwise I would have despaired of you long ago."

Dominic took her hands again, chafing at the mincing steps of the dance, remembering the one he'd performed at his wedding. An old elven dance, his father had called it. He only knew he'd followed his wife in a rhythm that had set his blood afire.

Aggie laughed again, bringing his attention back to her perfect face. He appreciated the distraction she always provided him. The way she never took offense to anything he said. She was as arrogant and vain as he appeared to be. And he hoped that others thought him as shallow of feeling.

They turned direction and he glimpsed another couple across the floor, almost losing his footing in surprise. Agnes widened her eyes at him in shock. The elven did not stumble.

"It cannot be," he said as he held her hand high and they minced steps to and fro.

She followed the direction of his gaze. "What do you mean?"

"The elven lords don't often leave their sovereignties. What would an Imperial Lady be doing here?"

Aggie snorted. "You aren't speaking of your wife, are you?"

"My wife?"

"Well, that's who you're staring at. And she doesn't look anything like an Imperial Lady."

Dominic stilled, hiding his surprise with an excessive force of will, staring over the heads of the other dancers at Cassandra. She wore a dress of honey gold, with jewels sewn into the cloth that winked with her every movement. Gold chains encircled her slim throat and elegant wrists. Her hair had been caught up at the sides and left to spill across her back, layered with pearls and ribbons as he'd seen it earlier this evening, but her little slave must have talked her into powdering her hair for a silvery white layer covered the warm brown.

With the silver hair of the elven she could easily pass for an Imperial Lady, the fine bones of her face more pronounced, the perfection of her skin accented by the color.

He preferred the warm brown of her hair, though. It made her look more human.

Agnes caught his hand and towed him back into the pattern of the dance. "Egads, Dominic, have a care—"

"Who is he?"

"Who is—oh, the handsome gentleman dancing

with Lady Cassandra." She licked her red lips as she stared at the golden-haired man. "He's just returned to court. Something about caring for his sick mother… but apparently she recovered. Charming man, that one. Beautiful too, despite his rugged human features. If he held more than one tiny manor in the country, I might even be tempted—"

"His name, Aggie."

She tittered. "I do believe you're jealous! Look at the way your jaw has tightened. But have no fear, darling, *I* would never prefer him over you."

Dominic caught the inflection in her voice, the way she swept her eyes over Cassandra with an accusatory look. Indeed, his wife appeared to be captivated by her partner, often breaking into laughter, their faces pulling too close together as if they exchanged private confidences. The man treated her with too much easy familiarity.

The general took eight steps instead of four, flustering a few dancers as they tried to adjust their positions to accommodate him. But it brought him closer to Cassandra and her partner. Yes, the other man gazed at his wife with adoring eyes. With a yearning that spoke of more than admiration. The fellow looked half in love with her.

"Name," choked Dominic, his fingers squeezing Agnes's.

"Ouch. Althorp. Viscount Thomas Althorp. Why is it so important to you?"

The general twisted his lips and closed the distance between his wife and that fellow. This time the other dancers dared grumble a complaint at him for interrupting the stately flow, but one glance and they lapsed into silence, quickly reforming their ranks.

Lady Cassandra's eyes widened and that Althorp fellow followed her gaze, wincing when he met Dominic's glare.

Aggie tugged on his arm. "I know what you're thinking; but don't do it."

Dominic looked down his nose at her. She scowled.

"If you call him out, you will make a scene," she huffed. "And all because of injured pride."

He nodded slowly, taking up Aggie's hands again to resume their pattern, catching glimpses of Cassandra's worried face. He appreciated his mistress more than ever. She'd stopped him from doing something extremely foolish, but she had it wrong. Pride did not prompt this sudden urge to run his blade through the viscount's flesh. Some other wicked emotion raged inside him, something he'd never felt before.

Fortunately his father had left his dais, pursuing some lady or retiring in boredom, he knew naught. But calling out another man for dancing with his wife would eventually reach Mor'ded's ears. And the elven were not prone to jealousy.

But his all-too-human heart appeared to be.

With a speed only his elven physique could manage, he'd dropped Aggie's hand and caught up his wife's. Althorp appeared to be a wise fellow, at least. He stood only for a second before snatching up the hand of Lady Agnes and leading her instead.

None of the other dancers appeared to notice the switch.

"What are you doing?" hissed Cassandra.

"Dancing with my wife."

"You could have waited for the next round, sir."

He raised a silver brow. "Why should I? Who is he to you?"

They parted. He bowed, she curtsied. Unfortunately, it gave his wife time to gather her composure. "He is an old friend of the family. That is all."

She lied. Dominic lowered his hand a bit in order for her to grasp it for the dance. The only reason he could think for her to lie was that the man had meant more to her than she wanted to reveal. Perhaps he still did.

It had not occurred to him before this that she might have had a previous relationship with any man other than her father. Mor'ded had been assured the school that boarded her was very exclusive. Very secluded. And he knew her to be a maid when he'd bedded her.

Yet why did his body fill with rage? Why did his fingers itch to summon fire?

This went beyond her role as one of his possessions. This trod into dangerous territory. He could not truly be jealous. His human heart could not be that weak.

And yet still the rage consumed him and Dominic found he could barely control it. He suppressed the urge to strangle her admirer, to sweep his wife up into his arms and carry her from the room.

Instead he bowed over her hand. "I suggest that you retire, my lady. I fear you have the headache."

Her brown eyes widened with confusion. "I have never felt better in my life, sir."

"How long do you think that will last if I challenge your Lord Althorp to a duel?"

"Whatever for?"

"For daring to touch what is mine."

She stared at him for a moment. The tune had ended and people started to watch them. "You would, wouldn't you?"

Dominic's mouth twitched.

The clever girl swept the back of her hand up to her forehead and swayed. The general caught her in his arms. Lady Agnes hurried over. "She will be fine," snapped Dominic. "She is overcome with exertion."

Aggie raised a doubtful brow.

Viscount Althorp, his golden hair glittering in the glow of the fire-washed ceiling, had the temerity to cock a grin. "Perhaps the general has already produced the child that his father so desires."

Dominic faced the shorter man, his face frozen, his voice quite calm and pitched so only the fop could hear. "Come near her again and I will kill you."

Cassandra stiffened in his arms. A flicker of something shadowed Viscount Althorp's pale eyes, but only for a moment, the smooth libertine quickly reappearing. "As you wish, General Raikes."

And Dominic swept his wife from the room—if not quite in the manner he had originally planned. He ignored the concerned queries from the nobles, knowing Althorp would have spread the word about his lady's supposed condition soon enough. Although the falsehood would be revealed in time.

He stopped for no one, including her two little slaves as they met them at the door. He ordered them to their rooms, tossed his wife on the mattress, and slammed the bedroom door.

"Pray tell me what has brought on this fit?" asked Lady Cassandra.

"Be quiet. You will make your headache worse."

She frowned but said no more as he pulled the ties from the curtains surrounding the bed, blocking off the glow of the fire in the grate.

He pulled her into his arms and she allowed it, although her body felt stiff as a tree. Dominic placed his mouth very close to her ear and whispered, "How do you know that man?"

"I told you—" He caught her face and brought her lips to his ear. "Why must I whisper?"

Dominic turned her head and breathed in her ear. "It is… a precaution."

She stilled for a moment and he could feel her mind working. Then he felt her soft lips at his ear again. "Spies?"

How would she guess such a thing? He had sensed his innocent wife hid a part of herself from him and now he felt certain of it. Dominic clasped her hand, the pad of his index finger finding the carved rose of her ring, the petals twisted in a tight bud.

He turned her head with his other hand. "You hired the servants who listen through keyholes. Answer my question."

"May and Gwen would never do such a thing."

She was probably right. But he never dropped his reserve within the palace walls, and his questions would not be those of an unfeeling elven lord's bastard.

"We shall argue in whispers?" she finally said in the taut silence.

This time she turned her own ear to his mouth and waited for him to speak. "So it seems."

"I told you, Thomas is an old friend of the family."

"You lie. He was too familiar with your person."

She caught her breath, as if she could feel his sudden rage. "He would come visit me at school sometimes."

Dominic waited, his finger stroking the still-tight bud of her ring.

"When I was very young, I thought I might be in love with him."

This sounded like truth and the slight unfurling of the rose ring confirmed it. He waited again.

His wife huffed. "He asked me to run away with him but I refused."

"Why?"

"Because you were—you *are* my destiny."

Despite his intentions for her to reveal something damning, he could not deny she spoke the truth, for the petals of the rose blossomed beneath his touch. Faith, he hadn't expected such an answer. He'd expected another lie—perhaps that she was in love with him, perhaps that she admired his features so much she wanted to be with him. He'd even hoped she might reveal the true reason she had married him.

But. Destiny. That was a powerful thing.

His rage faded as quickly as it had come.

"Now it's my turn," she softly whispered. "Tell me of Mongrel."

Dominic started. "How do you know of my dog?"

"Cook told me—nay, do not be angry. She sought only to comfort me with a bit of knowledge about the stranger I married."

He ran a hand over his forehead. Cook had known him since he was a lad, and although they treated each other with indifference, he'd always suspected that the redhead had a softer heart than she revealed. And Mongrel... just the name brought a memory of shared warmth and unquestioning loyalty. Words flowed from his mouth without thought. "The stable master tried to drown the runt, but he had more will to live than anyone credited. I found him on the bank of the Thames, weary and half-dead, and could only admire his spirit. I nursed him back to health and he shadowed me from that day on, until he died..."

The vision of fire blackening fur and the sound of Mongrel whining in agony brought Dominic back to himself. But too late. For his wife held his cheek in one soft hand, and the sound of her sigh held too much empathy. "I'm so sorry. You must have loved him so."

Dominic jerked away from her touch. This unpredictable creature had managed to warm his human heart, and he feared he'd revealed too much to her. Ador might be right. If he continued to spend time with her he might not be able to prevent himself from falling under her spell. Even now he felt... he felt... No, he would not admit it, even to himself. For if his father discovered the truth of his feelings...

He leaped from the bed as if she had the power to burn him and stormed from the room, heading for Ador's tower. The general took the stairs two at a time, not pausing for breath until he burst onto the tower roof.

The dragon snorted a noxious stream of smoke in his direction.

Dominic coughed.

Ador snorted again.

Dominic paced the length of that large black body, his hands curling into fists. "Damn. Damn. What do I do? How could I have let this happen?" He looked up at the star-sprinkled sky. "I cannot care for her! I don't have the power to protect her! Yet I find myself drawn to her again and again. The scent of her hair, the touch of her hand, those warm brown eyes fixed upon mine. I want to tell her all my secrets... and therein lies disaster. For my selfish need will only imperil her life."

The dragon stretched one black leathery wing, the tip of it grazing the general's shoulder, propelling him head over heels across the stone floor. Dominic flipped to his feet, shaking the hair from his face.

"When you were a child," Ador rumbled, "you forged a connection to the black scepter."

Dominic felt like he might still be tumbling. What was the dragon talking about? Yes, he'd touched the magical talisman, a forbidden thing he'd never mentioned to anyone. And whenever he'd looked at the scepter after that, he'd felt... odd. But he'd never even mentioned this to Ador.

"What does that mean?"

Ador opened his scaly lids, his eyes gleaming in the night, seeming to wash Dominic with a haze of their red color. "We were created from the scepters and still retain a link to them. They are more powerful than you humans have guessed and they have a will of their own."

The general struggled to grasp the dragon's words. "Are you saying the scepters are somehow alive?"

"Not like you and I. But aware, elven lord's son. And likely to destroy anyone who dares to wield them who is not of full elven blood. And yet it allowed you to touch it."

"Why?"

The red light faded as the dragon closed his eyes. "I don't know why it chose to protect you or to hide your growing magic of black fire from the mad elf."

Dominic stilled. It couldn't be. He'd thought he'd imagined the black fire magic within him. Thought it wishful thinking. A fantasy to stop his father's torture. "But... damn you! Do you mean to tell me I have had enough magic to be sent to Elfhame and—"

Ador snorted, a burst of red flame that washed the stones an ugly pink. "You foolish bastard. Do you really believe that's where the madman sends those who threaten his reign?"

Dominic's anger turned cold and his mind began to work at a frightening speed, the way it did on the battlefield when faced with a new strategy from his enemy. "If I believe these confidences you're suddenly willing to share with me... then I can see how it would be easier for the elven lords to have the children brought to them for the trials, to weed out any half-breeds who may have inherited enough power to threaten the Imperial Lords' sovereignty. That's if I believe what you're telling me."

If the talisman indeed had some kind of aware-ness—some power greater than his father's—it made sense, for he'd touched the scepter before his first trial. Magical gifts revealed themselves at puberty, but they could grow over time. The reason that his father kept his nobles close. But anyone possessing the higher gifts—like that of black fire—would be sent to Elfhame. But such children were rare; perhaps one in a thousand of those possessing elven blood were born with the powers to become a chosen one.

The general closed his eyes, unwilling to believe this but trying to remember. Had he touched the scepter through sheer accident or had he been impelled to do so? Damn, he did not like this feeling of being a pawn in some game he did not understand. He slowly opened his lids and narrowed his eyes at the black snout and unreadable features of the dragon. "Why are you telling me this now?"

"Because soon—ah but not yet—your powers will grow strong enough to challenge the madman, and you need to know the truth." Ador yawned, as if he hadn't voiced words that could change lives. "That is, if you survive long enough. But if you manage it and succeed in the coming battle, the scepter is one step closer to returning home... although it will be long and long before the gate to Elfhame can truly be opened."

Ah. Dominic caught a glimmer of understanding. So the dragon thought to use his human weakness just as his father did. Ador offered him the bait that Dominic did indeed have the power to protect Cassandra. But to what purpose? How could he discern the truth?

"Prove it."

"You humans are tiresome, half-elven or no," responded Ador, eyes still closed. "Very well, then. Your powers have at least grown strong enough to dispel the wards on Mor'ded's supposed door to Elfhame. The mad elf leaves the palace on the morrow. Go see for yourself."

Dominic rubbed his brow. Could it be possible Ador spoke the truth? The thought that he might have the power to protect Cassandra filled him with a savage elation. But it was tempered by the worry of what he might find behind that heavy oak door. It made him wish his wife had never awakened his human feelings again, and he stood for a time, staring at the stars in the cold night sky.

Ador finally succumbed to sleep, his rumbling snores shivering the stones beneath Dominic's boots.

Eight

CASS WOKE THE NEXT MORNING STILL IN HER GOLDEN
gown of the night before. A haze of silver powder
covered her pillow and memories came rushing back.
She pulled open the curtains surrounding the bed,
not surprised to find herself alone. Of course he had
not returned.

She rang for Gwendolyn and May, and they helped
her perform her toilette while her thoughts spun with
the events of the evening. It had been so grand to
see Thomas again, looking so handsome in the latest
mode of dress. Faith, he played the part of a mindless
coxcomb even better than he'd played a priest.

"How about this one, my ladyship?" asked Gwen,
holding out a fine wool mantua.

Cass sighed. She might as well give up on insisting
that Gwendolyn choose the plainer pieces in her
wardrobe. The girl had such a flair for the dramatic.
And last night… yes, the general had certainly appreciated the way she'd looked. His face, as usual, hadn't
revealed a thing, but she'd felt him staring at her far
too long.

"It's not quite appropriate for a walk on the grounds."

Gwen's face fell.

"But I suppose if you pin up the train, it shall suffice."

The girl nodded with enthusiasm and chose a soft leather girdle tooled with fanciful flying horses to belt the burgundy gown. She dithered over the choice of stays for they would show through the open bodice, but finally settled on an embroidered stomacher to cover it, heavily inlaid with garnet stones.

May had almost finished brushing the powder from her hair, and Cass closed her eyes at the heavenly feel of the older girl's gentle strokes. How would she find her husband today? She didn't know what to expect after his show of jealousy last eve. Her eyes flew open and stared at her reflection in the dressing mirror. Had he indeed been jealous? He'd certainly acted like it, and if she'd had any doubts, their whispered argument proved it. And when she'd asked him about his dog his voice had shaken with emotion. Only a man with a human heart could care for his pet the way Dominic had. But why had he left her bed and not returned? He had not finished telling her about Mongrel. How could she gain his trust when his actions were always so at odds with his feelings?

For she felt convinced that despite his elven blood, he had feelings just like any other human. He'd just become exceptionally skilled at hiding them. She could understand why, when he had such a horrid father.

May began to weave her hair, an intricate twining that Cass's eyes couldn't follow. Her new servants would never spy on her and if they did happen to overhear something, she did not doubt their loyalty. She wondered who would be interested in spying on the general. And then she flushed. Little did he know he harbored a spy in his very bed.

May positioned a pinner on her head with long lace lappets, and Gwen helped her into her mantua, the burgundy wool so finely combed it felt like velvet against her skin. The girdle unbuckled in front, and it made Cassandra feel much more confident as she left her apartments. The belt would make a fine garrote.

She intended to go for a walk about the grounds to consider her own feelings for her husband. Cass rejoiced that Dominic had shown jealousy over Thomas, for her goal had been to make her husband regard her enough to trust her. But did his possessiveness truly mean he cared for her?

For she cared for him. Despite knowing how foolish it would be, she might even have fallen in love with him. General Dominic Raikes had allowed her to glimpse his true heart once too often. And Cass hadn't been prepared for the beauty of it.

Consumed by her thoughts, still unfamiliar with the sprawling palace, Lady Cassandra soon managed to get lost.

A long hallway stretched before her, medieval armor flanking the walls as far as she could see, a glow of green fire within every faceplate, emanating through the links in the chain mail. Cass took a step into the hall and suddenly the armor came to attention, spears lifting and swords saluting. Her heart flew up into her throat and she froze.

A profound sense of relief swept through her at the sound of voices behind her. She whirled and went back the way she'd come, slowing as a couple approached her.

"Lady Cassandra," said Lady Verney. "How good to see you again." She nodded at her companion. "Have you met Sir Robert Walpole?"

The heavy man bowed his wigged head. "We haven't had the pleasure, my lady. But having met her husband, I have been looking forward to it." He looked quite somber in his gray coat next to Sophia's peacock-colored gown.

Cassandra dipped a quick curtsy, her eyes on the leader of the Rebellion. Had she heard something within his words? Her heart still fluttered with excitement. "I'm honored to make your acquaintance, sir. I got lost again, you see."

Lady Verney raised her elegant brows. "There are some rooms it's not wise to enter, Cassandra. You must allow me to show you a map of the palace. If I had known your servants failed to give you such instruction…"

Cass flushed, wondering if Sophia was truly unaware that she had hired slaves and not some of the castle staff.

"Capital idea," agreed Sir Robert. "Although I must say, we might not have had the pleasure of crossing paths today so fortuitously. But now that we have you must join us for tea, my dear."

He held out his arm and Cass took it without hesitation. She hadn't thought she'd have a chance to talk with him this soon. Perhaps they could find a moment to speak in private.

Her hopes were dashed as they entered a cozy parlor, nearly filled to bursting with the king's court. Some worked on their embroidery near the windows, taking advantage of the sunlight and the constant glow from the yellow fire outside the walls. Several tea trays lay scattered about the room, chairs clustered around them. The parlor lacked any magical enhancements and Cass wondered if that's why the court had chosen this small space.

Sophia and Sir Robert led her to an empty table, but it soon filled up with gentlemen and ladies. Most of them sent her glances of curiosity but Cassandra made herself as small as possible and managed to fade a bit into the background.

"The *other* court," commented a gentleman with a striped red coat, "is woefully in need of our guidance. Did you see what they wore to the ball last night?"

Another gentleman took a pinch of snuff. "I daresay they haven't the slightest idea that solid colors are not the mode. But don't worry; we'll set them to rights."

Lady Verney stiffened in her chair, teacup poised near her thin lips. "Although solids are not the rage, I heard that King George complimented General Raikes on the cut of his suit."

"That bastard could wear a gunnysack and manage to carry it off," replied the gentleman, then glanced at Cass and flushed. "Begging your pardon, my lady. But it's what they all call him."

Cass shrugged as if unperturbed but caught the sharp look from Sir Robert. As the conversation continued in a similar vein, mind-numbing in its inanity, she watched the leader of the Rebellion as he watched the others in the room. He listened more than he spoke, and at one point he got up and left, and Cassandra would have followed him but decided it would look odd. Instead she waited, hoping he would return and that the room might have cleared by then. But the nobles appeared to be engrossed in their conversations, speculating if black would be in and how their wigs would look with braids added to them.

She grinned as she imagined what Dominic would say about being an inspiration for fashion.

She'd just decided to leave when Sir Robert returned, a fold of paper in his hand. "Please accept this map, Lady Cassandra. It would be wise for you to know your whereabouts." This time she felt certain of the hidden meaning in his words.

"Oh," gasped Sophia, "it slipped my mind. I do have one in my room and will be happy to fetch it—"

"You do not need to trouble yourself," protested Sir Robert. "I have already memorized mine, so it's no longer needed."

Sophia appeared taken aback by this. "Good heavens, there are so many twists and turns I can't imagine ever knowing them all."

Sir Robert shrugged. "I've been trained to such tasks, your ladyship. It's not as difficult as it sounds."

His intense eyes stayed focused on Cass and she nodded, accepting the map from his hand. She would memorize it at once. She rose. "If you will excuse me, I think I shall take a turn about the grounds."

Lady Verney squinted up at her. "I could use a bit of fresh air myself. Sir Robert?"

A commotion at the door made them all turn

to see the king enter the small parlor. Sir Robert inclined his head regretfully. "Alas, but you'll have to excuse me. Duty calls."

Cassandra's heart sank. She had so hoped to speak with Sir Robert to see if he could help her puzzle out the mystery of her husband. Lady Verney rose and took Cass's arm and led her from the room, down several hallways and through some interesting formal rooms, until they reached a pair of doors that opened onto a garden.

Both she and Sophia took in deep breaths of the fresh air, and Cass reminded herself she should not look for help from anyone. Thomas had warned her she was on her own and if Sir Robert truly wished to speak to her he would find a way to do so.

Lady Verney giggled. "I think I owe you an apology. They are quite… set in their ways, are they not?"

Cassandra smiled. "It's beyond me how they can spend so much time discussing fashion. But I suppose that's all they're accustomed to doing."

"Indeed." Sophia frowned, seemingly as saddened by that fact as Cass. They walked along a white gravel path, the stones sparkling in the sunlight. A profusion of late-blooming flowers surrounded them, their scents combining into a heady perfume. Ahead of them flowed a fountain of yellow fire, the flames arcing out from a center column and spilling into the surrounding bowl.

"I had hoped," continued Sophia, "that the king's court would be more welcoming toward you than Mor'ded's. Lady Agnes hasn't had the opportunity to influence them as yet."

Cassandra stared up at her tall friend. She hadn't realized… well, it had been very kind of her. But how could she explain it didn't quite matter? "Thank you, Sophia. They *were* much more welcoming."

Her friend smiled a bit. "I suppose it will always be hard for you, being married to the champion and all."

They had reached the fountain and Cass leaned forward, allowing the yellow fire to wash over her hands, trickle through her fingers. "Like the fire on the palace walls; it's gently warm and yet doesn't burn. I think it's been harder for me to adjust to the wealth of magic."

"You'll get used to that. When I first arrived, I dreamed of fire every night and thought I'd wither from the heat. I should probably freeze if I lived anywhere else now."

Lady Cassandra looked up at the flaming walls of the palace and nodded. "I suppose one can get used to anything."

They walked the grounds for a time, idly talking. Cass occasionally brought up a question about the elven lord, but although Sophia had been surrounded by fire magic for many years, she knew little about the Imperial Lord himself. It seemed Dominic knew more about Mor'ded than anyone else at court.

And Cassandra couldn't be sure of ever getting her husband to trust her enough to share that knowledge.

"I'm sorry, Lady Cassandra. I must return to the palace for a fitting. Will you accompany me?"

They stood amid a hedge of bushes cut into swirling cones. Cass couldn't quite bring herself to return to the palace yet. "Do not worry, Lady Verney. I have the map Sir Robert gave me. I shall find my way back to the palace without getting lost."

Sophia patted her hand. "That's good, then. But remember; do not enter the shaded areas. They are places of strange magics." She frowned at Cass. "Perhaps I should show you."

Cassandra sighed. She'd never had a friend before to worry about her and couldn't decide whether she liked it or not. She removed the folded map from her skirt and opened it. A small sliver of paper fell from inside onto the clipped lawn, and she glanced quickly at Sophia to see if she had noticed. But the other woman had pulled the watch on her neck chain up to her face to squint at the numbers. Cass placed her foot over the paper and studied the map.

Nearly two-thirds of the palace interior and a third of the outside grounds had been shaded with wavy lines.

Lady Verney pointed at them. "These are the places to avoid. Now, this is where we are, see? There are three palace layouts, to show you each floor, and these are the stairs that will take you to each. Are you sure you can devise the sense of it?"

Cassandra had studied maps much more complicated than this one. "I shall manage, Lady Verney, never fear."

The taller woman took a step down the path. "I really must go. But perhaps next time you should take one of your servants with you for guidance. And for propriety's sake, of course."

"Of course."

Cass watched her gather up her peacock-colored skirts and hurry down the path. The moment she rounded a corner, Cassandra removed her foot from the paper and picked it up, reading it quickly before stuffing it into her mouth and chewing with a grimace. Feeling a bit like a goose, but unable to think of a lady-like way to dispose of it, she swallowed with a gulp. And then pondered Sir Robert's hastily scrawled note.

Your husband may be sympathetic to our cause. He hates his father.

Could it be possible? Could Dominic be capable of such a strong emotion? Apparently Sir Robert had noticed the undercurrents between Dominic and his father and come to that startling conclusion. She didn't know how he could be sure when she hadn't been able to understand their relationship herself. The elven did not act by human standards. And did Sir Robert really think that would be enough to sway Dominic to their cause? Just because the general held no love for his father didn't mean he would aid the Rebellion in having Mor'ded deposed. And what did Sir Robert expect her to do with the information?

Cass had the sinking feeling he was leaving it up to her to decide. But it had to be obvious to Sir Robert that although Dominic viewed her as his possession, he held no deep love for her. To approach Dominic with the truth about her marriage might very likely get her killed.

Or set her free. Their secrets from each other held them apart more than anything else. Was this the way to a true relationship between them? Her husband wanted her; she could be sure of that given his jealous reaction the other night. But would it be enough to protect her? She didn't know. And Thomas had told her to put her task before aiding Sir Robert.

Truth be told, she wanted to be honest with Dominic. She wanted to know if her feelings could ever be returned.

Cassandra folded the map, picked up her skirts, and headed back to the palace, determined to find her husband.

But it appeared he had left the palace, along with his father, and no one knew when they might return or where they might be. Rumor had it that Mor'ded had instigated a search for a family who refused to bring their child to the upcoming trials, but Dominic's absence remained a mystery. Cass retired early, but her husband did not return to their apartments that night. By the following morning, Cass had memorized the map Sir Robert had given her. And remembered Gwen's unique magical gift.

"Gwendolyn," she asked while sliding her arm into the sleeve of her day dress, "do you know where General Raikes has gotten himself off to?"

"Oh, my lady, I thought ye'd never ask! Ye've been moping about the apartments so."

Cass tried not to flush. "Can you use your gift to find him?"

"Of course," said Gwen, closing her eyes. "He's that way." And she pointed at the north wall of their apartments.

Cassandra frowned then picked up the map from where she'd placed it on the marble-topped table and opened it up. "Can you locate him using this?"

"La, I've never tried such a thing before, my lady." But the girl eagerly bent her blonde head over the paper and traced a finger across the surface of it, slowly coming to a stop outside the palace, on the farthest edge of the grounds. The area around her fingernail showed a miniature forest, with a square box drawn inside and shaded to indicate dangerous magic.

"What is that place?" breathed May, looking over their shoulders.

"I think"—Gwen squinted her hazel eyes at Cass—"he's in the elven garden. They say the Imperial Lord made it as a reminder of his homeland, but nobody's ever been brave enough to go near it, my lady, 'cept the champion. Even the Imperial Lord don't go there anymore. Mayhap ye should wait until he returns home."

Cass squared her shoulders. "Nonsense. I shall be perfectly fine."

The two girls exchanged worried looks.

"And I don't want either of you telling anyone else where I've gone, do you understand?"

Both girls quickly nodded, unable to deny their mistress a thing. Cassandra blessed the impulse she'd had to rescue the girls from the kitchens. She'd never had such loyal servants.

May and Gwen reluctantly announced their satisfaction with her appearance, and she bid them farewell, telling them she wouldn't return until evening. They both offered to go with her and Cass was sorely tempted. But she wanted to be alone with Dominic, so she refused them and gathered her courage as she made her way through the palace.

Lady Verney beckoned to her with a wave of her gloved hand as Cass passed the king's withdrawing room, but she pretended not to see. Although Sophia had tried her best to champion Cassandra, the king's court had quickly picked up the mannerisms of Mor'ded's and started to avoid her. Although they did so with pity on their faces instead of disdain. Cass couldn't be sure which felt worse.

But it did give her the freedom to roam the palace grounds, for no one would think to ask about her.

When Cassandra stepped out onto the manicured grass, she wished she had thought to bring a shawl, for the sun hid behind the clouds and the air felt chill. But she wore a wool gown with elbow-length sleeves and a flannel petticoat, and her wide hoops blocked most of the wind. Indeed, as she made her way across the lawn to the wooded area in back of the palace, the force of the gale against her skirts threatened to bowl her over. Gwen had insisted she adopt the new fan hoops, which extended so far out from her hips that she could rest her elbows upon them.

She hurried into the copse of trees, gasping as she caught her breath, the sturdy trunks protecting her from the increasing force of the wind. A storm brewed; she could smell it but she refused to turn back.

Lady Cassandra ventured deeper into the woods, her skirts more than a nuisance as they caught on every branch and twig. It seemed unnaturally silent under the canopy, a stillness about the woods that made her skin crawl. Something rustled in the brush, and a black shape skittered off into the greenery.

Cass eased off her girdle, grateful for the heavy buckle. If some animal threatened her it would make an adequate weapon. She stepped lightly now, avoiding the snap of twig or leaf, wary of breaking the silence of these woods. She followed a path for a time and then checked the map in her head again. Yes, she must leave this trail and strike out northeast.

She had a good sense of direction, but even then, when she finally clawed her way through some dense undergrowth to confront a wall of solid greenery, she couldn't be sure she'd found the elven garden.

Until she heard the singing.

Not singing, really, more of a chiming, whistling sound. What in heaven could create such a haunting melody? Or more accurately, what in that fabled land of Elfhame?

Lady Cassandra studied the wall of green, looking for some way to get inside. The leaves of the plants covering the wall—if indeed a wall lay behind them as she supposed—shivered as she took a step closer to the barrier. Surely the wind had caused that movement... but still Cass backed away suspiciously. Perhaps some animal hid within the undergrowth. She stepped forward and swung her belt at the vines, hoping to scare away anything lurking behind them, and glimpsed red stone beneath the green. The same brilliant red stone that comprised the walls of Firehame Palace.

And yet she'd not seen or smelled a hint of the magical fire that permeated the palace and grounds. Perhaps the shading on the map was just used as a deterrent to visitors. Or so she prayed.

Cass smiled grimly as she buckled her girdle back around her waist. Now she just needed to find the gate. But after several hours of walking the length of the wall, she could not find an entrance. The melody

within the private garden seemed to be calling to her more urgently, and Cassandra decided a more direct approach was required. She kicked off her shoes, untied her hoops and stepped out of them, and used her belt to hitch up her skirts. She would use the vines to climb the wall.

Not for a moment did she consider giving up. She would not go back to her apartments and sit around like a goose and wait for her courage to fail her. She feared she would change her mind and the opportunity would be lost forever.

Besides, she had climbed trees taller than this at her father's estate. She had enough elven blood to make her lithe and nimble, and her gift of dance kept her agile enough to scale a simple wall.

She had not counted on the capriciousness of the vines.

They shivered again when she clasped the sturdy trunk, and this time she felt certain the movement had nothing to do with the wind, for even though the breeze penetrated the clear area around the wall, it barely had enough force to stir her hair against her cheeks. She carefully placed a foot on a vine, and then another. They looked strong enough to hold her weight but as soon as she began to climb they bent beneath her, dropping her back to the ground.

"You will not stop me," she muttered as if the plants had some sort of intelligence. She huffed at her own foolishness and pushed through the greenery until she found the blocks of the wall. Like the castle, they weren't entirely smooth, and she fit her fingers within the cracks between them and pulled herself

up. Somehow her feet got tangled up in a web of interlaced vines and she fell backward, landing in a heap of dead leaves and petticoats.

She tried again and the same thing happened.

Cassandra got to her feet, eyed the trunk of the vine, and began to tear away the small tendrils that sprouted from it, determined to prevent her feet from getting tangled up again. The storm intensified; she could feel the gale finally penetrate the woods behind her, and the vine shuddered and creaked from the force of it.

She tossed away the ripped greenery and reached for more when she felt a pressure about her waist. She glanced down to discover that a vine had wrapped itself around her. Indeed, as she watched, another snaked around her feet, and she tried to jump to avoid it, but the one about her waist held her firmly in place.

Another vine curled around her left arm and Cass tried to tear it off, a wave of horrified panic overwhelming her. She screamed, scrabbling at the leafy plant with her fingers while simultaneously trying to twist her body from the hold of the one about her waist. She screamed again while even more vines reached out to trap her, until one fleshy tuber managed to wrap itself around her head and over her mouth, effectively smothering her cries and pressing against her nose until she couldn't breathe.

Lady Cassandra continued to struggle until her vision faded to black.

Nine

A STRANGLED SCREAM PULLED DOMINIC FROM HIS DARK thoughts. It came from over the garden wall, and it sounded like… "Cassandra!"

Dominic vaulted off the pavilion that he'd been standing in and ran through the orderly garden, skirting small ponds and beds of flowers and sculpted bushes. Had he truly recognized her voice in that cry?

He mentally scoffed. Who else would dare to breach the elven garden's walls?

Without hesitating a whit, Dominic leaped up the stone wall surrounding the garden, grateful for the elven blood that allowed the feat, and crouched like a cat on the narrow capstone. He scanned the guardian vine covering the outside wall, looking for a hint of movement, but the gale from the coming storm shook all the leaves in his vision and the screams had been too far away for him to judge the location.

"Damn."

The wind tore the hair away from his face and billowed his linen shirt out behind him as Dominic leaped again, over the green vines to the ground outside the garden. Dirt puffed up from his boots as he landed and he rolled, then sprang to his feet with a grace and speed that would have had the peasants crossing themselves in fear.

Dominic kept his eyes on the greenery as he ran beside it. His cursed father and his clever traps. Why should Mor'ded waste his magic when the plants that the Imperial Lord of Verdanthame created with his power could prove just as deadly? Although Dominic had been grateful the vines guaranteed his solitude within the elven garden, that had been before he'd married Lady Cassandra.

He wanted to curse her, but he could not. For he suspected that she'd sought him out, and the thought that she could not stay away from him almost made him smile. He quickly suppressed the desire, another thing he had to blame her for, but ran faster, scanning the leafy greenery. He had no doubt the nimble girl had tried to scale the wall to get to him. She possessed a reckless bravery and a willful heart that betimes he admired, and at others, terrified him.

Dominic had given some thought to the condition of the men who had kidnapped Cassandra and he'd come to the conclusion that her repertoire consisted of more than just love dances. Someone had taught her a death dance, and she had killed both of those men with seemingly little effort. She could have learned such a thing only from a few sources, the most likely being the Rebellion.

His wife had been trained as an assassin.

She hadn't been the first assassin the Rebellion had sent against an Imperial Lord, nor did he doubt that she would be the last. But they'd been clever this time, keeping the girl innocent while training her. Using Dominic to position her so closely to his father.

Dominic had little reason to expose her. He knew she'd fail in an attempt to kill Mor'ded, just as he had failed so long ago...

He tried not to think of Jack. Indeed, he ran faster, hoping the exertion would wipe the sudden thought from his mind. But he feared that his wife had managed to thaw his frozen heart for he could not stop the visions from replaying through his memory this time.

He saw himself young and brash, having just won his first skirmish against the finest of Imperial Lord Breden's troops. He'd entered the hall amid cheers and adoration, and he'd been so green he'd allowed it to go to his head. He had gotten drunk and cocky... and his father had told him he was due for another trial. Dominic had told him to go to hell and had tried to gut him with his sword.

Mor'ded had his guards haul Dominic to his room and had held him there with a ring of gray fire. The Imperial Lord had then summoned Jack. Jack, another slave who had not been raised from his lowly status because of his skill for battle. Jack, who had done nothing more harmful than befriending Dominic.

At first Dominic had thought that his father would only threaten to harm Jack.

But Mor'ded had made his son watch his best and only friend burn to death, while taunting him the entire time to call forth his black magic to defend him. And Dominic had failed. Just as he'd failed later to save Mongrel. After that Dominic had sought out Ador, relieved that the dragon, at least, could survive his company unscathed.

With a will borne of desperation, Dominic erased the vision of Jack's bones appearing through a haze of red fire.

He'd thought he'd buried that vision so deeply that it would never resurface. Damn his wife for making him acknowledge his human heart. It opened up too many old wounds.

A flutter of lace in the wall of green caught his eye, bringing his feet and, thankfully, his thoughts to a skidding halt. He reached out and tore the lace cap from the grasp of spiky tendrils and caught a flash of burgundy wool beneath the green. He knew these vines, had watched as they'd caught rabbits and unwary robins within their coils. They twined around their catch until nothing could be seen but leafy greenery and then belched out fur and bones like some great toothy beast.

Off to the far left, partially hidden in a thatch of tall grass, lay a set of hoops and a pair of low-heeled shoes. But thank the king for his fondness for lacy caps to adorn women's heads, for otherwise Dominic might never have found the exact place the foliage had swallowed his wife.

Dominic spread his fingers, calling forth orange fire instead of red, hoping to avoid harming Cassandra while he burned away the vines. He made his fire a narrow stream, cutting through the smaller vines first, hoping to reveal the rest of his wife's body. He had faced battle time and again but had yet to feel the sort of panic he felt now as he spied a stomacher laden with garnets, a tiny waist encircled with a leather belt.

For the garments did not move. She wasn't breathing.

The plant sent out a questing vine in his direction, moving so stealthily he did not see it until it wrapped around his leg, injecting those barbed thorns into his flesh. He cursed, cut the vine away from the mother plant, and shook the thing off his leg. He felt the thorns rip out of his flesh with the movement.

With calm fury Dominic slashed around the outline of Cassandra's body, the vines oozing purplish sap, quivering wildly from his assault. If it wouldn't have harmed his wife, he would have burned the entire garden wall of greenery. For when he'd cleared enough of the bush away he could see where green spikes had plunged into Cassandra's own flesh, seeking to suck her dry.

He cursed and took a step toward his wife.

A foolish mistake. For now the plant fought back with renewed desperation, no longer trying to be stealthy. Two vines wrapped around his ankles but he had to ignore them for the six that whipped toward his arms. He fried four of them, but the lower two each encircled an arm, preventing him from directing his magic at the trunk of the plant.

One breath and barbed thorns sprouted from the vine, piercing his flesh again. Another breath and he could feel the pressure as the plants sucked the blood from his veins.

Dominic smiled. Red fire bloomed on his body, his magic insulating him from the heat. But the plant had no such protection, and it could not unwrap itself from his limbs fast enough. Green twisted to black and thorns withdrew and shriveled, an odd sort of thumping noise emitting from the plant, like a stick beating a drum full of water. Dominic shook himself, black ash flew, and he raised his arms again, calling the red fire back to his fingertips alone, burning a wider swath around Cassandra.

When Dominic had burned all the limbs surrounding the trunk that held her, the tendrils hastily withdrew from her flesh, leaving small puncture wounds of dark dripping red on her soft pale skin.

He stopped the flow of fire just before she fell into his arms.

Dominic sank to the ground, cradling her body, looking for any sign of life. "Cassandra?"

Her lashes did not stir. Her breast did not rise.

He called forth blue fire, ran his hands quickly over her body, caressing, healing with a desperation that he'd never felt before.

The small puncture wounds closed; the droplets of blood dried and flaked to the ground. And still she did not breathe.

Blue fire could heal, but it could not call back the dead. Still, Dominic fed his magic to her, refusing to give in to the overwhelming despair that threatened to overtake him.

A weight settled in his chest, a pain far worse than his father's black fire. This pain would drive him mad. He could not lose her. He had barely just found her.

"You must live," he whispered to her. "For without you, I am done. Done and done with this

torment that I have been living. You cannot bring such light to my life and then take it from me, do you hear? Damn it, Cass, do you hear me?"

And suddenly her chest rose on a sigh. And rose yet again.

A wash of sweetness flowed through him, the likes of which he'd never known. A shiver that raised the flesh on his arms to little bumps.

Dominic could not ever recall shedding tears. If he had once known how, they had dried up long ago. But his eyes burned and he had to blink to stop it. He gathered her up in his arms, whispering nonsense and rocking her like a child.

His outburst had astonished him. It had come from his heart, which he had ignored for so long that he wondered at his words. Had his life indeed become brighter since Cassandra had come to share it with him?

Despite the turmoil she brought to him, the struggle to maintain his distance from the world, he realized that in his fear for her he'd spoken truly for once. The time before he'd kissed her in the abbey seemed like a smoke-shrouded dream. He would not wish to go back to it.

So and so. Her life had become precious to him, and yet she brought the threat of the greatest despair he could ever imagine.

The wind twisted his hair with hers, made the garden beyond the walls ring and chime with their haunting melody. Dominic kissed her hair, the smell of roses filling his senses. He ran his lips across her smooth forehead, gently fluttered them over her

lashes. Kissed the tip of her pert nose and the softness of her rounded cheek, at last finding her lips and hoping she would wake.

But she only sighed and Dominic feared she might not ever wake. But he refused to allow his emotions to overwhelm him again.

He would just have to be patient.

The wind suddenly changed direction and Dominic looked up with a frown. A flash of black wing shadowed him for a moment, and with another burst of conflicting currents, Ador landed near. The beast should have looked less enormous out in the open. He did not.

Dominic held Cass tighter, tucking her head beneath his chin. "Your timing is impeccable, dragon. Have you come to gloat?"

The beast folded his wings close to his sides, blocking the gale that had battered Dominic, and turned first one doleful eye on Lady Cassandra and then the other. "Do not make the mistake of transferring human attributes to my kind, bastard. Besides, what would I have to gloat about?"

"That you were right. That I cannot stop from caring for her."

Ador snorted, gray smoke dispersing like spinning dervishes in the wind. "I am always right. Does she live?"

"Of course. She is but asleep." Dominic narrowed his eyes up at the great beast. "Why does it matter so much to you?"

"She is important."

"Important how?"

Ador widened his eyes in a human attempt to look innocent. He failed miserably.

Dominic did not like the dragon's interest in her. He did not want Cassandra tangled up in whatever schemes might be afoot. "Keep her out of this."

Ador huffed, filling the wind with noxious fumes. His talons raked the earth, deep gouges of uprooted grass and dark soil. "I can no more keep her out of this than you can, bastard. Take my advice. You cannot fight the hand of fate."

"The hell I can't."

That enormous scaled head wove back and forth. "You have been forced to become a warrior. To fight for your survival. But there are some things you cannot fight. The girl is caught up in this as surely as you, because love binds you both."

"I will not let it," insisted Dominic.

"Still you fight it. Human stubbornness defies all reason!" The sky chose that moment to rumble with thunder, the wind increasing with the sound, ruffling the edges of Ador's leathery wings. He spread them, pitting his strength against that of the tempest. "Heed my advice, bastard. Stop fighting your love for the girl. Allow it to strengthen you, for I fear that you will have need of it. And do not fight the girl's role in your life. You will have need of that as well."

"I am tired of your advice, Ador. It has brought me nothing but confusion. Nothing but pain."

"You speak of more than the girl. You have seen inside Mor'ded's door to Elfhame."

Yes, Dominic had seen. And he wished he hadn't. Guilt and sadness washed through him. "Does Elfhame really exist somewhere?"

The sky crackled again. "Of course it does. But it takes more than one elven lord to open the gate."

A drop of rain smacked Dominic on the head. He rose, his wife a negligible weight in his arms. "I must get her to shelter." He walked along the vine-covered wall, noting wryly that Cassandra had been but a few steps away from the gate. Of course, she would not have recognized it as such, nor would she have known the elven word to open it. He would have to teach it to her. "*Shez'urria.*"

The vines shuddered, untangling leaf and thorn, peeling back from a wall with naught but a jagged crack between the stone blocks to indicate the gate. With a moan and a teeth-jarring screech of rock shifting on stone, the gate opened.

Cassandra stirred in his arms, a frown marring the smoothness of her brow. Dominic stroked the back of his hand across her cheek, and although she still did not wake, her skin smoothed and she returned to a peaceful slumber.

The sky rumbled again and Dominic looked back at Ador. A crack of lightning split the gray clouds, illuminating the dragon for a moment, the light reflecting off the black shiny scales, making them glow an unearthly hue.

Dominic took a few steps toward the gate and realized that Ador would not follow. He had never entered the elven garden.

"You never come inside," he shouted over the rising storm.

The wind buffeted the dragon's wings, raising him up and down, talons scrabbling in the earth. "No.

The garden is but a sad, pale copy of Elfhame, as much an illusion as Mor'ded's doorway."

Dominic fought for calm, grief washing through him again. "Damn you for telling me of that, Ador. Damn you for making my life even more of a lie than it already is."

"I see you're in no mood to talk of it yet." The dragon bowed his massive head, as if he grieved as much as Dominic. "Just remember that Mor'ded has made your life. I but seek to help you change it." And then he quickly took flight. The wind robbed him of his usual smooth glide through the sky, throwing him back and forth, Ador battling to keep to his path back to the palace tower.

"Do you?" muttered Dominic, entering the relative shelter of the walled garden. "Will the changes you seek make my life any better?"

But the dragon was no longer here to answer him, and only the frantic melody of the garden responded to his words. He crossed the gravel paths, keeping close to the walls to shield Cassandra from the storm. The rain held its breath until he reached the shelter of the pavilion and then came down in a sudden deluge, as if the sky had tilted a bucket over the garden.

Dominic hoped Ador made it safely back to his tower.

He settled in the middle of the pavilion, warming the surface of it with his magic, and adjusted his wife in his arms. He did not have to let her go. Not yet, for his father's attention was elsewhere and he feared no spies in the garden.

He smoothed the hair back from her face, allowed himself to look his fill of her. The arch of her brow, the fullness of her mouth. She looked like a princess, despite her torn dress and wild hair. A damsel from some fairy tale, where wickedness could be fought with the honesty of a steel blade and evil spells could be broken with but a kiss.

He lowered his mouth to hers with a tenderness he did not have to hide.

But this was no fairy tale and she did not wake. He frowned down at her, quickly suppressing a rise of panic. She would wake. Soon. He would think no other way.

He spared a thought to heal his own wounds; then with the patience of a man who had won many a skirmish with the surprise of an ambush, the general settled in to wait, while the man reflected on his conversation with a dragon and the discovery of a lie too evil to be borne.

No, his life was no fairy tale with the promise of an easy happy ending.

Ten

CASSANDRA WOKE TO THE SOUND OF A HAUNTING melody and the feel of warm arms about her. Her eyes fluttered open to the sight of her husband's beautiful calm face. She caught a flicker of emotion in those midnight eyes, a sadness that startled and confused her. He blinked, and they returned to their usual cold hardness, but Cass still sensed something vaguely different in his demeanor.

"What the hell did you think you were you doing?" he said in dulcet tones.

Cass sat up, and he dropped his arms, moving a bit away from her. "Where am I?" she asked, knowing perfectly well the answer, for the melody she'd heard from within the walls of the garden now rang clearly in her ears. But it gave her time to collect herself, and she glanced around with wide eyes.

The storm she'd predicted had broken, and they sheltered in a pavilion that looked to be made of marble but felt soft and pliable beneath her bottom. The rain created a sheer curtain beyond the roof and fell atop what she thought might be flowers of some sort, but their flat, round surface also reminded her of drums, except that when the rain beat upon them, they made ringing notes. The wind blew strongly now, and the whistling she'd heard before accompanied the ringing in harmony, and she searched for the source of that sound, her eyes widening even more as she discovered it.

The wind lifted the lavender petals of a plant and expanded them into long tubes that appeared to produce that whistling sound. As they waved and danced with the breeze the harmony changed, like the way fingers on a flute produced different notes. Just beyond that bed of flowers lay a patch of scarlet petals shaped like bells, the wind swaying them and producing the sound of thousands of tinkling chimes.

Cassandra looked up at Dominic in wonder. "Is this what Elfhame is truly like?"

His usually unexpressive face softened, and again Cass thought she detected an odd sort of sadness intermingled with anger before he quickly looked away and leaned against a pillar, the surface giving slightly with his weight. "I suppose."

Lady Cassandra stood and walked to the edge of the pavilion, breathing in the strange scents while her brain tried to match them with something familiar to her. Honey and roses, cinnamon and vanilla… perhaps clove and brandy? A myriad of fragrances she couldn't identify, and yet they seemed somehow familiar…

She glanced over her shoulder at her husband. "It smells like you."

He blinked, a sweep of long black lashes. "I come here often."

Cassandra looked out over the garden. Strange trees shaped into perfect circles, peculiar bushes growing in neat rows, white sparkling stones raked into smooth grooves, still ponds beneath miniature waterfalls, and clustered betwixt and between, tidy beds of bizarre flowers. "It's so… orderly."

"Indeed." His voice dropped so low, Cass strained to hear his next words above the sound of the music. "Father once told me that's why he made this place. To remind him of what he left behind."

She turned and faced him. "He must miss his homeland very much."

"Father finds order very boring, Lady Cassandra."

She frowned, trying to puzzle that out, but he moved closer to her and her body tingled with awareness and she lost her thought. He wore no coat, just fawn breeches tucked into brown boots and a white linen shirt carelessly buttoned, revealing his smooth throat and the upper contours of his muscular chest. The cloth, and even his leather boots, had been punctured and torn, a testament to the fight he'd waged to save her from the vine guardian.

"What are you doing here?"

She blurted the truth. "Looking for you."

"Why?" He reached out for her hand, fingering the damp sleeve of her gown, revealing the jagged tears in the fabric from the grip of those deadly vines. "It could have killed you, you know."

Cass shuddered. "This place. Everywhere I turn there are hidden dangers. How do you manage to live like this?"

"You get used to it." His beautiful face lay

perilously close to her own. "What do you want from me?" he murmured.

Cassandra looked into the devil's face. If only he didn't have the beauty of an angel, her body might not have betrayed her. All thought of the Rebellion and her task and even the plight of England faded from her mind. She almost hated herself for the way she longed for him, and shyness made her admit it in a roundabout manner. She blushed. "You have been neglecting your duty."

He narrowed those deep black eyes. "I forget you're anxious to secure your place here as mother to my children."

Fie, she liked that excuse. "Indeed. I do not want to give your father a reason to be angry with me."

"Father's anger is nothing to fear. His boredom and suspicion are another matter." He stepped away from her, leaned casually against the pillar again, looking out over the garden. The wind plastered his linen shirt against his chest, blew his loose silver hair in streams behind his elegantly pointed ears. "But you needn't have worried. Father's attention is… elsewhere."

Cassandra hugged her shoulders. The temperature had dropped considerably with the storm, but her chill came from his manner. "He left the palace?"

"Aye."

"What for?"

"That's none of your concern. You should have just been grateful his absence allowed me to stay away from you."

She should never have admitted to herself that she was half in love with him. That realization prevented

her from dismissing his rejection as she once had…
and suddenly Cass could no longer keep up any
pretense with him. She felt as if he'd run a dagger
through her heart, and she allowed her voice to reflect
her feelings. "I did not believe you found your duty
so distasteful."

He continued to stare at the falling rain, but his
muscular shoulders stiffened beneath the white linen.
"Do not—"

"I am a fool," confessed Cassandra. "I thought
you found pleasure with me. Despite everything… I
thought you had come to care a bit for me." Why had
she even imagined she could ever mean anything to
him? She collapsed on the soft surface of the pavilion,
hugging her shoulders even harder.

"Stop this," commanded Dominic.

"What?" Cass almost laughed. "Admitting what a
simpleton I've been? I should have listened when you
told me you had no human feeling. But I have no
standard to judge a man, no experience with court-
ship and love games. Instead, I run after you like some
love-struck little schoolgirl. I allow myself to become
a laughingstock among the ton."

He turned toward her then; she could feel his eyes
upon her but she refused to look up into that cold
black gaze.

"You do not understand," he whispered.

"Oh, but I do. This shall be my final lesson, sir.
I should thank you, I suppose, for teaching me the
different ways a man can tell falsehoods with his
touch."

"Stop it," he commanded again. She felt him crouch

next to her. His warm hands fell on her shoulders and gave her a gentle shake. "I can bear no more of this."

Cass nodded. Oh, how well she understood. His embarrassment from her declarations surely equaled her humiliation in having stated them. She took a deep breath, gathering her composure. A fine spy she made. She had let her heart interfere with her task when she knew all along that her marriage to Dominic could be nothing but a falsehood. She had handled this very badly.

"Cassandra." He breathed her name like a benediction. She finally looked up at him, and her heart stopped. That controlled mask of his had crumbled. Cass felt as if the man who had made love to her within the shelter of their curtained bed now faced her in broad daylight. Finally she could fully see the true nature of the man she'd married.

Those deep black eyes shimmered with warmth. "You *are* a little fool for making me care for you."

And he gathered her into his arms, the heat of his body taking the chill from the air. And then he kissed her, so tenderly it took the chill from her heart. Her heart, oh, had she heard him aright? Did he say he cared for her? The elven half-breed who possessed no human feelings? Cass wrapped her arms around him and kissed him back with all the wonder and delight that she possessed. The wind played with her hair and the melody of the garden sang with her heart, and for one glorious moment she forgot herself in the warmth of her husband's embrace.

And then he pulled away from her mouth and gazed into her eyes. She'd had only glimpses before, but now he revealed his entire soul in those black crystalline depths, and it stunned her.

"You have completely destroyed my last desperate attempt to protect you," he said.

"I—I don't understand."

Dominic smoothed the hair away from her cheeks. "I know. And I will tell you, for I'm done fighting this thing between us." He sighed and sat down next to her, keeping her within the circle of his arms. "Ador was right… and very wrong, for I think I started to feel again from the moment I first kissed you. In that one single act you unraveled years of effort in burying my human heart."

Lady Cassandra's head spun. She looked up into his face, trying to fathom his words. What did Mor'ded's dragon-steed know of her? She feared to ask. "But why would you do such a thing?"

"Because everyone I have ever held dear has been used against me. And I swore to myself no one would ever suffer again because of me."

Cass shivered, and he pulled her closer. "Your father," she guessed.

"Indeed. Have I told you that your intelligence is one of the things I admire about you?"

"You certainly have *not*."

He smiled down at her and her stomach did funny little flips. She still couldn't quite believe that he truly cared for her. Cassandra, the little brown wren.

Dominic turned his face away then, a frown tightening his mouth. "You deduced that we might be spied upon in the palace. Did you not wonder who?"

"There are too many factions within the ton to guess."

"The nobles, ha. As if they would have the means or power to threaten me."

Cassandra wondered what he might think if he knew of the Rebellion. No, best not to pursue that. Not yet. She would be selfish and enjoy this closeness before she made any confessions that might completely destroy it. "Your father, then. But why?"

"Oddly enough, because he fears me. He fears I have the power of black fire, the most potent of his magics. And I think he might be right."

Cass glanced around the pavilion, the rain that still curtained them in, the music of the garden that muffled their words, and still her heart jumped. "Do not say such things. What if he's spying on us now?"

"I told you; his attention is elsewhere."

Still, she lowered her voice to a whisper. "What is this black fire?"

"It's the fire that burns in the mind, and all the more powerful for that."

"But wouldn't he have discovered that unusual gift at your trials? And if you indeed possessed it, wouldn't you have been sent to Elfhame?"

"Sent to Elfhame," he whispered as if to himself and then shook his silvery blond head, raised his voice again. "Ah, dear wife. I cannot use the black fire. It's been hidden from me, and therefore my father cannot find it. But he suspects. I am the strongest champion of all the elven lords, and this makes him fearful. He does not want to find his tool able to turn against him."

Cassandra gripped her hands tightly in her lap. She could not believe Dominic finally spoke to her about his life, finally decided to trust her. Perhaps he had not been able to before, if he feared that his father spied upon them.

She no longer cared about the Rebellion or Sir Robert. She considered only Dominic, how tormented he seemed, and that if only she knew more about him she could in some way help. And she sensed more... "What does he do to you?"

"We are all given a trial at puberty, when our gifts appear the strongest. Don't you remember yours?"

"Vaguely. I felt challenged. As if that black scepter of your father's attacked me and I had to defend myself. And then... then I danced, and your father laughed, and it was done."

Dominic dropped his head, that thick silvery hair falling over his cheeks, the wind twisting it to hide his face. But not before Cassandra saw his tortured expression. "The more powerful the magic, the greater the challenge. When Father suspected I might be hiding my gifts from him, he tried using... stronger incentives. He thought... he thought I would reveal myself to save those whom I cherished."

"Mongrel," breathed Cass. So that's how his pet had died. And Cook had mentioned his best friend... "Jack?"

Dominic did not ask how she knew of him too. His shoulders slumped with a pain she could only imagine. "In a fit of rage, I once tried to run my sword through my father. Jack paid the price for it."

No wonder he took such care to control his emotions. Cass could not comprehend what he had gone through watching his friend burn and being unable to stop it. She reached out and caressed his cheek, and he turned his face into her palm for a moment, and she could only feel grateful that her touch seemed to bring him some comfort.

Dominic straightened. "But I could not find the magic within me," he continued, "no matter how hard I tried. I could not save them. And now…"

He raised his head and Cass stared into eyes that resembled black velvet.

"And now I can't be sure if I'll be able to save you."

Cass felt humbled. All this time he'd been protecting her by treating her with disdain, by trying to keep his distance from her. And yet he'd come to care for her anyway. It occurred to her she'd done the same, trying to avoid involving her emotions with him, telling herself she only sought his affection because she wanted to use him. And she'd been just as unsuccessful as he.

The last two people in England who could afford to desire each other had managed to do so, despite their best efforts not to. He had not said that he loved her; indeed, she couldn't be sure his elven blood would even allow him that deeper feeling. But she knew she loved him. And she couldn't help but wonder if her love would be strong enough for what would come.

Eleven

DOMINIC WATCHED HER DELICATE FEATURES SUBTLY shift as she considered the meaning of his words. He'd expected to see fear, but his bride surprised him as usual.

"I won't need your protection. Now that I have your trust, we can defeat him together."

For a moment he could only stare at her in stunned amazement. Then he threw back his head and laughed, his voice a wild accompaniment to the song produced by the flowers of Elfhame.

She pulled a bit away from him, and her lips twisted into a disgruntled frown. "I do not jest."

Dominic wiped his sleeve across his eyes. "Oh, my girl, that's what I'm afraid of. You have no idea of the power my father possesses."

She rose with the grace of a dancer and he sobered, watching her pace the confines of the pavilion. Now that he'd revealed his secrets to her, perhaps she would feel free to do the same. "What makes you think you can take on an elven lord, Cassandra? Do you truly think a few elven death dances can kill him?"

She froze, slowly turned her head to stare down at him where he still sat. Her tussle with the guardian vines had mussed her hair, strands of silky brown curling about her cheeks and forehead. Her stomacher fell sideways, half the cording stripped from its holes. Her abandoned hoops made her hem drag where it had escaped the girdle meant to hold it up. The sleeve of her gown had been torn half off, dirt streaked her bodice and skirt, and her toes peeped through holes in her stockings. She looked ravishing.

"You knew?" she breathed.

"I suspected," he countered, "when I found you over the dead bodies of your two captors."

"Oh." She started to pace again, but this time her feet appeared to pick up the rhythm of the flowers' song. "And yet you said nothing?"

"At first... should you have managed to kill him, I would have only been grateful. Do you think you're the first assassin sent against my father? Although I have to admit, the Rebellion is getting clever. Who would have suspected that my innocently raised wife had been trained in the art of—"

She moved then, faster than he would have credited, possibly even fast enough that if she managed to catch his father unawares, she had a slim chance of being successful. She had her girdle half around his throat when he encased her in dull gray fire.

"You are good, my lady. But not good enough."

Her brown eyes blazed with a fire of their own. "You knew I would try. But Mor'ded won't. I have a chance."

Dominic shook his head. "You will not risk it."

"I must try."

"Damn it, you little hoyden. Must I keep you imprisoned to ensure your safety?"

Her mouth narrowed in a stubborn line. Faith, how he admired this slip of a woman.

"You will stay like that until I have your promise."

She glanced down. Fire ringed her body in shimmering flames of gray, held fast her hands with her girdle still clutched between them, trapped her waist in a bent-over position. Dominic sighed and slipped away from her garrote, rose to walk around her, a half smile crooking his mouth. "The position has its merits."

"You wouldn't."

"No, I would not. But my father…" And he let the threat hang between them, for he'd seen Mor'ded perform acts that had threatened to make him ill. He did not want to expose Cassandra to the atrocities his father committed. Despite her ties with the Rebellion, she had been raised innocent of the brutal natures of men and elvenkind.

He released the gray fire and caught her up in his arms. "I will kill the one who coerced you to be the Rebellion's tool," he muttered.

She laid her head against his shoulder with a sigh. "I chose to do this, Dominic. I would willingly give up my life to free the people of England."

"Well I am not so unselfish," he replied. "I will not give you up for anything or anyone. You cannot succeed, Cassandra. Promise me you will cease this notion of trying to kill my father. Allow me to *try* to keep you safe."

She looked up at him, a wealth of sadness on her face. "I love you, Dominic, but I fear you carry too much elven blood to truly see the world the same way that I do."

Her words, ah, her words made his heart sing and fear plunge through him like a knife. "You will get used to it."

"Nay, I shall not. I will never get used to the slavery of my people."

Dominic held her quietly in his arms for a time, while the wind died and the flowers ceased their song. "I have tried to kill him," he whispered. "And I could not succeed."

She twisted out of his arms and stood at his side, a tiny girl with a will of iron. "But together we might."

Dominic shook his head. She still did not understand. He could not protect her innocence in this matter. He would have to show her.

❧

He showed her the hidden gate in the garden, taught her the word to open it, and then brought her into the palace by way of another hidden passage, lighting their path with a handful of warm yellow fire. Dominic hadn't used this particular entrance since he was a child, sneaking out to the elven garden that his father had forbidden him. Since Father rarely went there now, he hadn't the need for such secrecy.

The passage had sprouted a wealth of cobwebs since he'd last been inside, and he'd taken wrong turns twice, but he finally arrived at the door that led into the great room. He turned and held his flame closer to his wife's face. "Are you sure you still want to do this?"

She nodded, brushing at a strand of web at her cheek. Cassandra had barely said a word since he'd dragged her from the garden and shown her the hidden door to the passage. She looked frightened. And very determined.

Dominic squelched the fire in his palm and lowered his head and kissed her, wanting to linger the moment his lips touched hers but not daring to do so. He straightened and pushed the lever that unlatched the door, slowly opening it and peering around before stepping into the great room. Cassandra followed, and the door shut behind her with the slightest of creaks.

They stood behind a stone pillar, over a hundred paces from the dais that held Mor'ded's throne.

His father would not be back for at least another couple of days, and his attention would be focused on hunting the gifted elven children. Still, the general led Cassandra from pillar to pillar, avoiding the sconces of red fire that lit the long hall, listening for the clacking heels of the gentry or the softer footsteps of a slave.

His shoulders finally relaxed when they reached Mor'ded's throne without discovery. He opened the door in the wall behind it, calling back the yellow fire to light the way. He stopped at the stout oak door halfway down the passage and took a deep breath. If Ador had not told him that he possessed the power to dispel the wards on this door, he never would have attempted it the other night. Father's spells glowed with deadly threat in a sparkling web that covered the oak.

"Beware," he murmured to Cassandra, gently pushing her small body behind his. He raised his hands to the door, calling to the gray fire, encasing each strand of the seeming web with the dull flame. It took him much longer to neutralize the wards than it would have taken his father, and they wouldn't stay down permanently—as he'd discovered last night, to his infinite relief. He didn't want Mor'ded to know his secret had been uncovered. As he reached the last strands, flames shot toward him as if they protested against his meddling with their final strength. His magical defenses quickly responded with a blaze of their own, squelching the attack. Dominic encased the remaining strands, lowered his arms, and turned to his wife.

"Down this passage," he said, pointing to his left, "is the entrance to Mor'ded's private chambers. It's not warded with a spell of fire, as it saps even an elven lord's energies to keep up an active ward like this one, but there's a plant within that's nastier than the vine guardian."

"I understand," she said. "I will be careful, Dominic."

He raised a brow. She'd already proven how little she valued her life when it came to her passion for the Rebellion. He only hoped that what he now showed her would convince her of the futility of matching her powers against Mor'ded's.

Dominic opened the heavy door and tried not to breathe too deeply of the dust inside the passage. With a handful of yellow flame he followed the twisting tunnel, his wife hard on his heels, and they descended deep into the earth, the walls becoming rough and jagged as they neared their destination.

The tunnel abruptly ended at an opening that widened into a large underground cavern. The general put one foot into the chamber, gently catching Cassandra about the waist as she attempted to brush past him. "Do not go any farther."

"What is it?" she whispered. "Is it warded here as well?"

"No. But you don't want to… ah God, I shouldn't have brought you here."

"Do not take the Lord's name in vain," she whispered.

Her faith continued to puzzle him. "That was a prayer to him, my lady. If he should indeed exist."

Her eyes widened in surprise, but he didn't have time to debate theology with her. He itched to be gone from this place. He exchanged the yellow fire for white, the brighter flame spilling from his hands to light the rough-hewn ceiling, revealing the contents of the cave in horrid detail.

Cassandra blinked and stared in confusion.

Dominic did not blame her. If it hadn't been for Ador's words, he wouldn't have understood what lay within this cavern.

A black platform made of stone stood in the center of the chamber. Mounds of grayish white dust layered the back of the cavern, spilled over to small trickles near their feet.

"Behold the fabled land of Elfhame," said Dominic.

"I don't… what do you mean? What is all this ash?"

"Children."

Her soft brown eyes blinked in confusion as she stared at the powder near her feet, and he saw horror slowly harden them to a glittering bronze when the full import of his explanation dawned on her. Cassandra gasped a wordless denial, and she shivered while he clutched her tightly to him.

"This is where the children who hold too much of the elven power are sent. After they are put to the flame by the Imperial Lord."

"No," she breathed. "They are sent to Elfhame. To a better life of richness and happiness."

"Think on it, Cassandra. Would families bring their children to the trials if they knew what fate awaited them? But with the promise of being sent to the fabled land of Elfhame, it's easy for the Imperial Lords to gather together children who might be a threat to their rule. Even then some still refuse."

She covered her face with her hands, her words muffled by her fingers. "But only one or two a year are chosen. There is so much ash here... Dear heaven, the generations of innocents..."

Dominic could not stop the self-recrimination that flowed through him. "That's why my father left the palace. To hunt down the families who refused to give up their children to the trials. *And I sent him after them.*"

She slowly lowered her hands and looked up at him.

"I didn't know. Do not look at me like that." Dominic wanted to shake her, so he loosed her, and she swayed. "*I did not know.* I did not know I had enough power to dispel the wards until Ador told me last eve. But I should have tried. I know better than anyone the madness of the elven lords. I should have guessed something more lay behind the trials. Instead I chose to turn my back on everything human, including that which lay inside of me."

She put her small hand against his chest, covering his heart with her palm. "You are *not* the monster, Dominic. Your father is."

"And powerful enough to destroy you with a flick of his scepter," he pressed. "Powerful enough to enslave an entire country. You have been lied to, my dear. You have no hope of killing him. The Rebellion is nothing but the hum of an angry insect against Mor'ded's ear. If they become too much of a nuisance, he will swat them."

"He knows of the Rebellion, then?"

Dominic reined in his patience. When would she think of the danger to herself? "Not yet. I haven't chosen to share their existence with him yet, although I'm sure he's aware there *is* a resistance. I've been saving it for when he becomes bored."

"Bored?"

"You may say it with contempt, my dear, but you do not know the danger when an Imperial Lord becomes bored. Why do you think they left their perfect land of Elfhame?" Her hand made a fist against his heart, and he saw the tight furl of the petals on her rose ring. He covered that fist with his larger hand. "Oh yes, Elfhame does exist, but I don't know if the elven lords can even return, much less how they first shattered the barrier between our world and theirs. But my father once told me that's why they left. They became bored with peace and perfection."

She made a strangled sound and it tore at his soul. It made him wish his elven blood hadn't betrayed him and allowed his human heart to rule. He did not like feeling her pain as if it were his own.

"Please, Dominic," she whispered. "No more. Have mercy and take me from this wretched place."

He called back the white fire and plunged the cavern into darkness, but it could not change what lay there. He lifted his wife into his arms and carried her back up through the tunnel, unburdened by her weight but worried for her soul. Perhaps he had pushed too hard. But she would heal; he knew her inner strength. And he hoped he'd convinced her to give up the Rebellion and their futile attempts to win back England.

Luck stayed with him and he found the great hall empty, used the servants' stairs to carry her up to their rooms. Her two little slaves waited for them at the door to their apartments, both of their faces twisting with alarm at the sight of their mistress.

"What happened?" demanded the younger, always the cheekiest.

"She got tangled up in a guardian vine," he deigned to reply. "She's not injured. She but needs some care."

"Yes, yes, of course," whispered the older one, her hazel eyes soft with concern. "Oh, my lady. Your hair. Your dress!"

Lady Cassandra rallied in his arms. "It's all right, May. The vine got the worst of it. Truly, Dominic, you can set me down. I shan't faint."

His lips twitched, but otherwise his face felt rigid as stone. He felt relieved his defenses had not fully abandoned him. It felt… easier to sink back into his elven demeanor.

Lady Cassandra swayed on her feet, but as promised, she did not faint. The oldest girl fled out the door with a bucket, promising her lady a warm bath and a hot meal. Dominic's stomach growled and he realized with surprise that he felt ravenous. But he hadn't the heart to eat.

"You're leaving," said his wife in a toneless voice.

The smaller slave girl watched them with too much wisdom in those young eyes.

Dominic lifted Cassandra's chin, but she refused to meet his gaze. "Do not blame the messenger."

Her breath hitched.

He wanted to enfold her in his arms and comfort her, but a lifetime of training made him deny the impulse. "I will be back soon."

She nodded and turned away, disappearing into their bedchamber.

Her servant looked up at him. "She had great faith in the power of her God." And then she scurried after her mistress.

Dominic spun and strode out the door. The little chit saw too much. He knew it would be dangerous to have servants about. But his wife needed someone to soothe her right now, and despite how he wished it might be otherwise, it couldn't be him. Not yet. For now the general needed a bit of soothing of his own.

He dragged his feet up the tower stairs, feeling as if the steps had multiplied since the last time he'd gone up them. As he climbed his anger faded, and when he stepped through the tower door he felt nothing but sadness left inside of him. For him, for his wife, for the whole damned country of England.

Ador sprawled against the merlons at the far end of the tower, his black snout wedged within a crenel, his red-striated eyes gazing at the gray sky. But for once Dominic felt no urge to talk to the beast. He'd sought only the quiet of the tower, the fresh smell of rain-washed breezes, the softness of gathering dusk.

A gentle breeze stirred his hair and brought the fishy smell of the Thames along with it. Dominic leaned over a crenel, not far from Ador, the stone cool and rough beneath his hands, the solid feel of it helping to anchor him to the earth again. Helping him to lock the horror of the cavern back into the small box in his mind that protected his sanity.

But he could not do the same with his feelings for his wife. He'd admitted it to himself and her, and now he could never go back to feeling nothing again. She had breached his defenses and he would be vulnerable. And he would do anything to keep her safe... and happy. Fie, he hadn't considered the concept of happiness for so long, he wasn't sure if he could even offer it.

"I would change the world for her if I could," he whispered to the deepening night, to the stars, to that God of hers that she would no longer believe in. Not after today.

Ador's sigh sounded like a great bellows, tingeing the air with the scent of sulfur and smoke. "I have waited long and long to hear you say those words."

"I'm not in the mood for your confidences tonight, Ador."

The dragon made a loud harrumphing noise like an indignant old man. "So now that you know what the madman has been doing to those children, what will you do about it?"

"I don't know," he wearily replied. "When will my powers be strong enough to challenge him?"

"Only you can answer that."

Dominic's hands clenched into fists. "I have tried to find this greater power within me, and to no avail. The scepter keeps it from me just as surely as it keeps my magic hidden from my father." His fists loosened and he dropped his head in his hands, feeling suddenly weary. "And if I do indeed possess it, as you say, I dread the task before me. Damn this human heart, but the man *is* my father."

Scales slithered on stone, and the general felt hot breath against his back. "That's the problem with opening yourself to human emotion. You become capable of such great love... and great sorrow. Will you allow it to strengthen your power or weaken it?"

Dominic sighed. His feelings for Cassandra could only make him more vulnerable. They did not have some mystical way of strengthening an elven's power, or the Imperial Lords would have been defeated long ago. He did not tell this to the dragon, his weariness beyond anything he'd ever felt before, tired of answering hopeless questions.

Tired of feeling the utter desperation of his life. What would it matter if he defeated Mor'ded anyway? England still had six other elven lords ruling the rest of the country, and they would rise against him as soon as they discovered the death of his father. He could not stand against them, and Firehame would fall. Millions more innocents would suffer. As he thought of that harsh reality, a weight of despair unlike any he'd ever felt before settled about his shoulders.

He did not lift his head when he heard the dragon rise, when he felt the displacement of air from the mass of the beast's movement. Humid wind pushed against his body from the beat of leather wings and then calmed.

"It's an excellent night for a star dance," rumbled the dragon. "I offer you the skies of your true homeland, elven lord's son."

Dominic's head snapped up. And higher still, Ador suddenly appearing larger than he could imagine. Had he heard the dragon aright? After so many years, did the beast volunteer to carry a human upon his back?

The dragon snorted. "Unless your newly awakened human emotions include that of fear."

Dominic used his elven grace and strength to mount in one fluid motion, as he'd so often seen his father do. He grasped the edge of a scale near the dragon's neck, tucking his legs in front of the joints of Ador's wings.

The dragon's laughter shook the stones of the tower, shivered the calm night, and made the hairs on the back of Dominic's neck rise. The crushing despair he'd felt but moments earlier faded, to be replaced by a rush of excitement as Ador beat his wings harder and faster. With a lurch that nearly unseated the general, they rose into the lavender night, wind rushing past his ears, air chilling the higher they climbed.

Dominic threw back his head and laughed, surely sounding like the madman Ador professed his father to be. But the general didn't care. The freedom of flight, the absence of earth beneath his feet, made him drunk with exhilaration. It felt more magnificent than he had ever imagined.

Ador showed off for his rider, swinging smoothly from side to side, catching swift pockets of air currents and shooting along them with a speed that made Dominic's eyes water. The dragon climbed higher and higher until the general thought they'd surely reached the stars, for they glowed so brightly, seeming close enough to touch. And the dragon danced between them, a lilting glide that put Dominic in mind of Cassandra's elven dances. And he wished she could be with him.

Ador finally slowed and dropped lower, until they flew above the shadowed land of England, Mor'ded's red fire geysers scattered across the landscape, lighting up valley and road, fingers of flame seeming to threaten everything Dominic loved. Within a trice, they flew over London, the silvery ribbon of the Thames, minuscule lights blinking from the buildings below them. They flew toward Firehame Palace, the yellow flames that licked its walls making it shine like a sinister beacon within the city.

Or at least, that's how Dominic viewed his father's occupation of England.

Ador landed sooner than the general would have liked, a solid thud that shook the tower, snapped Dominic's teeth together. He sat for a moment, enjoying the up-and-down motion of the dragon's labored breathing, the way his own frozen cheeks and hands slowly thawed, and hoping Ador would take flight again. Dominic finally sighed, slid down a lowered wing, surprised to find his legs a bit shaky beneath him.

He bowed to the beast, the sweeping gesture the only way he could think of to properly thank Ador.

The dragon grinned at him, a flash of pointed yellowed teeth that had Dominic hoping never to see such a gesture from the beast again.

"Feel better, elven bastard?"

Dominic frowned. Had the dragon indeed taken him on that wild ride just to make him feel better? He would never have suspected that the beast knew him that well, but then again… "Aye, I do. You have reminded me I fight for more than just myself, dragon. I'll keep that in mind next time I'm tempted to wallow in self-pity."

"Good. Then I can tell you that your father will return on the morrow."

Dominic calmly nodded.

"And," continued Ador, "he has found the children who fled from the trials."

"Do any of them possess enough power to be sent to… Elfhame?"

The dragon did not question Dominic's choice of words. Better to continue the charade than to slip in front of his father.

"I would not mention it otherwise. There is one girl who promises to be more than even the scepter can guess at."

Dominic ignored the guilt that threatened. "Then have the scepter hide her magic from my father as well."

"Must I explain everything to you? The black scepter holds only an affinity for the power of fire.

Even then it is more of an... amplifier of that power. It cannot hide another Imperial Lord's magic."

"So this girl comes from another sovereignty. Which?"

"Dewhame."

Dominic cursed. She would have the magical ability of blue sky and water, then. Breden's realm. That elven lord continued to be a thorn in his side. "The elven lords like to keep their nobles close. What is she doing in Firehame?"

"Hiding."

"Ah. The Rebellion raises its annoying head again." Dominic didn't feel particularly surprised when Ador just nodded. Of course the dragon knew of the Rebellion. The general hesitated to think of how many things Ador truly knew. And how he managed to acquire the information. "The trials are to be held in two days' time."

"Then you had best determine how to save her," rumbled Ador. "The scepter feels she may be important."

It didn't matter to Dominic how important the girl might be to the game between the elven lords and their scepters. If indeed all the scepters were as duplicitous as his father's and sought to return to Elfhame as well. Dominic had brought the child into harm's way and honor demanded he save her. But how?

"My power is not strong enough to challenge my father yet."

"No."

"Then how can I save her?"

"I don't have all the answers, bastard. Isn't it about time you used your human heart to answer your own questions?"

The general spun, then quickly held up his arms to shield his face from the force of Ador's wings beating back up into the air. He watched the black speck dwindle into the stars and tried to contain his frustration.

So the dragon would help him only so far, and Dominic must figure out the rest for himself. He feared he could be only a pawn in this game between the dragon and his father. Yet hadn't he done that his whole life? Become a player in his father's war games? And he'd become a champion of them.

He vowed he would become a champion of this more deadly game.

The thought made his lips twitch. Then his stomach rumbled. Loudly.

He could stand here and allow his head to spin with a million questions and still not have any answers. Or he could go to the kitchens and snatch some dinner and then go comfort his wife.

※

The curtains around the bed had been drawn and the fire banked for the night. Dominic stripped off his clothing and slipped into bed, the wonder of his night ride with Ador still making him feel a lingering joy. But Cassandra had not been given a wonder to comfort her, and she lay with her back to him, her body stiffening when he ran a hand over her shoulder.

He knew of only one way to comfort a woman. One way to make her cry out with joy.

Dominic stroked the hair away from her cheek, his fingertips lingering on the softness of her skin. He could feel the muscles in her jaw as she gritted her teeth. He slid his hand beneath the covers, along the smooth curve of her waist, over the sweet mound of her bottom.

She pulled away from him. How could he comfort her if she would not let him touch her?

"So," he growled. "You do blame me after all."

Her voice sounded as if it came from a great distance. "No… I… I just wish the elven had never come to our world. With their games and their dragons and their damned magic."

Dominic sat up, spreading his fingers, calling forth the yellow flame from the magic that sang in his veins. The mellow fire played along his fingertips, lit their curtained cocoon with a soft golden glow. She did not blame *him*. Precious girl.

He flicked his fingers, sending the small yellow flames upward to dance along the carved wooden ceiling of the box bed. He called forth the magic again and again, flicking it upward, watching it create a spatter of light that resembled the stars in the night sky Ador had just showed him.

"Magic is not so bad," he murmured. "It's up to the user whether it brings pleasure or pain. Your elven love dance brought me great pleasure."

She made a dismissive sound deep in her throat.

He felt a smile curl his lips, looked down at her then, his ceiling of fire casting her in a golden glow, making her brown hair look like silken honey, her skin like shimmering silk. She still lay stiffly with her back to him, the covers snug about her waist, revealing only the smooth curve of her back and one bare arm.

"Will you not look and see the ceiling of stars I've made for you?" he asked.

She stubbornly shook her head.

Dominic called down one yellow flame, his eagerness making it dance and swirl. It touched her shoulder, made a circling motion, and her arm twitched at the gentle tickling heat. He called down another, sweeping the flame against the curve of her back. The next one he brought to her neck, made it curve beneath the fall of her hair and weave its way through the satiny strands of golden brown.

He envied his fire, for he wanted nothing more than to trace his own fingers across the paths on which he sent them.

But he could touch her in a thousand places at once with the myriad flames, and it brought him pleasure to imagine her own. So he sent the tiny flickers to her more quickly. Some to warm her back. More to weave within her hair. Yellow flames wove between her fingers, lightly moving her hands as they spun within her palms.

She pretended to ignore them.

Dominic traced her cheek with flame, eased more across her lips, and imagined his own mouth upon them when she sighed. He made the flames catch the covers and lift them up, draw them down her body until he could see the curve of her hip, the long length of her legs, the small soles of her feet. A shiver went through her from the chill air and he quickly sent more whorls of yellow to caress her legs, play with her toes, flick over her hips.

He narrowed his eyes in concentration as she

continued to ignore his magic, ruthlessly skimming her bottom with tendrils of flame, finally sending some to tickle the crease between her buttocks.

Cassandra let out a startled yelp and flipped onto her back.

Dominic continued to play with his fire as if he stroked the keys of some erotic instrument, his entire being caught up in bringing pleasure to his wife. He hadn't realized what intense satisfaction it would bring him.

Twelve

"WHAT DO YOU THINK YOU'RE DOING?" GASPED CASSANDRA.

"Showing you the pleasure of my magic."

She knew that as soon as she looked at him she would fall under his spell and would not be able to resist him. And she'd tried very hard to keep her back to him, to shy from his touch. Not that she blamed Dominic for the sins of his father, but she felt as if she needed some distance from him to settle her beliefs with what he'd shown her.

But when he'd astonished her with that intimate touch of his magic, she could not suppress her reaction. And now she could only stare at his beautiful face and body and feel every fiber of her being long for him.

He smelled like starlight. Faith, he'd created a starry night above her, small flickers of yellow diamonds atop the wooden ceiling of their bed. But those stars kept falling as his fingers wove a pattern in the air. Falling to land on her exposed skin.

His midnight eyes reflected those tiny specks of light, his beautiful brow furrowed in concentration as he orchestrated their dance. The rest of his face retained its usual smooth calm, his full lips set in a soft line, the rigid planes of his cheeks and jaw arranged in that ethereal composure of his.

But when she looked back into his eyes she noticed the subtle difference. They shimmered with a warmth that made her heart melt, that made her want to reach out to him and apologize for her earlier indifference.

But she could not speak, could not move other than to wriggle beneath the onslaught of his magic. As soon as she'd flipped over he'd rained more of his yellow flames down upon her. She'd watched them fall, anticipated their gentle, warm touch with an arch of her back that she could not suppress. Her breasts had been covered with tiny yellow diamonds, except for her nipples, which felt coldly neglected in comparison. Flames danced across her stomach, burrowed into her belly button, skimmed down the length of her legs, and curled about her toes. Each flame brought warmth and the lightest of touches. Lighter than a feather swept across her skin. And yet they did not tickle… Fie, she could not describe the way they felt. She could only feel. Thousands of caresses that soothed and titillated all at the same time.

Her scalp tingled from their weaving in her hair, from their strokes along the strands of it. Her mouth trembled beneath the warm flow against her lips. She wiggled her fingers and felt the flames move with her, pulsating around her fingertips and brushing across her palms.

Cassandra tore her gaze away from Dominic's and glanced down at her body. Merciful heaven, she glowed with fire. Her entire body writhed with it, and it should have frightened her.

"Look at me," he commanded, and she could not refuse him. Could not help losing herself in the bottomless depths of his dark eyes. He glowed golden in the reflected light, the muscles in his broad shoulders rippling as he continued to sweep his fingers over her body.

And then he smiled at her. With such tender passion that Cass could not help smiling back at him. And when she raised her arms above her head in absolute surrender, his smile grew wider. Triumphant.

Fire licked up her underarms and set her to quivering again. And suddenly tiny warm flames entered every crevice of her body. Her ears warmed from the inside. Her lips parted and tendrils stroked the insides of her cheeks, curled around her tongue. She blew out a breath of flame and tossed her head, for the fire had curled between her legs, filled the space between them, a gentle pressure that drove her mad for want of more. It filled her up, but so gently and teasingly that she could not help—

"Look at me."

She'd forgotten he would not allow her to look away from him. He wanted to see the pleasure in her eyes, as if it somehow brought him the same. And indeed, he looked just as maddened as she felt.

Thousands of gentle caresses with only two areas exposed to the cold night air. When the heat finally came to her nipples, to the nub of pleasure between her curls, she could no longer suppress a moan. Some of the flames stroked her; some whorled so fast they created a vortex that plucked at her skin, making her flesh rise higher and higher.

Dominic's eyes had become fierce. She reached out a hand to him and he clasped it, flames dancing between their entwined fingers. And when the spasms shook her body, he held her rooted to the earth, and when her moans threatened to turn into screams, he leaned down and covered her mouth with his own, taking her cries into his lungs while he continued to weave his magic.

Her pleasure lasted forever. Her pleasure lasted but a moment.

Cass had never felt anything like it before. Hadn't imagined such wonders of feeling aroused in her body.

Dominic pulled away from her. The yellow flames suddenly died, plunging her into cold and darkness.

And she realized it hadn't been enough.

"Dominic."

"I'm here." She felt the bed move, but he did not touch her.

"You have proven your point. Magic can be wonderful. But…"

She heard his intake of breath, the shaky release of it. Had her pleasure affected him so strongly, then?

"But I need more," she continued. "I need you."

And suddenly the heat of his body covered her, so much stronger than the tiny flecks of his magic. She reveled in the heavy feel of him between her legs, in the firm press of his lips against hers, and then the heat of his breath against her ear.

"Demanding wench, aren't you?"

Cass answered by wrapping her legs about his waist and pulling him unerringly into her. Ah, this was the pressure she'd craved, the feel her body had trembled for. She reached up and wrapped her fingers in his hair and pulled his mouth down to hers again.

He made a strangled sound and ground his lips atop hers, a pleasure-pain that made her tug at his hair and tighten her legs about him. She knew she'd taken him by surprise when she'd guided him so quickly into her, and she didn't want to give him a chance to recover. She pressed against him, not allowing him to pull out of her, deeper and deeper until he shuddered, plunging his tongue into her mouth as his own release rocked him, his groan of surprise muffled by her lips.

Something wonderful spread deep within Cassandra, a flow of warmth much stronger than magic. She held him to her with a strength she hadn't known she possessed. And in that moment her soul accepted his own as a part of her, and she knew she'd never be able to separate herself from him again.

Dominic rolled off her, taking her with him, so they lay on their sides facing each other, one of her legs still wrapped around his hip. Cass kept her hands twined in his hair, felt his breath stir the top of her head and the slight pressure of his chin, which rested upon it. She did not want to move. She wanted to stay like this forever, allow the happiness that filled her to stay a little while, for she'd never expected to feel such joy. Had never expected she'd fall in love with the elven lord's son.

Or that he might care for her in turn.

But she had to get up to brew the herbs that prevented pregnancy. For just a moment she allowed herself to think of what it might be like to conceive a child with him and felt such a fierce sort of joy it astonished her. She hadn't thought herself capable of such a feeling.

"Dominic?"

"Mmm," he replied, sounding half-asleep. Cass knew how much using her own bit of magic drained her, befuddling her mind afterward and sapping her body of strength. He must be so very tired after wielding the greater power he had at his disposal, despite his stronger elven blood.

But she had to ask.

"What will happen if we have a child?"

"You mean when."

He sounded so arrogant it made her smile. "All right then… when. If the child possesses this black fire as you fear *you* might, what will we do?"

He stiffened, disentangled himself from her arms, and rolled onto his back.

"We cannot give our child to your father," she continued. "Now that we know about—"

"Do not speak of it. Not within these walls."

Fire appeared in his hands, but not the warm flare of yellow and, fortunately, not the burning heat of red. Balls of orange flame rolled along his palms, lighting up the confines of their bed, the stiff beauty of his face.

Cass pulled the covers over her and propped herself up on an elbow. Despite the fact that the orange fire could burn her or the bedding, she had complete confidence in his ability to control it. To protect her from it. A very odd feeling for a girl who had been taught to rely on no one but herself.

Dominic made no move to cover his own nakedness and she guiltily felt glad. She could look at the beauty of his perfect form for years and never tire of it. But since she didn't have years, she tried to make up for it by drinking in the sight of him with desperate intensity.

Despite the stern look upon his face, he still resembled a Roman statue, with his long, smooth nose and full lips, the high cheekbones and square jaw. But his hair did not curl like the busts she'd seen; indeed, it lay thick and straight down his head, a luxurious fall curving over his broad shoulders and flowing down to his ridged abdomen.

Cass leaned over and twisted a hank of it about her fist, marveling at the silver glow that shimmered from the strands.

"I will fight him then," he finally said, "and as usual, it will be my father's whim whether I live or die."

She loosed his hair. "Then I will be at your side."

Dominic tossed the fireballs in the air, his midnight eyes reflecting the orange flecks of color in crystal glitters. "You and what army?"

"We don't need an army, Dominic. We will have God with us."

He glanced at her in surprise, the fire suspended in midair, twirling like small dervishes. "You still cling to your faith? After what I have shown you?"

Cass set her mouth in a stubborn line.

"Devil a bit, woman. If this God of yours exists, why would he allow such atrocities to happen?"

"Because he gave us free will. Do not blame the devil's actions on him… and do not try to debate theology with me. You shall lose."

"Indeed?" The orange flames shifted to yellow and danced up to the bed's ceiling again, swirling across the top of it like ribbons of golden light. "We could talk all night and I'd still call you a fool."

She could hear the anger, the bitterness in his voice. Her mouth softened and she put her hand over his heart. "You shall see. God will help us win."

He spoke again, and this time she heard the despair. The pain of a man who had felt abandoned for far too long. "Damn it, Cassandra, what has your God ever done for me?"

She allowed the covers to fall, scooted closer, and leaned over him, her breasts pressed against the smooth hardness of his chest. "He brought you… me."

He blinked and then gave a great sigh. Her body lifted and fell with his. Dominic brought his hands up to her face, the palms still heated from his magic, and gently smoothed back her hair. Cass half closed her eyes at the tenderness of his touch. His thumbs smoothed over her lips and traced a path across her cheeks.

His lip quirked. "How can I argue with that?"

She gave him a brilliant smile. He blinked again and then pulled her mouth down to his, sweeping his lips across her own again and again, until she pressed against him for something deeper. He obliged, opening his mouth, allowing Cassandra to sink into him as deeply as she could.

When she finally pulled away, they both were breathing hard.

"I love you," she said, suddenly feeling shy and vulnerable, but unable to stop the words from tumbling out of her mouth.

"I know," he replied without arrogance or conceit. "I can recognize it in others. But it's been long and long since I've found it in myself. You have become more important to me than my own life. Is that love?"

Cass couldn't answer him. He would have to discover that on his own. And perhaps if they had enough time, he might. She let her head relax on his shoulder, burrowed her face into his neck. Silky warmth.

She felt the muscles in his arms contract, and he pulled her close against him until she all but straddled his body full length. "I *will* protect you. And any child of ours. I will find this greater power within me. Ador says I will be strong enough soon. I will make it sooner."

"Dominic, you are crushing me." He relaxed his hold and Cass could breathe again. "I do not understand how your power could be hidden from you... how the dragon knows all this."

"Ador is connected to the scepter somehow. And the scepter—fie, I don't understand the half of it myself, only that it amplifies an elven lord's power and therefore possesses magic of its own. But when I touched the talisman as a child—"

"Touched it? And it did not harm you?" blurted Cassandra. The Rebellion had tried often enough to steal the scepters, much to the instant demise of the thieves.

Dominic shrugged. "I have seen Father carelessly brush it up against people time and again with no harm to them. But once a foolish courtier tried to wrest it from my father, and the man burned to ash where he stood. Perhaps it didn't harm me because I didn't try to wield it, or because I have so much elven blood running through my veins… I can't be sure. But I do know it somehow forged a connection with me when I touched it. One strong enough to hide my magic from my father. The scepter is… aware. And it wants to return to Elfhame, or so says Ador."

"And you believe this?"

"I have sensed the magic within me for years; so yes, I believe he speaks the truth. But they play a deadly game, Cassandra, in their quest to return to their homeland. One in which I do not want you caught up."

She had no intention, of course, of staying out of it. But it would do no good to argue with him. His will had been tempered in fire, and his strength astonished and humbled her. And despite her belief that God would help them win against the elven lord, she couldn't be sure she would survive the battle.

So when his breathing finally steadied, and he succumbed to exhaustion, Cassandra scrambled from the bed and set a kettle to heat on the fire. She washed herself and wrapped a robe about her shoulders, and while her herbs steeped, she prayed to God that he would protect Dominic. She could not bear the thought of a world without him, even if she no longer lived in it.

❧

The next morning, when Cassandra again woke up alone, she no longer felt dismayed by her husband's absence. For she'd become his lover… the son of an elven lord. A fire lord himself. The thought terrified and excited her all at the same time. And even though she knew he would rebuff her in public as he always did, she could not wait to see him again.

Gwendolyn's pretty face lit when Cass allowed her to choose a gown—a chocolate velvet with gold trim along the sleeves and hem. Wide hoops and a stomacher layered with golden bows. A woven gold pinner for her hair, heeled shoes with a bow perched on the toes. A dress fit for the court of the king and finer than Lady Cassandra would normally wear to break her fast.

But she hoped to call forth that glimmer of feeling within her husband's crystal black eyes, if only for just a moment, before he shuttered them again.

The confidence his lovemaking had instilled in her made her bound down the stairs, cursing the heels of her shoes but admiring the gold bows whenever they peeped from beneath her hem. She brought herself up short near the entrance to the dining room, the loud conversation of the nobles giving her pause.

Lady Cassandra couldn't care less what they thought of her. She'd told herself that the moment she'd entered the palace. But a small part of her shied away from their disrespect. It felt… exhausting sometimes. To keep her head raised high while they whispered scathing comments about her behind lacquered fans and gloved hands.

She sailed through the doorway, eyes searching for a tall man with silver-white hair, and for a moment her heart flipped when she spied him across the room. But she quickly realized it wasn't Dominic, but his father. She collapsed into the nearest seat and didn't acknowledge the two nobles who hurriedly excused themselves and vacated their spots next to her.

Mor'ded had returned to Firehame. She now had no chance of engaging Dominic in public, for he would surely return to his rigid demeanor with his father back. And he would use Lady Agnes as a shield again. Fie, what would she do when she saw them together?

Could their secret feelings for one another sustain her while she watched the general's mistress fondle him in public?

Lady Cassandra glanced up from her fork, where she'd made a complete muck of the scrambled eggs that the footman had served her, and felt compelled to meet Mor'ded's intense gaze. The image of mounds of gray ash came unbidden into her mind, and she struggled to control the hatred that twisted her mouth. She tried to copy Dominic, smoothing her lips and brow to an indifferent calm. She nodded at her father-in-law, and he narrowed his black eyes at her in response, hastily rising from the table and quitting the room.

Several other nobles quickly followed him.

She looked back down at her plate, forcing another mouthful of fried potato between her lips, trying to swallow past the tight feeling in her throat.

How could she fall so deeply in love with the son, when she detested the father so very much?

Lady Cassandra concentrated on her meal, nodded at the liveried footman when he brought a tray of watered wine near her elbow. She drank greedily, hoping to numb her shattered nerves.

"That's a useful talent you have."

Cass choked and quickly brought her napkin to cover her mouth, looking up into the piercing eyes of Sir Robert Walpole. "I beg your pardon?"

He took the seat next to her, flipping back the skirt of his somber blue coat. "The way you manage to clear a room." He waved a heavy hand about the table. Other than a few couples sitting far down the linens from them, the room lay empty.

Cass felt her face heat. The hope of the future of England sat next to her and she valued his opinion. Yearned for his respect and admiration. She took the napkin away from her mouth and slowly placed it on the table.

"A neat trick," he continued. "I wish I had the knack of it."

His face did not betray a hint of sarcasm. Indeed, he managed to look most sincere, his dark heavy brows lowered in earnest, his mouth curved into a gentle smile. He wore an enormous white wig, liberally powdered with the finely crushed stone that mimicked the elven's silvery sparkle. Only one of his bulk could manage to look distinguished in it.

Cass smiled tentatively back at him, relieved he hadn't been making fun of her. Perhaps he thought she'd cultivated the court's disdain on purpose.

He leaned closer to her. "It is most fortuitous for me, for at last I have a moment to speak with you alone."

She nodded, a tremor of uneasiness running through her. Surely he meant to ask about his note, his suggestion that Dominic hated his father. He would want to know what she had discovered, and she had to warn him. But how much could she reveal to him without betraying her husband? How far could she trust the Rebellion?

Cass suddenly realized that although she would gladly give her life for England, she could not do the same with Dominic's.

Sir Robert's voice dropped to a murmur. "We haven't much time. Thomas needs your help."

It was the last thing she'd expected to hear. She studied the portly man, realized that he struggled with some other, greater matter than the conversion to their cause of the elven lord's son.

"Where is he?" she breathed. "Is Thomas all right?" She struggled to keep the hysteria from her voice. It had never occurred to her that Thomas might need her help, that he would be in danger. He'd been her teacher and she'd held the utmost confidence in him.

"He's fine. You haven't heard the rumors?"

"Of what?"

A footman passed their seats with fruit tarts on a silver tray, and Sir Robert gave a hearty laugh and helped himself. "These will be the death of me, I'm sure." He bit into the sugary crust and waited for the footman to reach the other stragglers at the table. His voice lowered again. "Mor'ded has returned with a young girl destined for tomorrow's trials. She's one of Breden's half-breeds and has potential for great magic, powers that could be useful to our cause. Her mother agreed to allow us to hide her, and the girl agreed to give up the promise of Elfhame to aid our cause, but—what is it?"

This secret Cassandra had to share. She could not allow the atrocities to continue and she felt sure Dominic would agree. "The children—those who prove powerful enough to be sent to Elfhame…"

He did not ask questions, just waited for her to continue with his eyes riveted to hers.

"They… are destroyed. I do not know if the elven lords can even return to their home world. There is much I still—you are not surprised."

"No. We have long suspected, but… are you sure?"

"He showed me." She did not need to say who. "I saw the children's ashes."

This time Sir Robert betrayed a reaction, the blood draining from his face. But he quickly recovered. "What else did you find out from him?"

Cass shook her head, gold thread winking from her lappets. "You will have to ask him that yourself."

"So that is the way of it?"

"I have not wavered from my intentions," she hastened to assure him. "But as far as my husband goes… he will have to make a commitment himself."

"I believe he will—if only to protect you. In the meantime, keep our secrets as securely as you keep his. You will help Thomas?"

Cassandra knew what he asked. "He wants to free the girl?"

Sir Robert nodded. "A traveling company will perform *Romeo and Juliet* tonight." He grimaced, well-known for his distaste of the theater. "No one else in the palace will want to miss it. You must devise a way to leave after the first scene and meet Viscount Althorp in the small parlor where we first spoke. Do you remember?"

The same footman neared them again, this time with a tray of sugared fruit. Sir Robert did not wait for her answer. Instead he rose with a muffled grunt and gave her a small bow. "So you will ask the general to join the king in his box tonight?" he said in a loud voice. "We would be most honored. The king admires the cut of his suit, you see."

Cass gave him a watery smile, and he turned and left, snatching a sparkling strawberry from the footman's tray as he passed. She was the only one left in the dining room now, and slaves began to slip in to clean up the mess. The liveried servants ignored them as one would a dog beneath their heels, but several times Cass caught the slaves glancing her way with hidden smiles, which she returned with muted delight.

She'd made some friends in the palace, at least.

❧

That evening Lady Cassandra sat at her dressing table and frowned at the mirror, thinking that since she'd come to live at the palace, she spent entirely too much time changing her wardrobe.

"No, Gwendolyn, not that one."

The girl held up the silk gown that required enormously wide hoops and tsked. "But I'm sure all the other ladies will be wearing the like. The king admires the fashion—"

"Not tonight. Fetch me the black wool."

Gwen's face fell and Cass immediately felt contrite for snapping at the girl. But she had to wear something less restrictive, for she felt sure they wouldn't rescue the captive girl without a fight, and the black would help her blend into the shadows.

And she should admit to herself that she felt on edge with nerves. Thank heavens Dominic had been absent from the palace today, training his men. He surely would have realized something was afoot. And she couldn't tell him what she intended to do. He would only stop her in his personal quest to keep her safe.

Gwen slowly dragged out the black gown and scowled at the unadorned woolen. "It won't fit yer hoops."

"I know. Just fetch the black flannel petticoats."

The girl grudgingly obliged, then with a wicked gleam to her crystal eyes, held forth a stomacher sewn with jet beads. But Cass did not want anything that would catch the light, and when she told Gwen she would wear the plain embroidered one instead, the child looked on the verge of tears.

The child's obsession with fancy clothing would drive Lady Cassandra mad.

When Cass stood fully dressed before the looking glass, pulling on a long pair of black silk gloves, she nodded in approval while Gwen hung her head in despair.

"Ye shall look so drab, my lady."

"That is the point, Gwendolyn." Cass hesitated. She felt sure Thomas had a plan. But Thomas did not have Gwen. And unlike her husband, she trusted in her servant's loyalty. The court was now abuzz with the gossip of the trials and of the children who had been sequestered for the honor. No mention had been made of a powerful girl who had to be dragged to the palace for them. Would Mor'ded be so arrogant as to keep the girl with the rest of the other children?

Never underestimate the enemy.

"Shall I call for May to do yer hair?" asked Gwen, her voice rising hopefully. "She can twine it so lovely no one might notice the plainness of yer gown."

"Not yet." Cass fetched the map of the palace from the drawer and laid it out flat on the marble table. Gwen glanced from the paper to her mistress with growing curiosity.

"I want you to find someone again for me."

Gwen bounced to her side. "The champion is on the west grounds, my lady. I don't need my magic to tell ye that."

"That's not who I want you to find. Have... have you heard of the children awaiting the trials?"

Gwen smiled dreamily. "Aye, and lucky they be. But everyone knows where they are. Even the servants. In the old guest rooms of the palace."

Cass's suspicions solidified. "I think it's possible one of the children may be... housed in a different location."

"But why?"

"It's hard to explain. Can you do this for me without asking too many questions?"

Those wise hazel eyes took in Cass's appearance again, flicked to the map, and the girl nodded. "I trust ye. But I don't see as how I can help. I wouldn't know what to seek, ye see."

"I'm not sure I understand."

"Well, when ye asked me to look fer the champion, I could see his light clear as day on the map."

"His light?"

"Oh aye." Gwen scratched her head. "The champion's light is near as bright as his father's. He's easy to find."

"So everyone has a light?"

"Aye. May's light looks like it's woven. Cook's light slowly spins like a pig on a roast."

"And mine?"

"Yours *dances*, my lady. Like it's doing a merry jig."

Cass smiled at the bemused look on her servant's face. This light that Gwen saw must be a reflection of each person's magic. But how would she be able to recognize someone's light if she'd never seen it in relation to the person before?

"You said the general's light shines brightly? What does it look like compared to mine?"

"Oh, his shines much brighter and wiggles like a flame. Yers is soft, my lady, but... ye see, everyone with the fire magic has a bit of black about it. Mor'ded is the only one whose is completely black."

"I think I see. Not only do you see the strength of their magic, Gwen, but you see what kind of magic they possess as well."

"Then why don't our lights shimmer with red flame, my lady?"

Cass thought of the black fire Dominic told her about and suppressed a shudder, unwilling to reveal that knowledge to the young girl. "Perhaps because Mor'ded rules with a black scepter. Now, most of the nobles here are related to the fire lord, but there are many who possess magic from other sovereignties. Do you see those as clearly?"

"So that's why some have blue or brown or silver lights! Their magic matches the elven lord's scepter. I should have thought about that before. But it's always been something that's just there… and I never thought about looking for their lights on a map, my lady. Until you had me search fer the champion, that is."

"Be careful not to tell anyone about this, Gwendolyn. You have a unique gift and if it were known… others might want to use it for ill. Can you understand that?"

"Aye. There's some things that shouldn't be found."

Cass nodded and spread her palms across the map. "What lights do you see?"

"Mor'ded's." A frown. "The champion's. And yers and mine"—she stabbed her finger on the paper—"right here. And May's, in the other room. And Cook's, here in the kitchens. And May's stable boy, outside, here."

Cass glanced up with a smile.

Gwen shrugged. "He likes May. And he's got a gift with the horses. *I* like horses."

Lady Cassandra sighed. It seemed Gwen could focus on the people she knew well, or who were important to her, easier than the others. "Can you see the lesser lights of the nobles?"

Her brow wrinkled in concentration, her pink tongue appeared briefly at the corner of her mouth. "Oh aye, but they're so faint, it's very hard. Except for this here blue one."

Hadn't Sir Robert said the girl was one of Breden's nobles? He ruled with the blue scepter of sky and water! And if she held as much power as the Rebellion guessed… "Where?"

Gwen pointed to a tower near the western end of the palace. "That's an old part of the building and the stones of the tower are so ancient and crumbling, no one dares climb it. Why would they keep one of the children there?"

"Indeed." Cassandra's suspicions had proven right. They'd kept the girl in a different location than the other children, in a place no one would think to look for her. Thomas might already know this, but if he didn't, she'd just increased their chances of rescuing the girl.

Cass leaned down and hugged Gwendolyn. She was so young, and yet… "You must speak of this to no one. And if you hear any gossip, don't question anyone about it. Just understand that I'm doing what's best. I'm counting on your loyalty, my dear. My very life may depend upon it."

Those hazel eyes widened to alarming proportions, and Gwen practically whispered her next words. "Of course, my lady."

Cass folded the map and tucked it back into the drawer. "Now you may call May to arrange my hair. And while she's about it, tell me about this stable boy of hers."

Thirteen

Dominic felt a keen sense of disappointment when he entered his empty apartments. He'd thought of his wife all day and had anticipated the sight of her lovely face. Now he would have to wait to see her at the theater and be doubly cautious in guarding his reaction. But he'd had to stay late with his men, for his distraction had caused several of them to deliver some lucky blows in hand-to-hand combat, and he'd been honor bound to trounce them to prove his ability to lead.

And then it had taken some time to change the guard assigned to protect the tower holding Breden's half-breed. Mor'ded did not know the men the way his general did, would not recognize that only the most bumbling of his fighters had been chosen for the task. It would just make freeing the girl tonight that much easier for Dominic.

Then he'd had to secure some extra mounts and make sure they were stabled in the farthest paddock away from the palace. And while he'd gone about it, the stable boy had told Dominic that he'd finally discovered who had ordered the black stallion be given to Cassandra on the day they'd ridden to fetch the king.

Dominic entered his bedchamber and sat in the sturdy oak chair next to the hearth, pulling off his dusty boots while glancing about the room. Cassandra's feminine touch now permeated the very walls, and to his surprise, he found himself most comfortable among the frippery. It made him feel even more masculine by comparison.

His court clothes had been laid out neatly on the bed, and a cold bath awaited him with a bucket of hot water over the fire to warm it. He grudgingly admitted to himself that servants could be useful in preparing for the constant amusements one had to endure in the palace. While he quickly cleaned and changed, he wondered who had suggested *Romeo and Juliet*. It bored him to tears. He much preferred *Hamlet*.

Although tonight it really didn't matter what amusement the court had planned, for his sole purpose in joining them would be the opportunity to see his wife.

He took the stairs two at a time, grateful that his position as general allowed him the freedom of boots instead of heeled shoes. Gwen had a flair for fashion though, and he had no doubt the girl had chosen his coat of elaborately embroidered red birds with wings of flame and the matching dark red breeches. But his black shirt of ruffles at the throat and sleeves toned down the color, and it suited his fiery mood, and damn if he didn't care what he wore, as the only thing that concerned him was his desire to see…

A woman stood in the doorway to the antechamber of the theater. Dominic's heart sank while his face stiffened, and he bowed with fierce precision. He supposed it would be best to get it over with. "Lady Agnes."

She looked flamboyant in a gown that matched the color of her eyes. "La, my champion. I have missed you." She glided to his side and linked her arm with his. "I would ask where you've been, but rumor has already told me."

They entered the antechamber, with its pastel-painted murals of fairies and fauns covering the walls and ceiling. Gilt molding surrounded the artwork and crystal chandeliers exploding with yellow fire made the gold gleam with molten color. Linen-covered tables lined the room, a riot of food overflowing silver platters and china bowls.

"Rumors are often untrue, Aggie," he said, leading her to a private corner of the room. "Beware what you believe."

She went willingly, her eyes shining as she assumed the wrong reason for his want of privacy. "Oh come now, General! Surely you can't deny this rumor, when it would only lead to your… satisfaction again."

Dominic tried very hard to keep his attention centered on Lady Agnes, but his eyes kept sweeping over the top of her coiffed head for a glimpse of dark brown hair and a smile that could make his chest ache.

"What are you talking about, Aggie?"

"You. In my bed."

The very subject he'd been meaning to talk to her about, although in a more oblique manner. With a sigh of impatience, he folded his arms across his chest, leaned back against a faun making indecent advances upon a fairy. "I succumb to your skill at provoking my curiosity. What is the gossip?"

His position made his groin jut a bit away from his body. Agnes leaned her skirts up against him, but she didn't stir him in the least. Indeed, he found it most annoying.

She lowered her voice, for they had managed to acquire a few onlookers. "That you have managed to get your bride with child. And now that you have accomplished the formidable goal you shall be free to return to my bed."

Ah. So the hastily uttered words of Viscount Althorp had managed to circulate among the court. Cassandra's supposed headache had accomplished more than he had planned. He almost smiled when an unsettling thought occurred to him. Could it be true?

No. Cassandra would have told him.

"I had an interesting conversation with a stable boy this evening."

The sudden change of subject set her aback for a moment, but she quickly recovered with her usual aplomb. "La, General, why would that interest me, when we were having such a... promising tête-à-tête?"

"Because the conversation concerned you, my pet. Regarding a certain black stallion you insisted the lad give to my wife as a mount."

Aggie waved her silk-gloved hand in a dismissive gesture. "What of it?"

Dominic pushed his shoulders off the wall, grabbed those slender fingers in a painful grip. "Lady

Cassandra could have been killed, or at the very least, injured."

Her eyes widened as she stared from his black eyes to his tightened hand. "For which you would have been grateful."

"She belongs to me. You should have respected that."

"Fiddle!"

Dominic dropped her hand, afraid he'd crush her fingers. People had started inching their way toward the shadowed corner, their ears pricked to the discussion. He kept his face very calm, his voice smoothly composed. "If you ever threaten to harm her in any way again, you shall regret it."

She sniffed, tossing her blonde curls, completely unruffled by his threat. "I knew it. After all the years I've invested in you, you... bastard. You've fallen in love with your wife."

"I'm incapable—"

"So I thought—"

"Shut up, Aggie." And he could think of only one way to do that. One way to silence her accusations that he'd fallen in love with Cassandra. He kissed her. Hard. Without passion or consideration for her bruised lips. If Dominic hadn't had such iron control over his facial expression his mouth would have twisted with disgust.

She melted against him, throwing her arms eagerly about his shoulders. He heard a few startled gasps from their onlookers at such a public display, and then a few titters of amusement. When he broke the kiss, he looked up and stared at the few brave souls who'd dared to venture so close. They hastily backed away.

When Dominic looked back down at Aggie, her eyes told him she saw through the lie of his kiss. And when he glanced over her head, he spied Cassandra.

Her face flushed a bright red and she appeared to stumble, throwing out an arm to the man who stood by her side. Viscount Thomas Althorp smoothly caught her and turned her away from Dominic and his mistress, leading her to a table sparkling with decanters of brandy and port.

"He dares," hissed the general. "I told Althorp to stay away from her."

Lady Agnes looked over her shoulder, turned back to him with more expression on her features than he'd ever seen before. Such an ugly look on so beautiful a face. "Go ahead. Call him out. It will only confirm what I've told your father."

The fury of seeing his wife in the arms of another man faded at her words. He focused his complete attention back on Aggie, and she blanched.

"What, exactly, have you told Mor'ded?"

She shrugged but refused to meet his gaze. "I told him the truth. That you haven't shared my bed since you married."

"And why would you tell him that?" His voice dropped dangerously low. She took a step back from him. He followed. But she didn't need to answer, for he knew her ambition. "Did you succeed in getting into *his* bed?"

She shrugged.

"Listen to me, Aggie. You're playing with fire. Literally." He placed his hands on her narrow shoulders. "Stay away from my father. He's more dangerous than you guess. You would have a better chance with the king."

He'd spoken figuratively, but when she looked up a wicked gleam appeared in her eyes. "Do you think so?"

If he could have indulged in humor he might have laughed. "That's something you'll have to find out for yourself, now isn't it?"

Aggie gave him a tentative smile. Dominic had always thought Lady Agnes only pretended to be unfeeling, just as he did. But he now realized her shallowness might be a true part of her character. Had he so easily distracted her then? He could only hope, for the antechamber began to empty as the orchestra's opening song filtered into the room. He saw Althorp disappear into the king's box with his wife and quickly followed, Lady Agnes right on his heels. But when he entered the box Althorp had disappeared, and Dominic decided the man wasn't as witless as he'd thought.

The theater had been added to the palace years ago, when the baroque style had been the rage. Grand columns of marble circled the room and enclosed the boxes, a fresco of the sun's rays amid a sky of clouds adorned the ceiling, and the walls had been painted with trompe l'oeils of the English countryside, making the entire room appear to be open to fields of rolling hills and flowered meadows. A glamourist from the sovereignty of Dreamhame must have been a part of the theater troupe for the paintings moved, trees and grass swaying in the wind, the sun's rays shifting and sparkling, completing the illusion.

Only the elven lord's box, crawling with yellow flame, shattered the deception.

But it appeared that Mor'ded had decided to grace the king's court with his presence this evening, for he sat in the king's box on the older man's right. Walpole, as usual, sat at the king's left, and he rose and bowed to Lady Agnes, who quickly took a seat in front of the king, laying her arm on the back of the velvet chair and turning to bat her eyes at him. The rest of the court goggled at her. Dominic saw only his wife, who sat alone, just behind the king—the court shunning her as usual—her eyes rooted to the empty stage.

When he took the seat next to her a becoming blush heightened her cheeks. Cassandra snapped open her fan and placed it as a barrier between her face and his.

King George turned his head and nodded over his shoulder at Dominic. "Ah good, you have come. And this time I meet your wife. I see now why she wears the black, to complement the scarlet of your jacket."

Dominic raised a brow as he appraised his wife's understated gown, and shrugged. "Her servants are clever."

Mor'ded turned then, although he couldn't quite meet Dominic's eye, as the man sat directly in front of him, and instead settled his black gaze on Cassandra, who responded by fanning her cheeks. "It seems that congratulations are in order," he said as the house lights lowered with magical precision.

"Indeed," replied Dominic in a carefully neutral voice.

"It appears you have proven your virility."

Cassandra fanned herself even harder but did not waver from her concentration on the stage. Dominic did not respond either. Let the elven lord assume what he would.

"Your… dedication to your wife is commendable. Or so I have heard."

The curtain rose. Aggie quickly ceased her efforts in trying to gain the king's attention and turned to the stage. Mor'ded also turned and settled deeper into his chair, Cassandra letting loose a breath of relief. But the king continued to face Dominic, ignoring the actors as they entered onto the platform.

"I must demand the name of your tailor," blurted King George.

The opening music rose in a crescendo and Dominic leaned forward to catch the other man's words, brushing his leg against Cassandra's. She slid away, smashing her skirts into the opposite arm of her chair. A trickle of annoyance made the general lean forward and sideways even more, trapping her leg beside his.

"I beg your pardon," said Dominic, giving his wife a quick glance. He could see the color on her cheeks even in the dim light, but she pretended to ignore his presence.

"Your tailor," repeated King George. "I must have his name."

Dominic could not believe the man's obsession with clothing… although, since it appeared to be the only power he had, he supposed it was understandable. "I'm afraid it's not someone you would recognize, Your Majesty."

The lights on the stage lit with a brilliance that suggested magical fire, and he heard his wife gasp at the scene they revealed on the stage. The troupe must have more than one half-breed possessing the power of Dreamhame, for the set looked remarkably real. Italian towers eclipsed one another as they faded into the background; the river snaking its way across the right flowed with a sparkle atop its waves and birds winged their way across a gray sky that threatened rain. When blades clashed between the Montagues and Capulets, the blood that flowed not only looked real, but Dominic could swear he smelled the iron tang of it from his seat.

Mor'ded suddenly straightened in his chair and leaned forward. Did he fear that the power of the illusion might come from one too-powerful half-breed instead of the combined efforts of the smaller skills of many?

"Bah," said the king, "you just do not wish to tell me who the tailor is."

If Dominic didn't have the distraction of Cassandra at his side, he felt sure the man's obsession would have driven him mad. She held her fan with one hand, but the other lay loose upon her lap. He laid his hand lightly over the silk of her glove. The stubborn girl didn't even twitch.

"Nay, Your Majesty. I just fear you will be disappointed when I name her."

"Ah. A woman. She does not have a shop in London, then?"

"I'm afraid not."

Dominic curled his fingers between the top of the glove and his wife's warm skin, slowly peeling down the silk. She trembled. Sir Robert suddenly glanced back at them, his sharp eyes taking in their postures. He gave the general a smile laden with meaning before focusing back on the stage.

So then. Dominic had been right about Walpole's intelligence. Within the other man's expression lay an interest in Cassandra that surpassed the norm. And Dominic didn't think Walpole had revealed that without careful intent. Could he be a part of the Rebellion? There had been a certain smugness in that look, and Dominic felt sure he would be finding out soon.

The Rebellion would never have snared him if it hadn't been for his wife. He didn't think it had been a part of the plan; indeed, he felt sure they hoped to strike a lucky blow against his father using his innocent-seeming wife. But the impossible had happened, and he'd fallen under Cassandra's spell.

"You must stop this torture, General Raikes! If you do not wish to name your tailor, tell me so this instant."

Dominic frowned at the king. "I had no intention of keeping it from you, Your Majesty." He'd just been too preoccupied with his wife. He'd completely removed her glove and now encased her small hand within his. "My tailor is no one more than a talented kitchen maid."

"Devil a bit! A slave?"

Dominic traced a finger over the rose gold ring he'd given his wife. The petals had uncurled just a bit. "She's a prisoner of war from Verdanthame. Imperial Lord Mi'cal's half-breeds possess extraordinary powers in weaving the plants that his magic has introduced to England."

The king's face brightened. "I have never been captured by that sovereignty. I hope—ah well. You must send this person to me, General."

Dominic unconsciously tightened his grasp on Cassandra's hand. Perhaps the king had misheard him. "She is a *slave*, Your Majesty." As he had been. A person with no one to care enough to pay their ransom. A person like him, without consequence— until he'd proven his worth to the elven lord. Because his mother had been nothing more than a kitchen maid, taken in war from another sovereignty. He could only guess that her incredible beauty had caused Mor'ded to bed her.

His wife gave his hand a small squeeze before going back to ignoring him.

"I still wish you to send me this slave, General."

Dominic nodded, hoping he would be doing the girl more good than harm. "As you wish."

The king finally turned back around to the performance and Dominic had no further excuse to lean forward. He settled back into his seat, missing the heat of his wife's leg against his own. He now couldn't bear being near her and unable to touch her. She had shattered his control with the confession of her love for him, and as he focused on the play he realized that in some ways it echoed the relationship he had with Cassandra. Love entwined with death and sacrifice.

Dominic slowly picked up the black silk glove that lay discarded on his wife's lap. He faced her profile, her eyes still riveted to the stage, but he felt sure she was aware of his every movement. He brought the glove to his mouth and kissed it, breathing in the scent of her skin. Never would he have thought he'd act the dandy in this way. But he took the slip of silk and put it in his inside coat pocket, so it lay against his heart.

The general hoped she would understand the gesture, for he felt... badly about kissing Aggie. The look on his wife's face when she'd witnessed it had twisted something inside of him. He could not abide bringing her pain, even in such a small way.

The rush of pleasure that swept through him when he saw the slight curl of her lips made up for the thought that he'd acted like some silly court fop. If it managed to make her happy, he felt determined to learn every gesture of romanticism with which humans displayed their affection.

The curtain fell with the end of the opening scene and Dominic stood to stretch his legs, his hand twitching to assist his wife when she started to rise to her feet. But the sudden glow from the magically created sun's rays above them would reveal his actions, and he stilled his body to indifference once again.

They milled about the box, the intermission too short to return to the antechamber for refreshments, although a liveried footman brought round a tray of wine and sweetmeats.

Halting the performance after each scene made the short play interminably drawn-out.

Sir Robert engaged the Imperial Lord in whispered conversation, leading Mor'ded to the far side of the box, both of them focused on the stage. Perhaps he sought to ease his father's fears over the magical powers of the troupe, or to incite them. Dominic could only feel glad his father's attentions were otherwise engaged.

Lady Agnes immediately jostled the king's mistress out of her way, capturing the older man's arm within her own. The king gave her a look of mingled surprise and speculation, and his wife watched the two of them with a puzzled frown.

Dominic bent over to reach Cassandra's ear. "It seems Agnes has set her sights on a nobler conquest," he murmured.

She fluttered her hands, flushed at the sight of one of them ungloved, and quickly removed the remaining silk, stuffing it in the slit of her skirt along with her fan. "She's a fool," his wife replied with enough heat in her voice to please her husband.

"You aren't satisfied that my mistress has publicly declared that our affair is over?"

"Certainly not." She shifted from one foot to another, her hands still aflutter at her sides. "Now you will only have to find another one."

He didn't need to see her glance at Mor'ded for him to understand her meaning. Without the shield of a mistress, his attentions to his wife would become suspect. But an idea had occurred to Dominic and he wished he could speak of it to her. Regretfully it would have to wait until they were alone.

His wife continued to fidget. Dominic accepted the glass of brandy handed to him by the footman and downed it in one swallow, then studied Cassandra with a frown. He had seen her so nervous only once before, when they had stood together at the altar on their wedding day. The ring on her finger had tightened into a stiff bud once more, and he wondered if his gallant gesture had completely erased her hurt over seeing him kiss Lady Agnes. Or perhaps she truly feared the loss of his mistress would set Mor'ded's sights upon her.

And with that thought flowed another. Did her feet move to some silent music in her head? Did she prepare her magic for a death dance, hoping to catch Mor'ded unawares when the lights lowered? Perhaps that's why she'd chosen to sit behind him. Dominic glanced at her waist. She wore a thin black girdle of sturdy-looking cloth. He glanced over at his father. "Do not even think it. Do you realize how many will die if you attempt such a thing?"

She followed his gaze and quickly shook her head. "No, Dominic. I wouldn't... I know you're right about..." Then she clutched her head and swayed on her feet.

It took every ounce of his self-control not to reach out and sweep her up into his arms. "What is it?"

She rubbed her temples. "I fear I have a dreadful headache."

Lady Verney, who stood near the rail of the box with a gaggle of ladies, noticed his wife's actions and approached. "Are you well, Lady Cassandra?"

"I... I don't know what's come over me. My head just started to pound like a drum."

The taller woman smiled with maternal indulgence, the feather boa wrapped about her thin neck fluttering with the sigh of her breath. "My dear, that's to be expected in your condition."

"Oh, but I'm not—"

"Now, now. I know how strong you are, but even the best of us can be weakened by the changes in one's body. You will need to take better care of yourself, my dear." And she punctuated her words with a sharp glance at Dominic.

He could only study Cassandra in bewilderment. They both knew she wasn't with child and that her first "sudden" headache had been nothing more than a charade. She felt fine but a moment ago, and other than her continued skittishness and a crease in her brow, looked exceptionally well. He called blue fire to his fingertips, ready to ease her head with his magic. But she hastily stepped away from him.

"Do not trouble yourself, my lord. I prefer to seek a more… natural remedy." She glanced between the two of them, seemingly annoyed by their concern. "It's naught but a head pain after all. I'm certain I'll be fine after I rest for a while."

"Shall I accompany you to your rooms?" said Lady Verney, again giving the general a pointed look.

But Dominic did not think his wife wanted him to escort her. Devil a bit, he suspected she had no headache at all. That it was just a ruse to escape from him. Despite his attempt to make it up to her, she must still be angry with him for kissing his mistress. His wife had revealed her love for him and it had changed everything. He must take more care of her feelings.

"No, please. I would feel worse if I thought I'd deprived anyone of the joy in seeing the rest of the play. I can manage to make it to my rooms with nary a worry."

"If you are sure—"

"Faith, Sophia, it makes me feel worse to have anyone fuss over me." And with those parting words, his wife swept up her skirts and left the box.

"Sometimes I think she is too independent for her own good," grumbled the taller woman, her final parting shot at Dominic before returning to her cluster of court ladies.

He supposed Lady Verney suggested that he take his wife to hand, but the general had little desire to do so. Despite his fear for her safety, he liked Cassandra just the way she was. Self-sufficient nature and all.

But Dominic decided that it would seem an eternity sitting through the entire performance before he could he join his wife in their rooms. Before he could prove he had no further interest in Aggie or even acquiring another mistress to replace her. That he might no longer need such a shield.

He watched Lady Verney and her bevy of court ladies continue to whisper and glance his way while they took their seats for the next scene. His wife's false headache this eve would only solidify the rumor of her pregnancy among the entire court, and he did not regret it. Indeed, he vowed to make the rumor true within a fortnight.

Dominic made it through the performance by envisioning his wife's face lit with golden fire. He had never shared his magic in that way with another woman... had never had the desire to. But he had wanted to bring her pleasure in a way she'd never experienced before. In a way no other man could give her. And judging by her tremors, he'd managed to do so with startling success.

Before his marriage, he would never have guessed the serene little woman to whom he'd been affianced would possess such a fire for passion within her.

His thoughts flew in ever-creative ways as he considered the benefits his magic could bring her. Perhaps he could endeavor to experiment tonight, assuming he could manage to make her forgive him.

His thoughts made the time pass so quickly that he started with surprise when the performance finally came to an end. It took all the general's composure to slowly rise, to exchange pleasantries with debutants and dandies, to appear serenely oblivious to his wife's absence. His father spoke with Walpole again, and Dominic felt gratitude for the way the prime minister engaged Mor'ded. Clever man. Despite Walpole's all-too-human features, he must have inherited more than his fair share of elven charm from somewhere in his family line.

Dominic had just managed to extricate himself from another boring conversation, this time purposefully heading toward the exit of the box, when one of his lieutenants stepped through the open door.

"Sir."

"What is it?" The general's men rarely bothered him with trivial matters.

"The girl has escaped, sir."

Dominic didn't need his man to specify which girl. He'd given special orders to his men regarding only one prisoner. And with those few words, the general suddenly *knew*. He knew why his wife had looked so nervous this evening. Why she'd pretended a headache and excused herself without escort. Knew who had helped Breden's half-breed escape. He quickly positioned his body between his lieutenant and Mor'ded's line of sight.

"You have dispatched men in pursuit?"

"Aye, sir."

"Then they won't get far." Dominic knew he lied. With Cassandra to aid them, they had a better-than-average chance of escaping his men, especially with the fools he'd set as guards. Or so he hoped. But he didn't want to alert the lieutenant to the fact that he knew Breden's bastard had help in her escape. "Report directly to me when you've returned her to the tower."

"Aye, sir."

The man dallied and Dominic knew his lieutenant expected him to join the pursuit. Indeed, he would have, if only to find a way to protect his wife from exposure. But although he had some faith his wife would find a way to outwit his men, he knew she wouldn't stand a chance against his father. And despite his attempt to shield the lieutenant from Mor'ded's line of sight, he could feel his father's eyes boring into his back.

"Dismissed," he snapped, no longer capable of suppressing his fury. Cassandra had acted without confiding in him, had risked herself for no reason, since he'd had every intention of rescuing the girl tonight... without alerting half the palace guards. And his father.

The lieutenant practically leaped out the door, and Dominic slowly turned. Walpole waved his hands, trying to keep Mor'ded engaged in their conversation, but his father stood facing Dominic, curiosity flickering in those cold black eyes.

The general suppressed his fury. Snapped his spine rigid and forced a calm indifference on his face while his mind spun with some way he could protect Cassandra. He could reassure his father he had the situation well in hand, that he had complete confidence in his men to return the half-breed to Firehame. But if his father sought some amusement this evening, chasing a frightened child through the streets of London would certainly appeal to him.

Dominic strode toward Mor'ded and Walpole, and the short distance seemed incredibly long... and far too short. He could think of only one way to protect Cassandra. Only one way he knew for a surety that would distract Mor'ded's attention from the missing girl.

The memory of black fire sang through his mind, made his muscles twitch with just the memory of the pain.

Father had never tested him in public before. He preferred to keep the torture private, as he kept so many of his amusements private. The elven lords preferred to foster the facade of a benevolent overlord not only among the court, but more importantly, for any visiting dignitaries from the world outside the barrier surrounding England. Dominic had to find a way to goad him into it.

He tossed his head with arrogant pride, the last few of his steps turning into a strut.

A mocking smile broke across Mor'ded's mouth. "What news did your lackey bring, champion?"

Dominic bowed to him, a short bob lacking the full sweep with which he usually honored the Imperial Lord. He sent a pointed look in Walpole's direction. "A prisoner has escaped the tower."

They held all the prisoners of war in the old tower, far from the delicate sensibilities of the court, until the inmates were either ransomed or had fully accepted their new lowly status in the world. Mor'ded had decided not to keep the girl with the other children awaiting the trials, since he didn't want the court gossiping about why he felt it necessary to surround them with a contingent of guards. Dominic had followed his father's orders without question as usual but felt relieved at the new location. It would have made it easier for him to rescue the girl. If his impulsive wife hadn't made the attempt first.

Mor'ded knew exactly to which prisoner Dominic referred. His midnight eyes sparkled with anticipation. "Perhaps I should assist in this matter."

Dominic raised a brow, his head still tilted with smug arrogance. "But why trouble yourself over something so minor? My men will track her down soon enough."

Mor'ded's face fell with disappointment.

"Is there something special about this particular prisoner that interests you?" interjected Walpole.

"Nay, of course not," replied his father.

Dominic again felt gratitude for Sir Robert's presence, for his father could not reveal the reason for his interest. And the very question that Walpole had offered made Dominic suspect the man knew more about the prisoner than he pretended. Knew about his wife's involvement. His earlier impression that Walpole might be a part of the Rebellion solidified. How priceless to consider the possibility of the king's prime minister directly involved with the Rebellion.

But the general had to put aside speculations about Walpole for the nonce, for he knew his father might excuse himself at any moment, get involved with the girl's recovery just to relieve his boredom.

How he hated the arrogance of elven boredom.

Dominic had never felt as if he looked into a mirror of his future more so than he did at this moment, as he faced his father with the sole intention of provoking the man. Mor'ded's face held the same contemptuous superiority that he felt on his own.

"I have felt a change, Father." A pure lie. If Dominic held the greater power of black magic inside of him as Ador had revealed, he'd felt not a hint of it. The general knew without doubt that he would fail to withstand the test. He ignored the whisper of the memory of pain.

Mor'ded ceased glancing at the exit of the box and focused his full attention on his son. "What are you talking about?"

"My powers. Tonight I felt as if something has grown inside of me." He took a step toward his father, every nuance of his body language taut with challenge.

"Ah, Walpole. The young pup thinks that just because he managed to impregnate his wife it makes him a man." He kept his voice low.

Sir Robert replied by taking a step backward, and Dominic's estimation of the man's intelligence reached a new height.

"Not a man. But an elven lord. Isn't that what you fear, Father? That I hold enough power to challenge an Imperial Lord himself?"

Mor'ded's face twisted. "You dare."

"Yes. Here and now." And with those words, Dominic called his magic. Not the orange nor the red, but the insidious power of the black. The sound of the chattering court faded from his ears; the smell of mingled perfume and human body odor cleared from his nose; the sight of marble columns and painted frescoes blurred as he focused all his senses on the magic within him.

And he felt it.

A shadow of black fire. A mere suggestion of the flame.

But he could not call it forth.

Still, it was enough. Enough for Mor'ded to forget his surroundings, for his fear to launch an attack at his son in front of the entire court.

Dominic staggered backward from the force of the black blaze. He felt his clothes melt into his skin, his skin crackle and flake to the floor. Then the force of it slowed, as if his father sought to prolong the torture. To punish Dominic for arrogantly challenging him in public. Black flame lazily curled into his lungs, sizzled along his nerves, bringing an agony that surpassed any pain he might have experienced before.

Blackness covered his eyes and Dominic forced himself not to claw at them as they began to burn. To fry like an egg in a pan, the outer edges bubbling, the yolk hardening as the heat reached the core.

Ah, faith, it went on for a very long time.

Twice he felt himself almost collapse. But the thought of Cassandra kept him upright. His feelings for his wife could not make him strong enough to defeat his father, but this time he did not fall to his knees.

"Stop it, man," cried a voice. Walpole? Dominic couldn't be sure, for the flame crackled in his ears and muted all sound.

"Don't you see he hasn't the power to defend himself? You're killing him!"

And like a candle snuffed by a breeze, the burning stopped. Dominic tried to stand upright. He had hunched over from the pain. But his muscles screamed in protest, and he gritted his teeth as he straightened his back. He could not stop the tremors that racked him, the harsh gasp of his breath in the silence. He blinked his eyes as his sight returned, although they still throbbed in time to the memory of pain that still sang through his body.

Mor'ded gave him a look of triumph mingled with disgust as he pushed past his son and out of the box. A collective gasp followed his departure, and Dominic became aware of the court staring at him with open mouths. Indeed, even the lesser nobles in the seats below had turned to stare upward at the king's box, quizzing glasses held up to shocked eyes.

Walpole strode forward, grasped his arm. But his skin felt so sensitive he shook off the touch with a grunt of misery.

"Let me help you, man," he murmured in Dominic's ear.

"Get away from me." Ah, his voice croaked from his throat, the smooth elven richness of it burned away by fire. "I am used to this."

Another gasp went round the box and Dominic looked up in fury, straggles of dull white hair creating a curtain over his face. He would not suffer the court's contempt. Not when his every nerve felt seared with heightened awareness.

But the eyes he met did not hold the indifference he'd expected. Shocked horror, yes. And pity. Mingled with an anger that, oddly enough, he did not feel directed toward him. But toward his father. Yet they could not have seen the burning of his skin, the conflagration of his very bones, for the fire had blazed only in his own mind. Perhaps they had seen the black magic as it had enveloped him and guessed at what had happened.

Dominic did not care. He only hoped the drain on his father's power from the assault would be enough to keep him from pursuing the escaped child and Cassandra. Or that he had already bought them enough time to gain freedom.

He thought to take a step, the exit door of the box seeming ridiculously far away, but the moment his clothing slid against his skin a grunt of agony escaped his parched throat. Walpole made a strangled sound and again reached out to steady him, but Dominic ignored the gesture. He curled his hands into fists. Called forth every ounce of his elven blood to combat his human weakness. And strode forward, the silence in the theater near-deafening in the complete absence of sound.

And made his way toward Ador's tower, to lick his wounds as he always did after a trial.

The dragon turned his head when Dominic entered his domain, those red eyes narrowing with something akin to the human pity he'd seen on the court's faces below.

"Don't," he croaked. "I will not stand for any more."

Ador blinked, then gave a mighty yawn, the force of it stirring Dominic's hair against his cheeks, creating a new type of pain for him to disseminate.

"Did she escape?" whispered the general.

"I do not know."

Dominic sighed, slowly began to peel off his clothing, until he finally stood in nothing but his breeches. Better. But he wished the wind would stop blowing, for even that gentle breeze felt like small knives etching his skin.

He felt like railing against the dragon, whose knowledge always seemed sketchy at best. But tremors of fatigue still shook him, and only the thought of his wife's danger kept him on his feet. Ador could fly faster than the swiftest horse, could scent better than the huntsman's most skilled hound. He would not beg the dragon for his own life, but for Cassandra's... "Help me save her."

"I cannot."

"Or will not."

The dragon swished his tail, scale screeching on stone. "They are one and the same to me, bastard. Only an elven of great power can wield the scepter, and the scepter cannot move directly against him, for it is bound by the wielder's desires. I am already walking a fine line, revealing so much to you."

Dominic clenched his fists in frustration. "I must break the bond between this scepter and my magic."

"You cannot."

"Then do it for me."

If the dragon had a brow, it would have risen high above his pointed head. "Your estimation of my abilities flatters me. But have I not made it clear I am but a tool of the scepter? And the relic has motives beyond the comprehension of man, dragon, or elvenkind. But I do know it will not reveal your magic until you have enough power to destroy the mad elf."

"By then it may be too late."

"Then we will have failed. And it will be long and long before we see our homeland again." Ador sighed, gazing up at the starry sky, those brilliant eyes dulling to a red sheen, as if he saw a different sky above him, dreamed of a different world that held the comfort of home.

Dominic hung his head. Ah, faith, he felt tired unto death. One last tremor shook him, the memory of pain fading to nothing more than a dull ache. He gathered up his clothes and for the first time in his life, did not stay until his mind had healed from one of Mor'ded's trials. Instead he returned to his apartments to wait for the return of his wife. Or the summons from his men that they had captured her… or that his father had killed her.

And then he would make sure Mor'ded destroyed him.

Fourteen

LADY CASSANDRA LEANED LOW OVER THE NECK OF HER horse; her eyes squinted against the force of the wind, hooves pounding a staccato rhythm beneath her. Only a sliver of moon shone tonight, the pockets of the elven lord's fire across the countryside their only light. They had left the road far behind them, and Cass prayed that none of their mounts stumbled from a hidden hole. Thomas rode to her left, the child and her mother on his other side, and Cass sneaked a glance behind them.

Breden's half-breed, Cecily, had refused to leave without her mother, and since the girl looked younger than Cassandra had expected, they'd taken the older woman along with them without a fuss. But the combined weight of mother and daughter had slowed their horse, and the guards had caught up to them on the outskirts of London.

And they were gaining on them.

She'd felt grateful that the bumbling guards assigned to watch the girl had allowed them to free her without Cassandra's having to kill any of them. But despite their lack of skill, they had managed to rally quickly in pursuit.

A shot rang out behind them and Cass pressed her body even lower in the saddle. She glanced across at Thomas, whose face had hardened with grim determination. He must have felt her gaze and met her eyes, a curious mixture of fear and glee sparkling within the gray.

"We cannot outrun them," shouted Cass.

He nodded, hair streaked like a golden banner behind him. "I will stop and engage them, give you time to lose them in the forest ahead."

Cassandra didn't think it a likely plan, one man against so many, nor would she allow him to stand alone. But she didn't get the chance to respond to his suggestion, for the girl's mother, Eleanor, shouted her own response first.

"No!"

The look of surprise on Thomas's face nearly made Cass grin, despite the peril of their situation. For she'd noticed the adoring gaze Eleanor had bestowed on Thomas the moment he'd entered their cell and announced he was there to rescue them.

Cecily sat within the shelter of her mother's arms in the front of the saddle and had to turn her head back to stare up at her mother. Without the silver-white hair of the elven, the girl didn't appear to have inherited so much of her father's gifts, until one noticed her eyes. Like the Imperial Lord of the blue scepter, they glittered an inhuman crystal blue, large and wondrous in such a tiny face.

Cecily leaned over a bit farther to look around her

mother's body at their pursuers, and Cass felt grateful that the intensity of those crystalline eyes hadn't been directed at her.

Eleanor's arms tightened even more firmly about her daughter. The child then lifted her hands up to the sky, her fingers curling as if she beseeched some pet to come to her. It seemed as if the very air shifted, a sharp tang scenting the sudden breeze.

Within the shelter of the tower, the girl's sky magic might not have been useful, but here in the open...

Cass murmured soothing words to her horse. "Easy, boy. It will be just a bit of noise, a bit of rain."

She glanced behind her again. Fie, but she spoke falsely. Gray clouds gathered above their pursuers, following them as swiftly as any steed. Thunder rumbled and lightning flashed with blinding brilliance. Although they rode at the edge of the cloud, their own horses still shied at the noise, and they caught the backlash of the rain that the skies released.

Although it looked more as if a bucket had been dumped on their pursuers, a flood of water that washed their horses' legs from under them sent them twirling in circles of water. Men fell from their mounts, their cries muffled by the deluge. Lightning hit the very ground among them, outlining quaking bodies with a glow before they collapsed into the puddles that had already started to combine into one shallow lake.

Lady Cassandra turned back around, gritting her teeth against the pellets of rain that struck like a flail on her face. She did not look at the child or at Thomas. She'd hoped they would accomplish their task without a loss of life. She prayed for the souls of the general's men as they left them far behind.

Thomas called a halt just within the forest, beneath a stand of oak, the heavy canopy of their leaves protecting them from the rainstorm the child had created. Cass leaned over and patted the neck of her lathered horse while Thomas had a whispered conversation with the girl's mother.

Cass glanced at the shivering girl. Cecily did indeed possess astonishing power. The descendants of Dewhame's ruler could alter water in small ways, but only Breden could call a storm. The girl surely would have been chosen, would have perished in an agonizing death by fire by Mor'ded's hand or... what? Did Breden drown his powerful offspring? Cassandra felt a sudden rush of *rightness* in rescuing Cecily, and thanked God for it.

Thomas walked his horse over to hers.

"How is she?" asked Cass, nodding at Cecily, who had collapsed within her mother's arms.

"She's just drained from the use of her magic. Eleanor is strong and can take care of the girl." His gray eyes appeared as dark as Dominic's in the dim light, but Cass thought she detected a glimmer of warmth as he spoke of the girl's mother. And indeed, Eleanor was remarkably beautiful.

"Thank you, Cass," murmured Thomas with feeling, and she noticed that the heat of his breath frosted the chill air with his words.

"Whatever for?"

"If it hadn't been for you, I wouldn't have found them. How did you know?"

Lady Cassandra shrugged. "An advantage to knowing the son, I suppose. I didn't think Mor'ded would risk keeping Cecily with the other children. He wouldn't risk exposing his charade."

"Clever, yes. But why did he surround them with such inept guards?"

Cass suspected Dominic had had a hand in that. Had he hoped the Rebellion would attempt to free the child? He'd felt so guilty for bringing the existence of Cecily to Mor'ded's notice.

Raindrops peppered the canopy above them, smacked Cass's head like dollops of melted ice, plunked against the ground in spreading puddles. Thomas reached over and took her hand, the warmth of it enveloping hers even through the cloth of his heavy gloves. "Come with us."

"I cannot. Even if I wanted to."

"You truly love the bastard, then?" Thomas shook his head, his golden hair plastered to his skull in a dark cap. "He will be the death of you."

Cass shivered, and not from the cold. She nodded at mother and child. "Can you hide them?"

"I'm skilled at stealth and disguise, you know." He gave her that rakish grin of his. "Your efforts tonight will not be in vain, I assure you. I will keep them safe."

Cassandra nodded.

"Lord Althorp?" interrupted the girl's mother. "We must get Cecily to shelter. She cannot withstand the cold in her weakened state."

Thomas quickly dropped Cass's hand and dug in his pouch, pulled forth a blanket and led his horse back over to theirs, gently wrapping the damp wool over the two. His strong hands lingered on Eleanor's thin shoulders, giving her a gentle squeeze of reassurance.

"I must return before I'm missed," said Cassandra, feeling suddenly uncomfortable by Thomas's attentions to Cecily's mother. He had been her friend and admirer for such a long time.

Viscount Althorp tore his gaze from Eleanor's and frowned at Cass, as if he'd forgotten her presence. "Are you sure you won't come with us?"

She felt Eleanor's gaze upon her. "Very sure. Farewell, Father Thomas." His teeth flashed white in the darkness. "I hope... I hope that one day we can meet again."

And she turned her horse around as he led the others deeper into the forest, knowing she'd never see him again. He would have to hide deep to keep them safe. New identities. A new life. Until the Rebellion had need of the child's gifts.

As Lady Cassandra made her way back to London, giving the newly formed lake a wide berth, she wondered if a half-breed's magic could ever be strong enough to stand against an Imperial Lord's. Once the Rebellion spread the word about the true fate of a chosen one, the people of England would fight to hide their children from the trials. Like this eve, many more men would die in their efforts to keep them safe.

Assuming the people would believe that the children weren't sent to Elfhame. It would be hard for many, who led such difficult lives, to give up the dream of a better life for their children.

And would the Rebellion save the children to challenge the elven lords, and lose their lives anyway when they failed?

Cass couldn't be sure. She only knew she could not stand by and let any child be sent to certain doom.

She avoided the streets when she entered the city, using what elven gifts she had to make her passage as silent as possible through mews and alleyways. She came upon the palace through the forest that sheltered the elven garden where she'd professed her love for Dominic, the faint sound of the musical flowers almost bringing tears to her eyes.

To love among such misery only made it feel all the sweeter.

She left her horse with May's smitten stable boy, the yawning lad asking no questions about Lady Cassandra's wet and bedraggled appearance. The entire palace seemed to sleep, for she managed to make it to her apartments unseen. She had concocted a story about tending to a sick friend at her old school to explain her absence in the dead of night, but fortunately she didn't have to use it.

Her shoes still squelched as she entered her silent bedroom, and she quickly removed them, setting them quietly down by the door. The curtains around the bed had been drawn and only a soft glow from the fireplace lit the room. She cocked her head, listening for the sound of her husband's deep breathing. Cass had left him a message that she would explain her absence when she returned. She would tell him the truth, and despite his ridiculous notions about her safety, she felt sure he would understand why she'd had to help Thomas.

She peeled off her wet stockings, managed to struggle out of the sodden dress and bodice, and had just started on the ties of her stays when she saw him.

He sat in a shadowed corner of the room, and at first she could see only the glimmer of his crystal eyes.

"Dominic?"

He did not answer. She slowly made her way across the room to him, almost afraid to approach his still form. He must be more angry with her than she had supposed. She started to babble.

"I *had* to help Thomas save her. Breden's half-breed child. I... I could not let her face the trials. I know I've probably worried you, but I knew how guilty you felt about telling your father about the girl and so I thought you would forgive me—"

"Are you hurt?"

His voice sounded odd, the smooth elven richness of it changed to a gravelly whisper. She had reached the front of the chair, her damp petticoats brushing against his knees. He wore nothing but his breeches, his skin pale in the dim light.

"No. Just wet. Cecily, the half-breed, called down a storm on our pursuers and we caught the edge of it. But it allowed us to escape them, for Thomas to take them to safety—Dear Heavenly Father. Dominic, what's wrong with you?"

For her eyes had adjusted enough to see that his skin lacked its usual luster, that his face had seams of lines across his forehead, along the sides of his full lips. She reached out and laid her fingers on his arm, and he winced, pulling away from her.

As if her very touch brought him pain. Then he leaned forward, every muscle in his body tense with sudden anger.

"I had planned on freeing her tonight, *after* the play," he growled. "With enough skill that no one would have suspected her absence until the morrow. When it would be too late to launch a successful pursuit. If you had but confided in me, I could have told you."

Cass tried to keep the sullenness from her voice. "You wouldn't have allowed me to help."

"No. Unlike your Thomas, I have a concern for your safety."

Would he never accept her competence in taking care of herself? "Thomas has faith and confidence in my abilities."

"Do not say that man's name again." His anger abruptly died and he collapsed back into the chair with a groan.

Cassandra fell to her knees. "Dominic, please tell me what's wrong with you. I see no sign of hurt, and yet..."

"Foolish woman," he whispered, as if his voice could no longer retain its usual timbre. "Did you not think that my father might come after you?"

"We had thought to take her in stealth but it did not go as smoothly as we had planned." Fie, she hated to admit that.

"It went better than you know."

He sounded so weak, as if he'd just returned from a battlefield. Had he been with the men who had pursued them? Had Cecily's spell caught him unawares? Cass did not understand, but instead of asking more questions she waited for his reply, a dreadful feeling twisting her belly.

"Father saw my lieutenant when he brought me news of the girl's escape. I could not keep it from him, nor could I ride after you, for Father would have joined the hunt. Fortunately *your* Sir Robert stood with us—"

She gasped.

"Ah yes. He's part of this Rebellion of yours, is he not? A clever man to have on your side, I wager. He questioned the importance of the girl, and of course, my father could not admit to it. So it gave me the chance…"

His voice faded, as if parched beyond speech. The feeling that had grown inside of Cass now solidified into a vague sort of terror. She rose on wooden legs, fetched a glass of water, and returned to hand it to him.

His hand shook as he brought it to his lips. She could not bear to see him so weakened, and collapsed at his feet again.

The water appeared to help, and as Dominic set the glass down on the delicate mahogany table at his side, his posture straightened. "I could think of no other way to distract him. I told him I felt the black magic within me, goaded him to test me in front of the entire court. And it worked."

Cass dropped her face into her hands. He'd made his father torture him with magic. For her sake. Dear Lord, how could she live with this? She had never had anyone make such a sacrifice for her, would never have expected it. She hadn't realized the way love could entangle lives. She had a greater responsibility for him now than she ever did for the Rebellion.

She lifted her head, met his eyes. "To say I'm sorry cannot erase your pain. And I cannot ask for your forgiveness when you have suffered so greatly. All I can do is promise that I shall never act without your knowledge again."

He grunted, leaned forward and clutched her shoulders, dragging her face up to his. "That is enough," he whispered. "Damn, it is enough that you have returned to me unharmed."

And then she could no longer stop the flow of her tears. But at least they were silent ones, running down her cheeks with nary a sob. He kissed her then, so tenderly it made her tears flow the faster, for surely just the touch of her lips caused him more pain.

"It has been long and long since anyone has shed a tear for me," he said as he pulled his mouth away from hers. "Father's black fire has an uncanny knack for lingering inside of me for a time, making me sensitive to the slightest touch. But it will fade."

"Is there naught that I can do?"

His lip twitched. "Get out of those wet underclothes and join me in bed. It will help if I'm nude atop the covers. Can you manage to lie beside me without touching me?"

Cass sniffed. "You are entirely too arrogant in regard to your beauty."

"Will it help to know that it will be torture for me not to touch you as well?"

Lady Cassandra rose to her feet and considered. He looked a bit better already, the hint of a smile lingering on his mouth. "Yes, my love. It does."

When they finally settled beside each other on the bed, Cass could not help admiring the lean sight of his body. "Does your hair hurt?"

"It wouldn't surprise me if it did; but no, I think not."

She wrapped her fingers in the long length of it. It lacked its usual silver sheen but still felt like silk within her palm.

"I told you," he murmured smugly.

Cass sighed and brought the locks to her cheek, breathing in the faint spicy scent. No, she could not help but touch him.

"My magic is still not strong enough to defeat my father. Despite Ador's words, I fear it may never be."

"God will grant you the strength when you have most need of it."

She felt his body stiffen in doubt, but he did not shush her when she began to pray. Indeed, he drifted off to a peaceful sleep on the sound of her words.

❧

Cassandra felt as if she'd barely closed her eyes when the stench brought her awake. Dawn light filtered into the room, highlighting the planes of Dominic's body, making his skin shimmer. She glanced at his hair still tangled about her fingers and breathed a sigh of relief when she saw it had regained its silver luster.

And then she coughed.

Cass rose as quietly as she could and followed the smell, staring out her window with disbelieving eyes. A ribbon of blackness stretched from the palace through the city almost as straight as a road, nothing but rubble in its path, the far end of it flickering with red fire, a cloud of black smoke hanging above it.

She felt Dominic join her, heard him curse, but could not tear her eyes away from the devastation.

"What has happened?" she breathed.

"My guess is that Father regained the full strength of his powers this morning. And that your Thomas has managed to get Breden's half-breed out of Firehame. Mor'ded hasn't had a tantrum like this for many years, and never through the heart of London. The nobles will be annoyed by the loss of their fine mansions." He turned and began to pull clean clothing out of the wardrobe.

"What are you doing?"

"I must stop the fire before it does any more damage."

Cass quickly retrieved her own clothing. Black. Again. Yet she could think of no better color to wear in soot. "How?"

"With fire, of course. I will start a blaze to combat the one still burning—what do you think you're doing?"

"Coming with you."

He stilled for a moment, those fathomless midnight eyes staring into her own. "This is not your fault."

She did not agree but knew the futility of arguing with him. "So many people will be hurt, Dominic. I must help them if I can."

He pulled on the coat of his red uniform, secured a black cloak about his broad shoulders. "Do not slow me down."

Cassandra nodded, snatching a plain woolen mantle, struggling into it while following on her husband's heels. She pulled the hood over her head as they made their way through the eerily silent palace, and stayed beneath that covering while Dominic gathered up a troop of his men, gave orders to many others. She rode her black stallion, who had become hers by the simple fact that he allowed no other to approach him.

They rode hard through the streets of London, on parallel roads untouched by the fire, until they reached the end of the blaze. Dominic guided them directly in its path, behind several buildings that the fire had not yet reached. He ordered his men to clear the buildings, but most people had already fled, except for a lame old man and his grandson who had refused to leave his side.

At first the pair stared at Dominic with cold hatred, and Cass suspected they thought he was Mor'ded, but when they caught sight of Cass and studied her husband's uniform and face, their expressions changed, and they waited and watched with the rest of the general's men.

Dominic seemed to struggle to call his power, perhaps still not fully recovered from last night's ordeal, and Cass sidled her horse up to his, reached out to touch his arm. He glanced at her but a moment, his eyes shimmering with determination, then held up his hands. Gray flame burst from his palms, crawling over the buildings before them, smothering the red fire from the top down. But the red slid beneath his magic, igniting the buildings, smoke pouring through open windows.

The heat of the flames burned Cass's cheeks and robbed her of breath.

Then Dominic cursed and slammed down both his arms; a gray shimmer flashed before them, and the red fire snuffed out.

He gave a satisfied toss of his head and turned his mount.

"Where are we going?" asked Cass, blinking tears from her eyes, the smoke still shrouding the street.

The general frowned at her. "Back to the palace."

"But... but what of the people?"

"I have dispatched men to assist where they can, to quell any ensuing riots. The healers will see to the injured."

Cass prayed for patience. She must remember that he'd walled off his heart a long time ago, and even now he'd opened only a part of it to her. And she might be asking more of his power than he possessed. "But the city healers have but a whisper of the blue fire that you can call. Did the summoning of the gray flame exhaust you, then?"

"Of course not."

Ah, how she loved his arrogance. "Then we must do what we can. Even if we save only one life, it is worth the cost."

Without another word, the general turned his mount in the direction of the black wreckage, ordered his men to find and bring the injured to him. He dismounted near the edge of the burned street, sat upon an old planter as if it were a throne. Within moments, his men started bringing him the injured. Cass stayed by his side, made sure he did indeed have the power to use the blue flame without draining himself completely. He became absorbed in the healing as his soldiers brought one after another person to him.

After barely an hour, Cass felt near tears. So much suffering... and all of it her fault. She had to do something, anything to atone for what she'd done.

"Dominic," she murmured. "I'm going to help the men find more survivors."

He looked at her with dazed eyes, his face composed despite the suffering he witnessed. Despite the magic he was expending. Cass held her breath. She had promised to tell him her intentions, but she could not stop from doing what her heart bade her to. She didn't know if he had understood that.

Dominic nodded and turned back to his task, and Cass could breathe again. Her husband did indeed accept that she wouldn't be a normal wife. He would not deny her freedom in fear for her safety. With the exception of her challenging Mor'ded, he seemed to think she could take care of herself. Or at least, that's what his agreement proved to her.

Lady Cassandra leaned over and kissed her husband's cheek, much to the astonishment of several of his men, and then leaped onto her stallion's back.

And quickly joined the general's troops in the hunt for more survivors.

The buildings along the fire's path had suffered from the strength of the blaze, parts of them collapsing, especially the older structures. Her stallion picked his way through the rubble, suddenly perking up his ears in the direction of an old workhouse. It took a few moments for Cass to hear the cries as well.

She dismounted and gingerly made her way through the fallen stone and mortar, entered the

collapsed building by ducking under fallen beams.
"Where are you?" she shouted.

A faint response came from the left. Cass crawled
through the wreckage, heading toward the sound,
hoping that the way ahead wasn't completely blocked.
She coughed again and again from the smoke and
black dust, and the half-buried people continued to
call out hopefully toward that sound.

Cass was brought up short by a tower of rubble with
no way around it. For a moment she could hear nothing
but the pounding of her heart. She focused on that
rhythm, using it to build a dance. But she hadn't been
taught one that could make her scale small mountains.

So she would have to improvise. She took the
speed and power of a death dance, the strength of a
love dance, and combined them into a new pattern
that allowed her to spin and twist her way up the
wreckage, through the small crevice that brought her
face-to-face with four small children.

Their faces were so layered with soot that the
whites of their eyes stood out in startling contrast.

"Bugger me, it's a lady."

Cassandra smiled at the boy. "Indeed, but I shall
need the help of a man to get us all out. May I depend
upon it?"

Green eyes widened, and he quickly nodded.

"What's your name, sir?"

"Henry, at yer service, me lady." He pointed at the
ground beside him, explaining why he hadn't already
rescued the others by himself. "This one here's too
heavy ta carry, and I couldna jest leave her."

She glanced down in surprise at a black, unmoving

bundle. Without the whites of her eyes, Cass hadn't seen her. She picked up the child, who despite her size, didn't weigh as much as she should.

"Now then, Henry. Please take the hands of the other children and lead them after me. It will be easier going down than up, but we must take care not to jostle anything and to go as quickly as we can." She stepped out of the dark crevice, squinting at the comparative brightness of day shrouded by black smoke. "Step where I step, do you understand?"

All the children nodded warily. Cass descended the mountain of rubble, the dance still thrumming through her blood, and managed only one misstep. The blackened beam gave way beneath her and she slid, holding the girl up as high as she could, praying they wouldn't slide all the way to the bottom. But another beam brought them up short; the pile shivered in response for a moment, then settled again.

"That was a close one, Henry," she called behind her.

"We'll be more careful, me lady."

And indeed, they were. Without further mishap they reached the bottom, snaked their way through the rest of the collapsed building. To Cassandra's relief, the stallion stood waiting for them, nickering at the sight of her. She had feared he might be stolen while she was inside, but apparently no thief dared to approach the devil of a horse.

The rest of the children followed the horse, giving him a wide berth, while Cass carried the unconscious girl with her in the saddle. When she returned to where she'd left Dominic, her brown eyes widened with surprise. Tents had been erected in the bare area, pallets beneath them, and now several healers, distinguishable by their blue robes, mingled alongside the general's men.

Cass awkwardly dismounted, the girl now heavier than she had been at first, and approached the largest tent. Word had spread quickly for a line of people awaited the healing blue fire of her husband's magic.

A stout woman with a blackened apron and a motherly smile herded the rest of the children over to a steaming pot above an open fire, although Henry refused to be ambushed and stuck by Cassandra's side, his eyes fixed on the girl within her arms.

A healer with a soldier escorting him appeared at her side, lifted the eyelids of the girl. "You should take her to the general's tent." He nodded his head at the line. "This isn't something my powers can heal."

Henry rubbed stubbornly at his eyes.

"She will be fine," Cass assured him, glancing down at the boy.

The soldier standing next to the healer gasped. "Lady Cassandra?"

He looked so astonished that she felt sure she must look a sight. "Yes?"

"Please follow me." The soldier gently but firmly grasped her arm, as if afraid she would disappear, and tugged her toward the large tent. The healer stared after them with an open mouth. The soldier took the girl from her arms and then nodded for her to enter first, and Cass sighed, knowing she deserved whatever scolding Dominic would give her. But she hadn't realized she'd been gone so long—it felt but a few moments since she'd heard those first cries.

But he gave her only one long look and turned his attention to the soldier. "Put her on the table."

"Aye, sir."

Dominic held his hands over the child while Henry shuffled from one foot to another, his green eyes widening as the general's hands began to glow. Blue fire bathed the girl, and Cass watched in admiration as the child's eyes blinked slowly open.

Dominic collapsed onto a stool. "Take her back outside to the other healer. She needs a splint on her right leg that time will heal. I must conserve my magic."

"Aye, sir."

"You." And he focused his eyes on Cass. "Take the boy to get some food. Then return to me. I have need of you here."

He would not berate her, then. Just remind her of her duty to her husband. He looked tired beyond endurance. "Have you eaten?"

He frowned. "I can't remember."

"Faith, it is past noon." She spun around, almost barging into the soldier, who stared at her with widened eyes. "Why are you still standing here? You heard the general. Come along, Henry." And she snatched up the boy's hand, dragging him in her wake.

Whispers followed her as she made her way through the makeshift camp but she paid them nary a mind. Her husband needed her. She took him a bowl of soup and loaf of bread, watched until he'd eaten it all. "Do you feel better?"

"Yes. Send in the next one."

And that was how it went for the rest of the day, Dominic healing with blue fire while Cass fed him when his strength seemed to falter, until dusk shadowed the corners of their tent.

"Enough," she finally announced, sending the few remaining injured to the other healers. "You cannot do more without risking harm to yourself."

"You are one to talk."

Cass frowned, hands on hips. "Dominic, you look dreadful."

"Look in a mirror, my dear. I wager I look better than you."

"I took a tumble; that's all."

"Your face is black with soot."

Cassandra's hands flew up to her cheeks, but since her gloves had already been blackened beyond repair, she could not wipe her face clean. She glanced down at her torn gown and grimaced, knowing the back of her skirts looked far worse from her slide down the rubble. But saving those children had been worth it. It had helped her with the guilt she felt at causing this entire fiasco. If she had just spoken with Dominic first, he wouldn't have challenged his father. And Mor'ded wouldn't have lost his temper and flamed a ribbon of black through London.

"I suppose I do look a sight. But I saved five children, Dominic. Although I should say four, since you are responsible for the recovery of the girl."

He raised one silver brow.

"It is worth a bit of soot, don't you think?"

He moved so quickly with that elven speed and grace of his that Cassandra barely blinked before she found herself in his arms.

Shadows flickered across his face, highlighting his high cheekbones, his square jaw. "You have taught me to care for others again. That is worth more to me than a bedraggled wife."

Before she could take mock offense at his description of her appearance, he swept his lips down on hers, making her stomach flip, causing her to rise to her toes. Cass clutched his shoulders and he gathered her closer, his hands exploring every inch of her torn dress.

When he pulled his mouth from hers, some of her soot had transferred onto his pale skin. "It doesn't matter what you're wearing, my dear. You always look beautiful to me."

Heavens, would she ever get used to such romantic remarks from her once rigidly composed husband?

"But I suppose you want to be clean, anyway. It will probably take me all night to scrub the soot off you, so we'd best be on our way."

Cass felt her cheeks heat, imagining such a thing, but she couldn't stop the eager nod at his words.

Dominic led her from the tent and they both stopped in astonishment as the crowd in the makeshift camp suddenly broke out in cheers. Although her husband didn't betray a hint of it on his handsome face, Cass knew he must be feeling just as confused as she by the outburst.

But as they walked through the crowd toward their mounts, it became clear.

"Thank you, my lord," said the old man who'd witnessed Dominic's squelching the blaze.

Dominic did not have the chance to object to

the honorific when the boy next to him echoed the same words.

The children Cass had rescued brought her a ragged bouquet of flowers, and although she suspected they'd snatched them from someone's garden, she took them and buried her nose in the blossoms—for the first time that day smelling something other than smoke.

Henry led the children away, but not before he gave Cass and Dominic a bow worthy of the most elegant courtier.

It took them some few minutes to reach their horses as they made their way through a throng of healed people eager to praise them with kind words, and in Lady Cassandra's case, reach out just to touch her.

But finally Dominic swung her up in the saddle, his face shadowed with concern, but his lip twitching into an almost smile. "You have made the people love you."

"You are the one who healed them."

He swung onto his horse in one smooth movement. "At your bidding."

"You are not the kind of man to be forced to do anything you don't want to."

A few of his men surrounded them so he did not reply, but as they rode back to the palace, she felt his eyes upon her again and again.

Fifteen

As it had been that morning, the palace corridors and salons lay quiet and empty, so Lady Cassandra had no witnesses to her disreputable state. She winced to imagine the scathing gossip she would have supplied for the court.

Especially after Gwendolyn opened their apartment doors and saw her mistress. "My lady!" she gasped. "Ye look… famous!"

"I've always known you were a hoyden at heart," teased Cass, "despite your flamboyant taste in dress."

Gwen glanced up at the general and lowered her voice. "Ah well, I don't care for them black dresses of yers, so one less is no loss. I heard ye went into the city to help with the fire and I have warm water waiting for ye and—"

"She will not require your assistance tonight," interrupted Dominic.

"But, sir, it will take a good scrubbing to remove… Oh." Gwen turned a beet red and fled to her room.

"She is more intelligent than her years, Dominic."

He started to undo the buttons on the back of her bodice. "I told you it was a bad idea to hire servants."

Cass led him into the bedroom by the simple expedience of his nimble fingers, because he would not cease in popping out her buttons. She closed the door behind them and locked it for good measure.

Her bodice fell to the floor, followed even faster by her skirt, which had been held up only by her girdle, which somehow her husband had managed to remove without her even noticing. Before he could start on the ties of her stays, Cass stepped over to the bath, which looked half-full. "We cannot submerse ourselves. We have so much soot that we will be sitting in black soup."

"We?"

Cass lifted her chin. "Despite your elven propensity for avoiding dirt, you're rather smudged yourself."

His eyes glittered and he started to remove his soiled garments. "Then, indeed, we shall wash each other."

"I'm sure you're too tired to—I can manage the task myself."

He peeled off his breeches and fastened those dark eyes on her, proudly displaying the fact that he wasn't too tired to make love to his wife. He looked like some Roman statue with that perfectly sculpted, pale skin glowing in the candlelight. Muscles ridged his flat stomach, rounded in his shoulders and arms. The bit of soot across his cheeks and brow only made him appear more rugged.

He crossed the distance between them with but a step and to her embarrassment she felt like swooning. Within moments he had joined her undergarments to those already on the floor and had his hot skin pressed against hers. Dominic held her for a moment, then began to pull pins from her hair until its heavy weight fell about her shoulders. He easily lifted her in his arms and stood her in the tub. The water barely reached her calves, but it was *cold*.

"Close your eyes and hold your breath," he warned, then dumped a bucket of heated water over her head.

Cass sputtered in surprise, but truth be told, it felt delicious. And when he began to soap her body, she could only close her eyes in sheer ecstasy. His big hands started with her hair, massaging her scalp until it tingled. Gentle fingers washed the grime from her face, lingering on her lips before slowly sliding down her neck. He paid extra attention to her breasts, which she felt sure hadn't acquired a speck of soot, but she couldn't complain when her nipples tingled from the attention. His hands lowered to her stomach, crept around her back, as if he sought to explore every inch of her with this new slippery sensation. When he caressed her bottom she moaned, heard his soft chuckle in response, but she kept her eyes closed, delighted with this new experience.

Dominic washed her legs with long strokes, forced them apart with a gentle nudge. And then he finally slipped his big hand between her legs, the pleasure of it making her knees tremble.

"My magic has been drained near dry," he murmured. "There will be no fireworks tonight. Just me."

"That's all I need, Dominic."

He chuckled again, joined her in the tub, his hot skin warming the chill that had started to creep over her, his fingers still petting her. Her pleasure caught her by surprise, a sudden contraction that ripped through her body in wave after wave of glorious feeling.

Dominic rinsed her with another bucket of water, and she opened her eyes.

"Your turn," she said, the huskiness of her voice making it sound odd to her own ears.

He said nothing in reply, just watched her with those black glittering eyes.

Cassandra could not dump the water over his head though; she couldn't reach that high. But he took it from her and managed the task himself, his head thrown back as the liquid sluiced down his skin. She retrieved the soap from a china saucer atop a small enameled tray and worked a lather in her hands before smoothing it through his hair. The wet length of it reached the middle of his bottom and now looked more silver than blond, a beautiful unearthly color. With the remaining soap Cass followed the same path he'd taken with her, paying extra attention to his lips, the nipples on his broad chest, the feel of his muscular buttocks beneath her palms. He had fine hair on his chest, down the length of his legs, with the rest of his skin nearly as smooth as hers.

She looked her fill of every magnificent part of him.

He hadn't said a word, indeed, had barely moved, so when she cradled his shaft in her hand his sudden groan startled her from her intense concentration. Dominic reached over and picked up the remaining bucket, dousing the both of them, and then she felt his hands beneath her back and legs. The room spun briefly, she felt the mattress of the bed beneath her, then his hard length inside of her before she had a chance to realize what happened.

Soon, she no longer cared.

Her husband pleasured her with long slow strokes, until the room spun again, and she didn't know which way was up. A slow warmth spread inside of her. When he arched his back and drove deeply with uncontrolled thrusts, that warmth flared to breath-taking satisfaction.

They lay still for a time, trembling with exhaustion. Dominic finally rolled her to the middle of the bed, snuggled his face against her neck, and fell instantly asleep.

Her husband had been wrong. He'd said there wouldn't be fireworks tonight. But she'd seen the most marvelous display, all behind the lids of her eyes.

~◦~

Lady Cassandra woke with a start, sensing something amiss. She disentangled herself from her husband's arms, threw on a robe of watered silk, and walked over to the window. The distant sounds of hammers met her ears; the sight of fresh wood beams stretching upward met her eyes. She needn't have worried about returning to the damaged area of London, for it appeared the worst was over if rebuilding had already started. Then she realized that the sun hung low in the sky.

"We slept all night and half the day through," she murmured. Cass went back to the side of the bed and studied her husband for a moment, making sure he still breathed. He must have drained himself beyond exhaustion, for she'd never seen him sleep so soundly or for so long.

She tiptoed to the door and closed it softly behind her. "Gwen?" she called.

The girl popped her head around the doorway of the dining room. "Oh, my lady. I didn't want to wake ye, but it's near dinnertime and ye missed breaking yer morning fast and the noon meal…"

Cass's stomach growled loudly enough to halt the girl's words.

"Fiddle," said May, following the other girl out of the dining room with a silver tray in her arms. "Ye can see she needed the rest and if ye stop blathering, she can eat."

Gwen gave the other girl a disgruntled look but nodded.

Lady Cassandra did appreciate May's quiet manner, but she valued Gwendolyn's penchant for gossip even more. Had Mor'ded discovered that she'd helped Breden's half-breed escape? "Dinner can wait just a moment, May. What's the news about the palace?"

Gwen's hazel eyes regained their usual sparkle. "La, nothing's happening in the palace… The Imperial Lord still hasn't come out of his room and half the court's following his example." She dug into the pocket of her apron and pulled out a crumpled pile of papers, handing one to Cass. "But in the city, the dodgers are scattered on the streets like snow."

Cass scanned the cheaply printed circular. A cartoon of a soldier, his pointed ears hugely exaggerated beneath his cockade hat, knelt before a tiny woman who held a dripping heart in her hands. Beneath the drawing read the caption, *A discovery that hath shocked the cit.*

Her stomach growled again. Angrily this time. What would happen if Mor'ded saw this? Would he laugh it off or wonder if she had indeed captured Dominic's heart?

Gwen handed her another one, this time a drawing of a small woman with a torn dress and bedraggled hair, leading several children from a burning building, and this one read, *The champion's new wife.*

And another one, with the soldier's hands over a severed limb, with the next drawing showing it reattached and healed. Cass wondered if Dominic's magic could truly do such a thing.

Each successive circular proved to be more outlandish than the last.

"These are highly exaggerated," muttered Cass.

"Ah, but don't ye see?" piped Gwen. "It just shows how much the people love ye and the champion."

They'd had no choice but to help the people. But it had brought more danger to Cass than she could have imagined.

"Cook heard about what ye did in the city," said May, holding out the tray as her own offering. "She made all the champion's favorites but didn't know yers, and said she hopes she guessed rightly."

From the delicious aromas coming from the covered dishes, Cass didn't doubt Cook's decisions.

"There's lots of chocolate," whispered Gwen with reverence.

That did it. Cassandra could no longer ignore the demands of her stomach. She curled the papers in her hand and took the tray from May, who allowed her mistress to carry it without protest, used to keeping out of Dominic's notice.

"If you see any more of these circulars," whispered Cass as Gwen opened the door to her bedroom, "please burn them."

The servant gave her a puzzled look, but apparently she'd grown used to her mistress's odd demands for she quickly nodded and hushed May to silence when the other girl's mouth opened.

The door snicked shut behind Lady Cassandra, and she set the tray and circulars next to the bed.

Dominic sat up with a start, raking the hair away from his face.

"I'm sorry. I didn't mean to wake you."

He wiped a hand over his stubbled jaw. "Good morning."

"Um, that would be evening."

One silver brow rose. "I must have drained myself more than I thought—"

"No, no, do not get up." Cass put the tray on the bed, crawled in beside it. If she hadn't been so hungry she wouldn't have been able to ignore all that smooth expanse of muscled skin. Thankfully, rumpled bedding covered his lower half. "The danger is over, judging by the rebuilding that's been going on, so I don't think we're needed in the city anymore. And Gwen reports that neither the court nor Mor'ded have left their rooms, so no one will note our absence."

"My duties…" he mumbled.

"Can be put off for a day." He still needed to rest, and besides, she wanted him near. Would he ignore his duties for her? "Cook said she made your favorites," she added, uncovering some of the dishes.

He sniffed, and both their stomachs growled together.

Cass laughed and stabbed a fork into beef covered in a thick gravy, held it up to his lips. He dutifully opened and chewed with blissful intensity, washed it down with a glass of wine from the tray.

"This is my favorite dish," he said.

She waved her hand at the shiny silver. "Apparently they all are."

Dominic picked up his own fork and eagerly uncovered one plate after another, sampling from each. "What's the occasion?"

Cass kept her face smooth. "I'll tell you after we eat."

And they both fed each other from different plates, snatching their own mouthfuls in between, until Cass leaned back in pure satisfaction and waited for Dominic to finish.

Watching him eat shouldn't have given her so much pleasure, but it did. He moved with such grace that each sweep of his hand, every bunch of his muscular arms, delighted her. And Lady Cassandra felt content for the first time in her life. She wished it could last, that they could share many more quiet meals together.

He wiped his mouth with a napkin and slowly sipped his wine, his eyes studying her from head to toe. "Take off that robe."

"No." Cass gave him a smile to soften her reply.

"You've grown entirely too used to giving commands, General Raikes."

"Please take off that robe."

She laughed, a long peal of notes that made his lips twitch. When a full smile curled his mouth, Cass had to stop herself from nearly *tearing* off the silk and instead gathered her robe more tightly about her shoulders. It should not be possible that he could be any more beautiful than he already was. But his smile changed his features and lit his eyes until he near glowed. She squashed down the butterflies in her stomach and wished she could make him smile all the time.

"I can be quick," he drawled.

Her breath caught at the sultry look in his eyes. The devil couldn't be more tempting than this man. "There's… there's something I have to show you first."

Cass sat up and started putting the covers back on the dishes. She retrieved the circulars from the table and handed them to her husband. While he looked them over, she went to the door and called the servants to clear the tray and clean up their bath from the night before.

She noticed that the water had indeed turned into a black soup.

Gwen and May performed their tasks quickly, keeping their heads bent and their eyes down. Lady Cassandra sighed. She really must get Dominic used to the presence of servants; they couldn't always be sneaking about.

And wondered when she would quit thinking that they somehow had a future together. If Dominic hadn't already half convinced her, the devastation Mor'ded had released on the city fully did so. She no longer thought she might be able to accomplish an assassination, no matter if she took the elven lord by surprise. No matter how strong her faith might be. But even though she would not attempt to accomplish her task, they still had a short time together. The papers in Dominic's hands proved they could no longer keep their true relationship a secret.

And Mor'ded would be the one to assassinate her.

Dominic did not speak until the servants left the room, and even then he kept his voice so low that she had to join him in the bed again, her face close to his own.

"Where did you get these?"

"Gwen says they are all over the streets of London."

"My ears are not that big." He tossed the papers aside, caught up a locket of her hair, and twisted it around his finger.

The gentle tugging made her scalp tingle. "You are not worried that Mor'ded will see them?"

"I have thought this through, and I believe you are now safe from my father."

"What do you mean?"

"The rumors, my dear." He released her hair and ran a finger down the middle of her chest to her belly, parting the fold of her robe in the process. He traced circles around her navel, making Cass shiver. "The court believes you carry my child."

"But I'm not…" Her voice trailed off as she suddenly remembered that she hadn't brewed her herbs after they'd made love last night.

Dominic shrugged, muscles rippling from shoulder to chest. "No matter. You soon will be. I'll make sure of that."

His voice dripped with arrogance. Cassandra backed away from him to the far edge of the bed. "I still don't see what difference that will make."

"My father wants a new champion. Despite my resemblance to him, I have only the life span of an ordinary human." He rolled over onto his back, clasped his hands behind his head, silver blond hair spilling around him like some heavenly cloud. "Mor'ded will need a replacement. If he thinks you carry a child, he won't dare harm you."

Cass considered. "Not until I give birth, I suppose."

"And I will think of something else by then. Perhaps my powers will be strong enough—" He sat up in one fluid movement. "Come, let me help you get dressed."

"Why?"

"There's someone I think you should meet... while you're awake this time."

"What do you mean?"

And Dominic explained Ador's visit to the elven garden.

❧

The smell of sulfur and musky beast grew stronger the higher they climbed. Cassandra hesitated at the top of the tower stairs. She'd seen the dragon only from a distance, and even then the sight had terrified her. "Are you sure he won't mind?"

"With Ador, I'm never sure about anything," replied Dominic. "But don't worry; he won't hurt you. Despite the rumors, he prefers the taste of live-stock to people."

For obvious reasons, that didn't reassure her. But she followed her husband as he opened the door and strode out onto the tower roof. The flagstones beneath their feet had long gouges through them, which she assumed had been made from the dragon's claws. In some places the stones had cracked. Night had fallen but the fire that licked the walls of the palace made it appear to glow, and the stars seemed brighter here on this high perch, providing more than enough light for her to see the black form of the dragon.

Even curled into a ball, the beast's size over-whelmed her.

"He's asleep," she whispered. "Perhaps we shouldn't disturb him."

"He's always sleeping." Dominic held her hand and towed her closer. "Ador. I have brought my wife to meet you."

If her husband hadn't grasped her so tightly, she would have fled when the dragon opened his eyes. They appeared as large as the sun, and even brighter, with red glowing orbs split oddly enough into several sections, like a pinwheel. He blinked at her several times and then snorted.

Cassandra coughed.

"So we finally meet face-to-face," growled the dragon in a voice that reminded her of tumbling stones. "I can see how you managed to find the bastard's human heart."

"Er, thank you?"

The beast laughed, stone grating on stone. Cass

winced at the brief sight of his open maw, the size of those sharp yellow teeth. She gathered her courage. "Dominic says that you've told him he would one day have the power to defeat Mor'ded. Can you not do anything to hasten the process?"

"If he's told you that much, then you also know I'm forbidden to interfere directly with the mad elven lord. I cannot change the bastard's fate any more than I can change yours. If either of you tempts it, you will have to face the consequences." He rose then, a mountain of shining black scales and sharp edges, spreading his wings to their full length, revealing the jagged beauty of them. The gesture reminded Cass of a strutting peacock and lessened her fear. But only a bit, for the dragon was *huge*.

But still. "You are beautiful," she said.

Dominic snorted, and Ador cast him a baleful eye.

"However," said the beast, "a bit of flattery and a pretty face can always sway me."

Dominic made a choking sound this time.

"I can reveal this much, bastard's wife. The scepter is the key."

"To what?"

"Ah, now *that* you will have to find out for yourself." And he beat those glorious wings, whipping back Cass's hair and making her eyes water. Dominic stepped in front of her, sheltered her body with his own as the dragon took flight, even his tall solid body swaying with the force of the maelstrom from Ador's leap into the sky.

She watched him for a time, enjoying the shelter of her husband's arms, until the dragon blended with the black of the night.

Then she mentally shook herself and sighed. "He's rather annoying, isn't he?"

Dominic grunted. "He reveals more questions than he does answers." He loosed her slightly to look into her eyes. "But I find your choice of words fascinating. How can you find a creature who can gobble you up in one bite annoying?"

"Faith, he's not the ravening beast kind. He loves a game as much as Mor'ded, although he seems to like to play differently."

"I had hoped that once Ador met you, he would tell me a way to save you. I should have known better."

The night's breeze curled around her shoulders, played with Dominic's hair, tangling his silver locks with her dull brown ones. His arms felt so warm in contrast. Cass leaned her head on his solid chest, listened to the strong steady beat of his heart. "I forgot to take my herbs last night," she said.

"What herbs?"

"The ones that I have taken every night since our marriage to prevent pregnancy."

He stiffened then sighed, resting his chin atop her head. "I suppose I can't blame you. Are there any more secrets you'd like to confess?"

"No. That is the last." The lonely sound of a ship's horn drifted up to the tower from the Thames below. "I hope we don't have a child, Dominic. I'd rather your father kill me than give one up to him."

"Hush. I will think of something."

"And if I don't conceive, he will find out soon enough, and then what will we do?"

He moved his arms up to her shoulders and set her

from him, studying her face. "What happened to that faith of yours, Cassandra?"

"After what we saw in the city, how can you ask me such a thing?"

He brushed the backs of his knuckles across her cheek. "Because it is one of the things I admire the most about you. Your obstinate belief in this God of yours. Now that you have me half believing in him, I refuse to allow you to falter."

His words made hope spring in her heart. "Do you mean it?"

"Indeed. I prayed while I waited for you to return from freeing Breden's half-breed. I told him that if he kept you safe, I would place my trust in him."

Tears burned her eyes.

He bent his head and laid his cheek next to hers, his stubble gently scratching her face. "Besides, I know there are devils in this world. Why should I not believe in angels as well?"

❧

It felt odd the next afternoon to encounter the court on her husband's arm. Although Mor'ded had still not left his rooms, the court had apparently decided they'd had enough. They'd gathered on the west lawn for tea, enjoying an unseasonably warm autumn day.

The absence of the Imperial Lord had a marked influence on the court. Those who held a trace of elven magic usually displayed only the talents inherited through Mor'ded's line, but as Cass neared the scalloped-edged pavilions, she could see that those

who'd inherited gifts from other sovereignties now
showed off their talents as well.

Illusions of winged monkeys flew about the roofs
of the pavilions, swooping in occasionally to caper
for a courtier. At least Cass thought they were illusions, for they looked a bit transparent about the
edges. But the magic of Dreamhame paled next to
that of Stonehame, for the singing crystals adorning
several courtiers emitted a haunting melody reminis-
cent of the elven garden. The settings of the gems
had surely been crafted in Bladehame, for the silver
appeared to move like liquid about the throats and
wrists of the wearers. Eternally blooming roses grew
up the sides of the pavilions; odd trees with palms
shaped like fans brushed cool air on the courtiers,
surely from the talents of those with descendants
tracing back to Verdanthame.

Lady Cassandra tried to mentally match gifts from
the remaining sovereignties, but she felt Dominic
stiffen beside her and she tugged on his arm, stopping
him before they went any farther. He looked sublime,
of course, in a coat of chocolate velvet trimmed with
shiny gold buttons, the white lace at his sleeves and
throat a perfect foil for the white lace dress that she
wore. May had twined white silk roses in her brown
hair, making it look dark and lustrous by contrast, and
Gwen had chosen a stomacher embroidered with white
roses that boasted lace bows beneath each blossom.

The lace at her arms fluttered delicately as she
reached up to adjust his cravat. Which didn't really
need adjusting. "I am determined to enjoy my first
public appearance with my husband."

"We have often been together in public."

"Ah, but not as a true couple. Try not to let a few of the sillier nobles annoy you."

"A few?"

She laughed and felt him relax, his handsome face not quite as rigid. Cass lifted to her toes and kissed his jaw, and he moved quicker than lightning, capturing her mouth with his full lips for a few heart-stopping moments. When she managed to take a breath again, he looked entirely too pleased with himself.

She traced a finger over the tip of a pointed ear. "They aren't *really* that big."

He smiled, a dazzling display of white teeth and curved cheek. The sunshine made the silver sparkle in his hair, his skin glow a luminescent pearl, his eyes glitter with crystal fire. Cass suppressed a thrill of wicked desire, clasped his arm, and turned toward the pavilions.

The entire court stared at them in shocked silence. Even the crystals had ceased their songs.

Dominic patted her lace-gloved fingers and led her to an empty table, where Lady Cassandra sat with but a minor adjustment of her hoops and skirts. He pulled his chair about to face hers, sitting with one smooth flip of his coat skirt.

Instantly the cacophony started up again, crystals singing, monkeys flying, nobles chatting.

"You enjoyed that," muttered Cass.

"It felt highly satisfactory to finally be able to express the value I place on my wife. Their stupefied faces were but a… bonus."

A liveried footman brought them tea in porcelain so fine it appeared transparent in the sunlight. A tray

of sweetmeats was set before them: pastries drizzled
with honey, gingerbread shaped into oak leaves, tiny
cakes frosted with bows and ribbons. Truffles, fruits,
and jellies had been artfully arranged on another
platter by complementing color. Cold asparagus stood
up like a stack of bound hay in the center of pink-
fleshed shrimp arranged in a spiral.

"I don't quite know where to start," said Cass.

Dominic removed his fine leather gloves and began
to peel a shrimp, discarding the shell on the lawn and
holding it up to her mouth. "It matches the color of
your lips."

Lady Cassandra flushed and ate the offering, a
sudden rush of happiness overwhelming her, although
she knew this couldn't last. Mor'ded would emerge
from his lair, bringing fear and the threat of peril in
their midst again. But for now she tried to pretend
that this would be her life forever, being fed treats
from an attentive husband in front of a laughing court
beneath a sunny sky.

"Excuse my intrusion," said Lady Verney, "but
I must know how you fare, Cassandra. Any more
headaches?"

Cass looked up at the tall woman squinting down
at her, that thin face taut with genuine concern. It
took her a moment to remember her false headache…
and her supposed condition. "Oh no, Sophia. I am
quite well."

Her friend gave a sigh of genuine relief. "When
I heard you had accompanied your husband to see
to the welfare of the citizens affected by the fire,
I feared the stress might affect you adversely." She

shot Dominic a scathing look, apparently determined to blame him for not taking better care of Cass. As if her husband did not deserve her. It made Cass smile.

But then Lady Verney's face softened, and she inquired of Dominic, "And you, General Raikes. Are you well?"

He glanced at her with but a flick of his midnight gaze, but Cass could see he'd been caught by surprise. "Of course."

"Well then, I shall leave the two of you alone. It is truly a delight to see a couple so obviously taken with one another." And with a bob of her feather-topped coiffure, she took her leave.

And Lord Blevin immediately took her place. "I daresay, you make a fine couple, wot? I admire the cut of your coat, sir, and the way your attire complements one another."

Dominic's jaw flexed and Cass quickly spoke. "Thank you, my lord. The, um, braids in your wig are quite becoming."

"I did this in honor of the general's battle braids, although I think a multitude of them a bit more eye-catching." He preened his powdered hair, speckles of silver and white dotting his coat. "General Raikes, we are about to start a round of lawn bowls. Would you care to join us?"

Dominic's brows near met his hairline, and he didn't answer for several moments. Blevin tossed Cass a worried look, to which she responded with a weak smile.

"I would be honored," Dominic finally rasped. "But we haven't finished our tea yet."

"Oh, quite right, then. I'll leave you to it. But don't disappoint us now, General!"

Lord and Lady Somers appeared determined to take Blevin's place next to their table as soon as he walked away, but they had been stopped by one of the monkeys, who found the lady's coiffure an interesting place to squat and hunt for bugs.

"What the hell was that all about?" whispered Dominic, nodding at Blevin's departing back.

"I have no idea," replied Cassandra. Although she'd expected some of the lords and ladies to treat her with more respect once Dominic showed his true regard for her, she hadn't anticipated this change in attitude toward *him*. They always treated the general with respect, of course, but their fear kept them at a distance. "Perhaps they approve of the healing you performed for the citizens."

"They don't give a damn about anyone without a title." He broke a pastry in half, and fed part to Cass while he chewed the other, washing it down with a dose of tea. "Lawn bowls," he muttered. "I play elven war games. Not… party games."

"It is a game of skill, and I'm sure you will enjoy yourself. I shall stand on the sidelines and cheer you on—"

"I daresay," interrupted Lady Somers, who had managed to rid herself of her rider. "What fun to see the magic from other sovereignties. Although I can't say as I care for the monkeys—what say you, Lady Cassandra?"

Dominic's astounded gaze flew from his wife to this newest interloper. Cass pretended not to notice.

"Perhaps you can suggest to the magic user that they be changed to butterflies. Wouldn't that be grand for a garden party?"

"La, it would be an improvement. Although the lady in question would most likely give them feelers to tickle us with."

"She has a sense of humor, then?"

"Quite," interjected Lord Somers.

"I don't think you've been properly introduced to her yet," said his wife, giving her husband a quelling look. "I shall be happy to take you to meet her."

"We haven't quite finished our tea, but—"

"Oh, you might as well," growled Dominic. "I don't see as how we'll finish it one way or another."

Lady Cassandra rose to her feet, leaned over, and pecked Dominic on the cheek, who suddenly didn't seem as disgruntled after her affectionate gesture. She walked off with Lady Somers, leaving the two men alone, although they didn't stay at the table long. She spied them heading for the jack and bowls.

"I have always wanted to visit Dreamhame," she told Lady Somers. "I've heard that Imperial Lord Roden can cast illusions so real they can be tasted and smelled."

"I long to visit Stonehame... Have you seen Viscountess Rothermere's necklace? Oh, my dear, you must. How fortuitous, there she sits."

And so it went the entire day. Suddenly the ladies of the court found every excuse to speak with Lady Cassandra. To compliment her hair and dress and inquire as to her health. She received more advice on child rearing than she felt obliged to know, but she discovered to her surprise that she enjoyed the companionship of the other ladies. Fie, she felt as if she blossomed among the attention and glanced down at her wedding ring. She had never seen the gold petals quite so open before. Except when her husband made love to her…

He played lawn bowls exceptionally well, of course. With his elven strength and skill she'd expected him to become bored with the game, but several of the other men had magical powers to assist them and that appeared to provide him with enough of a challenge. Cass stood with several ladies of the court—Sophia firmly entrenched by her side—and admired the way his coat stretched over his shoulders when he tossed his ball. The way his breeches outlined his firm bottom when he bent over.

She near swooned when he discarded his coat and waistcoat, loosening the ties of his white linen shirt to grant him easier movement.

Sophia patted her hand in complete accord.

The sun had long set before Dominic sought her out, drawing her away from the group of ladies, Cass following more reluctantly than she would have ever dreamed.

He slung his arm about her shoulder as they headed for the palace, the flame licking the walls turning the night golden.

"You enjoyed the game, didn't you?" she asked.

He grunted.

"Oh, come now. I saw your lip twitch more than once."

When he spoke, she heard the laughter in his voice. "I thought I'd forgotten how to play…"

Within a trice he'd swept her beneath an archway of golden fire, the walls beneath the old stone warm on her back as he pressed her against it, his arms gently imprisoning her on both sides. Shadows played across the planes of his face; golden fire flickered in his hair. He kissed her then, long and slow, until her knees felt wobbly as jelly.

He pulled away and she thought she might lose herself in the dark depths of his eyes.

"First the citizens and now the court. You have made everyone care for me."

Cass widened her eyes. "On the contrary, you earned the love of the people when you offered to heal them."

"You made me do it."

He protested too much for her not to see beyond the indifferent expression on his beautiful face. "And as far as the court goes, *you* made them accept *me*. I had nothing to do with the men urging you to join in the game, but... Lady Verney mentioned something."

"Yes?"

"She said that she wished she'd known how Mor'ded made you suffer. That your true character would have been easier to understand."

"Ah, I see. You made me do that too." He smoothed back the hair from her face, dropped his hand to stroke the skin of her throat, sending tingles of pleasure clear down to Cass's toes. "But I can't say I regret it. I regret nothing from the moment I've met you, Cassandra. Not even falling in love with you."

Her heart skipped at his words. "So you have figured out what love is?"

"Indeed. I love you, my dear. Even if it leads to—"

Cass covered his lips with her fingers. "Do not say it. Let's not think of tomorrow. For today has been the most wonderful, most perfect day of my life."

"Has it?" He took a step back, spread his arms, yellow fire springing to life in his fingers. "Give me but another hour, my love." He waved his arms in one fluid movement and a wall of yellow fire ringed them in, creating a cocoon of privacy beneath the golden arch of the bridge, cutting off the coolness of the night air and surrounding her with gentle warmth.

Dominic leaned forward, placing his hands against the brick wall at her back, trapping her within the warmer heat of his arms. Gold light danced in his pale hair, playing along his strong jaw, his high cheek-bones. He glowed like an angel yet his voice tempted like the very devil. "You will now tell me that you love me too. Then I will make love to you. Right here. Right now."

Cass blinked. They stood in a bubble of fire, with brick at her back and gravel beneath her feet. "I don't think this is quite the place—"

"Ah, but I cannot wait a moment longer." He lowered his mouth to hers with a fierce possessiveness that stole her breath, her very thoughts. Her desire flared and held her trapped more surely than his arms.

His lips traced a path to her neck, making her lean her head back, her coiffure cushioning her head against the brick. Cass reached up and anchored herself by clasping his arms, taut with muscle as he braced himself over her.

"Tell me," he growled, his words shivering the skin at her neck.

"I love you."

He swept his mouth lower, over the swell of her breasts above her bodice. "Again."

"I... I..." Somehow she'd lost the ability to speak. She couldn't seem to take a proper breath within the confines of her stays. It made her head spin and her skin tingle with awareness.

He pulled away from her then, his eyes deeper than night, softer than velvet. His full lips pressed together while his sculpted jaw hardened with intensity. "Tell me, Cass. And I'll make love to you. For I'm never sure if it will be the last time and I can't seem to get my fill of you."

Her hands curled over his broad shoulders, the velvet fabric of his coat soft against her palms, the silky texture of his pale hair a tickle atop her skin. His hands clasped her waist and he swept her up against him then, his mouth but a movement from her own. She quickly wrapped her arms tightly about his neck, her toes barely touching the gravel at her feet. She didn't know how he might manage it, but she wanted him with a desperation that made her no longer care for anything but the dance of his lovemaking.

Cassandra gathered enough air into her lungs to give him what he demanded. "I love you, Dominic. I have loved no other as much as I love you."

His lips curved into a full smile, and he covered her mouth with his, demanding she open with the force of his tongue, tasting the depths of her when she complied. She felt the wall again at her back, but one of his arms cushioned her while the other gathered the lace of her skirts up to her waist. The strength that had once frightened her only made her heart thrill with rapid beats while he uncovered her legs, still holding her aloft.

"Wrap them around me."

Thank heavens the bulk of her hoops lay at her sides, for she could do naught but what he asked. Her stockings slid halfway down her calves and she felt the velvet of his coat, the firm solidity of his waist. And then his fingers, ah, they found her inner thighs and stroked her with promise.

She gasped and he broke the kiss, only to move his mouth downward, across her breasts again. Cass couldn't bear the teasing any longer. She released her hold about him, not surprised that he held her full weight without any assistance from her and with barely any effort due to the low cut of her gown, pulled her breasts out of the top of her bodice.

Dominic eagerly latched on to a nipple and she gripped his shoulders again, this time not to hold on but to enable her to arch her body upward, offering herself to his mouth with a moan of sheer delight.

His fingers had found her inner core and his touch quickly silenced her, for it took all her concentration just to continue to breathe.

Dominic held her against the wall for what could have been an eternity or mere moments, his mouth and fingers dancing over her body with intimate torture, until Cassandra shattered into a thousand pieces, her tremors of pleasure fierce and furious.

He raised his head and looked up into her face as he slowly withdrew his hand, slick with her wetness. She could only continue to gasp for breath as he reached for the buttons of his breeches.

The intensity of his gaze transfixed her, until Cass thought she could see to his very soul. But the desperation on his face frightened her. Would they never be together again? Would this be the last time they would dance as one?

He slowly leaned his lower body to hers, just as slowly eased the hard length of him inside her. Lady Cassandra shivered.

One arm continued to support her back, while the other grasped her bottom beneath the layers of her lace skirt. He pushed her against him, raising her up and down his tall body. Up and down his hot shaft. Cass wrapped her legs tighter about him, clasped her arms more firmly about his neck, until only Dominic supported her full weight.

He moved her gently against him at first, but she could feel his struggle for control in the rigidity of his muscles. She kissed his jaw, nipped at his ear, the thought that this might be their last time together filling her with a desperate urgency of her own.

Dominic responded by increasing the tempo of their dance, until that deep longing for release built to near madness inside her. His fire magic flared to new life, no longer a shimmer of golden curtain around them. Flames twisted and throbbed, climbing over their heads, swirling about Dominic's boots, occasionally bursting in sparks of glittering yellow that fell on his shoulders, on Cassandra's brown hair.

When Dominic flung back his head and groaned with his own release, a deep pleasure throbbed within her womb, spread throughout her body in the same pattern as the golden fire that surrounded them.

He held her within his arms for a very long time.

Then he finally leaned his head down and whispered in her ear, "In case this is the last time I'm able tell you, my lady, I love you."

Tears burned in her eyes as they separated from each other, Cass adjusting her mangled hoops and smoothing down the lace of her skirts. She could not speak. Her coiffure had surprisingly stayed intact, so that by the time he dispersed their cocoon of fire Cassandra felt sure she looked quite like her normal self.

Dominic escorted her from beneath the archway of the bridge, and they casually strolled across the palace grounds as if they hadn't just spent the last hour making wild passionate love to each other.

"And now," said her husband with an arrogant tilt to his head, "you can say it has been the best day of your life."

Sixteen

MOR'DED SUMMONED LADY CASSANDRA TO HIS PRIVATE chambers the very next morning.

Cass had been lazing about, reliving the garden party of the day before, determined to never forget one single golden moment of it... or the precious moments afterward.

Dominic had risen before dawn, brushing his lips across her cheek before he left to attend to his military duties.

Now the morning sun slanted across the foot of her bed, and Cass watched the dust motes dance in the light. She felt as if she glowed inside brighter than that sunbeam, brighter than any fire her husband could summon. For he'd told her he loved her. Not that he cared or felt protective, but that he truly loved her.

She'd never thought to hold such happiness in her heart.

Gwendolyn opened her bedroom door in such a rush that Cass sat up with a start, swallowing a yelp.

"Oh, my lady," panted Gwen, her cheeks flushed a bright pink. "There's a fearsome creature in the hall asking to see ye."

"Faith, Gwen, you startled me." Lady Cassandra fought to keep calm. "And keep your voice down, dear. You don't want to offend our visitor." Cass couldn't imagine what person would inspire such fear in Gwen, but they both performed her toilette in record time, and she walked through her apartments to the main entrance, Gwen right on her heels.

The girl hadn't exaggerated. When Cassandra opened the door, she did indeed face a *creature*, not a person. Crimson fire shaped a wraithlike being, with emaciated limbs and a face that constantly broke into oozing bubbles of black sludge.

"You are summoned by the Imperial Lord," said the creature, spewing flaming spittle onto the stone floor. "To his private chambers."

Cass tried to speak. Nothing articulate would come from her throat. This thing appeared more solid than anything she'd seen the courtiers produce with their meager gifts. Further proof, if she'd needed it, of the enormous power that Mor'ded could call upon.

Fortunately the creature didn't seem to need a reply. Once he'd delivered his message, he started to burn hotter, seemingly from the inside out. Both Cass and Gwen backed up, held their hands up to their faces to shield them from the wash of heat. Within seconds, the creature shriveled to black, only coarse ash and several black smudges in the flagstone to mark the spot where he'd stood.

"Mor'ded sends a fire messenger only when he's angry at someone," whispered Gwendolyn. "Oh, my lady, ye cannot go alone! We must fetch the champion."

Cass slowly closed the door, blocking off the heat that still lingered from the creature. Dominic. Faith, no. He would only die in an attempt to protect her. Despite his belief that Mor'ded wouldn't harm her because of her supposed pregnancy, Cassandra knew the time of reckoning had come. She hadn't really thought otherwise. She just hadn't expected it to be so soon.

"No, Gwen. Say nothing of this to the general. Indeed, speak of it to no one. And If I don't return... take care of my husband with the same unquestioning loyalty you've shown me."

The girl studied her with those crystal eyes that gleamed with too much knowledge of the cruelty of the world for one so young. The panic that had shown on her face since she'd announced their messenger suddenly faded. "Before ye go, please come with me." She held out her hand.

Cass stared at the small fingers in confusion. She needed music, some rhythm to focus on to gather her skills. She doubted if she'd even have a chance to use an elven death dance, with Mor'ded alert and waiting for her, but she would not easily go like a lamb to slaughter.

"My ladyship," prodded Gwen, taking Cass's hand in her own and leading her to the servants' room.

"I have to go," whispered Cass.

"In but a moment, lady." Gwendolyn opened the door, revealing their cozy room with May seated on a chair near a small window. The older girl stood, exchanged an indecipherable look with Gwen, and then went to their wardrobe and opened the bottom drawer.

Cass snapped out of her stupor. While Gwen enjoyed socializing, Cass had understood that May preferred the solitude of her own company, her fingers always twitching with the desire to weave. So she'd kept the girl supplied with cloth and ribbons, and Lady Cassandra wore the most ornate stomachers and patterned shawls of any of the ton.

The elven lord would not care that she wore a new shawl, and Cass cared only that a sturdy leather girdle encased her waist. But when May held up her arms, the words of protest died on Cass's lips. For the girl appeared to hold nothing but air, even though she held her fingers clasped together as if she displayed a length of cloth.

"May?"

The girl smiled, a proud tilt to the angle of her lips. "'Tis a mantlet."

"Indeed." Had the girl gone mad? Did she now weave cloaks in her imagination?

Gwen tugged on Cass's sleeve. "Look closely, my lady."

Cassandra squinted. "Have you managed to weave air, May? For I see nothing but that within your hands."

May shook her blonde head. "What use would a cloak of air be? Although I hope ye don't mind that I made this, my lady. Because of yer... habits, I feared ye might need some protection." She gave a pointed glance at the younger girl. "And it seems we were correct."

Cass reined in her patience. She didn't have time for this. Only the thought that the girls meant well managed to curb her tongue. "What have you done, May?"

The servant flushed. "I have woven yer dreams."

"My dreams?"

"Oh aye. And sorry I am that I took them from ye without telling."

"She couldn't have done it without me," added Gwen. "I had to find them for her, don't ye see? And their light is faint, and they float for such a short while that we had the devil of a time catching them."

May nodded enthusiastically. "They kept trying to float away while I wove them. It took all the skill I had to bind them together."

Cass could only stare at the two girls with bewilderment while they each took a pinch of air and wrapped it about her shoulders. To her astonishment, she did feel *something*, a hint of weight that felt as light as the touch of a gentle breeze.

"You wove me a cloak of my dreams?" Enthusiastic nods. "And this is supposed to protect me?"

"Oh, well, we can't be too sure of that," said Gwen.

May scowled. "Of course we can. Sometimes our dreams are all that we have to protect us—isn't that right, my lady?"

"I don't know, May. I've often relied on my faith, but never my dreams." Cass hugged her own shoulders, and a wisp of memory slipped through her mind. A dream she'd once had, of a child with Dominic's pointed ears peeking through curls of her own brown hair. "But it certainly can't hurt, and I thank you for making it for me."

Two pairs of hazel eyes welled up with tears and Cass frowned.

"My dears, I'm just going to meet with my

father-in-law, nothing more." She swallowed, trying to believe her own words. Surely Mor'ded wouldn't harm her, not when he thought she carried his new champion, not when he risked alienating the ton. But she saw the burning fire through London too vividly in her mind. He'd harmed thousands of innocents with a temper tantrum because Cecily had escaped his evil hands. Had he discovered she'd helped the girl to freedom? And what would he do to her for such a transgression?

No, she would not lie to herself. Mor'ded would not send that fire creature to her very door unless he'd found out some of her secrets. She would trust her first instinct. The time had come.

Cass suppressed a shiver of fear and smiled rather shakily at her two servants. "Remember what I said, Gwendolyn. Take care of the general."

"Aye, my lady." She placed a hand on her friend's bent head. "And stop crying, May. Have a bit of faith in your weaving."

Cass spun in a swirl of silk and left the room before her servants could see the look of doubt on her face. A cloak of dreams. What chance did such a weaving stand against the power of an elven lord? Absolutely none. But if she could surprise him with a death dance...

Her footsteps made a pattern of sound on the floor, through the long hall. She crafted a song from it, one that called to her magic, made it swirl inside of her, strengthening her muscles, bringing speed and grace to her movements.

She didn't have a prayer of succeeding.

But she prayed anyway.

She'd seen the door to Mor'ded's private chambers only from a distance, a glow of gold etched with a design that had made her curious, but not enough to venture closer. As she neared she studied the engraving—a map of England, sliced like a pie into seven sovereignties, the lines radiating from a center point somewhere within Oxford. It made her wonder why the elven lords had divided their lands in that particular pattern. Perhaps Sir Robert had some theory about it.

When she raised her hand to knock, she noticed that her fist shook. Fie, she would never have the opportunity to ask the leader of the Rebellion anything.

The door flew open and the song that flooded her veins skipped a beat in response. Her eyes met Dominic's from across the room, and for a moment she didn't recognize him. Her husband stood beside his father, reminding her again that he looked like a younger version of Mor'ded. His black eyes glittered as coldly as his father's, the expression on both men's faces near identical. Very calm, very controlled rage.

And then Dominic's mouth softened and he took a half step toward her.

Her heart fell. Why was he here? He would only die trying to save her from Mor'ded's wrath... but perhaps the Imperial Lord had summoned them both together for just such a reason. A hard knot formed in her chest. She would not allow that to happen.

Cass took in the room in one sweeping glance before she curtsied, keeping her head and body lowered until the Imperial Lord gave her permission to rise. For such a large chamber, it held very little furniture, and most of it unrecognizable as such. A few flower petals shaped like chairs, a large bird-shaped piece that might be a bed, a covered desk. Plenty of room for her to maneuver. The clear rock by the balcony doors didn't trouble her, but the plant on the adjacent wall with its enormous pink pods worried her. She remembered all too clearly the suffocating vines of the plant guarding the elven garden.

"Welcome, Daughter," said Mor'ded, only a slight sneer in his calm, clear voice. "Or should I say welcome to my would-be assassin?"

Cassandra jerked upright, her heart in her throat, her gaze flying to Dominic's face.

"Oh, don't think he has the power to help you," snapped Mor'ded. "He has proven to all the court that he is but a weak human." Then he softened his voice to its usual velvet smoothness. "*I* will decide your fate, my dear."

Lady Cassandra raised her chin and met the elven lord's eyes squarely, determined not to look at her husband again. She didn't know what Mor'ded had discovered but she would give nothing away. Especially not the existence of the Rebellion and Sir Robert Walpole's role in it. "I'm not sure what you mean, Your Most High. I thought my fate had already been decided—to give birth to your next champion."

"Don't play the innocent with me, girl. Do you think I don't know what you've been up to?"

She tried to turn the fear that flooded her limbs into strength for her dance, but it proved too much for her and shook her legs with weakness instead. "I hardly know what you mean..."

Within a blink Dominic stood next to her, his heavy hand a welcome warmth on her shoulder. But she couldn't allow him to intercede on her behalf. She knew what awaited her when she'd taken up the vow to the Rebellion, and despite her newly found love and the promise of happiness, she would face the consequences alone.

She stepped away from her husband.

"You will not play with her as you do with me," said Dominic. "Tell us what you are accusing her of."

"You reveal her treachery as you stand before me," replied Mor'ded, rolling his scepter between his pale hands. He wore a suit of such a dark emerald green that it appeared black, mirroring the color of the abyss of his eyes. The flared skirt of the coat, the lace at his neck and sleeves, did not give him the appearance of femininity in the least. Indeed, it made the man within the costume seem ferociously male by comparison.

"She has done nothing," said Dominic, and Cass could only wince at the lie.

"She has turned my son against me."

They both stilled at his words. Dominic sucked in a slow breath, but Cass knew her face couldn't maintain his calm. She could not mask her surprise. She'd expected Mor'ded to accuse her of being an assassin, of betraying him by helping Cecily escape. Of anything but accusing her of stealing his son away from him. A son he tortured.

"You are mad," said Dominic.

"Yes, well, humans call it madness because they don't understand the superiority of a higher intelligence. But I thought my son was beginning to, that his elven blood would prevail. How... disappointing that I erred in judgment."

Cassandra suddenly realized this meeting wasn't about her. Either Mor'ded knew nothing about her part in the Rebellion, or he didn't care. The elven lord saw only her husband as a threat and Cass herself as nothing but a tool to trap him.

Cass stepped back to Dominic's side.

Dominic shrugged. "I admit I've become protective of the girl. After all, she carries my child."

Cass knew her husband thought to remind Mor'ded of the reason he could not afford to harm her. But the Imperial Lord looked disappointingly unruffled.

"But she has not turned me against you," Dominic added.

"Your wife's existence is but a minor nuisance," he replied. "Indeed, I look forward to *playing* with her, as you call it. But you, on the other hand, have become more trouble than you're worth." Mor'ded pointed the triangular-shaped head of his scepter at Dominic, punctuating his words with a sharp jab in his son's direction. The odd writing inscribed on the talisman swirled to life, making Cass's head spin for a moment.

She quickly tore her gaze away from those glowing runes and clutched Dominic's arm. Did he not understand that Mor'ded threatened him and not her? Or did he not care, seeking only to protect her? She would not allow it. "My husband has done nothing to betray you."

The Imperial Lord's cold black gaze settled on her, and Cass refused to allow her fear to show. When Dominic saw Mor'ded's attention shift to her he immediately tried to shield her with his body, but Cass stepped lithely around him, the song she'd created for her dance still humming in the back of her mind.

Mor'ded slowly waved the scepter in front of him with his words, like a black snake waiting to strike, ticking off each of his son's transgressions. "He has proven that he cannot overcome the weakness of his human blood by caring for you. He challenged me in front of my own court, and instead of laughing at his weakness, the fools felt compassion for him. He used his powers to heal the drudges in the city and now they print words of praise about his kind heart. He has turned away from everything I've tried to teach him, all because of you. And as your reward, I've decided that you will watch him die."

Lady Cassandra dropped her husband's arm, tried to lunge forward, but Dominic proved to be faster than her rage for he reached out and caught her about the waist.

"You are overreacting, Father."

His voice sounded so calm that Cass felt like screaming.

Mor'ded's attention shifted to Dominic. "Perhaps. But your insistence on your wife's condition made me realize that you are now expendable. Soon I will have a new champion and this time I will make no mistakes with him. I will make sure to destroy any part of him that is human."

Cass grasped at the faint hope that Mor'ded would turn his deathly gaze back to her. She did not want to live in a world without Dominic. "It's a lie. I do not carry—"

Her husband's strong hand covered her mouth and he whispered in her ear, "Hush, my love. Do not let my death be for naught."

She wanted to tell him that she refused to live without him, but his hand held steady over her lips, and nothing but muffled cries escaped her mouth.

Mor'ded laughed, and Cass noticed he'd lowered the scepter to his side. And she remembered what Ador had told her. That the scepter was the key. But the key to what? Cassandra went still and she felt Dominic's muscles relax their hold. The scepter enhanced the elven lord's powers and, by the dragon's admittance, held some sort of awareness. And wanted to return to Elfhame. Could the scepter somehow aid them?

"You humans are a constant source of entertainment," said Mor'ded with a chuckle, his pleasure a mocking, evil thing. "Always willing to sacrifice each other in the name of love. But remember, *Romeo and Juliet* is a tragedy, my dear Cassandra." And he lifted his scepter, pointed it at Dominic. A black haze formed around the triangular-shaped head, then slowly crept through the air toward Dominic.

"Leave my wife out of this, Father. She is no threat to you."

"You are hardly in a position to make demands." Mor'ded heaved an overly dramatic sigh. "But at least you no longer beg and cry for the human pets. I managed to break you of that habit, at least."

Black sludge reached the toes of Dominic's boots. The song of a death dance still vibrated through Cass's body.

Mor'ded shifted his weight to one leg, a negligent stance that belied his eagerness to see his son tortured to death. But Cass heard it in his words.

"We've known this day would come, haven't we, Son? You hold the command of my army, and I was willing to allow that. But even though your magic is still weak, you gained the support of the court and the people of London. The girl was but a catalyst, for I knew you would one day seek more power to try to defeat me. You have enough elven blood to desire the thrill of conquering a more formidable foe. It's been enjoyable to watch you struggle. I will miss the entertainment." His cold black gaze flew to Cass. "But perhaps the girl will make up for the lack. If your child proves not to be a champion, the girl might still breed true once I have a go at her."

Dominic growled low in his throat. The black sludge sprouted wings of fire, curling around his ankles and up his calves. Cass watched in horror as the dark flames pierced the leather of his boots, seeped into his breeches.

"It's sad that we true elven breed so rarely," continued Mor'ded, "but it means I will use her well. If she can come to enjoy a bit of torture, she should last several years. Does that comfort you, lad?"

More thick black fire had slithered up Dominic's legs, wrapping about his waist, threatening to envelop Cassandra as well. Her husband finally released her, trying again to put his body between her and his father, but Cass danced out of his reach. She realized she couldn't save him by revealing the lie of her pregnancy. Mor'ded's words convinced her that nothing would stop him from destroying his son.

The two men faced each other. Despite the fire encasing his feet, penetrating inside his very body, Dominic managed to take a few steps toward Mor'ded. He raised his arms, red fire blazing from his palms, making Cassandra step even farther back from the blast of heat.

"You're going to try again," said Mor'ded, shaking his head in mock sadness. But his eyes glittered with paternal pride. "I knew you would."

Gray fire encased Dominic's red blaze, a swirling battle of heat and nothingness. Mor'ded easily squelched that first attack, but her husband had just begun. He called forth the coldness of white fire, directing it at the black sludge beneath his feet, dampening the wicked heat. A misty vapor curled up from the floor, wrapped about Dominic's pale hair and handsome face. The blackness encasing his waist flickered and died.

Lady Cassandra's heart soared. Had Dominic found a way to combat the black flame without calling on that same power himself?

"Ah," sighed Mor'ded. "Clever, Son. You have concentrated your power in the cold flame... Look, you have grown strong enough to challenge the black. Well done! But the white fire cannot follow the black inside of you—it will only hasten your death. And I wish to savor this moment."

With a flick of the scepter, Mor'ded made the black

swallow the white blaze, created a new belt of dark
fire about Dominic's waist, and this time it did not
play about his body. It bored into her husband's skin,
making him gasp and stagger backward. Cass could no
longer see the blackness, but she knew that it now ate
inside of him, knew Dominic felt the burning of his
lungs and very bones.

She wanted to go to him, curl her body about his
for protection, cry and plead for his life. But it would
do no good. She must channel her fear into fury, must
use the skills the Rebellion had taught her and, at long
last, try to accomplish her task. Cass slipped her girdle
off her waist, held it in her hands, and strengthened
the song that shivered in her head.

Mor'ded pointed the scepter at her husband and
black fire sprouted from its deadly tip yet again. She
did not know if the scepter could aid Dominic or not,
she knew only that it was being used against him now.
And she must stop it.

Cass took a dancing step toward Mor'ded. Despite
Dominic's pain he saw the movement, opened his
mouth, but no words came forth. Just an anguished
sound of fury.

The Imperial Lord smiled.

His son called forth black fire.

It licked and wove its way to Mor'ded's very feet.
Then fluttered and died.

"So you have a bit of the black after all," said the
elven lord. "It's a pity it's not enough to provide me
with a satisfying challenge."

Cass watched his eyes carefully, making sure they
stayed focused on his son as she inched her way closer

to him, the girdle clutched tightly within her hands. She must get the scepter away from Mor'ded. It would not stop his attack, but perhaps it would lessen it enough to give Dominic a chance.

Lady Cassandra allowed the song to consume her. Her limbs vibrated with her magic and she danced across the space between her and Mor'ded in a heartbeat, catching the elven lord by surprise. She could not risk touching the scepter, so she snapped her girdle about the rod, the leather belt twining three times around it, and yanked it out of Mor'ded's hold.

The Imperial Lord turned to her with a look of blank shock, which instantly blossomed into a furious rage. "You dare."

He held up elegant hands and black fire flew from his palms to her breast. For a moment nothing happened, as if she held a shield around her.

May's cloak of dreams.

Again, Mor'ded's eyes flickered with shock, and for a timeless instant neither one of them moved.

Black fire curled around the Imperial Lord's throat, and they both turned to look at Dominic. Somehow he'd managed to close the distance between them. Sweat rolled down his forehead, the muscles in his neck taut with strain. He held his broad shoulders slightly bent, as if the weight of pain fought to shove him down to his knees. But her husband kept upright, muscled thighs quivering with the effort.

The black fire that crept around Mor'ded's throat came from Dominic's upheld hands.

Then Cassandra felt the force of Mor'ded's magic.

She staggered backward, clutching the girdle with a death grip. But the scepter spun out as the leather unrolled around it, clattering to the floor with a clear ringing sound. She stared helplessly at the talisman while flame twisted inside her chest, robbing her of breath. And Mor'ded had flung only a small amount of black fire at her. It twisted and roiled in her stomach, ripped at her muscles like knives. It destroyed the song that had given her the magic of the dance, and her muscles shook with weakness. She could barely see for the pain.

Good Heavenly Father. What had Dominic been forced to endure? What did he withstand at this very moment?

She focused her cloudy vision on the scepter that had rolled to the edge of her skirts, Ador's words again sounding in her mind. *It is the key.*

The key to power.

She knew it held power. But only a true elven lord could wield the scepter.

Yet Dominic had touched it and, by his own admission, somehow forged a connection with the talisman. Could he possibly have enough elven blood to actually wield it?

"This has been more entertaining than I anticipated," said Mor'ded. Cass looked up at him. With a negligent toss of his pale fingers, the elven lord dispersed the black fire from around his neck. "But I'm getting bored, my dear. And the thought of you in my bed—screaming—suddenly appeals to me."

Lady Cassandra's shoulders quivered, but not in fear. Indeed, an odd sort of calm descended over her, and a wisp of a dream soothed her mind. A vision of her husband making love to her in a garden of singing flowers. The pain that licked through her chest suddenly eased and she felt a bit of strength flow through her muscles again.

Mor'ded took a step forward, bent down to retrieve the scepter.

"No," screamed Cass, slapping her girdle at the rod. It rolled out of the Imperial Lord's reach and thudded up against Dominic's boots.

"You continue to surprise me, my dear," said the elven lord. "I don't need the scepter to destroy him—or you, for that matter. But I must say you've held up to my power quite well. You shouldn't be able to move. What a treat you will provide me when I bed—"

Cassandra lunged for the scepter, but Mor'ded had the superior speed and strength of the elvenkind and his body hit hers, slamming both of them to the floor. Cass grunted, but she'd landed half atop him and quickly scrambled forward, fingers reaching out for the rod.

"Don't touch it," growled Dominic, crumpling over and picking it up, his voice distorted by pain, his movements jerky from the torture of his muscles. "It will destroy anyone who wields it except…"

He stared at the shiny black talisman, the runes engraved on the surface swirling in a sudden mad dance.

"Except for your father," finished Cass. "And you."

Mor'ded barked a mad laugh. "If you try to use it, it will destroy you."

"Will it?" murmured Dominic. He glanced down

at the floor, where his father still crouched a hand's breath from Cass, who knelt in a puddle of skirts. "Does it hum to you, Father? For it's humming to me, feeding me a power beyond anything I've ever known."

Mor'ded's eyes widened, and for the first time since Cassandra had met him, he looked afraid.

"Only one of full elven blood can use the power of a scepter," insisted his father.

"Are you trying to convince me or yourself? Perhaps I have enough of the blood to try."

"It will kill you."

"Indeed?" Dominic pointed the tip of the staff at the pink pods of the plant across the room. Black fire burst from the scepter, disappeared inside the leaves, and within a trice they shriveled and drooped upon themselves.

The elven lord sprang to his feet, fire at his fingertips. He threw it at his son, and Dominic wavered on his feet; but with a curse he slapped the scepter at the black flames, curling them back upon themselves, straight at Mor'ded.

The Imperial Lord gasped, his body convulsing with sudden agony.

"Father, don't do this. We don't have to destroy each other—"

"Damn you! Do you think you can defeat me? A weak half-human bastard?" Cass felt a sudden yank at her hair and suppressed a shriek. Mor'ded lifted her nearly off her feet and shook her by the brown roots, making her eyes water from the sting of it. "*This* is why you're weak. Even with the power of the scepter, you cannot do it. Your human heart will not allow it."

Mor'ded had sneered while uttering the last few words. Cass looked at her husband and wondered how the elven lord could be so blind. Dominic looked anything but weak. He grasped the scepter with a firm grip, his body no longer pain-wracked but upright, head thrown slightly back and midnight eyes narrowed grimly at his father. He near glowed with strength, both inner and magical.

"Let her go," he snarled.

"They are nothing but animals," Mor'ded responded, shaking Cassandra again.

And she'd had just about enough. Cass spun, twisting her hair even tighter, and struck out with her fists, catching Mor'ded in the gut. To her satisfaction she heard him gasp, but then his big hand closed around her throat and she clutched at his fingers, trying to pry them off.

"This is the last time I will say it, Father. Let her go."

Cass saw starbursts as Mor'ded slowly squeezed. She could almost *feel* Dominic gather his magic. Whether the scepter had released the black fire that he'd held inside of him or just enhanced that trickle to a powerful strength, what blazed forth from the scepter far surpassed anything she'd ever seen Mor'ded command.

She felt the magic enter the Imperial Lord, his fingers twitching about her throat from the force of it. Then his hold loosened and she twisted from his grasp, fighting for breath and rubbing at her bruised neck. Unlike Mor'ded, who'd used the black fire in a slow release that prolonged pain, Dominic had thrown one powerful burst of magic at his father.

The elven lord did not suffer when he died.

Seventeen

DOMINIC STARED AT HIS FATHER'S BODY BUT A moment, then called forth a narrow stream of red magic, until nothing was left of the elven lord but a small pile of ash.

"Are you all right?" he asked Cassandra as he went to her side.

She opened her mouth to reply and then winced, rubbing at her throat. He called forth blue fire, still surprised at how easily the magic now responded to his will. The flame caressed his wife's throat and she smiled with relief.

Dominic gathered her into his arms, trying not to crush her. He had saved her. Despite all odds, he had managed to save the most precious thing in the world to him.

"I love you," he said, holding her from him and staring into those soft brown eyes.

"And I love you."

Dominic smiled at her, fighting the stiffness of his lips. He supposed he would have to get used to that expression now. She managed to call the reaction from him entirely too often. He lowered his head and kissed her, wanting to feel that connection that flared to life whenever their lips met. He lost himself in the feel of her for a time but eventually pulled away, knowing he could not indulge himself for long.

How would he continue to keep her safe?

He glanced over at his father's ashes. "What have I done?"

"You have saved the people of London from a tyrant, Dominic. He might have fathered you, but don't feel guilty for doing what you had to do."

"You don't understand." Any human feeling he might have left for the man had died the moment Mor'ded had hurt her. "I have just placed your life, and those of the people of Firehame, in even more danger. Once the remaining elven lords discover that fact, they will turn their combined fury upon our sovereignty. And the power of one scepter wielded by a half-breed against the might of six—"

Dominic spun when the balcony doors blew open with a gust of wind that couldn't be natural. He swept Cass behind him and raised his arms. A long black snout pushed into the room, red eyes blinking from the pile of ash to the scepter within Dominic's hands.

"Quickly," Ador said. "Change your clothing."

Had the dragon gone mad? "What, why?"

Those huge red orbs turned to his wife. "Through that door, yes, I knew you would be quick on your feet. Any coat will do, yes, the black velvet, plenty of lace, as Mor'ded prefers."

Cassandra returned to Dominic's side, holding out one of his father's more elaborate coats. He found himself stripping off his uniform and shrugging into the clothing without thought.

"Devil take you, Ador. Why am I putting this on?"

The dragon snorted with impatience, a gust of sulfur-tinted air that made Cass wrinkle her nose. "*They* felt the change in the magic barrier, bastard. You'll need to talk to them."

The dragon had gone mad. "What for? To beg the elven lords for mercy? I'm done with that—not that it would make a difference, mind."

"Do I have to explain everything?"

"You needn't bother with your help now. Where were you a few moments ago?"

"Stop it," snapped Lady Cassandra.

They both turned their gaze on the exasperated woman.

Ador sighed. "That was your battle to fight, fire lord. And now that you've proven worthy, I am free to help you."

Dominic crossed his arms over his chest, the scepter tucked within the velvet. "Damn. What good will it to do speak with the elven lords? And how do I manage that anyway?"

Ador backed his snout halfway out of the room, extended one long claw inside, and tapped the crystal rock that sat next to the door. "The Imperial Lady La'laylia made this stone for the elven lords to communicate with one another. Did you think we dragons flew back and forth between sovereignties as messengers?"

Dominic stepped forward, studying the translucent stone. He'd often seen his father place his scepter within the cavity on the top of it, but he'd just assumed he'd kept it there for safety. That it protected the scepter somehow.

"What did you mean," said Cassandra, "when you said the elven lords felt a change in the barrier?"

"The scepters are united to maintain the magical barrier around England, and they are tied to the magic of the elven lord who wields each one. When the bastard used it, his magic infused the rod and changed the protection."

Dominic frowned. "Weakened it, you mean?"

"Ah no. Do not underestimate yourself, fire lord. Your power is a match for your father's, but your human blood taints it enough to make it slightly different. The elven lords felt the switch."

The general erased all expression from his face. It was time to call on his skills of war. "So I try to negotiate with them?"

The sound of stone grating on stone as something akin to a laugh sprang from Ador's throat. "You can't negotiate with the mad ones. No, my dear bastard. You will convince them that you are your father."

"I will... what?" Dominic felt Cass's arm on his sleeve, and he turned to look down at her beautiful face. Her soft brown hair hung in straggles about her cheeks from Mor'ded's yanking out her coiffure, and he could not help but reach out and smooth it back. Her skin felt like the softest of rose petals.

"You do look enough like him to manage it," she said. "It might work, love."

A slim hope, but hope nonetheless. Perhaps Cassandra's God had indeed found a way to allow him to continue to protect her. To allow him to love her until they grew old and content, dangling their grand-children on their knees. Grandchildren who would never be sent to Mor'ded's version of Elfhame.

"How do you make it speak to the other lords?" he asked, touching the cold smooth stone.

"Place the scepter in the hole at the top, yes; allow it to slide all the way down into the groove. Lady Cassandra, please step back. Farther. We do not want you within the range of the farseeing. They will be suspicious enough as it is without wondering why Mor'ded allows a human to stand by his side. Good. Now look closer at the stone, fire lord."

"Quit calling me that."

"As you wish. Bastard, it is."

Dominic refused to rise to the dragon's needling. In an odd way, he felt grateful for it. Annoyance masked his fear. If he failed to convince the lords that he was his father, he would doom all of Firehame. And although he looked a great deal like Mor'ded, he was ten years younger and had a more muscular build from his years of warfare. And he did have a human heart; Cass had finally convinced him of that. If he allowed a flicker of it to show in his face or voice…

Dominic took a deep breath. Hadn't he spent his entire life masking his humanity? He could do this. He had to.

With the scepter within the stone, Dominic could make out odd carvings on the face of the gem that didn't look like natural striations. Like the door on

Father's chamber, a map had been carved in the surface, a small map that looked like the spokes of a wheel with a very distorted outline. He recognized each section and recalled the name of the elven lord who ruled the sovereignty.

Ador had been watching him carefully. "First you must press the piece that represents your sovereignty, Imperial Lord Mor'ded."

Dominic winced at the name but knew he would just have to get used to it. Better the dragon reminded him of this now.

"This will open the vision of you," continued Ador, "and allow you to call up visions of the other elven lords… if they have done the same."

Dominic pressed Firehame on the map, and immediately all the other sovereignties lit up in their respective colors. Blue for Dewhame, green for Verdanthame, gold for Dreamhame, silver for Bladehame, brown for Terrahame, violet for Stonehame.

"As you can see," murmured the dragon, "they are all demanding to speak with you."

"Which one first?"

"Mm. Dewhame, I think. Breden is close enough to send his dragon if he doesn't hear from you soon."

Dominic nodded and pressed the blue piece on the map. Immediately an image of the Imperial Lord appeared within the translucent surface of the stone, his silver-white hair hanging damply against his head, a spray of mist curling about his shoulders.

"Mor'ded," snapped Breden. "Why the hell are you messing with the barrier?"

Dominic narrowed his eyes, smoothing his face to calm. He should have thought of a likely excuse before he'd started the farseeing, but hell, he was used to thinking on his feet. And it would do him good to outwit Breden. He would not forget that the Imperial Lord had kidnapped his wife.

"You are overreacting," replied Dominic, tilting his head in imitation of his father when he spoke to an irrational human. "I had to draw on the scepter's powers to take care of a difficult problem. There may have been a... slight resonance in the scepter."

The warped vision of Breden's face stiffened to a mask of indignant arrogance. "What problem?"

His father would never divulge any weakness. "That's not your concern. I have taken care of it—that's all you need know."

"Several delightful possibilities come to mind," said Breden, his right hand idly toying with a ball of water. "I had a bastard girl worthy of Elfhame slip through my fingers, and it's rumored that she hid in Firehame."

Dominic didn't blink.

"And then there's that champion of yours—did he overreach himself, Mor'ded?"

"As I said, the problem has been taken care of. And I have several other elven lords waiting to speak with me, Breden." The storm lord laughed, crushing the ball in his hand, water spraying between his fingers. Dominic reached over and pressed the blue area of crystal, breaking the connection. He looked over in amazement at Ador. "He believed me. He thinks I am my father."

The dragon snorted, puffs of gray smoke swirling from his nostrils. "Of course. People see what they expect to see—even elven lords."

With a bit more confidence, Dominic pressed the violet portion of the map, and the elven lady of Stonehame flickered into view. "What is it, La'laylia?"

The painfully beautiful woman in the crystal frowned at him. "You interrupted my... pleasure, Mor'ded."

"My apologies. It will not happen again."

She leaned forward, revealing a generous bosom barely concealed by a bodice of netted diamonds. Large violet eyes glittered with as much brilliance as the stones she wore. "You know better than to interrupt the feed to the barrier. Perhaps you sought to garner my attention?"

Had his father and La'laylia once been lovers? Were they now? Dominic could only guess and chose to follow the elven lady's lead. "Perhaps."

She smiled, revealing even white teeth, except for two rather pointed canines at the corners of her full-lipped mouth. She held up an odd-shaped gem, with too many honed edges for Dominic's taste. "You are looking exceptionally... healthy. Bored, my pet?"

Dominic cocked a brow, hoping to look arrogant while hiding his alarm that La'laylia had noticed his youth. "Not yet enough to taste the pleasures of your bed, La'laylia. Just seeing your loveliness will have to sustain me."

She laughed, low and sultry, making Dominic swallow hard in reaction.

"Ah well. When you can withstand the sharper pleasures, my lord, I will be pleased to provide them. In the

meantime, I will have to amuse myself with the humans."
And with that, her vision faded from the crystal.

Dominic breathed a sigh of relief. And then spoke
with Mi'cal of the green scepter, Roden of the gold,
Lan'dor of the silver. None of the elven lords seemed
to even suspect he wasn't Mor'ded. And the elven
lady Annanor of the brown scepter did not appear
to care. Unlike La'laylia, she only radiated a strong
distaste for Dominic's father, quickly closing their
connection once he reassured her that nothing threatened the power of their rule.

Dominic straightened his back, stretched his arms
and shoulders, relieving the tension in his muscles.
Faith, he'd grown used to having men's lives depend
upon him in the battlefield. But having to perform
this sort of subterfuge, with thousands of innocent
lives hanging in the balance, was a different sort of
game. He supposed he would have to get used to it.

"But for how long?" he wondered aloud. "How
long before I am found out?"

"The elven lords rarely meet in person anymore,"
said Ador. "With the exception of La'laylia, who
craves the pleasure of a challenge in her bed. If you
do not disturb the power of the scepter again, they
will not suspect you."

"They have spies, Ador. Father has several of his
own within the courts of all the sovereignties. The
elven lords love rumor and gossip."

"Ah well. Unless they have a specific reason to
believe such an improbable story, they will dismiss the
rumors. You must move carefully, fire lord. Do not
think that this will be easy."

Dominic backed into the room as Ador took wing, the blast of air making his father's coat—no, *his* coat—flap wildly about his waist. When had his life ever been easy? And why would he expect it to be any different now?

He brushed his hands across the velvet and frowned. He disliked the dramatically flared skirts of his father's coats, the excessive ornamentation and flamboyant colors. But he supposed it would be a minor thing to get used to, compared to the enormity of the task that awaited him. Dominic strode back to the crystal and removed the black rod from within it, feeling the hum of the scepter's magic vibrate all the way down to his boots.

How much magic would he now be capable of wielding? He thought of the black swath burned straight through the heart of London and resisted the urge to fling the scepter from him. Would the power turn him into another version of his father? Would he become so consumed with the glory of it that his humanity would again be hidden from him?

No. For he had Cassandra. He had her faith and her goodness to guide him. She'd become more than a lover, more than a friend. She guided his conscience in all things; for he'd abandoned his so long ago he could no longer be sure of right and wrong. He hadn't realized he'd led only half a life until he fell in love with her. She completed him.

Dominic turned to her, standing all alone across the enormous room, her soft brown eyes looking almost frightened. Of him?

"What is it?" he demanded.

"You looked so much like Mor'ded for a moment. When you spoke with the other elven lords, I could not see a difference between them and you."

He crossed the distance between them in a trice. She did not start, having grown used to the superior quickness of movement with which his elven blood had gifted him, but she trembled when he reached for her, shying away from the scepter in his hand.

Dominic frowned at the black thing. "I suppose I will have to do something about this. I can make a sheath for it, like my sword, so it cannot accidentally touch you. Although I do not think it will harm you unless you try to wield it. How did you know?"

She blinked. "Know what?"

"That I would be able to use it."

"I… I wasn't sure. But you said you had formed a connection, and Ador said it was the key, so I hoped that you had enough elven blood to wield it."

"I have always admired your intelligence." He grinned, but she didn't return it. Dominic tossed the scepter across the room to land unerringly on Mor'ded's bed. His bed.

He held out his arms to her again. Yet she still trembled.

"You have never been afraid of me, Cassandra."

"But I've learned to fear your father."

"And I am not he. I never will be, as long as I have your love. Would you withhold it now, when I need it the most?"

Tears formed in her eyes. "No. No, of course not, Dominic. Nothing can stop me from loving you."

And she flung herself into his arms, and he held her tightly, feeling his heart melt with the tears that soaked the front of his shirt. "Don't fret, love; somehow we will make this work without losing ourselves in the process. But there is much to be done, and I will need your strength to help me. Can you do that?"

She looked up at him with red-rimmed eyes. "Of course I can. It's just that I almost lost you and then gained you back, all in a few moments, and then worried about what you might become with that scepter in your hand... Fie! Enough of this nonsense. What needs to be done, my lord?"

"I'm not—well, I suppose I am now. I shall have to get used to being called a lord, although I shan't like it. This is going to be harder than we can both imagine, my dear. So first I need you to kiss me."

Her eyes widened but she lifted to her toes, and he bent his head. For a moment her lips seemed hesitant beneath his, but he pulled her closer and she wrapped her arms around his neck, her fingers twining in his hair as she was wont to do, and her mouth melted beneath his. Dominic pulled as much sustenance from that kiss as he possibly could before he let her go.

He strode over to the bed, retrieved the scepter, and proceeded to burn the swan-shaped surround, the coverlet quickly catching fire, flames dancing merrily across the surface. He did the same for the rest of the remaining furniture excepting the desk, which might contain information he could use, and the crystal. His father had hidden many secrets from him and it might take him years to discover them all.

"I will not have it said that the champion did not put up a good fight," he murmured. "Now then, my love. You can have the servants clear the room of ashes and redecorate to your heart's content. I may have to sleep here, but I want as little of him left in this room as possible."

"What shall I do with the ashes?" she asked, eyeing the pile that comprised Mor'ded's.

"Have the servants take them all to the refuse pile… no, better yet, I shall spread them myself in the false Elfhame. It will be fitting that Father joins his victims."

His wife nodded. Damn, he supposed he would have to think of her as his mistress now. He could not afford any slips of the tongue. What a tangled web they would have to weave.

"I must see to my men. In this ridiculous garb. I must convince them that their general is dead and that I will be taking over the supervision of the army myself."

"You can tell them that you no longer trust another to do it. That *Dominic* betrayed you."

"Indeed. I'm now grateful I kept myself aloof from the men. They should not suspect… but the rest of the court… and the people…"

"Shh, love. One thing at a time."

He picked up her hand and brushed his lips across it. "It will be a miracle if we manage the charade for a day."

"You hold the scepter."

"Better yet, I hold your heart. I will manage it, Cassandra."

"*We* will manage it. With God's help. By the time you return to your room this evening, you will no longer recognize this place."

Thinking of the changes she'd made to his old—to Dominic's old apartments—he could well imagine it. He reached out and cupped her cheek, his hand suddenly seeming large against her tiny face. "Do not overtire yourself, Lady Cassandra. You have a ball to attend tonight."

She leaned into his hand and sighed. "Fiddle. I don't recall a ball scheduled for this eve."

He kissed her farewell then spun on his heel. "I'm giving one."

"You?" she said to his retreating back.

"In your honor." He opened the door to the hall and turned to give her a deep bow. "Word will spread through the palace that I have destroyed my son for challenging me and have taken his wife as revenge for his impudence. But I must formally introduce you as my new mistress—my father enjoyed flaunting his victories. And then we shall see if I can fool the court as well as my men."

Eighteen

CASSANDRA STEPPED INTO THE CHAMPION'S APARTMENTS, wondering how on earth she would explain everything to Gwendolyn and May. She wanted to tell them the truth but couldn't be sure if they could manage the deception. No, she would take Dominic's lead and pretend by all outward appearances that he was his father.

"Oh, my lady," breathed Gwen, launching herself at Cass's skirts. "Ye see, May? Yer coat *did* work. She's alive."

The older girl blinked away her tears. "My magic isn't strong enough to withstand an elven lord."

"Maybe not," replied Cass, thinking of that tenuous moment when a wisp of a dream had given her the added strength she'd needed. "But it gave me enough of a distraction to do what needed to be done, May. I thank you for the gift."

The girl smiled, but Gwen let go of her skirts and stared up at her with a frown. "What needed to be done?"

Cass took a deep breath. "The champion betrayed

the Imperial Lord. For his treason, Mor'ded... destroyed him."

"The champion?" Gwen's voice cracked and Cass could tell she fought a sob. Dominic would be gratified to know that their servants had become fond of him. Or rather, he would have been gratified if he could have continued to exist beyond this day. She must try to keep her thoughts consistent with their new reality, or she would likely stumble.

"We cannot refer to him ever again, my dears. Do you understand? But for May's coat, I would not have survived Mor'ded's wrath myself. My life is precarious at the moment, in more ways than you can ever know. I am only lucky that the Imperial Lord desires me in his bed."

"His bed?"

"Yes. He seems... intrigued by the idea that I can produce another champion for him. And so he will try himself."

"That's awful," breathed May.

"But the champion already got ye pregnant," said Gwen.

"It's untrue. And Mor'ded does not like to be deceived."

For the first time, Gwendolyn gave her mistress a look that lacked the usual gleam of adoration. "Why would ye lie about it? Why would the Imperial Lord flame the champion for that?"

"There is more involved, Gwen. Dominic challenged his father for possession of the scepter."

Both girls gasped.

"And he lost. A reminder to us all that we cannot

challenge the rule of the elven lords." Lady Cassandra drew herself up to her not-so-considerable full height and slapped her hands together. "Come now. I need your help. Mor'ded's rooms were left in a shambles after the… encounter, and I've been given strict instructions to clean up the mess and move in my things."

"Just like that, my lady?" whispered Gwen.

"We are to live in the Imperial Lord's apartment?" squeaked May.

"No, of course not." Cass ignored Gwen's whisper. "There is a small chamber adjacent to his rooms where you can sleep."

Gwen grimaced. "And ye will sleep with him?"

"And we will all make the best of it." Cassandra clutched her throat as her voice broke. It had been a long day already. "We are women and must be strong, no matter what the circumstances. I was given to the champion without a say in the matter. How is this any different?"

The girls both nodded and followed her down the hall, hesitating in the doorway, hazel eyes riveted to the floor of ash and blackened remains of the furniture. Several other servants were already at work cleaning up the mess, and Lady Cassandra directed them to box up the ash and give it to her. She took the box into the passageway to the door to the false Elfhame and left it there for Dominic to take within.

It took only a few hours to clear the rest of the room and scrub it clean. Cass draped a silk cloth over the crystal near the door and another over the desk across the room. She left the empty pots that had once held the pink pods, hoping to fill them with flowers

from the elven garden—those that did not sing, least-
ways. Then she oversaw the transfer of the furniture
from her old apartments to these new, larger ones.
She allowed only Meg and Gwen to carry her more
delicate pieces, the glassware and vases and display
cases. She instructed the girls to give Dominic's old
clothing to the servants, to be given to the poor.

The other servants spoke barely a word while
they worked, in awe of being in the elven lord's
apartments. They avoided looking at the iridescent
walls, which made Cass so queasy herself that she
decided to cover as much of them as she could with
tapestries. When most of the heavy work was done,
the servants nodded eagerly when she dismissed them,
near running out the door.

Lady Cassandra glanced around the room in satisfaction. It looked nothing like the bare apartment Mor'ded
had occupied, and her moving in as his mistress would
satisfy anyone's curiosity about the changes.

Good heavens, she could no longer think of herself
as Dominic's wife. She would become the Imperial
Lord's lover.

She sighed and allowed a very silent Gwendolyn to
assist in choosing her clothing for the ball. God knew
the truth of her love for Dominic, and that would
have to suffice.

He returned while May put the finishing touches
on her coiffure, looking entirely too much like his
father, his face frozen in a disdainful mask. But he
glanced around the room and his shoulders relaxed,
and he strode to her dressing table and placed a kiss
on her cheek. "Well done, love."

May dropped her brush and Gwendolyn let out a soft gasp.

Cassandra winced and pretended to pull away from Dominic, but it proved difficult. She ignored the girls' reactions. "How did it fare with the men?"

He nodded, silver hair falling about his cheeks, exposing the tips of his pointed ears. "They will not miss their general. And their fear of his fate will keep them in line until I can appoint another to oversee them."

They had believed him, then. They had not recognized their own commander.

"But I thought you wished to command them yourself."

"Ah, too boring, my dear. Let's hope you breed me another champion who can do the task better than my current choices." He strode to the door of the room that held his clothing and washstand. "Now make haste with your toilette. We have a trial to oversee before the ball."

"A trial?"

He spun, his eyes narrowed, his beautiful mouth grim. "There are several children awaiting their trials, and it was scheduled for this eve. You wouldn't want to deny them the right to go to Elfhame as quickly as possible, would you?"

Cass allowed her sorrow to reflect in her eyes and for a moment, saw it mirrored back at her within his own. Then he glanced at May and disappeared into his dressing room.

She had a sudden impulse to dismiss her two servants so Dominic wouldn't have to veil his words to her. So they wouldn't have to continue the charade in their private apartments. But she knew it would be best that they got used to their roles and maintained them at all times.

Just like Dominic had done for most of his life, pretending to have no heart.

Lady Cassandra stood and gazed at herself in the mirror. Gwen had chosen a silver satin mantua studded with tiny gemstones that sparkled with her every movement, the train flowing several feet behind her. Gemstones studded a narrow girdle and the toes of her shoes. May had woven even more gemstones in her hair, so skillfully that each gem could not be seen; instead her hair just appeared to glow from the candles' reflection.

May had retrieved the invisible mantle from where it had apparently been set down during her change of clothing, for she draped air about Cass then gave her shoulders a final pat.

Cass had stubbornly refused the powder in her hair and a patch on her face.

Dominic emerged from his dressing room. "Shall we go?"

Her pulse fluttered and she turned. He stood in a coat of silver satin, studded with buttons of gemstone, ruffles at his wrists and throat. His waistcoat and breeches matched, his shoes glittering with diamond buckles. The scepter lay at his side in place of his usual sword, in a sheath of soft leather bleached as pale as his outfit.

His skin looked a golden cream in contrast, his eyes deeper than midnight.

His lip quirked, and Cass could breathe again.

"It seems we are of the same mind this evening. You look ravishing, my love." And he strode across the room, gathered her in his arms, crushing her against him with a kiss that left her breathless.

When they parted Cass turned to Gwen and May to bid them good eve, when she noticed the look they exchanged.

They knew. They knew that Dominic stood at her side and not Mor'ded. Would others see through their lie as easily?

The girls had been sullen most of the day, near-terrorized when Dominic had entered the room. Now they both smiled, their hazel eyes winking as if they'd been studded with gemstones like Cass's hair.

"Good night, my lady," they said in unison, bobbing brief curtsies.

Cass looked deeply into their eyes. They knew, but they would not reveal the truth. When Gwendolyn winked at her, she gave the girl a tremulous smile. May quickly jabbed her elbow into the younger girl's side, frowning and shaking her head. No, they would not reveal the truth. But May stepped forward, pinching her fingers over Cassandra's shoulders, dragging the invisible cloak down her back. "I do not think you will need this any longer, my lady."

Because she lived her dreams with her true love at her side.

Cass nodded and allowed her husband—no, her lover—to escort her from the room into the private passage. She noticed with relief that the box of ashes next to the stout oak door had been removed, but

Dominic said nary a word of it, his face a mask of pure arrogant elf.

"Sometimes," he whispered as they walked through the silent, gloomy passage, "the children are hurt during the trials."

Cass squeezed his hand. She didn't remember any pain from her own trial but did not doubt that Mor'ded might often "play" with children from the lower classes. "You don't have it in your nature to hurt a child, Dom—"

He stopped and placed a finger gently over her lips. "Do not call me that, even in private."

She nodded and for a brief moment he replaced his finger with his lips, the warmth and tenderness of his kiss an affirmation of her faith in him. He laid his cheek atop her head.

"Father used the scepter to challenge the children with magic. Any of their own latent magic would rise in defense of the attack. If they lacked the higher powers…"

"I understand. Is there some way you can just pretend to test them? After all, we have no intention of sending any of the children to the false Elfhame."

"I thought of that," he replied, his jaw moving in her hair. "It would be too dangerous. A truly powerful child can cause a lot of damage until their magic is under control, and if they are discovered by the other elven lords—no, we must test them and keep them hidden until they can be of use." He stepped away from her and held her by the shoulders, looking deeply into her eyes. "I want you to find a moment to speak with Walpole this eve."

"Of course. But Dom—my love, we will have to expose our secret. Are you sure you want to take the risk?"

"I see no other way. Not if we are to help the children."

"You appear to have thought of a plan for the chosen already."

He let loose a sigh. "I do not know how long we will be able to keep up this charade, if we shall even make it through the night. But as long as we are able to, we can save the children born with enough elven blood to wield a scepter."

"But chosen ones are rare. There are only two of you in England right now and even that is unusual. And the other sovereignties will continue to cull them… It was sheer chance one of Breden's bastards had hidden in Firehame. It may take decades to save a child with the same power to match the other scepters."

His big hands squeezed her shoulders. "That's why I want you to tell Walpole to spread the word among the Rebellion. That the children are going to their doom, and they must avoid the trials and find refuge in Firehame."

"They have already been trying to save children from going to Elfhame… but now that they know the full truth, perhaps they will be more successful. Still, I don't think the common people will believe it. They won't *want* to believe it. For some it is the only happiness they can offer their children. Besides, even if a chosen one can wield the scepter, the odds of them looking enough like the Imperial Lord to take his place are unlikely."

"I doubt we will replace another impostor over a sovereignty," he calmly replied. "But their powers are weakened without the scepters. The disruption to the barrier when I took the scepter from Mor'ded is proof of that. Even if a half-breed can't wield the scepter, they can steal it. Perhaps if we managed to take every elven lord's scepter…"

"It is more hope than we've ever had before. I think you should speak with Sir Robert about your plan."

"I intend to. On the morrow. First we must see if we can even manage this charade for the night." He picked up her arm again and headed for the door that led to the throne. "After I find a way to protect the children from my—Mor'ded's trial."

Cass realized he'd almost said "myself." She realized at that moment how truly strong she would have to be. She must keep him from losing himself in the part he must play. "I have faith in you," she said as he opened the door. "As does God."

He threw her a disgruntled look, but she only smiled at him as he led her out onto the dais. Cass blinked a moment, adjusting her eyes to the light, and then she saw most of the court clustered about the room.

She watched their faces as Dominic took the throne and she stationed herself next to it, one hand lying atop the back of the smooth marble. She didn't know how many people usually managed to witness a trial, but it seemed to her that an extraordinary number had shown up. The nobles had dressed in their finest in anticipation of the ball that would follow. An eerie silence settled over the hall as they watched Dominic nod at the first child standing in line to be presented.

An eager-eyed father escorted the young boy up the dais then quickly abandoned the child to resume his position on the floor. Cass imagined Mor'ded didn't allow anyone upon the dais except for himself and the child to be tested, judging by the looks she received from the assembled.

She easily spotted Lady Verney, by her height and the feathers in her hair that accentuated it. A bewildered expression pinched her thin face as she looked back and forth between Cassandra and the Imperial Lord. Indeed, half the court watched her with expressions ranging from confusion to disgust to self-satisfaction… as if they'd known all along she sought nothing but the power of the throne.

Lady Agnes actually winked at her.

Cassandra cringed, her fingers turning white as they clenched at the smooth marble beneath them.

And then her eyes met those of Sir Robert Walpole, and the expression in that dark piercing gaze made her knees go weak. He suspected. But unlike May and Gwendolyn, he wasn't quite sure he recognized the son in the role of the father. He gave her a low bow of respect.

Lady Cassandra straightened her back and raised her chin.

The Imperial Lord frowned at the child presented before him, and only Cass could see the slight rise of his chest as he took a breath before raising his scepter at the boy. White fire sprouted from the tip of it; Cass could feel the cold from where she stood. It hit the child square in his small chest and he grunted in surprise, his grubby hands automatically lifted in defense. A small white flame of his own blocked the scepter's attack.

Dominic quickly followed with a twist of gray flame, then a measure of yellow, each time reducing the strength of each power. When the child countered them all, Cass inwardly groaned. The next fire would be the orange, and although not as damaging as the red, it could possibly hurt the child.

The Imperial Lord hesitated, the scepter falling onto his muscled thigh, and the assembled began to whisper among themselves, wondering at the delay.

She knew Dominic would not do it. He would not risk harming the child. And then their charade would be exposed. But she could not regret that he'd found his human heart, and would rather face the combined wrath of the elven lords than have her beloved reclaim his elven coldness.

Lady Cassandra moved her arm from the back of the chair to his strong shoulder, feeling the tightness in the muscles. "I have faith," she murmured.

He did not look at her, but she felt his determination as he raised the scepter again. A ray of the blue healing fire streamed from the rod, encompassing the child, making him glow from head to ragged foot. And the orange fire followed on the heels of it.

The child tried to defend against the greater power, but he couldn't combat the flame with orange fire of his own. He shook in fear but not pain, for the healing blue protected the boy from harm.

Cass almost sobbed aloud in relief. She'd married

a very clever man. Perhaps they would manage this deception after all.

Dominic halted the flow of magic and imitated the sardonic laughter of his father so well that Cass shivered.

"Sorry, boy. No trip to Elfhame for you. Next!"

The child stumbled from the dais, relief and disappointment warring on his freckled face.

As they had thought, none of the children showed the slightest inclination for the higher powers, and the flames they managed to raise in defense of the scepter barely blocked the small amount of magic Dominic threw at them. And only one of the children possessed the magic from another sovereignty, a child whose bloodline must have come from the elven lord of Dreamhame, for she crafted an illusion of red flame that nearly fooled them, until Dominic realized it did not counter his attack. Indeed, he'd had to quickly strengthen the protection of the blue flame around the girl.

Cass had been so absorbed in the trials that she'd forgotten their audience. As the last child left the dais, she glanced up at the sudden silence and froze in fear.

Sir Robert no longer suspected the truth. He knew. His eyes glittered with understanding and an odd sort of triumph, surely calculating how he could use this sudden development in the Rebellion's cause. Since Cass had intended to tell him the truth, his certainty did not alarm her.

But Lady Verney now gazed at Lady Cassandra in sudden understanding, a slow smile spreading across her thin lips. A few of the other lords and ladies

who'd looked confused by Dominic's wife standing at Mor'ded's side shared the same expression.

The blue flame. The Imperial Lord had never thought to protect those whom he tested. They suspected the truth.

Dominic rose and extended his strong hand to her, and as she slipped her fingers in it, she met his eyes. He knew as well that several of the court had guessed that he wasn't Mor'ded. He raised one pale brow and gave an almost imperceptible shrug of those broad shoulders.

They would play it out.

Lady Cassandra followed him down the steps of the dais while the crowd parted to allow them passage. As one, the assembled bowed to them, murmuring "Imperial Lord" over and over. Dominic halted when he reached the king, who of them all, was not required to bow in homage.

"Your Majesty," said Dominic, his voice smooth and strong.

"Your Most High," replied the much shorter man, craning his neck to look up at Dominic. "The trial was most interesting. You and your new mistress"— his eyes flicked to Cass—"look stunning together in your silver satin. I congratulate you on your new relationship. You have the loyalty of my court."

"Indeed?"

"Forgive me for interrupting," said Walpole, straightening his own bow with a quick grunt, "but it appears you have also managed to acquire the loyalty of the people as well, Imperial Lord. Most unusual for an elven lord."

Dominic gave the man a twisted grimace. "I hold the scepter, Walpole. I don't give a damn who is loyal." And with the lie on his lips he swept Cassandra from the room, guiding her through the silent passages leading to the ballroom.

"They know," whispered Cass as they trod a velvet carpet past crystal globes that held liquid fire. "The king assured us of the court's support and Walpole guaranteed the people's."

"I know." Dominic abruptly stopped, pulled her into his arms. "I just don't know why."

"Don't you?" Cass lifted a hand, caressed that strong jaw, stared into his beautiful face. He had never looked more like an angel than he did at this moment. "You gained the loyalty of the court by revealing your suffering to them. The loyalty of the people by using your power to heal them during the fire. They want the freedom of England even more than we do, and have placed their confidence in you to gain it. They will not betray us."

He frowned, the expression making his beauty seem a bit more human. "I am used to living a life of deception, Cassandra. But you…"

"Hush. I'm used to giving my life to the Rebellion, but now I have your love to sustain me. I ask for no more."

"Indeed?" He bent down and kissed her, a brush of warm lips. She would always feel her heart soar at the touch of his mouth.

When Dominic raised his head, his frown had turned to a hesitant smile. "Come," he urged, dragging her through the hallway, toward the open doors

of the ballroom. "If it were within my power, I would offer you a different life. Ours will be filled with intrigue and danger and difficulty, but I promise you that I will also fill it with nights like this."

Lady Cassandra stepped into the ballroom and gasped. The new Imperial Lord had used the power of white fire to create a sparkling wonderland. Tiny starbursts created strands of glittering threads that hung from the ceiling, occasionally dropping one shining flake to fall to the floor like a shower of radiant snow. Between the strands dripped stalactites of white fire, near meeting the stalagmites that grew from the floor. Glittering fire sparkled along the walls, created a smooth expanse of unbroken white at their feet.

White mist swirled in the air, reached out to curl around Cass's waist like a cool caress, urging her to join the dance. She knew that despite all the dangers they faced, it would be worth the nights she could spend with Dominic.

"Shall we, my lady?"

She nodded and held out her hand to him, smiling as she caught sight of her wedding ring. The petals had unfurled into a glorious blossom of hope and love and happiness.

And then her lover swept her into his arms, into a sparkling world of magic and mystery.